CANADA

MAINE

Montpelier
1 2 Augusta
Concord
3 Boston
4 Providence
5 Hartford

NEW YORK
Rochester Albany
New York

WISCONSIN
Madison
Milwaukee

St. Paul
polis

MICHIGAN
Lansing
Detroit

IOWA
es Moines

Chicago

PENNSYLVANIA
Pittsburgh Harrisburg
ton

ILLINOIS INDIANA OHIO
Indianapolis Columbus
Baltimore
8 7
Washington,D.C. Dover

WEST VIRGINIA
Charleston

VIRGINIA
Richmond

on City St. Louis Springfield
SSOURI

KENTUCKY
Frankfort
Lexington

Greensboro

Nashville
TENNESSEE NORTH CAROLINA
Raleigh

KANSAS Memphis

ttle Rock
Birmingham
Atlanta

SOUTH CAROLINA
Columb

MISSISSIPPI ALABAMA GEORGIA
Jackson Montgomery

reveport

LOUISIANA
on Rouge
New Orleans

Jacksonville
llahassee

Atlantic Ocean

1	VERMONT
2	NEW HAMPSHIRE
3	MASSACHUSETTS
4	RHODE ISLAND
5	CONNECTICUT
6	NEW JERSEY
7	DELAWARE
8	MARYLAND

FLORIDA
Miami

BAHAMAS

CUBA

★ National Capital
● State Capital
● City or Town

THE UNITED STATES OF AMERICA

Olympia • • Seattle
WASHINGTON

Portland • • Helena
• Salem

OREGON

MONTANA

NORTH DAKOTA
• Bismarck

IDAHO
• Boise

WYOMING

SOUTH DAKOTA
• Pierre

Cheyenne •

NEBRASKA
Omaha
Lincoln •

• Carson City
Sacramento • Salt Lake City
San Francisco • **NEVADA**

UTAH

• Denver

COLORADO
• Colorado Springs
• Pueblo

CALIFORNIA

Las Vegas •

Topel

KANSAS
• Wi

• Santa Fe

ARIZONA
• Albuquerque

OKLAHO
Oklahor

Los Angeles •
• San Diego
• Phoenix

NEW MEXICO

• Tucson

• Da

TEXAS

• Austin

• San Antonio

Pacific Ocean

MEXICO

HAWAII

Honolulu •

ALASKA

Anchorage •

Juneau •

開口就會
美國長住用語

Live and Speak in America

實踐大學應用外語系專任講師
黃 靜 悅 ◎著
Danny O. Neal

五南圖書出版公司 印行

　　麥克魯漢（Marshall McLuhan）於上世紀六〇年代首度提出了「地球村」的概念，當時他原本用這個新名詞來說明電子媒介對於人類未來之衝擊，實不亞於古騰堡（Johann Gutenberg）印刷術對西方文明的影響；曾幾何時，「地球村」在今天有了新的涵義：天涯若比鄰！

　　現代科技進步昌明，往昔「五月花」號上的新教徒花了六十幾天，歷經千辛萬苦才橫渡大西洋，今日搭乘超音速飛機只要四個多小時就可完成；網際網路的普及，世界上任何角落所發生的事情對千里以外的地方都會有不可思議的影響，亦即所謂的「蝴蝶效應」；語言文字的互通理解；東方的「博愛」和西方的「charity」使得普天下心懷「人溺己溺」之心的信徒，都能為營造開創一個由愛出發、以和為貴的世界而一起努力！這一切都說明了一個事實：人與人之間不再因距離、時空、障礙和誤解而「老死不相往來」！

　　當然，在這一片光鮮亮麗的外表下，隱憂依然存在。「全球化」（Globalization）對第三世界的人而言，竟成為新帝國主義和資本主義的同義字！造成這種誤解，甚至於扭曲的主要原因是對不同於自己的文化、風俗、傳統及習慣的一知半解；是不是用法文就顯得比較文明？使用義大利文就會比較熱情？德文，富哲理？英文，有深度？而美語，就「財大氣粗」？是不是有一套介紹書籍，雖不一定包含了所有相關的資訊，但至少對那些想要知道或了解異國風物的好奇者，能有所幫助的參考工具書？

　　放眼今日的自學書刊，林林總總，參差不齊。上

者，艱澀聱牙或孤芳自賞；下者，錯誤百出或言不及意！想要找兼具深度和廣度的語言學習工具書，實屬不易。現有本校應用外語學系黃靜悅和唐凱仁兩位老師，前者留學旅居國外多年，以國人的角度看外國文化；後者則以外國人的立場，以其十數年寄居臺灣的經驗，合作撰寫系列叢書，舉凡旅遊、日常生活、社交、校園及商務應用，提供真實情境對話，佐以「實用語句」、「字句補給站」讓學習者隨查隨用，並穿插「小叮嚀」和「小祕訣」，提供作者在美生活的點滴、體驗與心得等的第一手資訊。同時，「文化祕笈」更為同類書刊中之創舉！

學無止境！但唯有輔以正確的學習書籍，才能收「事半功倍」之效。本人對兩位老師的投入與努力，除表示敬意，特此作序說明，並寄望黃唐兩位老師在教學研究之餘，再接再厲，為所有有志向學、自我提昇的學習者，提供更精練、更充實的自學叢書。

前實踐大學 校長

張光正

自序

　　學習外語的動機不外乎外在（instrumental）及內在（intrinsic）兩類：外在動機旨在以語言作為工具，完成工作任務；內在動機則是希望透過外語學習達成自我探索及自我實現的目標。若人們在語言學習上能有所成，則此成就也必然是雙方面的；一方面完成工作任務而得到實質上的利益報償，另一方面則因達成溝通、了解對方文化及想法而得到豐富的感受。

　　現今每個人都是地球公民中的一員，而語言則是自我與世界的連結工具。今日網路科技的發展在彈指間就可以連結到我們想要的網站，人類的學習心與天性因刺激而產生對未知的好奇心及行動力，使我們對於異國語言文化自然產生嚮往；增進對這個世界的了解已不是所謂的個人特色或美德，而是身處現代地球村的每個人都該具備的一種責任與義務！

　　用自己的腳走出去，用自己的眼睛去看、用自己的心靈去感受世界其他國家人們的生活方式，用自己學得的語言當工具，與不同國家的人們交談；或許我們的母語、種族、膚色、性別不同，或許我們的衣著、宗教信仰、喜好以及對事情的看法、做法不同，但人與人之間善意的眼神、微笑、肢體動作、互相尊重、善待他人的同理心，加上適切的語言，對世界和平、國際友邦間相互扶持的共同渴望，使我們深深體會到精彩動人的外語學習旅程其實是自我發現的旅程！只有自己親自走過的旅程、完成過的任務、通過的關卡、遇到的人們、累積的智慧經驗、開拓的視野、體驗過的人生，才是無可替代的真實感受。世界有多大、個人想為自己及世人貢獻

的事有多少，學習外語完成自我實現內在動機的收穫就有多豐富！

今日有機會將自己所學與用腳走世界、用心親感受的經驗交付五南出版社出版叢書，誠摯感謝前實踐大學張光正校長慨為本叢書作序、前鄧景元主編催生本系列書，眾五南夥伴使本書順利完成，及親愛的家人朋友學生們的加油打氣。若讀者大眾能因本系列叢書增進英語文實力，並為自己開啟一道與世界溝通的大門，便是對作者最大的回饋與鼓勵！

願與所有立志於此的讀者共勉之。

作者　黃靜悅　謹誌

頁碼

→ 單元標題

1.8 家電設備與裝修
Home Appliances, Decoration, and Repair

Dialog 1 對話1

A: 哈囉，我們來修理你的屋頂。

A: Hello. We're here to fix your roof.

→ 依不同情境模擬對話

B: 好，房子後面已經漏水漏了好幾個星期。

B: Great. It's been leaking in the back of the house for weeks.

A: 知道了，我的夥伴跟我會上去查看。

A: I see. My crew and I will get up there and check it out.

B: 謝謝，要多久時間來修呢？

B: Thank you. How long will it take to fix it?

Word Bank 字庫

roof [ruf] n. 屋頂
exterminator [ɪkˋstɜmə,netə] n. 消滅者
sink [sɪŋk] n. 水槽

→ 重要單字解釋

Useful Phrases 實用語句 → 各生活場景常用句子

1. 浴室漏水。
   There's a leak in the bathroom.
2. 屋頂 [水管] 漏水。
   The roof [a pipe] is leaking.
3. 馬桶阻塞。
   The toilet is plugged.

住所
郵電通訊
日常活動
銀行與保險
交通
食品與飲食
購物
社交活動
教育
休閒活動
醫療
緊急情況

Notes 小叮嚀 ➔ 在美生活應注意事項

即使在網路服務已十分普遍的情形下，基於安全理由，美國多數公共服務要求顧客在第一次申請安裝時，必須親自到場辦理，出示身分證明、填寫住家及公司地址、申請人姓名及電話等資料才能申請。

Language Power 字句補給站 ➔ 補充相關單字

◆ 了解帳單 Understanding a Phone Bill

online billing	網路帳單
paper billing	紙本帳單
account summary	帳戶總結

Tips 小祕訣 ➔ 快速適應美國生活的妙方

10-10 繞撥系統 10-10 Dial Around Services

在美國撥打長途或國際電話，可以加入特定直接撥號 (direct dial) 節費計畫系統，也可以選擇使用 10-10-xxx 繞撥 (dial around) 系統，繞撥不需特定業者，多撥幾個號碼使用可能比較划算的費率，家用電話或手機皆適用，使用電話卡其實就是繞撥系統的應用。

Cultural Tips 文化祕笈 ➔ 介紹美國風俗習慣

📖 課堂學習與互動

在美國讀書的學習態度要主動積極，在各級學校都一樣，課前預習 (preview)，課後複習 (review)，在課堂上必須適時表達意見，這些都需要足夠的語言能力才能漸入佳境，除了了解教材及課外書籍內容之外，美國人強調創新及批判性的見解 (creative and critical thinking [feedback]) 而不是重複或抄襲教材或課外書裡的意見，抄襲交出去的報告可是會被退學的。另外，可以和同學討論上課內容，但同學的筆記是不可能借來影印的。

目錄

Unit 12 緊急情況 Emergencies

附錄 Appendixes

字句補給站 Language Power

Unit 1 Housing

住所

到美國的新環境找房子，人生地不熟，自己及家人的需要如學校位置、工作地點、購物、交通、公園、休閒設施、生活方式等都要列入考慮。無論買屋或租屋，都需要時間和耐性，才能找到一個可信賴的房仲商或不占便宜的房東。

住所

郵電通訊

日常活動

銀行與保險

交通

食品與飲食

購物

社交活動

教育

休閒活動

醫療

緊急情況

1.1 找房子
Looking for a House

1.1a 詢問房屋仲介 Asking about Real Estate Agents

Dialog 對話

A: 哈囉，我是傑克徐，我在找一位會說中文的好房屋仲介。

A: Hello. I'm Jack Hsu. I'm looking for a good real estate agent that can speak Chinese.

B: 嗨，我是莎莉施，我可以幫你。

B: Hi. I'm Sally Hsih. I can help you.

A: 太好了，我在本地報紙看到你們仲介商的廣告，我與家人正要搬到這區，需要找一間公寓。

A: Great. I saw your agency's ad in the local newspaper. I'm moving to this area with my family and need to find an apartment.

B: 好，告訴我你要找什麼 (房子)。

B: OK. Tell me what you are looking for.

A: 我們要找沒有家具、附近安全、有好學校及購物便利。

A: We'd like something not furnished, in a safe neighborhood, with good schools and convenient shopping.

Word Bank 字庫

real estate n. 不動產
agent ['edʒənt] n. 仲介
ad [æd] n. 廣告 (advertisement 簡寫)
furnish ['fɜnɪʃ] v. 裝置家具
neighborhood ['nebɚˌhud] n. 鄰近區域

Useful Phrases 實用語句

● 詢問房屋仲介 **Asking about real estate agents**

1. 我在找一位好的仲介。

   I'm looking for a good real estate agent.

2. 這附近有好的房屋仲介商嗎？

   Are there any good real estate agencies around here?

3. 你們有任何會說中文的仲介嗎？

   Do any of your agents speak Chinese?

● 詢問房屋內外狀況 **Asking about a house**

1. 我在找一間房子來租。

   I'm looking for a house to rent.

2. 我現在回應我在報紙上看到的廣告。

   I'm responding to an ad I saw in the paper.

3. 你何時可以帶我看房子？

   When can you show me the house?

4. 請描述平面圖。

   Describe the floor plan please.

5. 你今天可以帶我們看另一間房子嗎？

   Can you show us another house today?

住所
郵電通訊
日常活動
銀行與保險
交通
食品與飲食
購物
社交活動
教育
休閒活動
醫療
緊急情況

住所

郵電通訊

日常活動

銀行與保險

交通

食品與飲食

購物

社交活動

教育

休閒活動

醫療

緊急情況

4

1.1b 與仲介約定看房子

Talking to the Agent and Making an Appointment

 Dialog 對話

B: 你們要幾間臥房？

B: How many bedrooms do you want?

A: 我們至少要三間，我們還希望能住在安靜的地區。

A: We must have at least three. We also hope to live in a quiet neighborhood.

B: 我知道了，嗯，我們有幾個地方符合您的需求。

B: I see. Well, we have several places that fit your requirements.

A: 我們何時可以看這些地方？

A: When can we look at some of them?

B: 明天下午如何？

B: How about tomorrow afternoon?

A: 沒問題，我太太那時也可以。

A: No problem, my wife is available then too.

B: 如果你想的話，現在我們可以在電腦上看房屋平面圖。

B: If you'd like, we can look at floor plans on the computer.

A: 好主意。

A: Good idea.

住所

郵電通訊

日常活動

銀行與保險

交通

食品與飲食

購物

社交活動

教育

休閒活動

醫療

緊急情況

Word Bank 字庫

fit [fɪt] v. 符合
requirement [rɪˋkwaɪrmənt] n. 需求
available [əˋveləbl] adj. 有空的
floor plan n. 平面圖

Useful Phrases 實用語句

1. 我們在找一間環境好的房子。
   We're looking for a house in a good neighborhood.

2. 我們要住在安全的地區。
   We'd like to live in a safe neighborhood.

3. 我們希望找一個安靜的地區來住。
   We're hoping to find a quiet neighborhood to live in.

4. 大眾運輸的便利很重要。
   Access to public transportation is important.

5. 我們要找靠近好學校的房子。
   We're looking for a house close to good schools.

6. 購物要方便。
   Shopping needs to be convenient.

7. 我們要三間臥房的公寓。
   We want a three-bedroom apartment.

8. 我們要兩層樓的房子。
   We're looking for a two-floor house.

9. 我們要找一間附家具的公寓。
   We need to find a furnished apartment.

10. 這房子有什麼樣的安全系統？
    What kind of security system does the house have?

11. 這公寓社區有停車位嗎？
    Is parking available at the apartment complex?

住所

郵電通訊
日常活動
銀行與保險
交通
食品與飲食
購物
社交活動
教育
休閒活動
醫療
緊急情況

12. 這公寓 [房子] 包含什麼家電？

What appliances are included in the apartment [house]?

13. 有冷氣嗎？

Is it air conditioned?

14. 主要暖氣來源是什麼？

What is the main heat source?

15. (房子) 有什麼特色？

What special features does it have?

16. 後院有多大？

How big is the backyard?

17. 有遊戲區嗎？

Are there any playgrounds?

18. 房子朝哪個方向？

Which direction does the house face?

19. 這地區對寵物好嗎？

Is this a good area for pets?

1.2 租房子
Renting a House

Dialog 對話

A: 這裡房租多少呢？

A: How much is the rent for this place?

B: 月租是 950 元，含水、電、瓦斯。

B: The monthly rent is $950, and that includes utilities.

A: 其他的費用呢？

A: What about any other additional fees?

住所

郵電通訊

日常活動

銀行與保險

交通

食品與飲食

購物

社交活動

教育

休閒活動

醫療

緊急情況

B: 兩輛車免停車費。

B: Parking for two cars is free.

A: 訪客可以在哪裡停車呢？

A: Where can guests park?

B: 事實上在街上也有很多停車位。

B: Actually there is a lot of free parking available on the street, too.

A: 押金多少錢呢，還有我們必須先付幾個月的房租？

A: How much is the security deposit, and how many months do we have to pay in advance?

B: 房東要第一和最後一個月的房租及200元押金。

B: The landlord requires first and last month, and a $200 security deposit.

A: 好，我需要知道如果房子有任何問題的話要跟誰聯絡。

A: OK. And I need to know who to contact if there are any problems with the house.

B: 房東不管事，我們代為管理，所以你可以聯絡我。

B: The landlord is an absentee owner. We manage the property for him, so you can contact me.

Word Bank 字庫

utility [ju`tɪlətɪ] n. 水、電、瓦斯等公用服務
additional [ə`dɪʃənl] adj. 另外的
security deposit n. 押金
absentee owner n. 不管事的房東

住所

郵電通訊

● 房客詢問訂約承租及解約

Tenant asking about payments, fees, and contract details

1. 每月租金多少？

   What is the rent each month?

2. 包含水、電、瓦斯費嗎？

   Are utilities included in the price?

3. 有維護 (管理) 費嗎？

   Is there a maintenance fee?

4. 停車要收費嗎？

   Are there any charges for parking?

5. 我何時及如何付房租呢？

   When and how do I pay the rent?

6. 押金多少呢？

   How much is the security deposit?

7. 租約多久呢？

   How long will the lease last?

8. 合約何時到期呢？

   When will the contract expire?

9. 我要看合約的影本。

   I'd like to see a copy of the contract.

10. 公寓 [房子] 何時會準備好呢？

    When will the apartment [house] be ready?

11. 我要多一副鑰匙。

    I'd like to have an extra set of keys.

12. 我們要搬出去多久以前要預先通知？

    How much advance notice do we need to give before we move out?

日常活動　銀行與保險　交通　食品與飲食　購物　社交活動　教育　休閒活動　醫療　緊急情況

● 房東 [仲介] 回答訂約承租及解約
Landlord [Agent] talking about payments, fees, and contract details

1. 租金是一個月750元。

   The rent is $750 a month.

2. 水、電、瓦斯 (沒) 有包含在內。

   The utilities are (not) included.

3. 合約裡明訂房客要付所有公共服務如水、電、瓦斯等費用。

   The contract states the renter is responsible for all utility payments.

4. 有維護 (管理) 費，每個月25元。

   There is a maintenance fee of $25 a month.

5. 停車免費。

   Parking is free.

6. 停車另外收費。

   Parking costs extra.

7. 房租可以用個人支票付給我，或者你可以在自動提款機轉帳到我的帳戶。

   The rent can be paid by personal check to me, or you can transfer the money at an ATM to my account.

8. 房租每月一號到期。

   The rent is due on the first of the month.

9. 支票開給查爾斯提史密斯先生。

   Make out the check to Mr. Charles T. Smith.

10. 一年後合約到期。

    The lease expires after one year.

11. 我們將會每年談新合約。

    We'll talk about a new lease agreement each year.

12. 下星期房子會準備好。

    The house will be ready next week.

13. 如果你要搬走，你要在30天前預先通知。

    You need to tell 30 days in advance if you plan to move out.

住所
郵電通訊
日常活動
銀行與保險
交通
食品與飲食
購物
社交活動
教育
休閒活動
醫療
緊急情況

住所

郵電通訊

日常活動

銀行與保險

交通

食品與飲食

購物

社交活動

教育

休閒活動

醫療

緊急情況

Tips　小祕訣

　　「缺席房東」是指不管事或不住當地而請公寓經理代管租賃及修繕事宜的房東。租屋時繳交的押金 (security deposit) 是房屋如果受損時或房客不付房租時要扣除的的費用；簽約多為一年一簽，繳交第一和最後一個月的房租及押金，因為要搬出前30天必須預先通知房東，所以最後一個月不必付房租。在約定退還押金期限前，房東必須退還所剩下押金，否則依據多數州的法律，房東必須賠償房客兩倍的金額給房客。因此，搬進租屋前要與經理確定房屋狀況良好，若有必要，可以在雙方都在場時拍下當時屋況以備將來之用，租約樣本請見附錄。

Hello, I'm Jack Hsu. I'm looking for a good real estate agent that can speak Chinese.

Hi, I'm Sally Hsih. I can help you.

Language Power 字句補給站

房屋廣告 **Housing Ads**

- an apartment with all the amenities 設備齊全舒適的公寓
- comfortably appointed 設備完善的
- controlled gate [access] 門禁
- intercom entry 對講機進入
- fully equipped kitchen 設備完善的廚房
- pets welcome 歡迎寵物
- pet friendly 對寵物友善的
- heated outdoor pool 溫水室外游泳池
- walk-in closet 走入式衣櫥
- short-term [corporate] lease available 可以簽短期[公司團體]合約
- state-of-the-art fitness center 新穎先進健身房
- wood-burning fireplace 燒木炭壁爐
- professionally landscaped courtyard 專業修整的中庭
- ceiling fan 吊扇
- laundry facilities 洗衣設備
- garbage disposal 垃圾處理
- great view 景觀好
- convenient location 地點方便
- schools nearby 鄰近學校
- safe neighborhood 安全社區
- close to parks 鄰近公園
- shopping nearby 鄰近購物
- parking included 包含停車
- close to public transportation 鄰近公共交通
- newly remodeled 新裝潢
- spacious kitchen 寬敞廚房
- central heating 中央暖氣
- 24 hour security 24小時警衛

住所
郵電通訊
日常活動
銀行與保險
交通
食品與飲食
購物
社交活動
教育
休閒活動
醫療
緊急情況

12

1.3 買房子
Buying a House

買房子需先有財源、挑中合適的房屋、經過議價、成交、交屋等手續才算完成，之後還有裝潢，搬家後才能安頓。委託專業的仲介商雖須支付大約房屋成交價 6% (可以商議)的佣金，但能省去許多時間及麻煩，電話簿及網路上很容易找到信譽良好的仲介商，在僑民較多的都市裡，華商年鑑或電話黃頁內有許多會說中文的不動產經紀人。買房子前若先讓銀行核可你的貸款，可加速從成交到交屋的手續；因些微利率差距會影響每月支付貸款的金額，必須多比較後選擇最好的貸款條件。

1.3a 在銀行與貸款人員談論房屋貸款
Asking about Home Loan at a Bank

Dialog 對話

A: 嗨，我想要和貸款人員談貸款。

A: Hi. I'd like to talk to a loan officer about a mortgage loan.

B: 我可以幫你，請坐。

B: I can help you. Please sit down.

A: 謝謝，我太太和我想買間房子。

A: Thanks. My wife and I are interested in buying a house.

B: 我了解了，你們要先從核准程序開始嗎？

B: I understand. Would you like to get started on being approved?

A: 是的，我們找房子前想先通過核准貸款。

A: Yes. We'd like to get pre-approved before we look for a home.

住所

郵電通訊

日常活動

銀行與保險

交通

食品與飲食

購物

社交活動

教育

休閒活動

醫療

緊急情況

B: 好主意，我拿出需要的表格。

B: Good idea. I'll take out the necessary forms.

A: 需要多久才會核准？

A: How long will it take to get approved?

B: 平均 4-6 週，要視確認你財務狀況的難易度以及我們處理申請的量而定。

B: On average, 4-6 weeks. It depends on how easy it is to verify your financial status and how busy we are processing applications.

A: 好，我們開始吧。

A: OK. Let's get started.

✎ Word Bank 字庫

loan [lon] n. 借貸
mortgage [`mɔrgɪdʒ] n. 抵押
approve [ə`pruv] v. 核准
verify [`vɛrə͵faɪ] v. 確認
financial status n. 財務狀況
process [`prasɛs] v. 處理

住所

郵電通訊

日常活動

銀行與保險

交通

食品與飲食

購物

社交活動

教育

休閒活動

醫療

緊急情況

14

1.3b 與仲介對話 Talking to a Realtor

Dialog 1　對話1

A: 午安,我是羅德泰勒,我可以為你效勞嗎?

A: Good afternoon. I'm Rod Taylor. May I help you?

B: 可以,我是吉姆石,我太太和我想買一棟房子。

B: Yes. I'm Jim Shi. My wife and I are interested in buying a house.

A: 我知道了,你們想要新房子還是中古屋?

A: I see. Are you interested in something new or already lived in?

B: 都可以,要看我們是否喜歡。

B: Either is OK, depending on whether we like it or not.

A: 好,我們坐下來討論你要找什麼樣的房子。

A: Alright. Please sit down and let's discuss what type of house you are looking for.

B: 謝謝,我們要至少三間房間及兩間浴室,我們也想住在靠近市區。

B: Thanks. We want at least three bedrooms and two baths. We also want to live near the city.

A: 你想要離學校及購物近的地方嗎?

A: Do you want to be close to schools and shopping?

B: 要，我們想住在西區，因為離我工作比較近。

B: Yes. And we would like to live on the west end of the city because it is closer to my work.

Dialog 2　對話2

A: (電話上) 哈囉，石先生，我是羅德泰勒，我已找到幾間你會喜歡的房子，你何時可以看屋呢？

A: (on phone) Hello, Mr. Shi, this is Rod Taylor. I have located several houses I think you'd like. When are you available to look at them?

B: 我太太和我這個週六可以。

B: My wife and I could do that this Saturday.

A: 好，我會聯絡屋主並確定我們可以過去看房子。

A: Great. I'll contact the owners and make sure it is OK for us to come around and look.

Word Bank　字庫

realtor [`riəltɚ] n. 仲介
locate [`loket] v. 找到

1.3c 出價 Making an Offer

Dialog　對話

A: 或許這間房子我們該出價。

A: Maybe we should make an offer on this house.

住所
郵電通訊
日常活動
銀行與保險
交通
食品與飲食
購物
社交活動
教育
休閒活動
醫療
緊急情況

B: 我同意，我們都喜歡，而且它幾乎都符合我們的要求。

B: I agree. We both like it, and it has most of the features we want.

A: 仲介說定價是 250,000元。

A: The realtor said it is priced at $250,000.

B: 我們出210,000元。

B: Let's make an offer of $210,000.

A: 好，我會告訴仲介我們的出價。

A: OK. I'll inform the realtor of our offer.

Tips　小祕訣

在美國買屋也有所謂的斡旋金 (earnest money) 通常約為總價的 1%，買方為顯示有誠意買屋，必須交付此價金予第三造 (通常為處理所有房屋交易文件的公司) 暫時保存。如果房屋交易順利，此價金轉為支付售價的一部分，如果交易未成，此價金退還買方，但是如果是毀約行為，斡旋金並不退還；因此一旦簽約，雙方必須迅速配合履行未完成交易所需，如估價、檢查等購屋步驟，不過在簽約後不想買屋也是可以的，只是會損失合約上規定的價金。

1.3d 屋主還價、自備款、每月貸款
Counter Offer, Down Payment, Monthly Payment

 Dialog 對話

A: 他們還價 230,000 元，你覺得呢？

A: Their counter offer is $230,000. What do you think?

B: 我很喜歡那間房子，我想我們應該接受。

B: I really like that house. I think we should accept.

A: 接受這價錢之前，我們來算一下每個月必須支付多少。

A: Let's figure out how much we need to pay each month before we accept the price.

B: 我們要付多少頭期款？

B: How much are we going to put down?

A: 我們付10%。

A: Let's put 10% down.

B: 我覺得要付15%，我們每個月可以少付點貸款。

B: I think we should put 15% down; we'll have a smaller mortgage to pay on.

A: 明天我會打給貸款人員確定我們的月付金額。

A: I'll call the loan officer tomorrow to make sure about our monthly payment.

B: 好。

B: All Right.

住所
郵電通訊
日常活動
銀行與保險
交通
食品與飲食
購物
社交活動
教育
休閒活動
醫療
緊急情況

Notes 小叮嚀

　　貸款買屋有三步驟——交付頭期款、辦好貸款和繳清交屋及其他交易完成之費用。在美國買屋貸款有許多選擇，端看個人對資金運用方式而定，不付半毛錢的全額貸款也是可能的，但是付房屋總價10%-20%的頭期款，並以低利借貸其餘成數貸款，也可能是划算的，所以買屋需要好好盤算或找專家諮詢省錢之道。房地產其實是個複雜但規範嚴謹的行業，所有經紀人都有執照，但是買賣交易協商可能複雜且冗長，有些經紀人會直接帶著貸款合約文件，所以買方不需與銀行或貸款公司交涉就可辦好貸款，但無論貸款來源為何，買主務必要注意利息的計算及其他所有加上去的成本。

1.3e 成交 Closing the Deal

Dialog 對話

A: 房子成交了，我們明天會跟銀行簽約，下個月可以搬進去。

A: The deal is closed. We'll sign the contract with the bank tomorrow. We can move in next month.

B: 每個月貸款多少？

B: What is the mortgage payment each month?

A: 1,050元。

A: $1,050.

B: 那有包含房屋的保險嗎？

B: Does that include the insurance on the house?

A: 有。

A: Yes.

B: 我想我們最好開始準備搬家。

B: I guess we'd better start getting ready to move.

A: 對。

A: Right.

Useful Phrases 實用語句

1. 我需要準備多大一筆頭期款？
   How large of a down payment will I need to make?

2. 仲介費多少呢？
   How much is the realtor's fee?

3. 我們何時可以簽約？
   When can we sign the contract?

4. 我們何時可搬進去？
   When can we move in?

5. 合約有什麼條件？
   What are the terms of the contract?

6. 通知立約人 [承包人] 所需要的修繕。
   Contact these contractors for any needed repairs.

7. 我想讓我的律師看合約。
   I'd like my lawyer to see the contract.

8. 10號前你要付 25,000元。
   You need to pay $25,000 by the 10th.

9. 你可以寄支票或匯款。
   You can send a check or wire the money.

住所
郵電通訊
日常活動
銀行與保險
交通
食品與飲食
購物
社交活動
教育
休閒活動
醫療
緊急情況

左側縱欄：住所　郵電通訊　日常活動　銀行與保險　交通　食品與飲食　購物　社交活動　教育　休閒活動　醫療　緊急情況

Language Power　字句補給站

房屋種類 **Types of Houses**

town houses
（單棟或成排之）房屋，
較 row houses 寬敞

row houses 排屋（式樣相同）

brownstone
正面為褐色砂石砌成的房屋

detached [single] house
單棟房屋

duplex 雙拼

bungalow 簡單的木造平房

ranch house 單層平房（長條型）

two-story house 兩層樓房

farmhouse 農舍

cabin 小木屋

房屋種類 **Types of Houses** ②

住所

郵電通訊

日常活動

銀行與保險

交通

食品與飲食

購物

社交活動

教育

休閒活動

醫療

緊急情況

cottage 鄉下小屋

beach house 海邊度假屋

Tudor house 都鐸式

Victorian 維多利亞式

cedar house 杉木房

log house 木屋

apartment building 公寓

mansion 大廈

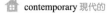 contemporary 現代的  custom built home 顧客定造房

condominium (住戶自有的)公寓

studio 套房，工作室 high rise 高樓

co-op (cooperative apartment) 住戶共同擁有的公寓

平面圖 **Floor Plan**

住所
郵電通訊
日常活動
銀行與保險
交通
食品與飲食
購物
社交活動
教育
休閒活動
醫療
緊急情況

① chimney 煙囪　　　　　② roof 屋頂

③ skylight 天窗　　　　　④ drainpipe/gutter 排水管

⑤ balcony 陽台　　　　　⑥ deck 露天平臺

⑦ storage 儲藏室　　　　⑧ garage 車庫

⑨ garden 花園　　　　　⑩ gatepost 門哨

⑪ fence 籬笆　　　　　　⑫ gate 圍牆門

⑬ lawn 草皮　　　　　　⑭ porch 門廊

⑮ stairs 樓梯　　　　　　⑯ patio 屋外鋪有石地板的露天空間(常用來聚餐、聊天)

⑰ deck chair 躺椅　　　　⑱ swimming pool 游泳池

⑲ driveway 車道　　　　⑳ hammock 吊床

㉑ backyard 後院　　　　㉒ playground 遊樂場

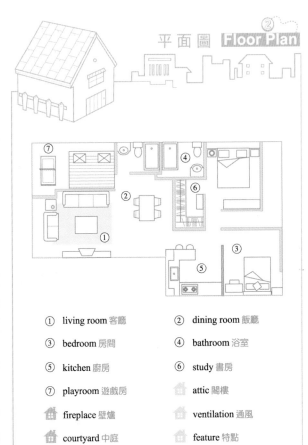

平面圖 Floor Plan ②

① living room 客廳　　② dining room 飯廳

③ bedroom 房間　　④ bathroom 浴室

⑤ kitchen 廚房　　⑥ study 書房

⑦ playroom 遊戲房　　attic 閣樓

fireplace 壁爐　　ventilation 通風

courtyard 中庭　　feature 特點

terrace 庭院陽臺　　basement 地下室

◆ 地點 Locations

city [urban] area	城市
the suburbs	郊區
small town	小鎮
country, rural area	鄉村
downtown	市區

住所　郵電通訊　日常活動　銀行與保險　交通　食品與飲食　購物　社交活動　教育　休閒活動　醫療　緊急情況

lakeside	湖邊
forest land	林區
agricultural zone	農業區
protected area	保護區
farmland	農地
residential area	住宅區
trailer park	貨櫃屋區
wetlands	溼地
business district	商業區
waterfront	濱水區

◆ 合約用字 Contract Vocabulary

contract	合約
get a loan	借款
undersigned	下方簽名的
buyers	買方
sellers	賣方
down payment	頭期款
amount financed	貸款金額
terms	期數
interest rate	利率
fixed-rate	固定利率
adjustable rate	浮動利率
promissory note	約定摘錄
lien	抵押權，債權
as is	如同
title	抬頭
transfer title	轉讓抬頭
transferring cost	轉讓成本
provisions and conditions	條款
monthly payment	月付
make an offer	議價
counter offer	還價

ownership	擁有權
closing	成交，結案
commission	佣金

1.4 搬家
Moving

1.4a 與搬家公司通話 Calling a Moving Company

Dialog 1 對話 1

A: 哈囉，我要請搬家人員過來。

A: Hello. I need to arrange for a mover to come.

B: 你要搬到哪裡？

B: Where are you moving to?

A: 我們剛從國外搬進一間新房子，所有的東西現在都在港口倉庫。

A: We just moved into a new house from abroad. Everything now is in the harbor warehouse.

B: 你有多少貨櫃，貨櫃多大呢？

B: How many containers do you have and how big are they?

住所
郵電通訊
日常活動
銀行與保險
交通
食品與飲食
購物
社交活動
教育
休閒活動
醫療
緊急情況

A: 兩個，都是10呎長、8呎寬及8呎高，你可以告訴我運費要多少錢嗎？

A: Two. Both are 10 feet long, 8 feet wide and eight high. Can you tell me how much the moving cost will be?

B: 我先去看，再告訴你價錢，之後才派搬運工人。

B: I'll go check first and tell you the cost before sending the movers.

A: 好，我們可以今天下午兩點在倉庫碰面嗎？

A: OK. Can we meet at the warehouse this afternoon at 2 p.m.?

B: 好，但請你先告訴我是哪個倉庫以及你的電話號碼。

B: Fine, but you need to tell me which warehouse and your phone number please.

Word Bank 字庫

arrange [əˋrendʒ] v. 安排
container [kənˋtenɚ] n. 貨櫃
warehouse [ˋwɛrˏhaʊs] n. 倉庫
mover [ˋmuvɚ] n. 搬運工人

Dialog 2 對話2

A: 我們要搬到城另一邊的一棟新房子。

A: We are moving across town to a new house.

B: 你可以告訴我有多少要搬的？

B: Can you tell me how much you have to move?

住所

郵電通訊

日常活動

銀行與保險

交通

食品與飲食

購物

社交活動

教育

休閒活動

醫療

緊急情況

A: 我們要把所有東西從四間房間的房子搬出來。

A: We have to move everything out of our four-bedroom house.

B: 我知道了，聽起來你有很多東西。

B: I see. It sounds like you have a lot.

A: 是的，你可以為我們搬家估價嗎？

A: Yes, we do. Can you estimate the cost of moving us?

B: 我去看一下比較好。

B: It would be best if I came over and looked.

A: 好，你可以今天來嗎？

A: OK. Can you come today?

B: 可以，今天下午兩點好嗎？

B: Sure. Is this afternoon around 2:00 OK?

A: 好的，我告訴你地址。

A: Yes, that's fine. Let me tell you our address.

B: 好，也請告訴我電話號碼。

B: Good. Please give me your phone number, too.

 Dialog 3 對話3

A: 我需要自己打包嗎？

A: Do I need to pack things myself?

住所

B: 你可以自己打包，省錢省時間，或者我們可以做。

B: You can do it and save time and money, or we can do it.

A: 你們會帶打包的箱子嗎？

A: Will you bring boxes for packing?

B: 我們可以帶，但是會加收費用。

B: We can, but they will add to the cost.

A: 你們打包怎麼算？

A: What do you charge for packing?

B: 兩倍收費。

B: If we pack things, it will cost twice as much.

A: 我們需要拆大件家具嗎？

A: Do we need to detach big furniture?

B: 我們會處理大件物品不加價。

B: We'll take care of big items for no extra charge.

✎ Word Bank 字庫

> estimate [ˋɛstəˌmet] v. 估價
> pack [pæk] v. 打包
> detach [dɪˋtætʃ] v. 拆卸
> furniture [ˋfɝnɪtʃɚ] n. 家具

 Useful Phrases 實用語句

1. 我需要打電話給搬家公司。

   I need to call a mover.

2. 我們租搬家卡車吧。

   Let's rent a moving truck.

3. 我們需要打包每件東西。

   We need to pack everything up.

4. 請小心打包 [搬運，拆裝] 這些易碎品。

   Please pack [move, unpack] those fragile things carefully.

5. 搬家人員會明天來這裡。

   The movers will be here tomorrow.

1.4b 在搬家卡車公司 At a Rental Truck Company

 Dialog 對話

A: 我想租搬家卡車。 → **A:** I'd like to rent a moving truck.

B: 你需要多大的尺寸？ → **B:** What size do you need?

A: 我想 20 呎載貨板就足夠。 → **A:** I think a 20 foot bed will be good enough.

B: 你可以租一臺，29.95 元可以租 8 小時，每英里加 99 分錢。 → **B:** You can rent one for eight hours for \$29.95, with a 99¢ per mile rate.

A: 車子含任何設備嗎？	**A:** Does it have any equipment with it?
B: 有，有固定繩、大物件的保護墊及一臺推車。	**B:** Yes. It has tie down straps, protective padding for big items, and a dolly.
A: 聽起來不錯，卡車有保險嗎？	**A:** That sounds good. Is the truck insured?
B: 有，已包含在租金裡面，是原本租金再加2元。	**B:** Yes. That's included in the rental price for \$2 more.
A: 好，我租了。	**A:** OK, I'll take it.
B: 請出示你的駕照、一張有效的信用卡並且填寫這張表。	**B:** Please show me your driver's license, and a valid credit card, and fill out this form.

住所 郵電通訊 日常活動 銀行與保險 交通 食品與飲食 購物 社交活動 教育 休閒活動 醫療 緊急情況

Tips 小祕訣

　　美國人較世界多數國家人民移動頻繁，其移動力 (mobility) 反映在搬家次數上，美國文化期待年輕人在高中畢業後搬離父母外出獨立，就學、就業及尋找成功機會，人們通常在工作穩定及成家後搬家次數才會減少，而經濟榮枯也直接影響搬家移動的多寡。

　　如果不是搬的很遠 (in town move) 或家當多又重，需要專業搬家公司的話，在美國許多人搬家是自己到搬家卡車公司租輛合適的卡車來搬家，可以選擇大點的車裝滿或小點的車來回幾趟搬完，如果搬到較遠城市，只搬一趟 (one way move)，可以在搬去後的城市還車。租車若以小時計價，要注意還車時間不要超過，租車前可以先在網路上查價挑選 (租車公司會列出幾房約需多大的尺寸供參考)，輸入租車尺寸、地點及租車時間後即可查詢租車價格並訂車。租車通常需另買保險，但有時租車公司已把最低額保險加入定價，如需搬家工具，租車公司也可以提供。

Language Power 字句補給站

◆ 搬家 Moving

capacity	容量，載貨量
three rolls of tape	三捲膠帶
furniture pads	家具墊
rope	繩索
lock	鎖
bubble wrap	泡棉
fragile	易碎的
mattress bags	床墊防護袋
appliance dolly	家電推車

住所
郵電通訊
日常活動
銀行與保險
交通
食品與飲食
購物
社交活動
教育
休閒活動
醫療
緊急情況

1.5 認識鄰居
Meeting the Neighbors

 Dialog 對話

A: 哈囉，我是徐珍，我們剛搬到你隔壁。

A: Hello. I'm Jane Hsu. We just moved in next to you.

B: 嗨，我是雪莉泰勒，很高興認識你。

B: Hi. I'm Sherry Taylor. Nice to meet you.

A: 我也很高興認識你。我先生、小孩和我才剛來兩三個禮拜。

A: It's very nice to meet you, too. My husband, children, and I just arrived a few weeks ago.

B: 歡迎來到這社區。

B: Welcome to the neighborhood.

A: 謝謝，我可以問你關於本地服務的幾個問題嗎？

A: Thank you. Could I ask you a few questions about local services?

B: 當然囉，你要知道什麼呢？

B: Sure. What would you like to know?

 Useful Phrases 實用語句

1. 嗨，我是徐珍，我們剛搬來。

   Hi. I'm Jane Hsu. We just moved in.

住所 郵電通訊 日常活動 銀行與保險 交通 食品與飲食 購物 社交活動 教育 休閒活動 醫療 緊急情況

2. 我先生、小孩及我才剛搬來這裡。

   My husband, children, and I just moved here.

3. 我們打算在這裡住兩年。

   We plan to live here for two years.

4. 我先生在 CS Chandler 公司工作。

   My husband works at CS Chandler Corporation.

5. 你可以告訴我怎麼安排電話服務嗎？

   Can you tell me how to arrange phone service?

6. 關於我們的小孩上學，我們要聯絡誰？

   Who should we contact about having our children enter school?

7. 這裡的商業區何時打烊呢？

   What time do shopping districts close here?

8. 我們期望我們的東西很快從國外寄到這裡。

   We're expecting our things from overseas to arrive here soon.

9. 我有時候可以向你請教嗎？

   May I ask for your advice sometimes?

10. 郵差什麼時候來呢？

    What time does the mail carrier come?

Tips 小祕訣

認識新鄰居通常不難，但各地做法不同。住在中小城鎮的人很容易碰到面，這時你可以走過去自我介紹，或敲他們的門自我介紹是這社區的一份子，有些鄰居會到你家自我介紹或送上歡迎禮，你也可以選擇要不要回送個小禮，但你的鄰居不認為你需要這麼做，送禮物也並不代表你就被新社區接受；在大城市，通常大家各管各的，所以鄰居多半不熟，但有些出租社區大家至少還知道鄰居是誰。

如果你受邀到別人家裡晚餐、烤肉或鄰居聚會，最好帶瓶酒或其他可以貢獻給這場合的東西，最好要準時，除非約定好要幫忙，否則不要早到。

住所

郵電通訊

日常活動

銀行與保險

交通

食品與飲食

購物

社交活動

教育

休閒活動

醫療

緊急情況

住所
郵電通訊
日常活動
銀行與保險
交通
食品與飲食
購物
社交活動
教育
休閒活動
醫療
緊急情況

1.6 水、電、瓦斯
Utilities (Water, Electricity, Gas)

Dialog 對話

A: 午安，賀福城電力及照明公司。

A: Good afternoon, Havertown Power and Light.

B: 嗨，我打電話來請人來接電。

B: Hi, I'm calling about having electricity hooked up.

A: 好，請告訴我你的名字及地址。

A: OK, Please tell me your name and address.

B: 徐珍，我先生是朗，我們的地址是格蘭街344號。

B: Jane Hsu. My husband's name is Ron. Our address is 344, Grant Street.

A: 謝謝，我明天會派人去那裡。

A: Thank you. I'll send someone there tomorrow.

B: 什麼時候呢？

B: What time?

A: 大約下午 2 點到 3 點間。

A: Sometime between 2:00 and 3:00 in the afternoon.

B: 有接線費嗎？

B: Is there a hookup fee?

A: 有，接線費35元。
A: Yes. The fee for hooking up is $35.

B: 我們要付錢給來接線的人嗎？
B: Do we pay the man that comes to turn it on?

A: 不用，你們之後會收到郵寄帳單。
A: No, you'll be billed by mail later.

Word Bank 字庫

hook up 連接
fee [fi] n. 費用

Tips 小祕訣

除了垃圾收集外，其他公用服務對話內容類似。

Useful Phrases 實用語句

1. 我要我的新房子供水。
   I'd like to have the water turned on at my new home.
2. 我們需要我們的新房子 [公寓] 供電。
   We need the electricity turned on at our house [apartment].
3. 我需要接一支電話。
   I'd like to have a phone hooked up.
4. 我必須知道長途電話選擇方案。
   I need to know about long-distance options.
5. 我打來是要求供應 (天然) 瓦斯。
   I'm calling about having the (natural) gas turned on.

住所
郵電通訊
日常活動
銀行與保險
交通
食品與飲食
購物
社交活動
教育
休閒活動
醫療
緊急情況

6. 我要停止服務。

   I'd like to have service discontinued.

7. 開始供應瓦斯要多少錢？

   How much does it cost to have the gas turned on?

8. 瓦斯 [電話，電力，水] 費一個月多少錢？

   What does gas [phone service, electricity, water] cost a month?

9. 我該如何繳款？

   How do I pay the bill?

10. 你們公司可以裝一個防漏偵測器嗎？

    Can your company install a gas leak detector?

11. 沒電。

    The power [electricity] is off [out].

12. 沒水 [瓦斯，電話]。

    The water [gas, phone] service is off.

13. 帳單10號到期。

    The bill is due on the 10th.

14. 沒有撥號音。

    There's no dial tone.

15. 有條線路斷了。

    There is a line down.

Language Power 字句補給站

◆ 公共服務 Utilities

natural gas (for cooking or heating)	天然瓦斯
phone service	電話服務
long-distance service	長途電話
electrical power/electricity	電力
hook-up	連接
connection	接線
disconnected	斷線

bill	帳單
start [stop] service	開始 [停止] 服務
pay the bill	付帳單
make a late payment	延遲付款
gas meter	瓦斯表
water meter	水表
electrical meter	電表
pay this amount	付這筆款項
due by 00/00/00	到期日
gallon	加侖
sanitation fee	清潔費

Tips （小祕訣）

　　申裝家裡水、電、瓦斯、電話服務，對話及手續通常很類似，除非所居住的地區有管線問題，一般情況在填表及出示證件後，很快就來服務。使用電、瓦斯或其他能源要看當地可使用能源的情況而定，在能源普遍的地區，每戶人家廚房、熱水器、暖氣等可以有電氣或瓦斯等不同選擇，在美國廚房使用電力烹調很普遍，若是租來的房子，不一定附有微波爐及洗碗機，但會有公共的投幣式洗衣機及烘乾機，雖然租屋條件可能大不相同，但是較熱及較冷地區的租屋通常包含冷暖氣，因為依照美國法規，租屋必須提供安全及合理的舒適環境。付款通常有幾種方式：個人支票、網上付款或銀行自動轉帳，但有些方式需要經過安排才可轉帳或扣款，想使用網路達成所需的服務有時可能是一項挑戰，一來透過網路設定必須要用英文且商業網路服務目前缺少一套公式可循，各家服務有不同的案件名稱及商業術語；是否可以將費用列入信用卡帳單也要看各家政策而定，面對面與服務代表溝通應該是最好的。停用服務通常很簡單，只要一個月前通知不再需要服務即可，但要安排最後一期帳單地址及繳款問題，還要記得將 (全部的或剩下的) 押金拿回。

住所
郵電通訊
日常活動
銀行與保險
交通
食品與飲食
購物
社交活動
教育
休閒活動
醫療
緊急情況

住所
郵電通訊
日常活動
銀行與保險
交通
食品與飲食
購物
社交活動
教育
休閒活動
醫療
緊急情況

1.7 垃圾處理及回收
Garbage Handling and Recycle

 Dialog 對話

A: 城市清潔，我可以為你效勞嗎？

A: City Sanitation, may I help you?

B: 是的，我要了解垃圾清運收費及時間。

B: Yes. I want to know about garbage pickup charges and times.

A: 好的，你住在哪一區？

A: Alright. What part of the city do you live in?

B: 我們的地址是格蘭街344號，我們在城市的南區。

B: Our address is 344 Grant Street. We're in the south end of the city.

A: 好，我看到我們的行程表，垃圾車在星期二及星期五早上大約9點到你們社區。

A: Fine. I see on our schedule that the garbage trucks come around 9 a.m. on Tuesday and Friday in your neighborhood.

B: 好，我還有回收的問題，這裡怎麼做的呢？

B: OK. I also have a question about recycling. How is it done here?

住所

郵電通訊

A: 我們會給你不同顏色的塑膠桶，上面貼有標籤告訴你放入哪種回收物。

A: We give you color-coded plastic containers. There are stickers on each container telling you what types of recyclables go in each one.

日常活動

B: 回收日與平常垃圾收集日一樣嗎？

B: Are the pickup days the same as regular garbage?

銀行與保險

A: 不一樣，我們只在星期二到你們那區收取回收物。

A: No, they are not. We only pick recyclable materials up on Tuesdays in your area.

交通

Word Bank 字庫

charge [tʃɑrdʒ] v. 收費
container [kən`tenɚ] n. 容器
recycle [ri`saɪkl] v. 回收
plastic [`plæstɪk] adj. 塑膠的
sticker [`stɪkɚ] n. 貼紙

食品與飲食

購物

Useful Phrases 實用語句

1. 垃圾清潔員星期幾來？
   What days do the garbage men come?
2. 我們何時該把要收走的垃圾拿出去而且要放哪裡？
   When and where do we put the garbage out for pickup?
3. 我們要把垃圾放在哪種垃圾桶裡？
   What kind of containers do we have to put our garbage in?
4. 回收物該怎麼辦？
   What should we do with recyclable materials?

社交活動

教育

休閒活動

醫療

緊急情況

Language Power 字句補給站

◆ 垃圾 **Garbage**

garbage, trash	垃圾
garbage pickup	收垃圾
garbage men [collector]	垃圾清潔人員
garbage truck	垃圾車
garbage can	垃圾箱
garbage dump	垃圾場 [堆]
sanitation department	清潔 [環保] 部門
dumpster	有蓋附輪子的大型垃圾箱
haul garbage	拖拉垃圾 (將大垃圾箱拉起倒進垃圾車)
recycle bin	回收桶
disposal	廚餘碾碎機 (裝置在廚房水槽，可將廚餘碾碎後沖掉)

 Tips 小祕訣

　　各地垃圾清運及回收時間表不同，通常大城市比中小型城鎮有較頻繁的清運。

　　在美國，人們使用垃圾桶及大垃圾箱，在收垃圾的那天，垃圾箱會被拖出來擺在人行道，清潔人員會來清掉垃圾及居民整理出來的回收物品，如果你住在公寓或社區住宅，可以將垃圾丟到公用的大型垃圾箱，如果住在鄉下，也用垃圾箱，垃圾車每個月可能只來兩次，你可以載垃圾到垃圾場，付錢讓人幫忙卸下來，而不必付費讓垃圾車來你家清垃圾，但是這樣比較不方便。各地垃圾清運費不同，但因為是基本服務，通常收費不高，大約為 $20-$30。

1.8 家電設備與裝修
Home Appliances, Decoration, and Repair

 Dialog 1 對話1

A: 哈囉，我們來修理你的屋頂。

A: Hello. We're here to fix your roof.

B: 好，房子後面已經漏水漏了好幾個星期。

B: Great. It's been leaking in the back of the house for weeks.

A: 知道了，我的夥伴跟我會上去查看。

A: I see. My crew and I will get up there and check it out.

B: 謝謝，要多久時間來修呢？

B: Thank you. How long will it take to fix it?

A: 要等到我們知道是什麼問題才能告訴你，但是我想應該要4到5個小時來修理。

A: I won't know until we know what's wrong, but I believe we will probably have it repaired in four or five hours.

住所

郵電通訊 日常活動 銀行與保險 交通 食品與飲食 購物 社交活動 教育 休閒活動 醫療 緊急情況

Dialog 2 對話2

A: 嗨，我是你找來的除蟲人員，你遭螞蟻蟲害，對嗎？

A: Hi. I'm the exterminator you called for. You have ants, right?

B: 是的，我很高興你來。

B: Yes, we do. I'm so glad you are here.

A: 帶我看牠們在哪裡。

A: Show me where they are.

B: 大部分在靠近廚房水槽這裡，但是其實到處都有。

B: Mostly they are in here near the kitchen sink, but they are generally everywhere.

A: 好，我先看看，之後再告訴你要怎麼做。

A: Alright, I'll look around, and then tell you what needs to be done after that.

Word Bank 字庫

roof [ruf] n. 屋頂
exterminator [ɪkˋstɝməˌnetɚ] n. 消滅者
sink [sɪŋk] n. 水槽

Useful Phrases 實用語句

1. 浴室漏水。

   There's a leak in the bathroom.

2. 屋頂 [水管] 漏水。

   The roof [a pipe] is leaking.

3. 馬桶阻塞。

   The toilet is plugged.

4. 馬桶不能沖水。

   The toilet won't flush.

5. 冰箱不夠冷。

   The freezer is not cold enough.

6. 冰箱不會自動除霜。

   The freezer will not self-defrost.

7. 熱水器壞了。

   The hot-water heater is not working.

8. 熱水器漏水。

   The hot-water heater is leaking.

9. 冷氣壞了 [不能正常運作]。

   The air-conditioner is broken [is not working well].

10. 我們的暖氣壞了。

    Our heater is not working.

11. 我們房子裡有蟲。

    We have bugs in our house.

12. 我們房子裡有很多螞蟻。

    We have lots of ants in the house.

13. 樓梯需要修理。

    The stairs need to be repaired.

14. 我們的房子需要油漆。

    Our house needs to be painted.

15. 我要裝潢室內。

    I'd like to have the interior decorated.

16. 我的洗衣機壞了。

    My washing machine is broken.

17. 我需要修理人員來這裡。

    I need a repairman to come here.

18. 我們家需要鋪新地毯。

    We need new carpeting in our home.

19. 我們要裝些新燈。

    We'd like to have some new light fixtures installed.

住所 郵電通訊 日常活動 銀行與保險 交通 食品與飲食 購物 社交活動 教育 休閒活動 醫療 緊急情況

住所
郵電通訊
日常活動
銀行與保險
交通
食品與飲食
購物
社交活動
教育
休閒活動
醫療
緊急情況

20. 我們要重新裝修這房子。

We need to completely remodel this house.

21. 我需要費用估價單。

I'd like a cost estimate.

22. 水管工人何時會到這裡？

What time will the plumber be here?

23. 你可以明天來嗎？

Can you come tomorrow?

24. 你的維修工作有保固嗎？

Is your work guaranteed?

25. 要花多久時間修理？

How long will it take to fix it?

26. 你今天可以修理嗎？

Can you repair it today?

27. 新的一個多少錢？

What does a new one cost?

28. 這可以修理或是需要換新的嗎？

Can you fix it, or does it have to be replaced?

29. 我有什麼選擇呢？

What options do I have?

Notes 小叮嚀

　　通常維修人員會在查看問題後，給你維修、更新或替換等建議，當然價錢也依照需求而有異。在美國，水管工、電工與線路工是分開的，各司其責，維修服務是以小時計費，因此在施工前要先估價 (get a cost estimate)，並請不同維修服務站估價後再施工，打聽口碑好的服務也是必要的，所謂貨比三家不吃虧，若是租屋的修繕，應由房東付費，所以要聯絡房東，並且要了解當地租屋法律以保護自己；美國人工昂貴，若是自家的房屋需要簡單的修繕或裝修工作，如油漆、組裝家具、簡單的水電工作、修剪庭院花草等，可以自己動手 (DIY)，許多美國人也樂此不疲。

Language Power 字句補給站

◆ 家電設備及修理工作 Appliances and Repair Work

refrigerator	冰箱
freezer	(冰箱) 冷凍庫
stove	爐子
oven	烤箱
dishwasher	洗碗機
air-conditioner	冷氣
central air-conditioning	中央空調
central heating	中央暖氣
heat pump	熱泵 (將熱氣由低溫移向高溫的裝置)
heating oil	暖氣油料
space heating	空間暖化
solar panel	太陽能板
water heater	熱水器
smoke detector	煙霧感應器
electrician	電工
plumber	水管工
lineman	線路工
remodel, renovate	裝潢，裝修
paint	油漆
dig	挖掘
scrape	刮除
replace	更新

住所

郵電通訊

日常活動

銀行與保險

交通

食品與飲食

購物

社交活動

教育

休閒活動

醫療

緊急情況

Unit 2 Communications

郵電通訊

美國雖是各國人士的大鎔爐，大城市也有其他語言的報紙、雜誌、廣播及電視臺，但要融入美國生活，就要能用英語溝通才行。

住所
郵電通訊
日常活動
銀行與保險
交通
食品與飲食
購物
社交活動
教育
休閒活動
醫療
緊急情況

2.1 家用電話
Home Phone

美國的電話是多家民營企業，申請電話時有分本地電話與長途電話 (國內/國際)，本地電話公司有 AT&T, Century Link, Qwest, Verizon 等，各有其特定的服務區域。撥打本地電話很便宜，基本月費多在 $20-$30 間。有些電話公司採用固定費率，其他公司以通話時間計價。申請電話通常需要支付押金，大約在 $40-$100 之間。有些公司會在你搬家後退還押金，但因為沒有強制性，有些公司並不退還押金。

傳統上當地電話服務基本上不提供長途電話服務，顧客必須在比過價格及服務後，自己選擇長途電話公司。大型長途電話公司有 AT&T, Verizon, Qwest, Century Link 等。但是現在也有當地電話公司搶進長途電話市場，並提出許多優惠方案。因此同一家公司可能在提供顧客當地電話服務外，另可提供長途電話服務。有些人選擇買長途電話預付卡來打電話，如此就不需要長途電話公司的服務了。另一個節費的選擇是使用越來越普遍的網路電話 Internet phone, wireless home phone 或 VoIP (Voice over Internet Protocol)。

電話公司的網頁提供服務項目、計價方案說明等訊息，輸入所在區域號碼即可查詢相關訊息，美國電話公司網頁 (如AT&T) 已提供中文網頁服務及中文專人接聽；新搬到一個地區，可以向鄰居請教他們選用的優惠電話服務。

因為競爭激烈，許多長途電話公司經常改變通話費率來吸引顧客轉換電話公司，各家公司業務員也經常打電話或在各商場以各種優惠勸進顧客轉換到該公司，電話公司也會整合所有提供服務之項目，如家用電話 (本地、長途、國際)、手機、網路等，推出優惠套裝服務，其中可能包含免費的家用電話線路。因災難發生時手機及網路未必能使用，使用地下電纜 (land lines) 的家用電話有其安全上的重要性。

2.1a 詢問方案及計價方式 Asking about Plans and Prices

住所

郵電通訊

日常活動

銀行與保險

交通

食品與飲食

購物

社交活動

教育

休閒活動

醫療

緊急情況

Dialog 1 對話1

A: 你可以告訴我本地電話的費率嗎？

A: Can you tell me the phone rates for local calls?

B: 可以，月費 19.34 元可以讓你無限制打電話。

B: Yes, you can make unlimited local calls with a monthly fee of $19.34.

A: 有任何限制或其他費用嗎？

A: Are there restrictions or additional charges?

B: 沒有，每天 24 小時都可以。

B: No, it's 24 hours a day, everyday.

Word Bank 字庫

unlimited [ʌnˋlɪmɪtɪd] adj. 無限制的
restriction [rɪˋstrɪkʃən] n. 限制
additional [əˋdɪʃənḷ] adj. 另外的
charge [tʃɑrdʒ] n. 費用

Tips 小祕訣

　　美國家用電話共有十碼 (與手機號碼數相同)，前三碼是區域號碼，後七碼是電話號碼，相同區域號碼是本地電話，不必打前三碼 (2010 年起已有十幾個州的特定地區必須撥十碼)。不同區域號碼為長途電話，需先打 1，再打區域號碼及電話號碼。電話公司在下班後及假日多有優惠時段。

住所

郵電通訊

日常活動

銀行與保險

交通

食品與飲食

購物

社交活動

教育

休閒活動

醫療

緊急情況

Dialog 2 對話2

A: 我想問家裡的長途電話計費方式。

A: I'd like to ask about the long-distance call plans for my home.

B: 你可以加入我們單一費率計畫。

B: You can sign up for our one rate plan.

A: 你可以解釋給我聽嗎?

A: Can you explain it to me?

B: 當然囉,我們提供每分鐘單一低價長途電話費率。

B: Sure, we offer one low per-minute rate for any long-distance calls.

A: 每分鐘多少錢呢?

A: How much is the rate per minute?

B: 我們有三種選擇,5分、7分及10分。

B: We offer three options. 5¢, 7¢, and 10¢.

A: 我要付月費嗎?

A: Do I need to pay a monthly fee?

B: 10 分計畫不必付月費。

B: There's no monthly fee for the 10¢ plan.

A: 那另外兩項呢?

A: What about the other two plans?

B: 7分計畫月費是 3.95 元，5 分計畫不需月費，但是有每月最低使用9元的規定。

B: The monthly fee is $3.95 for the 7¢ plan. There's no monthly fee for the 5¢ plan, but there's $9 monthly minimum usage requirement.

Word Bank 字庫

option [ˋɑpʃən] n. 選擇
minimum [ˋmɪnəməm] n. 最少，最低
requirement [rɪˋkwaɪrmənt] n. 規定

Dialog 3 對話3

A: 我想知道你們有什麼國際電話方案。

A: I'd like to find out what international call plans you have.

B: 我們提供超過200個國家的國際電話優惠費率，你最常打到哪一個國家呢？

B: We have great international rates for over 200 countries. Which country will you make the most phone calls to?

A: 臺灣。

A: Taiwan.

B: 每天任何時間，每分鐘7分。

B: It's 7¢ per minute anytime, everyday.

住所

郵電通訊

日常活動

銀行與保險

交通

食品飲食

購物

社交活動

教育

休閒活動

醫療

緊急情況

A: 我要付月費嗎？

A: Do I need to pay a monthly fee?

B: 要，但不多，月費是3.95元。

B: Yes, but not much. It's $3.95.

Useful Phrases　實用語句

1. 這裡的電話費率是多少呢？

   What are the phone rates here?

2. 你們有長途電話服務嗎？

   Do you have long-distance service?

3. 你們有什麼樣的長途電話服務呢？

   What kind of long-distance services do you have?

4. 何時打長途電話最便宜？

   When is the cheapest time to call long distance?

5. 有什麼額外費用呢？

   What additional charges are there?

6. 我要另外付語音信箱及電話插撥的費用嗎？

   Do I need to pay for voicemail and call waiting?

7. 月費包含許多電話服務在內。

   The monthly fee covers many features.

8. 每月 19.99 元你可以用每分鐘 4 分打美國長途電話和打到加拿大。

   With $19.99 per month you can make long-distance calls anywhere in the US and to Canada for 4¢ only per minute.

9. 每月 29.99 元你可以無限制打美國長途電話和打到加拿大。

   With $29.99 per month, you can make unlimited long-distance calls in the US and to Canada.

10. 我怎麼用家用電話 [手機] 撥打另一個國家的家用電話 [手機] ？

    How do I use my home [cell] phone to dial a home [cell] phone in another country?

住所

郵電通訊

日常活動

銀行與保險

交通

食品與飲食

購物

社交活動

教育

休閒活動

醫療

緊急情況

11. 從我家打到手機你們怎麼收費？

How much do you charge a call from my home to a cell phone?

Tips 小祕訣

　　長途電話 (包含打加拿大及加勒比海國家) 需先打 1，再打區域號碼及電話號碼；由美國打出的國際直撥電話，先打 011 (國際碼) 再打國家碼 (臺灣為 886) 及去掉 0 後的區域碼和電話號碼 (或手機號碼)。

Language Power 字句補給站

◆ 電話 The Phone

long distance	長途電話
overseas call	國外電話
extra line	另外的電話 [線路]
cell [mobile] phone	行動電話
Internet phone	網路電話
calling card	電話卡
flat rate	固定費率
unlimited calls	無限暢談
measured rate service	計時收費
per minute	每分鐘
feature	特點
weekend rate	週末價
lineman	線路工
unlisted number	(電話簿) 不列出號碼
call waiting	插撥
call forwarding	轉接
voicemail	語音信箱
caller ID	來電顯示
three-way-calling	三方通話
cordless phone	無線電話

call screen	電話過濾
anonymous call rejection	拒絕匿名電話
repeat dialing	重複撥號
speed calling	快速撥號

2.1b 申請與安裝 Application and Set Up

申請服務通常從填表及出示證件開始，申請各項服務的對話基本上大同小異，提供個人資料、了解是否有押金或到期日、額外費用、簽約、了解維修安排等都是常見的基本程序；如果有疑問，可以請教鄰居或致電公共服務委員會 (Public Utility Commission) 或相關單位幫忙解答疑惑。在移民多的城市，有專為不同國籍移民所設的電話服務中心，提供移民使用母語獲得所需服務，並有不同語言的電話簿或工商年鑑。

Dialog 對話

A: 哈囉，我是徐朗，我家要申裝電話。

A: Hello, my name is Ron Hsu. I'd like to get phone service started at my house.

B: 好，請告訴我你的名字及住址。

A: OK. Please tell me your name and address.

A: 徐朗，格蘭街344號。

A: Ron Hsu, 344, Grant Street.

B: 好的，徐先生，你要哪種服務？

B: Very well, Mr. Hsu. What kind of service would you like?

A: 呃，我不知道你們公司有提供什麼？

A: Well, I'm not aware of what your company offers.

B: 我們當然有本地服務，而且如果你連接我們的長途電話服務，會比其他長途電話公司便宜。

B: We have local service of course, and if you connect to our long-distance service, it's cheaper than other long-distance carriers.

Word Bank 字庫

offer [`ɔfə] v. 提供
connect [kə`nɛkt] v. 連接

Useful Phrases 實用語句

1. 我需要電話服務。

   We need telephone service.

2. 我需要轉接及插撥。

   I want call forwarding and call waiting.

3. 請盡快裝機。

   Please turn it on as soon as possible.

4. 我要填什麼表格呢？

   What forms do I need to fill out?

5. 我們要裝另一條線。

   We need another phone line installed.

Notes 小叮嚀

　　即使在網路服務已十分普遍的情形下，基於安全理由，美國多數公共服務要求顧客在第一次申請安裝時，必須親自到場辦理，出示身分證明、填寫住家及公司地址、申請人姓名及電話等資料才能申請。

住所
郵電通訊
日常活動
銀行與保險
交通
食品與飲食
購物
社交活動
教育
休閒活動
醫療
緊急情況

2.1c 帳單及付款 Billing and Payment

 Dialog 對話

A: 每個月帳單何時到期？

A: When is the monthly bill due?

B: 每月10號。

B: On the 10th of the month.

A: 每個月都有帳單明細嗎？

A: Will I get a detailed monthly bill?

B: 有，有不同服務的明細。

B: Yes, there are details for different services.

A: 我要如何付電話帳單？

A: How do I pay my phone bill?

B: 你可以用支票付款或在你的銀行設定自動轉帳。

B: You can pay by check, or you can set up automatic bill payment with your bank.

A: 可以在提款機轉帳嗎？

A: How about an ATM transfer?

B: 抱歉，我們沒有設定這個服務。

B: Sorry, we aren't set up for that.

A: 我可以用信用卡付款嗎？

A: Can I pay by credit card?

B: 可以的。

B: Yes, you can.

A: 萬一我過期才繳費呢？

A: What if my payment is late?

B: 我們有自動服務會打電話提醒你。如果你拖太久，服務就會被切斷。

B: We have an automated service that will call and remind you. If you wait too long however, service will be cut off.

A: 可以付現嗎？

A: Can I pay cash?

B: 可以，但是你要到我們服務處繳費。

B: Yes, but you'll have to come to our office to do it.

✏ Word Bank 字庫

automatic bill payment n. 自動轉帳
transfer [`trænsfɜ] n. 轉帳
remind [rɪ`maɪnd] v. 提醒

住所
郵電通訊
日常活動
銀行與保險
交通
食品與飲食
購物
社交活動
教育
休閒活動
醫療
緊急情況

Useful Phrases 實用語句

1. 電話帳單何時到期？

   When is the phone bill due?

2. 我們要如何付帳單？

   How do we pay the phone bill?

3. 我需要每個月帳單明細。

   I'd like a detailed monthly bill.

4. 請將帳單寄到我的地址。

   Please send the bill to my address.

5. 我不要號碼列在電話簿上。

   I want to have an unlisted number.

Language Power 字句補給站

◆ 了解帳單 Understanding a Phone Bill

online billing	網路帳單
paper billing	紙本帳單
account summary	帳戶總結
current charges	當期費用
recurring charges	循環費用
local telephone service	本地電話服務
charge for network access [subscriber line charge]	網路連線費 [用戶線路費]
local monthly charges	本地月租費
long-distance service charges	長途電話服務費
universal connectivity fee (universal service fund/carrier universal service charge)	全面電信接駁費 (電信業者有責任贊助聯邦政府補助低收入戶、偏鄉及公益性電話，但電信業者將費用轉嫁消費者)
Emergency 911	緊急電話
state TRS (telecommunications relay services)	州際電信撥接服務
Federal Excise Tax	聯邦賦稅 (帳單內一部分必須繳給聯邦政府)

Utility User Tax	基礎設備使用稅
state and local taxes	州及本地稅
domestic discount	國內折扣
state and local surcharge	州及本地附加費
single bill fee	單一帳單費
type	型態
rate	費率
minute	詳細的
place and number called	電話發話地及號碼
direct dial	直撥
operator assistance	接線生協助
directory assistance	查號臺

Tips　小祕訣

10-10 繞撥系統 10-10 Dial Around Services

在美國撥打長途或國際電話，可以加入特定直接撥號 (direct dial) 節費計畫系統，也可以選擇使用 10-10-xxx 繞撥 (dial around) 系統，繞撥不需特定業者，多撥幾個號碼使用可能比較划算的費率，家用電話或手機皆適用，使用電話卡其實就是繞撥系統的應用。

10-10的方案有許多種，例如：長途電話可以打 10-10-345-1-區域碼-電話號碼，國際電話打 10-10-345-011-國碼-區域碼-電話號碼；當然撥打的地區及國家不同，費率也不同。在網路搜尋引擎打上 10-10-345 即可查詢撥打各國的國際電話費率，如果是手機打海外手機，帳單會有一筆線路費，轉撥划算與否，有待消費者自行比價。

美國不像臺灣一樣可以在便利商店繳款，繳費有許多方式，包含寄出個人支票或從帳戶中自動扣款 (auto-billing)、使用網路銀行 (online banking)、撥打電話按照語音指示 (voice prompts) 輸入帳戶、信用卡號碼扣除，或下載電話公司之APP後，登入付費。若選擇去服務處繳納，付現金或個人支票都可以，如果錯過繳款日就必須到服務處去結清。

住所　郵電通訊　日常活動　銀行與保險　交通　食品與飲食　購物　社交活動　教育　休閒活動　醫療　緊急情況

住所

郵電通訊

2.1d 報修 Calling for Repair

 Dialog 對話

A: 艾迪生電力公司，我可以為你服務嗎？

A: Commonwealth Edison. How may I help you?

B: 我家停電了。

B: Power is out at my house.

A: 請告訴我你的名字及家裡的地址。

A: Please tell me your name and address.

B: 羅伯王，加菲街355號。

B: Robert Wong, 355 Garfield Street.

A: 好的，王先生，停電多久了？

A: Very well, Mr. Wong, how long has the power been out?

B: 我不確定，我剛到家，但這一區似乎都沒電。

B: I'm not sure. I just got home, but it appears no homes on this block have power.

A: 知道了，我會馬上派一組維修人員過去。

A: I see. I'll have a repair crew dispatched immediately.

B: 非常感謝你。

B: Thank you very much.

A: 不客氣，維修小組應該會在半小時內抵達。

A: My pleasure. The repair crew should arrive within half an hour.

Word Bank 字庫

block [blɑk] n. 街區
dispatch [dɪˋspætʃ] v. 派遣

Useful Phrases 實用語句

1. 我們需要維修人員來。
   We need a repairman to come.

2. 沒有電。
   The power is out.

3. 我們的電話壞了。
   Our phone is out of service.

4. 我們聽不到撥號音。
   We have no dial tone.

5. 我的留言服務壞了。
   My messaging service is not working.

6. 免費修理嗎？
   Is the repair free of charge?

7. 我需要在家等候嗎？
   Do I need to stay home waiting?

2.1e 停用 Termination

Dialog 對話

A: 哈囉，我可以為你服務嗎？	**A:** Hello. May I help you?
B: 是的，我打電話來永久停用我的電話。	**B:** Yes. I'm calling to have my phone service permanently disconnected.

住所 郵電通訊 日常活動 銀行與保險 交通 食品與飲食 購物 社交活動 教育 休閒活動 醫療 緊急情況

住所

郵電通訊

日常活動

銀行與保險

交通

食品與飲食

購物

社交活動

教育

休閒活動

醫療

緊急情況

A: 好的，你的名字及電話號碼？

A: Alright. What is your name and phone number?

B: 我的名字是瑞秋陳，號碼是 356-9981。

B: My name is Rachael Chen; the number is 356-9981.

A: 好，我現在在電腦上看到你了，你要何時停止服務呢？

A: OK. I see you on my computer now. When do you want the service stopped?

B: 10月20日。

B: October 20th.

A: 最後一期帳單你要寄到哪裡？

A: Where do you want the last bill sent?

B: 泰勒街528號。

B: 528 Taylor Street.

Word Bank 字庫

termination [ˌtɝməˈneʃən] n. 停用
permanent [ˈpɝmənənt] adj. 永久的
disconnect [ˌdɪskəˈnɛkt] v. 斷線

Useful Phrases 實用語句

1. 我要停止服務 [停話]。

   I want service discontinued.

2. 我要取消電話服務。

   I want to cancel our phone service.

3. 我不再需要長途電話服務。

   I no longer want long-distance service.

4. 我要停止網路服務。

   I want to stop my Internet service.

5. 我可以拿回任何押金嗎？

   Do I get any deposit back?

6. 何時會停止服務？

   When will the service be stopped?

7. 我可以現在付最後一期的帳單嗎？

   Can I pay the last bill now?

8. 最後的帳單請寄到這個地址。

   Please mail the last bill to this address.

2.2 手機
Cell Phone

手機服務在美國很普遍，各電信業者皆有不同方案可選。大型手機公司有 T Mobile, Verizon, AT & T, Sprint, US Cellular 等，但美國面積廣大，每家電信業者各有其經營地區 (coverage)。手機計價方案經常推陳出新與臺灣類似，顧客可選擇不同月費，不同通話分鐘數 airtime minute 的方案，月費包含長途電話費及美國國內漫遊 (domestic roaming) 費，但不包含國際話費，有的方案還可以將沒有打完的分鐘數累積 (rollover) 到下個月。若是越低資費超過所定分鐘數，每分鐘收費越貴。若是家庭成員，可以選擇共享計畫 (family plans)。顧客也可使用預付方案 (prepaid plans)。與家用電話一樣，使用手機在下班時間或週末費率較便宜。若需要購買手機，模式與臺灣相同，跟電信公司簽訂某一期限的合約，手機就有優惠。近來美國民眾每月約支付 $50 (或更低) 可使用手機上網。

Dialog 對話

A: 我想了解你們的手機服務。

A: I'd like to find out about your cell phone service.

住所

B: 我們有不收開線費方案，包含這支電話及500分鐘免費。

B: We have a no activation fee plan that includes this phone and the first 500 minutes free.

日常活動

A: 那以後呢？

A: How much does it cost after that?

銀行與保險

B: 每100分鐘10元。

B: Each 100 minutes costs $10.

交通

A: 有通話時段限制嗎？

A: Are there any restrictions on the times I can call?

食品與飲食

B: 沒有，你可以以此費率打到美國各地或加拿大。

B: No. You can call anywhere in the USA or Canada for that rate.

購物

A: 那打國外呢？

A: What about overseas calls?

社交活動

B: 我們這個系統可以讓你打到國外，但費率很貴。

B: The system we have will certainly allow you to call overseas, but the rate is quite expensive.

教育

休閒活動

 Word Bank 字庫

醫療

activation fee n. 開線費
restriction [rɪ`strɪkʃən] n. 限制

緊急情況

Useful Phrases 實用語句

1. 我要詢問手機服務。

   I want to ask about cell phone service.

2. 我想設定一個手機帳戶。

   I'm interested in establishing a cell phone service account.

3. 你們怎麼收費？

   What do you charge for service?

4. 你們有什麼手機？

   What type of phones do you have?

5. 我要一支可以傳簡訊的電話。

   I want a phone that can text message.

6. 這手機可以照相嗎？

   Does this phone take pictures?

7. 這是支照相手機嗎？

   Is it a camera phone?

8. 電池可以維持多久？

   How long does the battery last?

9. 開始的設定費是多少？

   What is the initial sign up fee?

10. 是一年期的合約嗎？

    Is it a one-year contract?

Language Power 字句補給站

◆ 手機相關字彙 Cell Phone

cell phone/cellular/mobile phone	手機
smart phone	智慧型手機
camera phone	照相手機
megapixel	百萬畫素
dual-band	雙頻
triband	三頻
quad band	四頻

住所 · 郵電通訊 · 日常活動 · 銀行與保險 · 交通 · 食品與飲食 · 購物 · 社交活動 · 教育 · 休閒活動 · 醫療 · 緊急情況

touch screen	觸控螢幕
features	特點
gimmick	花招
storage space	儲存空間
roaming charges	漫遊費
SIM card	手機晶片卡
ring tone	響鈴
speaker	擴音
Bluetooth earphone	藍芽耳機
signal strength	信號強度
text message	簡訊
voice mail	留言
speech to text	口說轉成文字
mobile power bank	行動電源
lockscreen password	螢幕上鎖密碼
fingerprint scan	指紋掃描
eye tracking	眼球追蹤
NFC (Near Field Communications)	近場通訊
sync (synchronization)	同步
smart phone addict/phubber	低頭族
phubbing offender	低頭族冒犯者
stop phubbing	禁滑手機

Notes 小叮嚀

　　短期到美國出差者可在臺灣購買預付卡 (如T–Mobile) 加值，抵達美國後將 sim 卡插入手機，填入 IMEI 手機序號 (International Mobile Equipment Identity) 即手機身分號碼，每支手機只需填入一次，選擇自動或手動搜尋 T–Mobile 訊號，即可以當地費率通話或上網，也可在美國購買或加值預付卡。

住所

郵電通訊

日常活動

銀行與保險

交通

食品與飲食

購物

社交活動

教育

休閒活動

醫療

緊急情況

2.3 公用電話
Pay Phone

手機的普遍使用大大影響到一般電話及公用電話的使用率，許多公用電話消失，全世界皆然，美國也不例外，手機沒電或是意外災難無法使用手機的人仍需公用電話。有些公用電話是民營的，費率可能稍高，公共電話上會註明費率、免費電話和使用方法。多數公共電話也可以接聽，如果沒零錢了，可以告訴對方公共電話號碼，請對方打來。或請接線生打對方付費電話 (collect call)，但金融風暴後有些電信公司怕收不到錢，已取消這項服務。公共電話上也有地址，萬一需要，可以聯絡。

2.3a 使用公共電話 Using a Pay Phone

Dialog 對話

A: 這裡有公共電話嗎？

A: Is there a pay phone here?

B: 當然有，在那兒。

B: Sure, it's over there.

A: 我要用零錢來使用它嗎？

A: Do I need change to use it?

B: 它接受硬幣或電話卡。

B: It will take coins or phone cards.

A: 我可以到哪裡買電話卡？

A: Where can I buy a phone card?

B: 去收銀員那裡。 ▶ **B:** Go to the cashier.

Useful Phrases 實用語句

1. 最近的公用電話在哪裡？

   Where is the nearest pay phone?

2. 我需要2元的25分錢。

   I need $2 worth the quarters.

3. 將硬幣投入投幣口。

   Insert a coin into the slot.

4. 等待通話音。

   Wait for the dial tone.

5. 撥號。

   Dial the number.

6. (錄音訊息) 對不起，您撥的電話是空號，請確定號碼後再撥。

   (recorded message) We're sorry. The number you have dialed is not in service. Please check the number you have dialed and try again.

7. (錄音訊息) 您撥的電話已停止使用，請撥查號臺查詢新號。

   (recorded message) The number you have dialed is no longer in service. Please contact directory assistance for the new number.

住所

郵電通訊

日常活動

銀行與保險

交通

食品與飲食

購物

社交活動

教育

休閒活動

醫療

緊急情況

Tips 小祕訣

　　打當地電話，多數地方需投 50¢，可以通話 15 分鐘，25¢、10¢、5¢ 都可以投。拿起話筒，先撥號，話筒裡的電腦總機會告訴你要投多少錢，通話後可以繼續投幣，電腦總機會提醒剩下多少時間。美國有些地方 (如紐約市) 已將公用電話加設熱點 (hotspot) 提供 wi-fi 上網服務，可投幣或以信用卡付費 (如免費服務，均含有大量廣告網頁，才提供極有時間限制之服務)。有些飯店的公共電話以觸控螢幕汰換舊式按鍵電話，提供電話與網路服務。無論如何，對出門在外者都是一大便利。要注意的是在任何公共熱點或設備傳輸資料，皆須考量網路安全。

2.3b 查號臺 Directory Assistance

Dialog 對話

A: 查號臺，我可以為你服務嗎？

A: Directory Assistance. How may I help you?

B: 哈囉，我要打到日本，但我不知道國碼。

B: Hello. I need to call overseas to Japan, but I don't know the country code.

A: 日本的國碼是81。

A: The country code for Japan is 81.

B: 謝謝，我要如何撥到東京呢？

B: Thank you. How do I dial Tokyo?

A: 打國碼，再打城市碼3，然後再打你要聯絡的號碼。

A: Dial the country code. Then city code, 3. Then the number you want to reach.

住所
郵電通訊
日常活動
銀行與保險
交通
食品與飲食
購物
社交活動
教育
休閒活動
醫療
緊急情況

B: 謝謝。

B: Thank you very much.

Useful Phrases 實用語句

1. 我要知道南波士頓的區域號碼。

   I want to know the area code for South Boston.

2. 我要打對方付費電話。

   I want to place a collect call.

3. 義大利國碼是幾號？

   What is the country code for Italy?

4. 我需要哈柏林公司的號碼。

   I need the number of Haplink Corporation.

Tips 小祕訣

　　911緊急電話可免費撥打，411是當地查號臺。接線生當地打0，外地打00。

　　1-自己的區域碼-555-1212為長途電話查號臺，1-800-555-1212為免費電話查號臺。區域碼800、888、877的電話是免費電話 (toll free number)。打美國國內長途電話為1-區域號-電話號碼，打國際電話回臺灣臺北為011 (國際碼)-886 (國碼)-2 (區域號去0)- 電話號碼。

住所

郵電通訊

日常活動

銀行與保險

交通

食品與飲食

購物

社交活動

教育

休閒活動

醫療

緊急情況

2.4 網路
Internet

申辦網路時，了解居住的社區有哪些電信業者可以選擇，大型網路業者包含 Comcast, Cox, Time Warner, AT & T，各家業者在不同州別各占優勢，電信業者經常推出促銷方案 (如辦網路送免費家用電話)，可與電話、有線電視一起綁約 (bundled services) 通常每月約 $80-$90，但收費因網速、頻道數與電話線數等條件而異。使用網路電話 (Internet phone/VoIP) 還可節省電話費，但要注意過了促銷後，回復原價是否仍划算。

都會已少見的電話撥接上網 (dial up access) 約 $10-$20，寬頻上網 (broadband Internet access)：使用有線電視 (cable) 線路約 $20-$30，使用數據機 (DSL Internet) 用原電話線快速上網約 $40-$50。另有大都會區使用的光纖 (fiber optics) 上網，無線 (wifi) 快速上網約 $40-$65，與偏遠地區適用之寬頻衛星 (broadband satellite) 上網。

Dialog 對話

A: 我家裡需要網路服務。

A: I need Internet service at my home.

B: 你要用數據機連線或是DSL連線？

B: Do you want a modem connection or a DSL hook up?

A: DSL月費多少？

A: How much is DSL a month?

B: 每個月 45 元無限使用。

B: Unlimited use costs $45 a month.

住所
郵電通訊
日常活動
銀行與保險
交通
食品與飲食
購物
社交活動
教育
休閒活動
醫療
緊急情況

A: 聽起來不錯，我何時可以接線？

A: That sounds good. When can I have it hooked up?

B: 我們先填這個表格，你明天下午就有網路服務了。

B: Let's get this form filled out. Then you should have it tomorrow afternoon.

Word Bank 字庫

modem [`modən] n. 數據機
connection [kə`nɛkʃən] n. 連線
hook up 連接

Useful Phrases 實用語句

1. 我要接網路。

   I'd like to get hooked up to the Internet.

2. 你們提供什麼網路方案？

   What kind of Internet options do you offer?

3. 你們的網路費率多少？

   What are your Internet rates?

4. 我們有一般數據機或寬頻的無限上網方案。

   We have an unlimited usage plan for a regular modem, or broadband.

5. 你明天下午前可以上線。

   You'll be online by tomorrow afternoon.

6. 有任何問題打電話給我們。

   Call us if you have any problems.

7. 請查閱我們的網址。

   Please check on our website.

8. 我們會送DSL數據機過去。

   We'll deliver the DSL modem.

住所

郵電通訊

日常活動

銀行與保險

交通

食品與飲食

購物

社交活動

教育

休閒活動

醫療

緊急情況

9. 我怎樣使用網路電話？

How do I connect to an Internet phone?

2.5 有線電視或衛星電視
Cable TV or Satellite TV

近年有線電視市占率前幾名的業者包含 Comcast, Time Warner Cable, AT&T U-verse, Verizon FiOS, Cox，電信行動及有線電視業者不斷拓展，互搶商機。有線電視或衛星電視都是一年合約，當然工程人員會來裝機或接線。有線電視或衛星電視公司通常提供大約一百臺左右 (甚至更多) 的基本頻道 (basic cable)，包含全國電視網的各頻道如 CBS, NBC, ABC, CNN, PBS, ESPN, FOX 等，月費約 $40-$50。如果要更多電影頻道 (premium cable)，如 HBO, Cinemax, Showtime, Starz 須加裝電視盒 (converter box)、現場直播運動節目或訂閱其他頻道，收費就更高。除有線電視外，選擇還包括光纖電視 (fiber-optic TV)、數位裝置 (digital device，如 apple TV) 或直播衛星電視 Direct Broadcast Satellite/DBS (如 direct TV) 觀看電視。

Dialog 對話

A: 哈囉，我可以為你服務嗎？

A: Hello. How may I help you?

B: 我想了解有線電視服務。

B: I'd like to find out about cable TV service.

A: 好的，你要知道什麼呢？

A: Sure. What do you want to know?

B: 有線電視基本費用多少？

B: What does basic cable cost?

A: 基本服務每個月45元。

A: Well. Basic cable service costs $45 a month.

B: 我能有什麼服務呢？

B: What do I get for that?

A: 你有120個頻道，包括本地州內的頻道及5個電影頻道。

A: You'll receive 120 channels including the local in-state channels, and the 5 movie channels.

B: 那運動頻道呢？

B: What about the sports channels?

A: 你也有4個頻道。

A: You'll get 4 sports channels as well.

B: 好，你何時可以來接線呢？

B: Great! When can you come connect it?

A: 明天早上可以嗎？

A: Is tomorrow morning OK?

B: 可以。

B: Yes, it is.

Word Bank 字庫

cable [`kebl] n. 纜線
satellite [`sætə͵laɪt] n. 衛星
channel [`tʃænl] n. 頻道

Useful Phrases 實用語句

1. 我需要有線電視服務。

   I need cable TV service.

2. 有線電視服務多少錢？

   How much is cable TV service?

3. 基本費率有什麼頻道呢？

   What channels can we get for the basic rate?

4. 我們家裡需要衛星電視服務。

   We'd like to have satellite TV service at our home.

5. 衛星電視可以有多少頻道呢？

   How many channels are available on satellite?

2.6 報紙
Newspapers

新科技新技術為傳統印刷報業帶來新的營運及消費模式，各大報章雜誌等媒體無不積極拓展疆域進行與其他行業 (如廣告、物流、資訊、娛樂、服務) 的融合 (media convergence)。報章雜誌現今透過網路平臺，即時免費呈現，隨手可得，或採用數位訂閱 (digital subscription)「額外費用模式」(premium model) 供訂閱者下載 app。

全國性的報紙銷量大，如 Wall Street Journal 華爾街日報，The New York Time 紐約時報，USA Today 今日美國報。地區性流通量大的報紙，包含 Las Angeles Times 洛杉磯時報，Daily News (紐約) 每日新聞報，New York Post 紐約郵報，Washington Post 華盛頓郵報，Chicago Sun-Times 芝加哥太陽報，Chicago Tribune 芝加哥論壇報。傳統報章雜誌訂閱 (print subscription) 以一年為期限，報社也提供兩年或三年的訂報選擇，當然訂越久每份報紙就越便宜。

2.6a 訂報 Subscribing to Newspapers

 Dialog 對話

A: 哈囉，我要訂早報。

A: Hello. I'd like to subscribe to the daily morning newspaper.

B: 好，你要送到哪裡？

B: OK. Where do you want it delivered?

A: 送到我家，住址是格蘭街344號。

A: To my house. The address is 344, Grant Street.

B: 好的。

B: Alright.

A: 你何時開始送？

A: When will you start delivery?

B: 我問幾個你個人資料的問題後，明天應該可以開始送。

B: After I get a little personal information from you, it should start tomorrow.

A: 多少錢呢？

A: How much is the cost?

B: 一年25元。

B: It costs $25 a year.

A: 我要怎麼支付呢？

A: How do I pay for the subscription?

B: 你可以郵寄支票、付給送報員或設定你的銀行自動轉帳。

B: You can send a check in the mail, pay the delivery person, or set up automatic bill payment at your bank.

Word Bank 字庫

subscribe [səb`skraɪb] v. 訂閱
subscription [səb`skrɪpʃən] n. 訂閱
delivery [dɪ`lɪvərɪ] n. 遞送

Useful Phrases 實用語句

1. 我想要訂本地日報。

   I'd like to subscribe to the local daily newspaper.

2. 訂本地報紙要多少錢？

   How much does a subscription to the local paper cost?

3. 訂閱一期時限多久？

   How long does a subscription last?

4. 今天的報紙沒送到我家。

   Today's paper was not delivered to my home.

5. 我要停止送報一星期。

   I want to stop delivery of the paper for one week.

2.6b 停報 Stopping Delivery and Termination

Dialog 1 對話1

A: 我要停止訂報兩星期。

A: I need the newspaper delivery to stop for two weeks.

住所

郵電通訊

日常活動

銀行與保險

交通

食品與飲食

購物

社交活動

教育

休閒活動

醫療

緊急情況

B: 好，你何時要停送？

B: OK. When do you want it stopped?

A: 下星期三開始。

A: Starting next Wednesday.

B: 我看一下日曆，那我們在 22 日再開始送嗎？

B: Let me check on the calendar. So we'll begin delivery again on the 22nd?

A: 是的。

A: Yes, that's right.

Dialog 2 對話2

A: 我想永久停止送報。

A: I'd want to permanently stop delivery of the newspaper.

B: 如果你要的話，我們可以送到你的新地址。

B: We can deliver it to your new address if you'd like.

A: 真的嗎？我不知道。

A: Really? I didn't know.

B: 當然可以，只要給我你的新地址，我們就轉送到那裡去。

B: Sure. Just give me your new address, and we'll forward it to there.

A: 好，但是我們要下個月才住到那裡。

A: OK, but we won't be living there until next month.

住所

郵電通訊

日常活動

銀行與保險

交通

食品與飲食

購物

社交活動

教育

休閒活動

醫療

緊急情況

B: 我們可以繼續送到你現在的地址，然後到你告訴我們的日期再轉過去。

B: We can continue to deliver to your present address. Then switch on the date you tell us to.

Tips 小祕訣

如果搬家是在同一區不是太遠的話，在更改地址後當地報紙可以繼續遞送，若是全國性的報紙刊物，就得用郵寄了。

2.7 郵遞
Postal Service

搬到新住所後，要盡快告知郵局啟動你的郵遞服務，尤其在完全沒有郵件寄達過的全新住所這點很重要，搬家也要通知郵局，郵件才會轉去新地址，更改地址可以上網或直接去郵局填地址變更表。如果需要，可以終止遞送服務，這樣就不會收到郵件。

Dialog 1 對話1

A: 我要怎樣開始在我的住址收信？

A: How do I get mail delivery started at my address?

B: 只要填表我就會處理。

B: Just fill out this form, and I'll take care of the rest.

A: 在填表前，我也想知道怎麼開郵政信箱呢？

A: Before I do that I'd like to know how I can set up a post office box, too.

住所

郵電通訊

B: 如果你也填這個表，我可以馬上安排一個信箱。

B: If you fill out this form too, I can assign one to you right now.

日常活動

A: 如果我要寄東西給某人，可以在這裡買寄送的信封及紙箱嗎？

A: And if I need to ship something to someone, can I buy shipping envelopes or boxes here?

銀行與保險

B: 可以，我們有各式紙箱及信封，也有包裝材料。

B: Yes, you can. We have all sizes of boxes and envelopes available, packing material, too.

交通

A: 謝謝你的幫忙。

A: Thanks for all your help.

食品與飲食

Dialog 2 （對話2）

購物

A: 我要寄這封信到臺灣。

A: I want to send this letter to Taiwan.

社交活動

B: 我先秤重。好，郵資是2元。

B: Let me weigh it first. OK. The postage for this will be $2.

教育

A: (付錢拿到郵票) 我也要交給你郵寄嗎？

A: (pay and get the stamp) Do I give it to you to mail also?

休閒活動

B: 是的，我會幫你處理。

B: Yes. I'll take care of it for you.

醫療

A: 謝謝你的幫忙。

A: Thanks for all your help.

緊急情況

 Useful Phrases 實用語句

住所

郵電通訊

日常活動

銀行與保險

交通

食品與飲食

購物

社交活動

教育

休閒活動

醫療

緊急情況

1. 我家需要開始郵件服務。

   I need to get postal delivery started to our house.

2. 我需要停止郵件服務一個月。

   I need to have postal service stopped for one month.

3. 如果有包裹送到，但沒人在家該怎麼辦？

   What should I do if a parcel arrives but nobody's home?

4. 我們會留一張送件通知。

   We'll leave a notice of delivery slip.

5. 你必須到郵局來取件。

   You'll have to come to the post office to pick it up.

6. 你可以在櫃臺或在郵票機買郵票。

   You can buy stamps at the counter, or from the stamp machine.

7. 我們也賣信封。

   We sell envelopes, too.

8. 我要寄包裹 [信] 。

   I want to mail this package [letter].

9. 我需要買些郵票，3張國內郵票及4張寄到臺灣的郵票。

   I need to buy some stamps, three domestic stamps and four stamps to send something to Taiwan.

10. 我要秤這郵件。

    I need this mailing weighed.

11. 郵資多少？

    How much is the postage?

12. 郵筒在哪裡？

    Where is the mailbox?

13. 你們有賣信封嗎？

    Do you sell mailing envelopes?

Tips　小祕訣

　　要寄普通信件很方便，不需到郵局或去外面找郵筒寄信。只要貼上郵票，把信放入家裡的信箱，將旗子豎起表示有信件待收，郵差看到旗子升起就會收走信件，並將旗子降下。如果郵差送信來，會將旗子豎起，提醒用戶收件。一般公寓成排的信箱沒有旗子沒關係，也可以放在自己的信箱裡面，但是要等到你下次有郵件進來時郵差才會收走。若不想拖時間或擔心信件安全問題，街上有許多郵筒可以寄信。

　　美國郵差不只是男士擔任，女郵差也很常見(各行業也是如此)。他們不像臺灣的郵差全身綠色裝扮，某些郵差制服看來倒頗像童軍裝，美國的郵務車是白色加上美國郵局老鷹飛翔的標誌。

I want to send this letter to Taiwan.

Let me weigh it first. OK. The postage for this will be $2.

Unit 3 Daily Activities
日常活動

對剛搬來美國的人而言，經常需要請教他人問題來了解日常生活所需的服務或有關項目的消息。使用簡單直接的英語溝通，加上禮貌應對是了解生活資訊的不二法門，也是融入當地生活的必要工具。

住所

郵電通訊

日常活動

銀行與保險

交通

食品與飲食

購物

社交活動

教育

休閒活動

醫療

緊急情況

3.1 自助投幣洗衣店
Laundromat

Dialog 1 對話1

A: 嗨，我是新來的，你可以告訴我怎麼用這些機器嗎？

A: Hi. I'm new here. Can you tell me how to use these machines?

B: 好，沒問題。

B: Sure. No problem.

A: 我該使用哪臺機器？

A: Which machine should I use?

B: 我看你要洗的不多，所以我想這些小機器的其中一臺就夠了。

B: I see you don't have a lot to wash, so I think one of the smaller machines is good enough.

A: 好，我要怎樣操作呢？

A: OK. How do I operate it?

B: 只要打開蓋子，放入衣物並加點洗衣粉。

B: Just open the lid, put your clothes in, and add some soap.

A: 那錢呢？

A: What about the money?

B: 將硬幣放入投幣孔，然後推進去，機器就啟動了。

B: Put the coins in these slots and then push them in. That will start the machine.

住所

郵電通訊

日常活動

銀行與保險

交通

食品與飲食

購物

社交活動

教育

休閒活動

醫療

緊急情況

A: 那這些按鈕呢？

A: What are these dials?

B: 是讓你選擇你要的設定，例如熱或冷水，水量 (依照你放入衣物的多寡)，或你洗的衣物有多細緻。

B: They allow you to choose the settings you want. For example, hot or cold water, water level depending on how much clothing you put in the machine, or how delicate the clothing you are washing is.

A: 我了解了，謝謝。

A: I see. Thanks.

 Dialog 2 (對話2)

A: 對不起，我有另一個問題。

A: Excuse me. I have another question.

B: 你需要知道什麼？

B: What is it you need to know?

A: 我不確定要怎麼用烘衣機，你如何使用？

A: I'm not sure about the driers. How do you use them?

B: 很簡單，放入衣物，關門，然後放入一個25分硬幣。

B: It's easy. Put your clothing in, close the door, then just put in a quarter.

住所
郵電通訊
日常活動
銀行與保險
交通
食品與飲食
購物
社交活動
教育
休閒活動
醫療
緊急情況

A: 只要一個25分硬幣？

A: Only one quarter?

B: 事實上，一個25分硬幣只能烘10分鐘，你差不多至少要放3個25分硬幣。

B: Actually one quarter will only buy about ten minutes of drying time. You'll probably need to use three quarters at least.

A: 我知道了，你們有賣柔軟精嗎？

A: I understand. Do you have softener for sale here?

B: 有，你可以在那裡的機器買，或我可以在櫃臺後面賣一些給你。

B: Oh, yes. You can buy it in that machine over there, or I can sell some to you from behind the counter.

A: 還有一個問題，你們這裡也有乾洗嗎？

A: One more question. Do you also do dry cleaning here?

B: 有，我們保證你的乾洗三天會好。

B: Yes, we do. We guarantee your dry cleaning will be ready in three days.

Word Bank 字庫

lid [lɪd] n. 蓋子
slot [slɑt] n. 投幣孔
dial [`daɪəl] n. 按鈕
delicate [`dɛləkət] adj. 精緻的
softener [`sɔfənə] n. 柔軟精
dry cleaning n. 乾洗

Useful Phrases 實用語句

1. 我需要找一家自助洗衣店。

   I need to find a Laundromat.

2. 我需要換一些硬幣。

   I have to get some coins.

3. 我可以換一些洗衣機用的硬幣嗎？

   May I have some change for the washers please?

4. 這些洗衣機用25分硬幣。

   These washing machines use quarters.

5. 將硬幣放入投幣孔，然後推進去。

   Put the coins in these slots. Then, push them in.

6. 放一些洗衣粉進去。

   Put some soap in.

7. 我需要多買些洗衣粉。

   I need to buy more soap.

8. 我在哪裡可以買到柔軟精？

   Where can I get softener?

9. 每個25分硬幣可以烘10分鐘。

   The dryer runs for ten minutes per quarter.

10. 不要讓你的機器無人看管，因為別人可能偷走你的衣服。

    Don't leave your machines unattended because someone might steal your clothing.

住所
郵電通訊
日常活動
銀行與保險
交通
食品與飲食
購物
社交活動
教育
休閒活動
醫療
緊急情況

住所
郵電通訊
日常活動
銀行與保險
交通
食品與飲食
購物
社交活動
教育
休閒活動
醫療
緊急情況

11. 投幣洗衣店何時開 [關] 門？

What time does the Laundromat open [close]?

12. 我們每天早上7點開，晚上10點關門。

We open at 7:00 a.m., and close at 10:00 p.m., everyday.

13. 我們這裡也有乾洗服務。

We also offer dry cleaning services here.

14. 乾洗何時可以好？

When will the dry cleaning be ready?

Tips 小祕訣

一般的公寓都有公用投幣式洗衣機及烘乾機，街上也可以找到投幣式洗衣店，有各式大小的洗衣機及烘衣機，小至衣物大至棉被、窗簾都可以清洗烘乾。大致而言，美國人沒有晒衣服、被子的習慣，所有衣物幾乎一律烘乾。

3.2 美髮店
Beauty Parlors and Barbershops

傳統上女士們到美髮院 (beauty parlor) 找美髮師 (hairdresser)，男士們到理髮店 (barbershop) 找理髮師 (barber) 整理頭髮，但髮型沙龍 (hair salon) 則男女顧客都有。大城市的髮型師 (hairstylist) 在這行業裡相當專業，提供顧客最好、最新的造型、諮詢、護髮用品及服務。

3.2a 女士 Women

Dialog 1 對話1

A: 嗨，我的頭髮要做造型，需要預約嗎？

A: Hi. Do I need an appointment to get my hair styled?

B: 今天不用，我們今天不忙，請進吧。

B: Not today. We're not too busy, so please come in.

A: 好，謝謝，我真的需要做頭髮，因為今晚我必須參加一個特殊的場合。

A: Great. Thank you. I really need my hair styled because I must attend a special event tonight.

B: 好，先讓我給你看些相片，你可以知道要什麼(髮型)，再給我看。

B: OK. First let me show you some photos. You can get some idea of what you want, and then you can show me.

A: 謝謝。

A: Thanks.

Dialog 2 對話2

A: 嗨，你要做怎樣的髮型？

A: Hi, how would you like to have your hair done?

B: 我想修短及部分挑染。

B: I'd like to have it trimmed and some hair highlighted.

A: 好的，你要修到什麼長度？

A: Alright. To what length would you like to have your hair trimmed?

B: 大約短1吋。

B: About an inch shorter.

A: 好,那瀏海呢?

A: OK. What about the bangs?

B: 請修一點,但不要太短,我偶爾想用髮夾。

B: Trim them a little bit please, but not too short. I like to use hair pins sometimes.

A: 我拿顏色給你看,你要挑染哪個顏色?

A: Let me show you the hair colors. Which color do you like for the highlights?

B: 淡褐色,我的頭髮挑染要多久?

B: Light brown. How long will it take to have my hair highlighted?

A: 大約 20 到 30 分鐘。

A: About 20-30 minutes.

(稍後 Later)

B: 我要吹乾頭髮。

B: I'd like to have my hair blow dried.

A: 好的,你要吹乾就好,還是要做髮型?

A: OK, do you need just a blow dry or do you want it styled?

B: 我要挽一個髮髻,前額留瀏海。

B: I'd like to wear my hair up in a bun. Keep the bangs on the forehead.

A: 好的。

A: Alright.

Word Bank 字庫

trim [trɪm] v. 修剪
bangs [bæŋz] n. 瀏海
highlight [`haɪˏlaɪt] v., n. 挑染

Useful Phrases 實用語句

1. 我要做一個新髮型。
   I'd like a new hairstyle.

2. 看這些型錄。
   Look at these style examples.

3. 我要染髮。
   I want my hair colored. / I want to dye my hair.

4. 我要修頭髮。
   I want my hair trimmed.

5. 我也要洗頭。
   I also need my hair washed. / I also need a shampoo.

6. 我要燙頭髮。
   I want a perm.

7. 我要預約嗎？
   Do I need an appointment?

8. 我要預約。
   I'd like to make an appointment.

9. 你們有護髮產品嗎？
   Do you have any hair care products?

10. 你可以洗直我的頭髮嗎？
    Can you straighten my hair?

11. 我要把瀏海修短。
    I'd like to have my bangs trimmed short.

12. 我要留瀏海。
    I'd like to grow my bangs.

住所
郵電通訊
日常活動
銀行與保險
交通
食品與飲食
購物
社交活動
教育
休閒活動
醫療
緊急情況

住所

郵電通訊

日常活動

銀行與保險

交通

食品與飲食

購物

社交活動

教育

休閒活動

醫療

緊急情況

13. 我想挑染成褐色。

I'd like to highlight some hair brown.

14. 我後面要打層次。

I'd like the hair in back layered.

15. 請剪掉分叉部分。

Please cut the split ends off.

16. 我要做護髮保養。

I'd like to have hair care treatment.

17. 我燙 [染] 髮要多久？

How long does it take to have my hair permed [dyed]?

18. 做 [剪，洗直] 我的頭髮要多久？

How long will it take to style [cut, straighten] my hair?

19. 我要把頭髮紮起來。

I like to wear my hair up.

20. 我後面的頭髮會翹起來。

My hair in the back often pokes out.

21. 我要如何整理我的新髮型？

How should I care for my new style?

22. 只要用手指梳就可以了。

Simply run your fingers through it.

23. 你可以吹乾我的頭髮嗎？

Can you blow dry my hair?

24. 我怎樣才能讓頭髮看起來柔順光亮？

How can I keep my hair smooth and shiny?

25. 你有防毛燥的產品嗎？

Do you have anti-frizz products?

Language Power 字句補給站

髮 飾 **Hair Accessories**

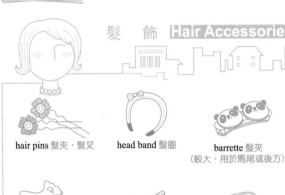

hair pins 髮夾，髮叉

head band 髮圈

barrette 髮夾
（較大，用於馬尾或後方）

hair clamp 鯊魚夾

hair stick 髮簪

elastic bands
橡皮筋髮圈

bobby pins
黑色U型髮夾

scrunchy 馬尾捲

hair clips 髮夾

Hi, how would you like to have your hair done?

I'd like to have it trimmed and some hair highlighted.

住所

郵電通訊

日常活動

銀行與保險

交通

食品與飲食

購物

社交活動

教育

休閒活動

醫療

緊急情況

髮型、造型 ①

Hair Styles,Styling

住所 | 郵電通訊 | 日常活動 | 銀行與保險 | 交通 | 食品與飲食 | 購物 | 社交活動 | 教育 | 休閒活動 | 醫療 | 緊急情況

perm 燙　dye 染　highlight/tint 挑染　cut 剪　trim 修剪

slice/thin 削薄　bangs 瀏海　curly 捲髮的　wavy 波浪捲髮的　straight 直髮

braids 辮子　dreadlocks 辮子頭　shoulder length 及肩長度　short 短髮

feather cut 羽毛剪　shaggy 蓬鬆雜亂的　bob cut 妹妹頭　blow dry 吹乾　part 分邊

coil 捲　wrap 包捆　fluffy 蓬鬆的　frizzy 毛燥的

Afro 黑人髮型（圓形大又蓬鬆）　pony tail 馬尾　bun 髮髻　wig 假髮

髮型、造型 ②
Hair Styles, Styling

- length 長度
- layered 有層次的
- pull up 拉
- sweep 抹
- damaged 受傷的
- brittle 易斷的
- strong 強效的
- mild/gentle/light 溫和的

- volume 髮量
- flip up 輕拍
- scrunch 揉皺
- backcomb/tease 逆梳
- thin/fine 纖細的
- perm solution 燙髮液
- medium 中度的
- split ends 分叉

美髮產品 Hair Products

shampoo 洗髮精

conditioner 潤髮乳

moisturizer 保濕劑

repair treatment
護髮用品

hair mousse
美髮慕斯

hairspray 噴髮劑

silk serum 亮膠

gel 髮膠

wax 髮蠟

3.2b 男士 Men

Dialog 對話

A: 嗨，請坐下，等一下就換你。

A: Hi. Please sit down we'll be with you in a little while.

(稍後 Later)

A: 好，換你了，請坐在這裡。

A: OK, we're ready for you. Please sit here.

B: 謝謝，我要修剪頭髮。

B: Thanks. I need my hair trimmed.

A: 你要多短呢？

A: How short do you want it?

B: 我要上面剪多一些，但兩邊不要太短。

B: I want it trimmed a lot on the top, but not too much on the sides.

A: 那後面呢？

A: How about the back?

B: 請讓它厚實點。

B: Block it please.

A: 好的，你要留兩邊的鬢角嗎？

A: Alright. Do you want to have your sideburns left alone?

B: 不要，鬢角也要修剪，但維持現在長度。	**B:** No. Please trim them too, but leave them the length they are now.
A: 沒問題。	**A:** No problem.

Word Bank 字庫

block [blɑk] v. 使厚實
sideburns [`saɪd͵bɜnz] n. 鬢角

Useful Phrases 實用語句

1. 我要修頭髮。

   I need my hair trimmed.

2. 我要右分。

   I want it parted on the right.

3. 我不要分邊。

   I don't want a part in my hair.

4. 請不要太短。

   Not too short, please.

5. 剪個頭髮多少錢？

   How much is a hair cut here?

6. 我要頭髮往後貼。

   I'd like to slick my hair back.

7. 我在留鬍子，所以不要刮。

   I'm growing a beard, so don't give me a shave.

8. 請幫我刮 (鬍子)。

   Give me a shave too, please.

住所
郵電通訊
日常活動
銀行與保險
交通
食品與飲食
購物
社交活動
教育
休閒活動
醫療
緊急情況

住所
郵電通訊
日常活動
銀行與保險
交通
食品與飲食
購物
社交活動
教育
休閒活動
醫療
緊急情況

Language Power 字句補給站

◆ 男士髮型 Men's Hairstyles

crew cut	平頭
buzz cut	用推剪理髮
tapered in the back	後面逐漸剪短
block in the back	後面厚實
hairline	髮線
part	分邊
slicked back	向後貼
moustache	鬍髭
beard	鬍鬚
punk	龐克
be balding	變禿
shave the hair off	剃光頭
go bald	選擇光頭髮型
bandana	頭巾

Hello, I'd like to have a manicure.

Certainly. Please sit down and the manicurist will be with you shortly.

Notes 小叮嚀

跟所有其他服務一樣，髮型業者收費依照服務及設備而有不同收費標準。在臺灣髮廊到處都是，一般收費的價格使女士們可以經常上髮廊洗髮做造型，洗髮或剪、燙髮之前的洗髮及之後的吹整並不再另外收費。

但在美國許多傳統髮型業者 (barbershop, beauty parlor) 對於每項服務是個別收費的，一般男士只剪髮費用約為 $8-$12，洗頭及吹乾每項大約收費為 $5。因此多數人自己洗頭後再出門剪髮(可以先吹半乾再出門以免著涼)，或剪完後不吹乾，而是自然乾或回家吹乾。若是不想那麼麻煩，就得多付些費用，或到髮廊去消費。

然而在美國髮廊 (hair salon) 消費並不算便宜，普通的髮廊剪髮費用在 $20-$25 間，較高檔的髮廊當然收費更高，有些髮廊會提供無線上網服務。若價格包含洗髮、吹乾、改變造型，男士收費約在 $30-$60 之間，女士為 $40-$75 間。髮廊也不是到處可見，而是要到商場才有。美國在 2008 年金融風暴後大量印鈔，物價普遍上揚，多數人只有在剪、染、燙髮換造型時才會上髮廊。在藥房或超市有許多自己動手整理髮型的工具，讓人眼花撩亂，女士在家自己上髮捲，甚至開車時頭上還上著髮捲的景象也見怪不怪。在移民較多的城市裡，有許多少數族裔開設的髮廊，可以為同族裔移民提供服務。

在傳統男士理髮店通常不需給小費，但到髮廊消費雖說小費依消費者的感受而定，一般多給 10%-15% 左右的小費。如果固定給相同髮廊設計師整理頭髮也滿意服務，不妨給到 20%。

3.3 指甲護理
Manicure

有些髮廊提供修手腳指甲護理服務，但另外計費。有些指甲護理店是自立門戶，像臺灣這兩年流行的指甲彩繪及指甲貼片，在美國可是歷史悠久。手腳護理依消費地點不同，收費從 $35-$100 都有。

住所
郵電通訊
日常活動
銀行與保險
交通
食品與飲食
購物
社交活動
教育
休閒活動
醫療
緊急情況

Dialog 對話

A: 哈囉，我想要修指甲。

A: Hello. I'd like to have a manicure.

B: 好，請坐，修甲師一會兒就過來。

B: Certainly. Please sit down and the manicurist will be with you shortly.

A: 謝謝。

A: Thank you.

B: 還有，你只要修指甲還是也要護手？

B: By the way, do you want only your nails cared for, or do you want hand care too?

A: 我要全套護理。

A: I want a complete treatment.

B: 好的。

B: Very well.

Language Power 字句補給站

◆ 指甲護理 Manicure

manicure	修手指甲
pedicure	修腳指甲
nail cutter	指甲剪
nail filer	銼刀
nail brush	指甲油塗刷
nail polish	指甲油
acetone , nail polish remover	去光水
coat	層

stroke evenly	塗抹均勻地
pumice stone	浮石
foot scrapper	磨腳棒
foot rasp	腳銼刀
antiseptic lotion	消毒乳液
foot powder	足粉
toe separator	分趾海綿 (塗腳趾時分開腳趾用)
Q tips	棉花棒
orange stick	(木製) 推棒
nail painting [art]	指甲彩繪
nail sticker	裝飾指甲的貼片

3.4 保姆
Babysitter

 Dialog 1　對話1

A: 嗨，我回應你們找保姆的廣告。	**A:** Hi. I'm answering your ad for a babysitter.
B: 喔，好，你叫什麼名字？	**B:** Oh, good. What is your name?
A: 我叫珊蒂，14歲。	**A:** My name is Sandy. I'm 14 years old.
B: 嗨，珊蒂，我是凱莉蘇，你是有經驗的保姆嗎？	**B:** Hi, Sandy. My name is Kelly Su. Are you an experienced babysitter?
A: 是的，我已經當保母三年了。	**A:** Yes, I am. I've been babysitting for about three years.

住所

郵電通訊

日常活動

銀行與保險

交通

食品與飲食

購物

社交活動

教育

休閒活動

醫療

緊急情況

住所
郵電通訊
日常活動
銀行與保險
交通
食品與飲食
購物
社交活動
教育
休閒活動
醫療
緊急情況

B: 很好，你這個星期五晚上有空嗎？

B: Great. Are you available this Friday night?

A: 有。

A: Yes, I am.

B: 好，你可以晚上6點到這裡嗎？

B: Good. Can you be here by 6 p.m.?

A: 可以，我會早一點，這樣你可以介紹我給你的小孩。

A: Sure. I'll need to be early, so you can introduce me to your child.

B: 對，事實上，我先生和我有兩個小孩。

B: Yes, right. Actually my husband and I have two children.

A: 喔，我知道了，我應該告訴你兩個小孩我每小時多收2元。

A: Oh, I see. I should tell you I charge $2 more per hour for two kids.

B: 我知道了，這樣每個小時你收多少？

B: I understand. So how much per hour do you get?

A: 你的情形是每小時8元。

A: In your case I'd get $8 an hour.

Word Bank 字庫

babysit [ˋbebɪ͵sɪt] v.當保姆
babysitter [ˋbebɪ͵sɪtɚ] n. 保姆
experienced [ɪkˋspɪrɪənst] adj. 有經驗的

Useful Phrases 實用語句

1. 今晚我們需要一個保姆。

   We need a babysitter for tonight.

2. 你有當保姆的經驗嗎？

   Are you experienced at babysitting?

3. 我們一小時付10元。

   We pay $10 an hour.

4. 我們會晚歸。

   We'll be back late.

5. 如果有緊急狀況，打這個電話。

   Call this number if there is an emergency.

6. 小孩晚上 10 點前要上床。

   The children must go to bed by 10 p.m.

7. 確定我女兒要吃藥。

   Make sure my daughter takes her medicine.

8. 你可以在冰箱拿任何你要的東西。

   Have anything you want from the refrigerator.

9. 請在晚上 6 點前到。

   Please be here before 6 p.m.

Dialog 2 對話2

A: 嗨，珊蒂，我看到你帶小孩兜風。

A: Hi, Sandy. I see you are taking your children for a ride.

B: 哈囉，卡蘿，事實上我要去參加一個重要會議，但我找不到保姆。

B: Hello, Carol. Actually I have to go to an important meeting, but I couldn't find a babysitter.

住所

郵電通訊

日常活動

銀行與保險

交通

食品與飲食

購物

社交活動

教育

休閒活動

醫療

緊急情況

A: 真的嗎？你可以把他們交給我，我會看好他們。

A: Really? You can leave them here with me. I'll watch them.

B: 喔，不行，我不能那樣麻煩你。

B: Oh, no, I couldn't bother you with that.

A: 不，真的沒什麼，我很了解你現在的處境。

A: No, really, it's no big deal. I know the situation you're in very well.

B: 看來我們應該彼此聯絡交換看小孩時間。

B: It seems that we ought to contact each other about trading baby-sitting time.

A: 那是個好主意。

A: That's a good idea.

 Word Bank 字庫

ride [raɪd] n. 兜風
leave [liv] v. 留下
bother [`baðɚ] v. 干擾，麻煩
contact [`kɑntækt] v. 聯絡
trade [tred] v. 交換

Useful Phrases 實用語句

1. 我們的小孩差不多年紀。

   Our children are about the same age.

2. 我們可以互相帶小孩。

   We can babysit for each other.

3. 我們可以互相幫忙帶小孩的需要。

   We can help each other with babysitting needs.

4. 當你要做事情，我可以幫你看小孩。

   When you have something to do, I can watch your kids.

5. 你今天可以幫我看小孩嗎？

   Can you watch my kids today?

6. 你在城裡忙時，我來幫你照顧小孩。

   Let me take care of your children while you run around town.

7. 真的沒什麼。

   It's really no big deal.

Notes 小叮嚀

　　托兒服務可能極為昂貴，有些地方以包月計算，有些則以鐘點計算。最近的調查顯示，平均美國人每週托兒費用在$80-$100之間。多數美國人自己將小孩送到托兒所，不像在臺灣等娃娃車來載。在美國托兒行業雖然受到很大的規範，但是保姆還是要父母仔細挑選。

　　父母出門將小孩單獨留在家而沒有保姆陪伴，可能造成極為嚴重的後果，除了可能發生的可怕意外，父母甚至會被以遺棄小孩或故意忽略小孩的罪名受到法律處罰；此外在美國沒有不打不成器這種事，小孩不乖是不可以體罰的，美國各州的法律也規範父母教養方式，不允許有語言暴力及肢體暴力。國人在臺灣見怪不怪的教養方式，在家或公共場合打罵教訓子女，讓小孩在公共場所亂跑大聲喧鬧，將小孩單獨留在家中等等行為，在美國的鄰居或旁人不會冷眼旁觀，而是積極舉發保護小孩，父母將因此而吃上官司。

　　小孩的照顧問題在美國有法律規定，父母必須選擇他們覺得有足夠能力及責任感的人來當保姆，十幾歲的青少年或十歲左右的兒童常打零工幫忙帶小孩，而送報童多由前青少年階段的男童擔任。青少年滿十六歲起可以開始工作，但對幾歲可以當保姆並無規範。

住所 郵電通訊 日常活動 銀行與保險 交通 食品與飲食 購物 社交活動 教育 休閒活動 醫療 緊急情況

住所
郵電通訊
日常活動
銀行與保險
交通
食品與飲食
購物
社交活動
教育
休閒活動
醫療
緊急情況

106

3.5 洗車
Car Wash

洗車在美國很方便,有人工啟動完全機械式自動洗車,也有完全無人的自助投幣洗車,還有人工洗車,提供和臺灣類似的服務。人工洗車多幾道手續,如人工刷洗、毛巾擦乾及打蠟。有些加油站在加入一定金額汽油後,提供免費洗車服務。一般簡單洗車約為 $5-$10,如要清潔車內灰塵,洗車處也有吸塵器。

Dialog 對話

A: 嗨,我要洗車。

A: Hi. I'd like my car washed.

B: 好的,你要洗哪一種?

B: OK. What kind of wash do you want?

A: 事實上,我從未洗過,你可以告訴我有什麼選擇嗎?

A: Actually, I've never done this before. Can you tell me what the choices are?

B: 好,我們有普通洗車還有豪華洗車。普通洗車收費5元,豪華洗車收費7元,包含兩次上肥皂及上熱蠟。

B: Sure. We have a regular wash and a deluxe wash, too. The regular costs $5. The deluxe costs $7 and includes double soaping and hot wax.

A: 我知道了,我想我要豪華洗車。

A: I see. I think I want the deluxe wash.

B: 好，先付錢給我，然後向前開，我們會先擦洗你的車。

B: Fine. Just pay me. Then pull forward, and we'll scrub your car down first.

A: 收音機天線沒問題吧？

A: Is the radio antenna OK?

B: 看來是很有彈性，應該沒問題。現在往前開到輪夾，再把車放到空檔。

B: It looks like a very flexible one, so there should be no problem. Now pull forward into the wheel clamp and put the car in neutral.

A: 好(向前開後停止)。

A: OK. (Pull the car forward and stop.)

B: 這樣對了，洗車機會做剩下的事。

B: Yes, that's right. The car washing machine will do the rest.

A: 吸塵器在哪裡？

A: Where are the vacuum cleaners?

B: 你的車經過洗車機後，等燈號變綠色，然後開出去，你會看到吸塵器就在你右邊，要用25分錢。

B: After your car passes through the washer, wait for the light to turn green. Then drive out. You'll see the vacuum machines on your immediate right. They require quarters.

A: 非常感謝。

A: Thanks very much.

住所　郵電通訊　日常活動　銀行與保險　交通　食品與飲食　購物　社交活動　教育　休閒活動　醫療　緊急情況

Word Bank 字庫

regular [`rɛgjələ] adj. 一般的

deluxe [dɪ`lʌks] adj. 豪華的

wax [wæks] n. 蠟

antenna [æn`tɛnə] n. 天線

forward [`fɔrwəd] adv. 向前地

scrub [skrʌb] v. 用力擦或刷

wheel clamp n. 車輪夾板

neutral [`njutrəl] adj. 空檔的

vacuum cleaner n. 吸塵器

require [rɪ`kwaɪr] v. 需要

Useful Phrases 實用語句

1. 我要豪華洗車，謝謝。

   I'd like a deluxe wash, please.

2. 你們有吸塵器嗎？

   Do you have vacuum cleaners?

3. 你們也有打蠟嗎？

   Do you wax cars, too?

4. 我從沒有這麼做過，你可以告訴我怎麼做嗎？

   I've never done this before. Can you tell me what to do?

5. 我現在付錢給你嗎？

   Do I pay you now?

6. 是軟布還是刷子？

   Is it soft cloth or brush?

7. 是什麼樣的刷子？

   What kind of brush is it?

8. 我想要用手洗。

   I'd like it hand washed.

9. 我想要用毛巾擦乾。

   I'd like it towel dried.

10. 洗車包含清潔內部嗎？

   Does the wash include cleaning the inside?

11. 你可以到大廳去等車子。

   You can go to the lounge to wait for your car.

12. 你的車子幾分鐘就好了。

   Your car will be ready in just a few minutes.

3.6 修改衣服
Clothing Alteration

買衣服時就有修改衣服的服務，平時需要修改衣服時可以拿到女裁縫師 (seamstress) 或男裁縫師 (tailor) 店裡修改。

3.6a 女士 Women

 Dialog 對話

A: 嗨，我需要修改這條裙子。

A: Hi. I need this skirt altered.

B: 你要修改多少？

B: How much do you want it altered?

A: 我要剛好在我膝蓋下面。

A: I want it to be just below my knees.

B: 你穿上我先量一下。

B: Let me measure you with the dress on first.

A: 好，我在哪裡換衣服？

A: OK. Where can I change?

住所｜郵電通訊｜日常活動｜銀行與保險｜交通｜食品與飲食｜購物｜社交活動｜教育｜休閒活動｜醫療｜緊急情況

左側邊欄：住所 | 郵電通訊 | 日常活動 | 銀行與保險 | 交通 | 食品與飲食 | 購物 | 社交活動 | 教育 | 休閒活動 | 醫療 | 緊急情況

B: 我們那邊有更衣室。

B: We have a changing room over there.

A: 謝謝，修改要多久？

A: Thank you. When will the alteration be done?

B: 明天下午就好了。

B: It will be ready tomorrow afternoon.

3.6b 男士 Men

Dialog 對話

A: 嗨，這條長褲太長了。

A: Hi. This pair of pants is too long.

B: 沒問題，我可以替你改短褲管。

B: No problem. I can shorten the cuffs for you.

A: 你可以改快一點嗎？

A: Can you do it quickly?

B: 我可以在一小時內改好，我先確定長度。

B: I can have them ready in an hour. Let me check the length first.

A: 謝謝。

A: Thanks.

Useful Phrases 實用語句

● 顧客 Customer

1. 我要修改這個。

   I need this altered.

2. 你這裡有修改衣服嗎？

   Do you alter clothing here?

3. 我要改短這個。

   I need this shortened.

4. 何時會好？

   What time will it be ready?

5. 要很久嗎？

   Will it take long?

6. 我可以明天 [今天下午，一個小時後] 來拿衣服嗎？

   Can I pick it up tomorrow [this afternoon, in an hour]?

7. 修改會看起來明顯嗎？

   Will the alteration be noticeable?

● 男 [女] 裁縫 Tailor/Seamstress

1. 請穿上。

   Please put it on.

2. 你要改什麼？

   What do you want altered?

3. 你要多長？

   How long do you want it?

4. 我要將裙子改成膝蓋上一吋。

   I'd like my skirt altered one inch above the knee.

5. 我要改短袖子，但還是要蓋住手腕。

   I'd like my sleeves shortened, but still cover the wrist.

6. 更衣室在這裡。

   Here is the changing room.

7. 我要量一下。

   I need to measure it.

住所
郵電通訊
日常活動
銀行與保險
交通
食品與飲食
購物
社交活動
教育
休閒活動
醫療
緊急情況

8. 站直不要動。

Stand straight and still.

9. 手臂向外伸直。

Hold your arms out.

10. 我明天會改好。

I'll have it ready tomorrow.

11. 只需一個小時。

It will only take an hour.

12. 在這裡，試穿看看。

Here it is. Try it on.

13. 你覺得如何？

How do you like it?

14. 可以嗎？

Is it OK?

 Language Power 字句補給站

◆ 修改衣服 Clothing Alteration

tailor	男裁縫
seamstress	女裁縫
alter	修改
alteration	修改
sew	縫
hemline	下擺
cuff	褲管
collar	領口
seam	接縫
take in	改緊
let out	放寬
shorten	改短
material	質料
fabric	布料
measure	丈量

Unit 4 Banking and Insurance

銀行與保險

搬家後要盡早到銀行開戶(美國的郵局與臺灣不同,並不提供理財服務),美國銀行營業時間較長,服務方便,多數提供類似服務,如存提款、支票帳戶、保險箱、匯兌、貸款及其他理財服務,但要特別注意各類隱藏的手續費,如提款手續費、帳戶管理費或信用卡相關處理費用等。平日營業時間各家不一,從早上 8-10 點起至下午 5-7 點都有,有些銀行晚上及週六也有營業。

保險是個人安全防護的工具,美國醫療及意外險昂貴,但雇主多有提供,人壽險因為選擇很多,必須貨比三家。在美國合約以英文簽立,即使是土生土長的美國人也需要保險經紀人替他們的保險解惑,例如:需要多少保障、如何看懂保單、了解保險術語等。因此新移民最好找可信賴的經紀人幫忙規劃自己需要的保險。

住所

郵電通訊

日常活動

銀行與保險

交通

食品與飲食

購物

社交活動

教育

休閒活動

醫療

緊急情況

4.1 開戶（活期存款及活期支票帳戶）
Opening Accounts (a savings account and a checking account)

一般人為了方便起見，常在銀行開幾個帳戶，通常都是開兩個帳戶——活期存款及活期支票帳戶。銀行為求安全起見，開立帳戶時除了檢查證件外，會要求提供社會安全號碼 (SSN, Social Security Number) 及母親的娘家姓 (mother's maiden name)，供後來必要時確認之用。因民眾不可能忘記母親的娘家姓，所以銀行用來當作確認工具。

 Dialog　對話

A: 哈囉，我要開一個存款帳戶。

A: Hello. I would like to open a savings account.

B: 好，你需要填這份表格。

B: Fine. You'll need to fill out this form.

A: 好，我也需要一個支票帳戶。

A: Alright. I also want to have a checking account.

B: 好的，你也要申請信用卡嗎？

B: Good. Would you like to apply for a credit card, too?

A: 是的，核卡需要多久？

A: Yes. How long does it take to be approved?

B: 大約一週。

B: Usually about a week.

B: 只要你帳戶隨時保持至少500元存款，我們這裡用支票免費。

B: We have free checking here as long as you keep at least \$500 in your account at all times.

A: 知道了，我想我可以做到，你們有個人樣式的支票嗎？

A: I see. I think I can do that. Do you have personalized checks?

B: 有的，你可以在上面印照片或選擇我們有的樣式。

B: Yes, we do. You can have your picture put on them, or select from the styles we have available.

A: 好，我等下再看，現在我要兌現這張支票。

A: OK. I'll look at those later. Right now I need to cash this check.

B: 我了解了，因為你剛在這裡開了帳戶，所以兌現不必收費。

B: I see. Because you have opened an account with us, there will be no charge for cashing it.

A: 太好了，謝謝。

A: Great. Thanks.

B: 請在背面簽名。

B: Please sign the check on the back.

A: 好。

A: OK.

住所
郵電通訊
日常活動
銀行與保險
交通
食品與飲食
購物
社交活動
教育
休閒活動
醫療
緊急情況

 Word Bank 字庫

apply [ə`plaɪ] v. 申請
approve [ə`pruv] v. 核准
personalize [`pɜsənəˌlaɪz] v. 個人化
cash [kæʃ] v. 兌現

Useful Phrases 實用語句

1. 我要開一個存款帳戶。

   I'd like to open a savings account.

2. 最低金額要存多少？

   What is the minimum amount I must deposit?

3. 存款利率是多少？

   What is the interest rate on savings?

4. 我要存這張支票到我帳戶內。

   I want to deposit this check into my account.

5. 我想建立信用。

   I'd like to establish a line of credit.

6. 我想開一個支票帳戶。

   I'd like to open a checking account.

7. 我想開一個聯名支票帳戶。

   I want to open a joint checking account.

8. 我可以有免費的支票嗎？

   Do I get free checks?

9. 我的支票何時會好？

   When will my checks be ready?

10. 我會收到多少張支票？

    How many checks will I receive?

11. 我要個人式樣的支票。

    I want personalized checks.

12. 我想兌現這張支票。

    I want to cash this check.

13. 我需要人幫忙設定網路銀行。

    I need help setting up online banking.

14. 我想取消一張我開出去的支票。

    I want to cancel a check I wrote.

15. 我要申請一張信用卡。

    I want to apply for a credit card.

16. 你們營業[休息]的時間是？

    When are you open [closed]?

Notes 小叮嚀

開戶要選擇有 FDIC (Federal Deposit Insurance Corporation) 聯邦存款保險公司標誌的銀行，存款才能獲得聯邦政府的保障 (10 萬元內)。較大的銀行有 JP Morgan Chase (摩根大通)，Bank of America (美國銀行)，Citibank (花旗)，Wells Fargo (富國)，HSBC (匯豐) 等。選擇大的銀行很重要，可以省下跨行提款的手續費。

社會安全號碼 (Social Security Number) 就像是個人身分號碼一樣，許多機構如銀行用它來設定帳戶、確定身分、核發信用卡等等。政府用它追蹤 (繳稅) 紀錄，決定你的社會福利資格，特別是退休後的福利，考駕照也要用到此號碼，所以非美國公民但必須長期居住者需要此號碼才行的通。社會安全號碼可以向當地社會安全局辦事處申請，也可以在社會安全局的官方網站www.ssa.gov上申請或致電 1-800-772-1213。

4.1a 存款 Saving

Dialog 對話

A: 我要把錢存入儲蓄 [支票] 帳戶。

A: I'd like to put the money into my savings [checking] account.

B: 好的，我需要你的存摺及存款單。	**B:** OK. I need your bank book and a deposit slip.
A: 好，在這裡。	**A:** Yes, here you are.

4.1b 提款 Withdrawing

Dialog 對話

A: 我想領300元。	**A:** I want to withdraw \$300.
B: 好的，我把你的支票兌現。	**B:** OK. I'll cash your check.
A: 謝謝，你可以給我20元的鈔票嗎？	**A:** Thanks. Can you give it to me in 20s?
B: 沒問題。	**B:** No problem.
A: 還有你可以找開一張20元，換成一張10元、一張5元、五張1元的嗎？	**A:** Also, can you break one twenty into a ten, a five and five ones?
B: 好，這裡是20，40…280，290，295, 96, 97, 98, 99, 300。	**B:** Alright. Here you are 20, 40... 280, 290, 295, 96, 97, 98, 99, 300.

住所
郵電通訊
日常活動
銀行與保險
交通
食品與飲食
購物
社交活動
教育
休閒活動
醫療
緊急情況

A: 非常謝謝你。

A: Thank you very much!

Tips 小祕訣

在美國存取款用自動櫃員機 ATM 非常方便，但跨行提領需手續費約 $3，每個月銀行會寄來每個帳戶連同利息在內的對帳單 (bank statement)，所以不需定期去刷存摺。網路銀行用戶，可上網隨時查看對帳單。如要存現金或支票可以用 ATM 或帶存摺到銀行填存款單 (deposit slip) 存入，有些個人支票簿後面也會附有存款條可用。如要提款可以用 ATM 或到銀行填寫取款條 (withdraw slip) 或開自己的支票給銀行兌現，有些美國銀行沒有提供提款條，個人支票即是提款條。近來銀行已不使用存摺，而是印出一張存款或提款收據。

4.2 提款卡及扣款卡
ATM Card and Debit Card

4.2a 詢問 Asking about the Cards

Dialog 對話

A: 我想要辦一張提款卡及一張扣款卡。

A: I'd like to get an ATM card and a debit card.

B: 事實上，你的提款卡就是扣款卡。

B: Actually, your ATM card acts as a debit card.

A: 我何時會收到 (提款卡) 呢？

A: When will I receive it?

B: 一週內會寄到你的地址。

B: One will be sent to your address within a week.

A: 我知道了。

A: I see.

A: 用提款卡提領現金有每日限額嗎？

A: Is there a daily limit on cash withdrawals at an ATM?

B: 有的，每天限額為1,000元。

B: Yes. There is a $1,000 a day limit.

4.2b 開卡 Activating a Card

Dialog 對話

A: 我需要開卡嗎？

A: Will I need to activate it?

B: 要，開卡說明書會附在郵件內。

B: Yes. Instructions about how are included in the mailing.

A: 我可以選密碼嗎？

A: Can I select my own PIN?

住所
郵電通訊
日常活動
銀行與保險
交通
食品與飲食
購物
社交活動
教育
休閒活動
醫療
緊急情況

B: 卡片附有一組密碼，但你可以更改，說明書會告訴你怎麼做，卡片及密碼會分開郵寄。

B: One will come with the card, but you can change it. The instructions will tell you how. The card and the PIN will come as separate mailings.

A: 我知道了，如果有問題可以來這裡請你們幫忙嗎？

A: I see. If I have trouble, can I come here for help?

B: 當然，沒問題，我們可以幫你設定。

A: Sure. No problem. We can help you set it up.

A: 謝謝。

A: Thank you.

Word Bank 字庫

daily limit n. 每日限額
cash withdrawal n. 現金提領
activate [`æktə‚vet] v. 開卡
PIN (personal identification number) n. 個人識別密碼
instruction [ɪn`strʌkʃən] n. 指示；說明書

Useful Phrases 實用語句

1. 我何時會拿到提款卡？
   When will I get my ATM card?
2. 使用提款卡怎麼收費？
   What are your ATM charges?

住所
郵電通訊
日常活動
銀行與保險
交通
食品與飲食
購物
社交活動
教育
休閒活動
醫療
緊急情況

3. 我要怎樣使用提款機？

   How do I use the ATM?

4. 我怎麼變更我的密碼？

   How do I change my PIN number?

5. 每天可提領現金的限額是多少？

   What is the daily cash withdrawal limit?

6. 我需要一張扣款卡。

   I need a debit card.

Language Power 字句補給站

◆ 存款及支票帳戶 Saving and Checking Accounts

bankbook	存摺
deposit slip	存款單
withdraw	提款
minimum amount	最低金額
teller	行員
ATM	自動櫃員機
drive-up window	開車族窗口
online banking	網路銀行
processing fee	手續費
debit card	扣款卡
overdraw	透支
NSF (not sufficient funds)	存款不足
penalty	罰金
overdraft protection plan	透支保護計畫
bounce a check	跳票

Tips 小祕訣

在銀行開戶時就會拿到提款卡，美國的自動櫃員機不只可以提款，還可以接受存款，非常方便。使用提款機時，可以選擇從活儲或支票帳戶提領現金，也可以在兩戶頭互相轉帳 (transfer)。近年銀行甚至像速食店一樣，設有免下車之「得來速」提款機 (drive through ATM) 服務，大多數銀行對使用自家銀行的顧客收取ATM手續費，跨行提款時再加上他行手續費，因此現今手續費從 $2-$6 元不等 (賭場內的最貴)。

提款卡也可以當作扣款卡使用。扣款功能與使用支票相同，且在外州為商店接受，因此使用廣泛。使用扣款功能時，商店螢幕會顯示從活儲或支票帳戶扣款，並且問你 Cash back? (是否需要順便提領現金，通常不超過 $60，如此可省下使用ATM 提領之手續費)，持卡人輸入是/否及 PIN 後，該費用便立即從帳戶中扣除，記得將收據收好以便對帳。

4.3 網路銀行
Online Banking

Dialog 1 對話1

A: 我可以問你幾個有關網路銀行的問題嗎？

A: Can I ask you a couple of questions about online banking?

B: 讓我為你找個專員，他們可以告訴你所有關於網路銀行的事。

B: Let me get a representative for you. They can help you with all of that.

A: 謝謝。

A: Thank you.

住所

郵電通訊

日常活動

銀行與保險

交通

食品與飲食

購物

社交活動

教育

休閒活動

醫療

緊急情況

Dialog 2 （對話2）

A: 我可以為你服務嗎？

A: May I help you?

B: 我要設定網路銀行。

B: I'd like to get set up for online banking services.

A: 我可以幫你，請坐。

A: I can help you. Please sit down.

B: 服務費多少？

B: How much is the service?

A: 免費，我們只要輸入一些關於你的個人基本資料以及你在我們銀行的帳戶。

A: It's free. All we have to do is enter some basic personal information about you and the accounts you have with our bank.

B: 用這系統很難嗎？

B: Is it difficult to use the system?

A: 不會，我會教你怎麼用，只要用滑鼠按鍵。

A: No. I'll show you how to use it. It just requires clicking around with the mouse.

B: 那安全性呢？

B: What about security?

A: 系統有重重加密，只要確定沒有人知道你的密碼。	**A:** The system is heavily encrypted. Just make sure no other people know your password.
B: 我可以用它轉帳到別的戶頭嗎？	**B:** Can I use it to transfer money to different accounts?
A: 可以，你也可以付款。	**A:** Yes, and you can make payments, too.

 Word Bank 字庫

representative [ˌrɛprɪˋzɛntətɪv] n. 專員
encrypt [ɪnˋkrɪpt] v. 加密

 Notes 小叮嚀

　　美國網路銀行設定免費，但帳戶可能無利息收入，如果不符銀行最低存款或其他標準 (如無紙化及不使用臨櫃服務或 23 歲以下學生身分)，就不能免去 (waive) 支付每月維護費約 $10 (e-banking monthly maintenance fee)。利用網路銀行或手機轉帳 (mobile transfer) 亦需支付手續費 (transfer fees)，依轉帳為當天或隔天，轉入或轉出，帳戶種類，一次或定期，國內州別或國際轉帳等不同，收費有別。銀行為維護網路銀行安全及更好的服務，提供客製化提醒功能 (customized alerts)，幫助用戶避免詐騙或異常帳戶活動及存款不足等風險。

住所　郵電通訊　日常活動　銀行與保險　交通　食品與飲食　購物　社交活動　教育　休閒活動　醫療　緊急情況

住所 郵電通訊 日常活動 銀行與保險 交通 食品與飲食 購物 社交活動 教育 休閒活動 醫療 緊急情況

4.4 個人支票
Personal Checks

網路銀行或手機 app 轉帳功能在某些狀況下已可代替開立支票，只要有對方 email、姓名及手機號碼即可轉帳，網路轉帳同時會以 email 及手機簡訊通知對方領取，如果對方也已註冊網路銀行，該筆帳款就已自動即時入帳。在其他狀況下，支票仍是主要的支付工具之一，各銀行也開始推出電子化支票 (echeck)。

4.4a 支票樣本及解說 Sample Check

支票在美國是重要的支付工具，多數的商店接受當地的支票。開支票時在 date 欄寫上日期，pay to the order of 寫上付款給誰，$金額 (阿拉伯數字)，dollars 欄以英文寫上金額。銀行名稱下方 for 是開票人備忘欄，寫上開票緣由 (如房租、電費)，之後在右下欄簽名。使用支票支付帳款時，商店會要求出示證件並查看證件上的簽名，證明是你本人開立的支票，所以支票可以說是安全的支付工具。

❶ PERSONALIZATION 開票人姓名地址 (電話)
❷ CHECK NUMBER 支票編號
❸ DATE 開票日期
❹ FRACTION 銀行分行資訊
❺ PAY TO LINE 受票人姓名欄
❻ DOLLARS BOX 金額數字框格

❼ AMOUNT LINE 金額欄 (以英文寫上)

❽ PADLOCK ICON 安全鎖標示 (銀行為防止支票詐欺所設)

❾ BANK INFORMATION 銀行名稱及地址

❿ MEMO/FOR (支票用途) 備忘

⓫ SIGNATURE 開票人簽名

⓬ ABA CHECK ROUTING NUMBER 美國銀行協會 (American Baking Association, ABA) 的編號

⓭ ACCOUNT NUMBER 持票人支票帳號

⓮ CHECK NUMBER 本張支票號碼

每張支票都為兩聯，第一聯使用時從支票本撕下交給對方，第二聯為本人留存，此聯並有記帳欄可供計算帳戶內餘款。保持支票帳戶紀錄正確很重要，如此才不會混淆或透支；每個月銀行會將被兌現的支票寄回給你對帳，並確認帳戶還有多少金額，自動櫃員機或網路銀行也可以讓你很方便的查到支票帳戶餘額。一般支票帳戶通常不要求保持最低餘額，但是如果要銀行支付利息的話，支票帳戶內就必須保持最低餘額。

網路銀行或手機 app 轉帳功能在某些狀況下已可代替開立支票，只要有對方 email、姓名及手機號碼即可轉帳，網路轉帳同時會以 email 及手機簡訊通知對方領取，如果對方也已註冊網路銀行，該筆帳款就已自動即時入帳。在其他狀況下，支票仍是主要的支付工具之一，各銀行也開始推出 echeck。

如果收到別人開給自己的支票，可以到銀行或使用 ATM 將支票存入自己帳戶，也可以使用手機 app 存入。

1. 在銀行櫃臺辦理：

攜帶銀行存摺，在銀行櫃臺員面前，於支票後面 endorse here (在此背書) 欄內簽名，寫上「For Deposit Only」(存款專用) 與自己的帳戶號碼，為防止支票遺失，被存入他人帳戶，未到銀行前絕對不要在支票後面簽名！帳號填寫並非絕對必要，除在銀行辦理手續外，應注意維護帳號以免遭人利用。

(支票背面)

```
ENDORSE HERE (在此背書)
                Your signature    你的簽名
                For deposit only  存款專用
                (Your bank name 銀行名稱
                account no. 帳號)
        DO NOT WRITE, STAMP, OR SIGN BELOW THIS LINE.
        (以下銀行專用，請勿寫字、蓋章或簽名。)
```

2. 在自動櫃員機(ATM)存款：

必須使用自己開戶銀行的櫃員機才能存款，當然必須有ATM卡及密碼，筆及存款單 (deposit slip) 在機器旁就有，在ATM選擇存款功能時，機器會打開信封夾 (deposit envelope) 供取用，支票背面簽上自己的名字並寫上「For Deposit Only」及自己的帳戶 (同上圖)，填好存款單，於信封內放入支票及存款單，置入櫃員機存款縫內，ATM印出帳戶餘額後，交易完成。

3. 將別人開給自己的支票背書可以轉讓第三人 (third party)：

在支票背面簽自己名字後，寫 pay to order of「付給指定人」及第三人名字，交予第三人，此人將支票存入帳戶或兌現時須在下方簽名。
(支票背面)

```
ENDORSE HERE (在此背書)
                Your signature    你的簽名
                Pay to the order of 付給指定人
                Third party's name 第三人
                (Third party's signature 第三人簽名)
        DO NOT WRITE, STAMP, OR SIGN BELOW THIS LINE.
        (以下銀行專用，請勿寫字、蓋章或簽名。)
```

4.使用網路銀行或行動裝置存入：

用戶也可下載行動銀行應用軟體 (mobile banking app)，直接使用平板或手機將支票前後拍照 (要背書)，按照流程輸入資訊，確認即完成。

4.4b 止付支票 Putting a Stop Payment Order

Dialog 對話

A: 哈囉,我想要止付一張我開出去的支票。

A: Hello. I want to put a stop payment order on a check I wrote.

B: 我知道了,你知道那張支票的號碼嗎?

B: I see. Do you know the number of the check?

A: 知道,這是我的支票本明細,上面有號碼。

A: Yes. Here is my checkbook statement. There's the check number on it.

B: 好的,沒問題。我有號碼、日期及你支票本的金額。

B: OK. No problem. I have the number, date and amount from your checkbook.

A: 你可以今天止付嗎?

A: Can you stop it today?

B: 可以,我現在馬上發出停止支付命令。

B: Yes. I'll put the stop payment order out now.

A: 非常謝謝你。

A: Thank you very much.

Word Bank 字庫

checkbook [`tʃɛk͵bʊk] n. 支票本
statement [`stetmənt] n. 明細
stop payment order n. 停止支付命令

住所 郵電通訊 日常活動 銀行與保險 交通 食品與飲食 購物 社交活動 教育 休閒活動 醫療 緊急情況

住所
郵電通訊
日常活動
銀行與保險
交通
食品與飲食
購物
社交活動
教育
休閒活動
醫療
緊急情況

Tips 小祕訣

　　如果有任何必要，必須停止支付某張尚未被兌現的支票，可以先打電話給銀行及時告知該張支票號碼、付款對象、金額、日期等確實資料，之後盡快 (14日內否則無效) 親自到銀行填寫書面通知 (stop payment order) 並簽名，銀行因須通知各分行追蹤該支票並承擔及時止付的風險，會收取高額手續費 (在帳戶內扣除) ，約在 $18-$32 之間，停止支付有效期限為六個月。若已到期但該支票仍未被提示，可以更新止付命令。

4.4c 支票兌換現金 Cashing a Check

Dialog 1 對話1

(在銀行 at the bank)

A: 我可以為你服務嗎？

A: May I help you?

B: 可以，我要兌現支票。

B: Yes. I'd like to cash a check.

A: 你有我們銀行的帳戶嗎？

A: Do you have an account with our bank?

B: 有，有差別嗎？

B: Yes. Does it matter?

A: 如果沒有，你就要多付5元的手續費。

A: If you don't have one, then you'd have to pay an additional $5 processing fee.

住所

郵電通訊

日常活動

銀行與保險

交通

食品與飲食

購物

社交活動

教育

休閒活動

醫療

緊急情況

B: 我知道了。

B: I see.

A: 你要付款還是要現金就好？

A: Are you making a payment or just getting some cash?

B: 我需要現金，我沒有用很多支票，我該把金額寫在這裡嗎？

B: I need some cash. I have not written many checks. Should I write the amount here?

A: 是的，寫在金額欄，支付對象欄寫銀行名字。

A: Yes. On the line that says, "for the amount of." And write the name of the bank on the line that says, "pay to the order of."

B: 我需要在右下角簽名對嗎？

B: I need to sign it here on the bottom right, correct?

A: 對，還有因為是要現金，你也要在背後簽名。

A: Yes, that's correct. Also, because it is for cash, you need to sign it on the back, too.

B: 好。

B: OK.

 Dialog 2 （對話2）

(在藥局 at a pharmacy)

A: 你收支票嗎？

A: Will you take a check?

B: 當然。	**B:** Sure.
A: 好，我該付給誰？	**A:** OK. Who should I make it out to?
B: 卡森藥局。	**B:** Carlson's Pharmacy.
A: 我需要一些現金，可以在寫購物金額外多寫20元嗎？	**A:** I need some cash. Is it ok to write the check for \$20 more than the amount of purchase?
B: 好的，沒問題。	**B:** Sure, no problem.

Tips 小祕訣

　　在不同銀行使用支票換現金可能會被收取手續費。在購物時若身上現金不多了，可以問店家是否願意讓你在支票上多寫一些金額換現金，店家通常會答應，如此付帳，身上也會有一些現金。

4.5 信用卡
Credit Card

雖然信用卡可以在各國使用，但要在美國長期生活，考慮匯率、手續費、國際清算費等相關費用及人在美國如何處理帳單問題，申請美國信用卡是必要的。信用卡從買雜貨到汽車都很好用，基本上較昂貴的物品，人們多以信用卡支付。

住所
郵電通訊
日常活動
銀行與保險
交通
食品與飲食
購物
社交活動
教育
休閒活動
醫療
緊急情況

4.5a 申請 Application

Dialog 1 對話1

A: 哈囉,我想申請信用卡。

A: Hello. I'd like to apply for a credit card.

B: 好,你在我們銀行有帳戶嗎?

B: Fine. Do you have an account at our bank?

A: 有。

A: Yes.

B: 好,請填好這張申請表後交給我。

B: OK. Please fill out this application. Then, bring it back to me.

A: 好。

A: Alright.

Dialog 2 對話2

A: 嗨,這是我的申請表。

A: Hi. Here is my application form.

B: 好,我會處理,你有完整填寫你的信用紀錄嗎?

B: Good. I'll have it processed. Did you write down your credit history completely?

A: 有。

A: Yes, I did.

住所 | 郵電通訊 | 日常活動 | 銀行與保險 | 交通 | 食品與飲食 | 購物 | 社交活動 | 教育 | 休閒活動 | 醫療 | 緊急情況

B: 很好，一星期內你會知道結果。

B: Very good then. You should know in one week.

A: 我需要來這裡領卡嗎？

A: Do I have to come here to get the card?

B: 不必，你會先收到核卡通知，過幾天會收到卡片。

B: No. You'll receive a notice of approval first. Then, a few days later the card will arrive.

A: 我需要到銀行來開卡嗎？

A: Do I have to come to the bank to activate it?

B: 不必，你可以在電話上開卡。

B: No. You can do that over the phone.

 Word Bank 字庫

credit history n. 信用紀錄
approval [ə`pruv] n. 同意

 Tips 小祕訣

　　要在美國申請信用卡，必須向信用卡公司或發卡銀行提供你的財務狀況，因此必須準備能證明財務狀況的資料及信用紀錄，如果是用電話聯絡還必須提供有關安全確認的資料。事實上美國的信用卡核卡容易，就算沒有信用資料，銀行也願意開始讓你建立信用，並在衡量你的財務狀況後，提供一個適當的額度給你。

4.6 保險箱
Safe Deposit Box

Dialog 對話

A: 我要開一個保險箱。

A: I want to open a safe deposit box.

B: 我們有不同尺寸，這裡是尺寸清單。

B: We have different sizes. Here is a list of sizes.

A: 好。我要一個 12x24吋的箱子。

A: OK. I want a 12 by 24 inch box.

B: 那種的一年要 25 元，可以每年自動從你帳戶扣款一次。

B: Those cost \$25 a year. It can be automatically withdrawn from your account once a year.

A: 聽起來很好。

A: That sounds good.

B: 好，請填寫這張表格，然後我給你一支鑰匙。

B: Great. Just fill out this form, and then I'll assign you a key.

A: 我何時可以到保險箱區？

A: When can I get into the safe deposit area?

B: 我們營業的任何時間，平時9點到6點，週六9點到2點。

B: Anytime we are open, which is 9 to 6 on weekdays, and 9 to 2 on Saturday.

住所
郵電通訊
日常活動
銀行與保險
交通
食品與飲食
購物
社交活動
教育
休閒活動
醫療
緊急情況

A: 我知道了，真謝謝你。

A: I see. Thank you very much.

Useful Phrases 實用語句

1. 我要一個保險箱。

   I'd like to have a safe deposit box.

2. 一年收費25元。

   It costs $25 a year.

3. 你會每年寄通知給我嗎？

   Will you send me a notice each year?

4. 我們會事先在兩個月前通知你。

   We'll inform you two months in advance.

5. 你可以登記自動扣款。

   You can register it for automatic withdrawal.

4.7 購買定存單
Buying a Certificate of Deposit (CD)

Dialog 對話

A: 我想買定存單。

A: I'd like to buy a certificate of deposit.

B: 你要買哪一種？

B: Which one do you want?

A: 這家銀行有什麼期限選擇？

A: What maturity options does this bank offer?

B: 我們有6個月、1年、18個月、2年、3年及5年的定存單。

B: We have 6 month, one year, 18 month, two year, three year, and five year CDs.

A: 2年的定存單利率多少？

A: What is the interest rate on a 2-year CD?

B: 如果存4,000元，是2％，如果存5,000元以上，是2.3%。

B: 2% if you invest $4,000. If you buy $5,000 or above, you'll get 2.3%.

A: 好，那買一張兩年期的。

A: OK. Let's set up a two year one now.

B: 我現在輸入電腦設定，我需要個人基本資料、你的帳戶號碼及簽名。

B: I'll set it up on the computer right now. I just need basic personal info, your account number, and your signature.

A: 我兩年後必須兌現嗎？

A: Do I have to cash it out after two years?

B: 不用，你可以續存到另一張新的定存單。

B: No. You can roll it over into another new CD.

Word Bank 字庫

maturity [məˋtjʊrətɪ] n. 到期
roll over n. 續存

Useful Phrases 實用語句

1. 我要買一年的定存單。

   I'd like to buy a one year CD.

2. 你們提供的定存單利率是多少？

   What interest rates do you offer on CD's?

3. 我必須至少 [最多] 投資多少？

   What is the minimum [maximum] amount I must invest?

4. 如果提早兌現有什麼處罰？

   What penalties for early cashing in are there?

5. 我要怎麼付定存單？

   How do I pay for the CD?

6. 這家銀行有什麼期限選擇？

   What maturity options does this bank offer?

7. 自動續存利息會變動嗎？

   Will the automatic roll over change the interest rate?

8. 如果不續存，錢會入哪個帳戶？

   Which account will the money go to if it's not rolled over?

9. 快到期時，你會通知我嗎？

   Will you notify me when it's going to mature?

10. 我何時會接到通知？

    When will I get the notification?

11. 是用電話還是信件通知？

    Is the notification by phone or by mail?

12. 利息何時會進來？

    When will the interest come in?

13. 你可以選擇每月、每季、每半年或每年讓利息匯進你的定存。

    You can choose to have interest credited into your CD every month, quarter, half year, or every year.

14. 哪一個是最好的選擇？

    Which one is the best choice?

15. 這種定存有任何節稅好處嗎？

Are there any tax advantages with this type of CD?

Notes 小叮嚀

定存單的購買多以 $500 為最低購買金額，利率 (fixed/ mobile interest rate 固定/機動利率) 及未到期解約 (early cash in) 罰則各家銀行規定不同，所以要多做比較才不吃虧。購買定存時可以選擇到期時是否自動續存 (automatic roll over)、利息何時入帳 (be credited) 及是否要接到到期通知 (notification)。

4.8 匯款
Wire Transfer

Dialog 對話

A: 我需要匯錢到香港。

A: I need to wire money to Hong Kong.

B: 你需要填寫這張表格。

B: You'll need to fill out this form.

A: 你可以幫我嗎？

A: Can you help me?

B: 可以，其實很簡單，只是一般個人資料、帳號以及你要匯過去的銀行地址。

B: Yes. Actually it is pretty easy. It's the usual personal information, plus the account number and address of the bank you are wiring to.

住所
郵電通訊
日常活動
銀行與保險
交通
食品與飲食
購物
社交活動
教育
休閒活動
醫療
緊急情況

A: 我知道了。

A: I see.

B: 你還需要有照片的證件。

B: You need a picture I.D. also.

A: 沒問題，今天的匯率是多少？

A: No problem. What's the exchange rate today?

B: 請查一下牆上的告示板。

B: Check the reader board up there on the wall.

A: 好的。

A: OK.

Useful Phrases 實用語句

1. 我要匯款到國外。

   I want to wire money overseas.

2. 今天的匯率多少？

   What's today's exchange rate?

3. 我要匯到這個帳戶。

   I want to wire it to this account.

4. 這是我的證件。

   Here's my I.D.

4.9 外幣
Foreign Currency

4.9a 兌換錢幣 Money Exchange

Dialog 對話

A: 我想換美金。

A: I want to exchange for U.S. dollars.

B: 要用什麼貨幣換？

B: What are you exchanging?

A: 英鎊。

A: British Pounds.

B: 知道了，沒問題。

B: I see. No problem.

A: 匯率是多少呢？

A: What's the exchange rate?

B: 今天的匯率顯示在這邊。

B: Today's rates are shown here.

Word Bank 字庫

exchange [ɪksˋtʃendʒ] n., v. 兌換
rate [ret] n. 匯率

住所 郵電通訊 日常活動 銀行與保險 交通 食品與飲食 購物 社交活動 教育 休閒活動 醫療 緊急情況

4.9b 旅行支票 Traveler's Checks

 Dialog　對話

A: 我想將旅行支票兌現。

A: I'd like to cash traveler's checks.

B: 什麼幣值呢？

B: What denomination?

A: 我想要兌現兩張100元支票。

A: I want to cash two $100 checks.

B: 好的，請確定它們都簽名了。

B: OK. Please make sure they are signed.

 Word Bank　字庫

traveler's check n. 旅行支票
denomination [dɪˌnɑməˈneʃən] n. 幣值
sign [saɪn] v. 簽名

Useful Phrases　實用語句

1. 你們兌換旅行支票嗎？
   Do you cash traveler's checks?

2. 我要10元及20元 (的鈔票)。
   I'd like tens and twenties, please.

3. 我要在哪裡簽名呢？
   Where do I sign?

4. 我需要買些旅行支票。
   I need to buy some traveler's checks.

5. 你們怎麼收佣金 [手續費]？

   How do you charge the commission [processing fee]?

Tips 小祕訣

交易時旅行支票其中一欄 ，必須在使用時當面簽名，但旅支的面額較大時，可以先去銀行換些小鈔，一般商店可能會找不開。

4.10 詢問資費及各項使用問題
Asking about Charges, Penalties, and Services

訂購新支票、用其他銀行提款機提領現金、轉帳、貸款手續費，甚至結束帳戶，有些銀行都要收取手續費，更別提早解約定存單、透支支票帳戶、遲繳信用卡款等可觀的手續費。所以要留意合約上或帳單上的細節，管理自己的帳戶並提出疑問。銀行及其他財務機構的規定未必相同，政府機構雖有規範商業行為，但通常對商業機制有利。美國人有句話說「caveat emptor」[ˋkævɪat ˋɛmptɔr] (拉丁文) 指的就是「Let the buyer beware.」(消費者自己要張大眼睛)。

Useful Phrases 實用語句

● **顧客 Customer**

1. 在提款機轉帳你們收費多少？

   How much do you charge for transferring money at an ATM?

2. 在其他銀行的提款機提款手續費多少？

   What's the service charge if I withdraw money from other bank's ATM?

3. 語音轉帳你們收費多少？

   How much do you charge for a voice transfer?

4. 我需要支付支票帳戶的月費嗎？

   Do I need to pay a monthly fee for the checking account?

5. 我每個月可以開的支票有限額嗎？

   Is there a monthly limit of the checks that I can write?

6. 如果存款不足，支票會跳票還是銀行會先墊付？

   Will the check bounce if there are insufficient funds, or will the bank cover it first?

7. 如果銀行代墊存款不足，罰金是多少？

   How much is the penalty if the bank covers for insufficient funds?

8. 除了不良信用紀錄，跳票還有何處罰？

   What's the penalty for bouncing checks, besides a bad credit record?

9. 利息在 6 月及 12 月底支付嗎？

   Is the interest paid at the end of June and December?

10. 重發幾個月前的信用卡帳單收費多少？

    How much do you charge for reissuing a credit card statement from a few months ago?

11. 如果我忘記繳信用卡帳單，處罰是什麼？

    What's the penalty if I forget about paying the credit card bill?

⊚ **行員 Teller**

1. 如果你用本行的提款機，不收費。

   There is no charge if you use our bank's ATM.

2. 如果你用其他銀行的提款機，要收費 3 元。

   There is a $3 charge if you use another bank's ATM.

3. 開支票免收費。

   Checking is free.

4. 我會為你訂新支票。

   I'll order new checks for you.

5. 請在這裡簽名。

   Sign here, please.

住所

郵電通訊

日常活動

銀行與保險

交通

食品與飲食

購物

社交活動

教育

休閒活動

醫療

緊急情況

6. 銀行會代墊透支支票，第一次不罰錢。

The bank will cover overdraws [overdrafts]. There is no penalty the first time.

4.11 遺失及補發
Losing and Reissuing Documents or Valuables

如果遺失了信用卡、支票簿、存摺或密碼，馬上通知銀行保障自己的權益後，最好是親自到銀行辦理手續，這樣確認會容易一些。每家銀行有不同手續，依照遺失物件不同，補發可能是當天或一週左右。

 Useful Phrases 實用語句

◎ **顧客 Customer**

1. 我丟了旅行支票，需要重發。

   I lost some traveler's checks and need to have them replaced.

2. 我的存摺似乎不知放哪了。

   I seem to have misplaced my bankbook.

3. 我不記得定存單放到哪裡去了。

   I don't remember where I put my CDs.

4. 我丟了我的保險箱鑰匙。

   I lost my safe deposit key.

5. 我遺失了我的信用卡。

   I lost my credit card.

6. 我這個月沒收到銀行帳單。

   I haven't received a bank statement this month.

7. 你可以電郵銀行帳單給我嗎？

   Can you email me my bank statement?

◎ **行員 Teller**

1. 我會發給你新的旅行支票。

   I'll get new traveler's checks for you.

2. 我會開一本新的存摺給你。

I'll arrange a new bankbook for you.

3. 我們可以做新鑰匙，費用 5 元。

We can have a new key made. It will cost $5.

4. 我會重發信用卡給你。

I'll reissue a new credit card to you.

5. 我會在電腦叫出你的銀行明細並且印一份給你。

I'll pull up your bank statements on my computer and make a copy for you.

6. 我們有網路銀行。

We have online banking services.

7. 你可以在網路查詢你的帳戶。

You can check your account online.

4.12 貸款
Loans

Dialog 1 　對話1

A: 我需要找個人談貸款。

A: I'd like to talk to someone about a loan.

B: 我把你引薦給我們的放款人員，請在那裡坐一下，我會確定他們知道你在這裡等。

B: I'll introduce you to one of our loan officers. Please sit down over there, and I'll make sure they know you are here.

A: 謝謝。

A: Thank you.

Dialog 2 (對話2)

A: 嗨，我想借錢買一部車。

A: Hi. I'd like to borrow some money to buy a car.

B: 好，首先我們要核對你的信用資料。

B: OK. First we'll have to check your credit references.

A: 我要做什麼來開始呢？

A: What should I do to get things started?

B: 我們要先知道你目前的就業狀況，並調查你過去的信用紀錄。

B: Well, we'll need to know about your current employment situation, and look into your past credit history.

A: 我有帶紀錄，請看一下。

A: I have records with me. Have a look.

B: 好，你可以告訴我你需要借多少錢？

B: Great. Can you tell me how much you need to borrow?

A: 我想我需要借10,000元。

A: I believe I'll need to borrow $10,000.

B: 我知道了。

B: I see.

住所 郵電通訊 日常活動 銀行與保險 交通 食品與飲食 購物 社交活動 教育 休閒活動 醫療 緊急情況

Useful Phrases 實用語句

1. 我想找放款人員談話。

   I'd like to speak to a loan officer.

2. 我要貸款買一部車。

   I'd like to get a loan to buy a car.

3. 貸款利率是多少？

   What's the loan rate?

4. 每個月貸款是多少？

   What is the monthly payment?

5. 核貸要多久？

   How long will it take to approve?

6. 我需要一個共同簽名的人嗎？

   Do I need a co-signer?

7. 我有抵押品。

   I have collateral.

8. 我想借不必抵押品的貸款。

   I want to take out an unsecured loan.

9. 我最多可以貸多少？

   What's the maximum I can borrow?

10. 合約多長？

    How long is the contract for?

11. 我要一個三年的合約。

    I want a three-year contract.

12. 我要合併我的貸款。

    I want to consolidate my debt.

住所
郵電通訊
日常活動
銀行與保險
交通
食品與飲食
購物
社交活動
教育
休閒活動
醫療
緊急情況

住所

郵電通訊

日常活動

銀行與保險

交通

食品與飲食

購物

社交活動

教育

休閒活動

醫療

緊急情況

Notes 小叮嚀

　　申辦貸款必須向銀行提供個人財務狀況且需要一些等待的時間，現在的信用查詢及貸款手續通常不必等太久，但貸款核准與否還是要看整體的經濟狀況。銀行彼此競爭客戶，所以要貸款要貨比三家了解貸款條件，要買定存或其他投資工具也一樣。

　　如果放款人員要求你要有共同簽名的人 (即保人) ，那該位人士也必須到銀行簽名，可能還要提供信用紀錄。如果貸款金額龐大，銀行要求提供抵押品，就必須簽定文件設定抵押給銀行，萬一將來繳款發生問題，銀行將出售抵押品彌補損失。

Language Power 字句補給站

◆ 貸款 Loans

credit reference	信用資料
collateral	抵押品
loan officer	貸款人員
co-signer	共同簽名人，保人
loan application	申請貸款
late payment	延遲付款
due date	到期日
lien against property	財產扣押權
amount borrowed	貸款金額
contract	合約
terms	條件
interest	利率
APR (annual percentage rate)	年利率

住所
郵電通訊
日常活動
銀行與保險
交通
食品與飲食
購物
社交活動
教育
休閒活動
醫療
緊急情況

4.13 解約
Closing Bank Services

4.13a 結清帳戶 Closing an Account

Dialog 對話

A: 嗨，我想結束我的支票帳戶。

A: Hi. I'd like to close my checking account.

B: 你有任何未兌現的支票嗎？

B: Do you have any outstanding checks?

A: 我想大約有兩三張尚未兌現的支票。

A: I think there might be two or three that have not been cashed yet.

B: 好，我們現在結束帳戶，但是我建議你還不要提款。

B: All right. We'll close it now, but I suggest you do not withdraw your money yet.

A: 為什麼？

A: Why?

B: 讓已經開出去的支票結清。

B: To clear the checks that have already been written.

A: 如果帳戶裡的錢不夠支付會怎樣？

A: What will happen if there isn't enough money in the account?

B: 會跳票。

B: The checks would bounce.

A: 我知道了,好,那我要等多久?

A: I see. OK, then how long should I wait?

B: 我們銀行建議兩週。

B: Our bank suggests two weeks.

A: 之後就可以提款嗎?

A: After that can I get my money?

B: 是的,我們可以寄張支票給你或你自己來領。

B: Sure. We can send it as a check, or you can come get it.

A: 我也會收到帳戶結清的通知嗎?

A: Will I receive notice of closure in the mail, too?

B: 是的,還有最後被處理的幾張支票。

B: Yes, you will, along with the last checks that were processed.

A: 我知道了,謝謝。

A: I understand. Thanks.

🖊 Word Bank 字庫

outstanding [aʊtˋstændɪŋ] adj. 尚未清償的
notice of closure n. 結束通知

4.13b 結束信用卡 Canceling a Credit Card

 Dialog 對話

A: 我想取消我的信用卡。

A: I want to cancel my credit card.

B: 好,給我卡號。

B: OK. Just give me the credit card number.

A: 我需要簽什麼嗎?

A: Do I need to sign anything?

B: 不必,但是記住你仍必須支付尚未付清的信用卡款。

B: No, but remember that you still must pay outstanding charges on it.

A: 我知道,你可以今天取消信用卡嗎?

A: I understand. Can you cancel it today?

B: 可以。

B: Yes.

A: 好的,謝謝。

A: All right. Thanks.

 Notes 小叮嚀

　　離開美國時,不再需要美國的信用卡,申請停卡後最後一期帳單如何處理,寄到哪裡,務必妥善處理確保個人信用。

4.13c 定存單解約 Canceling [Selling] a CD

Dialog 1 (對話1)

A: 我想賣一張定存單。

A: I'd like to sell one of my CDs.

B: 好,到期了嗎?

B: OK, is it mature?

A: 我想是的。

A: Yes, I think so.

B: 我看看,是的,本金加上利息,總共是 525.78 元。

B: Let me check. Yes, the original amount plus the interest. It comes to \$525.78.

A: 好。

A: OK.

B: 請在這裡簽名。

B: Please sign here.

Dialog 2 (對話2)

A: 我需要賣一張定存單,但是還未到期。

A: I need to sell a CD, but it's not mature yet.

B: 喔,那恐怕有罰金。

B: Oh, there's a penalty I'm afraid.

A: 我知道，罰金是多少？

A: I know, but what's the penalty?

B: 一個月的利息。

B: One month of interest.

 Useful Phrases 實用語句

1. 我想結清我的帳戶。

   I'd like to close my account.

2. 我想取消我的信用卡。

   I want to cancel my credit card.

3. 我想知道支票帳戶內有多少錢。

   I want to know how much money is in my checking account.

4. 如果錢被領走，支票會跳票。

   The checks will bounce if the money is withdrawn.

5. 你有任何未兌現的支票嗎？

   Do you have any outstanding checks?

6. 我要退掉保險箱。

   I need to close my safe deposit box.

 Notes 小叮嚀

　　定存解約時罰金的多寡常以購買的期限來規定，如3個月期定存解約罰金為1個月利息，24個月定存為3個月利息等。如果太早提前解約，產生的利息可能還不夠支付罰金的話，解約就會扣到本金了。

4.14 醫療及意外保險
Health and Accident Insurance

 Dialog 對話

A: 我想了解我和我太太的醫療及意外保險。

A: I would like to know about health and accident insurance for my wife, and I.

B: 好的,請過來這裡坐。

B: All right. Please come over here and sit down.

A: 謝謝。

A: Thank you.

B: 你們想要多少保障?

B: What kind of coverage are you interested in?

A: 我不知道,你可以解釋有何選擇嗎?

A: I don't know. Can you explain the possibilities?

B: 當然,我先拿些資料給你看。

B: Of course, let me start by showing you some information.

A: 我聽說醫療及意外保險很貴。

A: I've heard health and accident insurance is expensive.

B: 依照您的需求,我們有不同的保險計畫。

A: We have different plans to fit your needs.

住所

郵電通訊

日常活動

銀行與保險

交通

食品與飲食

購物

社交活動

教育

休閒活動

醫療

緊急情況

 Useful Phrases 實用語句

1. 我要醫療保險的報價。

   I want a quote on health insurance.

2. 你們的保單保什麼？

   What does your policy cover?

3. 請為我解釋保單。

   Please explain the policy to me.

4. 我要申請理賠。

   I have to file a claim.

5. 我要如何申請理賠？

   How do I file a claim?

6. 這份保單每年要多少錢？

   How much a year does the policy cost?

7. 你要何時開始投保？

   When would you like the insurance to start?

8. 我最少要買多少保障？

   What is the least coverage I must buy?

9. 我要退保。

   I want to cancel my policy.

10. 我要加保。

    I want to increase my coverage.

11. 我要多些醫療保障。

    I want more health insurance coverage.

12. 我要買人壽險。

    I'm interested in buying life insurance.

13. 你要怎麼繳保費？

    How would you like to pay for the premium?

14. 我何時會收到保單？

    When will I receive my insurance policy?

Language Power　字句補給站

◆ 保險 Insurance

policy	保單
deductible	自付額
claim	索賠
terms	條件
effect	生效
limits	限制
coverage	保障
compensation, reimbursement	賠償
benefits	保險金津貼
policy holder	被保人
beneficiary	受益人
adjuster	核算人
appraisal	估價
premium	保險費
fault	過失
annuity	年費
clause	條款
community rating	社區排行
grace period	有效期限後的寬限時間
on the premises	在被保險的財產內
insurance agent	保險經紀人
insurance agency	保險公司
lifetime policy	終身保障
minimum coverage	最低保障
compulsory insurance	強制保險
full coverage	全險
life insurance	人壽險
accident insurance	意外險
health insurance	醫療險
non-smoker	不吸菸者
pre-existing conditions	保險前情況
travel insurance	旅遊險

住所

郵電通訊

日常活動

銀行與保險

交通

食品與飲食

購物

社交活動

教育

休閒活動

醫療

緊急情況

cancer insurance	癌症險
auto insurance	車險
body repair shop	修車廠
burglary	破門竊盜
robbery	搶劫
theft	偷竊
flood	水災
fire	火災
storm	暴風雨
earthquake	地震
tornado (alley)	龍捲風 (肆虐帶)
hurricane (alley)	颶風 (肆虐帶)
tsunami	海嘯
tidal wave/storm surge	巨浪

All right. Please come over here and sit down.

I want a quote on health insurance.

Tips 小祕訣

　　因為醫療保險所費不貲，多數人希望獲得一份有醫療保障的工作省去這筆支出。醫療險需要繳交健康檢查報告，不吸菸的人保費比吸菸者低 (其他類別保險也多將此因素算入)，戒菸至少就可省下一些保費。

　　美國沒有全國性的健康保險制度，除了受雇單位所提供的醫療保險以外，一般人如果要有所保障，必須購買醫療及意外保險。聯邦政府提供給弱勢居民醫療補助 (Medicare)，資格為殘障或健康欠佳者或單親之原住民。退休老人若無法負擔醫療費用，可以申請醫療補助 (Medicaid)。民眾對於就業單位所提供的保險，應確認保險單是否提供應有的保障；儘管州及聯邦政府有基本條文規定，但小公司通常不能提供足夠的 (或根本沒有) 保障，兼差工作更是幾乎毫無保障，即使大型公司保障也經常是不足的。如果因公受傷，大多數的州提供就業傷害補償，以就業收入為基準，提供相當的金額作為補償，但補償有時限，通常幾個月就停止了。

　　如果沒有保險卻出了意外，醫院的急診室通常會收病患，但是費用照算，當然也有病患被醫院拒收的案件，但通常這些都不是緊急情況，如果生病必須持續治療卻無保險，在美就醫的帳單會輕易將人拖垮。

　　許多人難以理解為何美國國力強大，卻遲遲沒有全民健保？比較臺灣與美國差異即不難理解原因，臺灣民眾視全民健保為基本人權，政府以「扶弱濟貧」的概念提供單一保險，由「健保署」負責全民健保，高所得者負擔較高保費，可視為另類行善。

　　但美國人的觀念並非如此，美國為「資本主義」(capitalism) 及「個人主義」(individualism) 國家，強調選擇的自由 (freedom of choice)，個人必須為自己完全負責，包括健康及醫療。追求健康與追求財富一樣，必須努力獲取，選擇不健康生活方式者是咎由自取，後果自負，與他人無關。在此觀念下，美國政府「無法」令各州政府如臺灣及其他已開發國家一樣實施全民健保。反對者稱其違憲，人民有權拒保或選擇其他保險，難怪美國成為已開發國家中唯一未能提供全民醫療保險 (universal health care) 的國家。

　　為改善現況，美國歐巴馬總統競選最重要的政見之一Obamacare，經過重重困難後，終於在近期啟動，邁入將大多數人納保的階段。其政策立意良善，但對於不同經濟階級人民的受惠效果仍有待觀察。

住所
郵電通訊
日常活動
銀行與保險
交通
食品與飲食
購物
社交活動
教育
休閒活動
醫療
緊急情況

4.15 汽車險
Car Insurance

Dialog 1 （對話1）

A: 哈囉，我要了解汽車險。

A: Hello. I need to find out about auto insurance.

B: 好，我們從填表開始，你的大名是？

B: OK. Let's start by filling out this form. What's your name?

A: 我是山姆蘇。

A: I'm Sam Su.

B: 你開的車是幾年份的？

B: What year of car do you drive?

A: 我有一臺 2007 年的克萊斯勒城城鄉箱型車。

A: I have a 2007, Chrysler Town and Country van.

B: 你想要哪種保險？

B: What kind of coverage do you want?

A: 我不確定。

A: I'm not sure.

B: 我來為你解說不同的保單選擇。

B: Let me explain various policy options to you.

住所

郵電通訊

日常活動

銀行與保險

交通

食品與飲食

購物

社交活動

教育

休閒活動

醫療

緊急情況

Dialog 2 對話2

A: 如果你擁有這輛車的話，你可以買最低保障。

A: You can buy minimal coverage if you own the car.

B: 不是，我向銀行貸款買的。

B: I don't. I borrowed money from the bank to buy it.

A: 那銀行會要求你買全險。

A: Then the bank will require you to buy full coverage.

B: 等還清了，我可以少保一些嗎？

B: After the car is paid off can I get less insurance?

A: 當然可以。你可以依照你要的保障少買保險。

A: Yes, of course. You can buy less coverage depending on what you want to protect.

B: 你可以多解釋一點嗎？

B: Can you explain a little more?

A: 好的。比方說你可以只買州規定的保障，那是最低保障，之後你可以買財物及傷害保險保護到你要的程度。

A: Sure. For example you can buy coverage that covers only what the state requires. That is minimal coverage. After that you can buy insurance that protects against property and injury loss to whatever level you want.

B: 我買越多，費用就越貴，對嗎？

B: The more I buy, the more it costs, right?

A: 對。

A: Right.

Useful Phrases 實用語句

● 顧客 Customer

1. 我想買汽車險。

   I want to buy some car insurance.

2. 全險多少錢？

   What does full coverage car insurance cost?

3. 有自付額嗎？

   Is there a deductible?

4. 保險何時生效？

   When will the policy be activated?

5. 我付款有何選擇？

   What are my payment options?

6. 我要最低保障。

   I want minimal coverage.

7. 這是我的車籍登記。

   Here is my car's registration.

8. 我的保單何時到？

   When will my policy arrive?

● 保險經紀人 Agent

1. 我來解釋你的選擇。

   Let me explain your options.

2. 保單今天開始生效。

   The policy begins today.

3. 你可以每三個月付一次。

   You can pay every three months.

4. 你可以每六個月付一次。

   You can pay once every six months.

5. 我需要看你的車籍登記。

   I need to see you car's registration.

6. 你的保單這週會寄給你。

   The policy will be mailed to you this week.

7. 這張是臨時保險卡。

   Here's a temporary policy card.

8. 一直把保險卡放你車裡。

   Always keep the policy card in your car.

Language Power 字句補給站

◆ 汽車險 Auto Insurance

year	年份
make	車廠
model, body style	車型
primary use (commuting to work [school], pleasure, business, commercial)	主要用途 (通勤工作 [上學]，休閒，商業)
ownership (paid for, financed, leased)	所有權 (已付清，貸款，租賃)
liability	法律責任
bodily injury	受傷
collision	碰撞
bodily injury liability	身體傷害法律責任
property liability coverage	財損法律責任
VIN (vehicle identification number)	車輛製造號碼
actual cash value	實際現金價值
collision deductible waiver	碰撞免自付額
accidental death coverage	意外身故保障

住所
郵電通訊
日常活動
銀行與保險
交通
食品與飲食
購物
社交活動
教育
休閒活動
醫療
緊急情況

vandalism	惡意毀壞
declarations	保險聲明書
effective date	生效日
expiration date	到期日
exclusions	例外
indemnity	賠償金
income loss	所得損失
judgment	判決
limits	最高額度
medical benefits	醫療福利
medical payment coverage	醫療支出保障
towing	拖吊
theft	偷竊
burglary, robbery	強盜
claim form	理賠申請書
claims adjuster	理賠核算人

I'm afraid I've had a car accident. I need to file a claim.

Is the car here?

Tips 小祕訣

　　車險為強制險，車主必須至少買最低保障，每州的最低保障不盡相同，保險公司會告訴你需要的最低保障並報價給你，汽車險有許多選擇且保障經常改變。每州對保險經紀公司的規定也不同，最好能找三到四家報價，再選擇適合的保障。通常保單每半年就必須更新，有信譽的保險公司不至於欺騙客戶，但是有問題要釐清，且要印證你認為的保單條款內容就是確實的內容，才能保障自己的權益。

　　每位車主的保費依照駕駛紀錄及車型而定，四門房車的保費遠比拉風跑車低，如果車上裝有防盜追蹤系統(anti-theft recovery system) 保費也會較低。其他需提供資料，如駕照號碼、每年駕駛英里數及個人資料如年齡、性別等。25歲以上的駕駛比25歲以下者的保費低，女性比男性低，已婚者比未婚者低，所以駕駛紀錄良好的25歲以上已婚女性比年輕男性保費低廉許多。

　　如果是貸款買車，每個月必須支付一定金額償還車款，還完貸款前，車子還算是銀行的，必須照貸款銀行規定買全險才行，保費就比最低保障貴上許多。依照法律規定，車主必須將車險保單放置車內；在美國，車主多不願意將車子借給別人開，萬一出了事，保險公司不負責。

4.16 理賠
Filing a Claim

Dialog 對話

A: 我出車禍，我要申請理賠。

A: I'm afraid I've had a car accident. I need to file a claim.

B: 車子在這裡嗎？

B: Is the car here?

住所
郵電通訊
日常活動
銀行與保險
交通
食品與飲食
購物
社交活動
教育
休閒活動
醫療
緊急情況

A: 沒有，損壞太嚴重了，被拖到修車廠了。

A: No. It's too badly damaged. It was towed to a body repair shop.

B: 好，我們要派一個理賠核算人去看看。

B: OK. We'll have to send a claims adjuster out to look at it.

A: 我了解，這是修車廠地址。

A: I see. Here is the address of the shop it is at.

B: 謝謝，你有警察的車禍報告嗎？

B: Thank you. Do you have an accident report from the police?

A: 有，在這裡。

A: Yes, I do. Here it is.

B: 有任何人受傷嗎？

B: Was anyone injured in the accident?

A: 有，另一部車裡的人。

A: Yes. A person in the other car was.

B: 你有另一部車子的保險公司名稱嗎？

B: Do you have the name of the other party's insurance company?

A: 沒有。

A: No, I don't.

B: 我們要看是否有在車禍報告裡或打電話跟警局要。

B: We'll see if it's on the accident report, or call the police for it.

如果你駕駛的車子在美國發生重大車禍(major car accident)，先打緊急電話911，有時傷勢在當時不見得明顯，待在車內等待警車及救護車到達，你必須跟其他駕駛和警方交換保險資料，記得不要承認任何錯誤，警方會調查事故，作筆錄，釐清責任歸屬。警方會詢問你及其他駕駛和車禍現場目擊證人(witnesses)，如果有任何違法 (infraction) 情形，警方會在事故現場發出法院傳票 (citation)。

如果是輕微事故 (minor car accident)，你必須將車子移到路邊並與其他駕駛交換保險資料，不管是大小車禍都必須要通知你的保險公司。更多資訊請看第12章緊急情況。

4.17 房地產保險
Homeowners Insurance

Dialog 對話

A: 午安，我可以為你服務嗎？

A: Good afternoon. May I help you?

B: 可以，我想了解屋主保險。

B: Yes. I would like to find out about homeowners insurance.

A: 好，你是屋主嗎？

A: OK. Are you a homeowner?

B: 我即將買房子，且不喜歡銀行的保險費率。

B: I'm going to buy a house very soon, and don't like the banks insurance rate.

住所

郵電通訊

日常活動

銀行與保險

交通

食品與飲食

購物

社交活動

教育

休閒活動

醫療

緊急情況

A: 我知道了，你的房地產值多少錢？

A: I see. How much is your property worth?

B: 估價約 400,000 元。

B: It was assessed at $400,000.

A: 好，我們現在看看有一些要保項目，像暴風雨、火災及竊盜保險。

A: Fine. Let's look at some options now, like storm, fire, and theft insurance.

B: 好，我也要保水災險。

B: OK. I'm also interested in flood insurance.

A: 那包含在暴風雨保單項目內。

A: That will be part of the storm insurance section of the policy.

 Useful Phrases 實用語句

1. 我想保房屋險。

   I need to insure my house.

2. 我要怎麼保家當險？

   How do I insure my furnishings?

3. 我需要損失估價。

   I need an estimate on the damage.

4. 我想要保險經紀人來給我估價。

   I'd like to have an agent come out and give me an estimate.

5. 保單保障什麼？

   What is covered by this policy?

6. 我可以保水災險嗎？

   Can I get flood insurance?

7. 我的房屋暴風雨損失有保障嗎？

   Is my house covered for storm damage?

8. 我想加保。

   I want to add more coverage.

9. 我要申請理賠。

   I need to file a claim.

10. 我的房子要先被檢查嗎？

   Will my house need to be inspected first?

Notes 小叮嚀

　　房屋保險如同任何保險，必須貨比三家並弄清保障內容，把保單放在安全之處，若有需要可以立即找到。如果是貸款買屋，你必須要購買屋主險，這是必要的支出，可以和房貸一起支付，也可以分開購買。

住所

郵電通訊

日常活動

銀行與保險

交通

食品與飲食

購物

社交活動

教育

休閒活動

醫療

緊急情況

Unit 5 Transportation

交通

美國面積廣大，除了少數大都市 (如紐約) 有便捷的大眾運輸工具外，私人車輛是主要的交通工具。維修車輛費用是以小時計算，一小時 $50 的費用不算少見，找原廠或口碑好的維修廠貨比三家，先估價再決定是否接受維修。

買車對任何人都是個考驗，購買二手車更是如此。各州消費者保護法不同，對於售車業者剝削消費者不見得能予以完全保護。最好是找一位信得過的汽車技師一起去選購二手車，通常技師會收費 $30-$50。除非自己很懂車，否則不冒險購買狀況已經很差的車輛是保護自己的最好方法。

車輛的保險是強制的，各家保險費及保險項目各有不同，選擇適合自己的保險並將保險單隨時放在車內備查。

住所
郵電通訊
日常活動
銀行與保險
交通
食品與飲食
購物
社交活動
教育
休閒活動
醫療
緊急情況

5.1 考駕照
Getting a Driver's License

Dialog 1 （對話1）

A: 我抽到20號。

A: I pulled number 20.

B: 20號是下一個。

B: Number 20 is next.

A: 嗨，我要考駕照。

A: Hi. I want to get a driver's license.

B: 好，你要先填寫這張表格，然後考筆試。

B: OK. You'll need to fill out this form first. Then, take the written test.

A: 我要去哪裡考試？

A: Where do I take the test?

B: 那邊，考試用電腦考。

B: Over there. It's done on a computer.

(稍後 A little later)

A: 這是填好的表格，我可以現在考筆試嗎？

A: Here is the filled out form. Can I take the written test now?

B: 可以，請跟我來。

B: Yes. Follow me, please.

Dialog 2　對話2

A: 我已考完筆試。

A: I've finished the written test.

B: 好，我看一下。

B: Alright. I'll check it.

(稍後 A little later)

B: 恭喜！你通過了。

B: Congratulations! You passed.

A: 太好了！我現在可以考路考嗎？

A: Great! Can I take the driving test now?

B: 很快，你要等其中一位考官有空的時候。

B: Soon. You'll have to wait until one of the testers is available.

A: 你想要等多久呢？

A: How long do you think that will be?

B: 不會太久，我猜10分鐘吧。

B: Not too long. I'd say ten minutes.

A: 我知道了，我坐那裡等。

A: I see. I'll sit over there and wait.

B: 別擔心。考官好的時候，我會告訴你。

B: Don't worry. I'll tell you when the tester is ready.

住所

郵電通訊

日常活動

銀行與保險

交通

食品與飲食

購物

社交活動

教育

休閒活動

醫療

緊急情況

A: 謝謝。 ➤ **A:** Thanks.

Useful Phrases 實用語句

1. 我要如何申請駕照？

   How do I apply for a driver's license?

2. 請取一個號碼。

   Please take a number.

3. 請先填這張表格。

   Fill out this form first.

4. 機動車輛部門在哪裡？

   Where is the DMV?

5. 我要考駕照。

   I want to take a driving test.

6. 我需要一份駕駛手冊。

   I need a copy of the driver's manual.

7. 你們有中文的駕駛手冊嗎？

   Do you have a Chinese driver's manual?

8. 你們這裡有說中文的人嗎？我需要幫忙。

   Do you have Chinese speaking people here? I need some help.

9. 你需要測視力。

   You need to take an eye test.

10. 我何時可以考試？

    What time can I take the test?

11. 你要先考筆試。

    You must take the written test first.

12. 我要考中文版的駕照考試。

    I'd like to take a driving test in Chinese.

13. 考場在哪裡？

    Where is the testing room?

14. 你通過考試了。

You passed the test.

15. 我們要幫你拍照。

We need to take your picture.

16. 你要成為器官捐贈者嗎？

Do you want to be an organ donor?

17. 這是你的駕照。

Here's your license.

18. 我要考機車駕照。

I want to take the motorcycle test.

住所

郵電通訊

日常活動

銀行與保險

交通

食品與飲食

購物

社交活動

教育

休閒活動

醫療

緊急情況

Tips 小祕訣

　　到美國短期居住，可以使用國際駕照，但務必要隨身攜帶臺灣駕照備查，國際駕照合法使用期限，各州規定不同，30 天到一年都有，有的以母國駕照期限為準。在美國生活，多數地方出門就要用車，所以拿到駕照是一件很重要的事。如果在美國不開車又需要身分證件，可以到 DMV 申請非駕照身分證 (non-driver ID)，或稱為州身分證 (state ID)。為免大排長龍，DMV 接受上網或電話預約，但當天除外。

　　申請駕照時，除了填寫所需的資料外，表格會有是否願意器官捐贈的問題，在移民較多的州內，有不同族裔的服務人員為移民服務，也有多種移民語言的駕駛手冊 (driver's handbook)及考題可供選擇或可上網取得，DMV 也提供 app 供民眾下載，幫助民眾熟悉交通規則及模擬試題，準備好再考試，因為萬一答錯幾題就得過幾天再繳費重考。考筆試 (written test) 時間不會很長，有的地區筆試已電腦化，有些仍是紙筆測驗，筆試通過後，有時可以直接繳費給考路考 (road test)，但有些地方必須預約考試。筆試通過後，DMV 會發給學習駕駛許可 (learner permit)，可以在有執照的旁人陪伴下開車。

　　對開車沒信心的人可以找教練上幾個鐘點熟悉路況，再準備考試，路考時必須自己提供可以正常運作的車輛及該車行照 (car registration)，可以選擇用自排或手排車考試；要練習路邊停車，你只有兩次機會把車停好，如果路考失敗，多數州必須要等一星期才能再考，也必須再繳費。考照變換車道時，記得除了打方向燈外，要回頭 (一定要過肩) 查看後方車輛 (已習慣在臺灣開車的人務必注意)，確定盲點處沒有車輛，才可以變換車道。路試通過後，接下來是 DMV 拍照，幾分鐘後就可以拿到駕照了。

Language Power 字句補給站

◆ 駕照 Driver's License

driver's test	考駕照
automatic	自排的
manual's, stick shift	手排的
DMV (Department of Motor Vehicles)	機動車輛部門 (如臺灣的監理處)
defensive driving	防禦性 [小心] 駕駛
parallel park	路邊停車
front [back] in parking	車頭朝內停車 [倒車入庫]
driver's manual	駕駛手冊
organ donor	器官捐贈者
restrictions (on license)	(駕照) 限制

5.2 買車
Buying a Car

Dialog 1 對話1

A: 嗨,我可以為你服務嗎?

A: Hi, may I help you?

B: 我想買一輛新車,所以先看看。

B: I'm interested in buying a new car, so we're looking around.

A: 好,你知道你要哪種車款嗎?

A: Great. Do you know what kind of car you want?

B: 我想看看不同款的車。

B: We want to look at different ones.

住所
郵電通訊
日常活動
銀行與保險
交通
食品與飲食
購物
社交活動
教育
休閒活動
醫療
緊急情況

A: 我帶你到車場看看。

A: Let me show you around the lot.

B: 這部如何？

B: How about this one?

A: 這是新的本田雅歌。

A: This is a new Honda Accord.

B: 多少錢？

B: What is the price?

A: 大約 15,000 元，看你要選什麼配備。

A: It costs around \$15,000 depending on what options you want.

B: 這臺車有 CD 音響嗎？

B: Does it come with a CD player?

A: 有，還有兩個安全氣囊。

A: Yes. It is also equipped with dual air bags.

Notes 小叮嚀

　　不管是買新車 (brand new car) 或是二手車 (used car)，買車時盡量問問題，別急著完成交易，如果售車商服務不夠好，就到下一家去，沒有必要接受不夠優質的服務或不能充分合作的車商。

Dialog 2 對話2

A: 我想試開這部車。
A: I'd like to take this car for a test drive.

B: 好，沒問題，我只需要看一下一張有效的駕照。
B: Sure. No problem. I just need to see a valid driver's license.

A: 好，這是我的駕照。
A: OK. Here's mine.

B: 好的，我們去兜風一下吧！
B: Great. Let's go for a ride.

Useful Phrases 實用語句

1. 我想買一輛新車。

   I'm interested in buying a new car.

2. 我們去試車。

   Let's go for a test drive.

3. 你們有什麼付款方案？

   What type of financing do you have?

4. 我想看你們的二手車。

   I'd like to look at your used cars.

5. 這車跑了多少英里了？

   How many miles does it have?

6. 這車多少錢？

   How much is it?

7. 這車有什麼配備可以選擇？

   What optional equipment does it have?

住所

郵電通訊

日常活動

銀行與保險

交通

食品與飲食

購物

社交活動

教育

休閒活動

醫療

緊急情況

180

8. 這車是什麼年份？

   What year is it?

9. 你們有維修紀錄嗎？

   Do you have the maintenance records?

10. 告訴我保固的事。

    Tell me about the guarantee.

11. 我想找個技師來看車。

    I'd like to have a mechanic look at it.

Notes 小叮嚀

有時售車員會與你一起試車，將車開出，要確實完全的試駕，15-20分鐘的試車並不少見，試車時也必須包含高速試車。如果購買新車，保固時間通常為3年或36,000英里，視哪一個先到期；二手車保固期間就相對短了許多，頂多1年，如果是向私人買車，就完全沒有保固的保障。每家車廠之保固年限或里程數與售價相關，加買保固是另外的選項。

Language Power 字句補給站

買 車 Buying a Car

- auto dealer 汽車商
- car dealership 汽車代理商
- used car 二手車
- makes and models 車廠及車型
- high [low] mileage 高[低]哩程
- warranty 保固
- maintenance 維修
- body repair shop 車殼修理店
- oil 機油
- insurance 保險
- tune up 調引擎
- pickup truck 載貨卡車
- down payment 頭期款

- car lot (汽車商)停車場
- sales rep. 售車代表
- test drive 試車
- guarantee 保證
- mechanic 技師
- repair shop 汽車修理店
- disc brakes 碟煞
- gas 汽油
- lube job 換機油
- alignment 校正
- deposit 訂金
- auto loan 汽車貸款

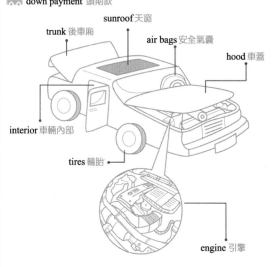

sunroof 天窗

trunk 後車廂

air bags 安全氣囊

hood 車蓋

interior 車輛內部

tires 輪胎

engine 引擎

住所
郵電通訊
日常活動
銀行與保險
交通
食品與飲食
購物
社交活動
教育
休閒活動
醫療
緊急情況

5.3 汽車維修
Auto Maintenance

5.3a 例行保養 Regular Maintenance

Dialog 1 對話1

A: 哈囉,我車開過來做例行保養。

A: Hello. I brought my car in for scheduled maintenance.

B: 好,我找一個服務人員來。

B: Good. Let me call a service rep.

(兩分鐘後 Two minutes later)

B: 好,把你的車開到後面服務區。

B: OK, drive your car around to the service bay area behind the building.

A: 謝謝,我要找誰?

A: Thanks. Who should I talk to?

B: 傑瑞,別擔心,他會找你,他知道你開什麼車。

B: Jerry. Don't worry. He'll be looking for you. He knows what you are driving.

Dialog 2 對話2

A: 嗨,你是傑瑞嗎?

A: Hi, are you Jerry?

B: 是的,歡迎你到服務區來。

B: Yes. Welcome to our service bay.

A: 謝謝,我要把車留在這裡嗎?

A: Thanks. Should I leave the car here?

B: 是的,沒關係,我會處理其他所有的事。

B: Yes, this is fine. I'll take care of everything else.

A: 好的,何時車子會好?

A: Good. What time will the car be ready to go again?

B: 應該只要兩小時可以完成所有的事。

B: It should only take us a couple of hours to do everything.

A: 好,我會在兩小時後回來。

A: OK, I'll be back in a couple of hours.

Word Bank 字庫

service bay area n. (修車) 服務區

Tips 小祕訣

在固定的代理商做新車例行檢查是免費的。

住所
郵電通訊
日常活動
銀行與保險
交通
食品與飲食
購物
社交活動
教育
休閒活動
醫療
緊急情況

5.3b 汽車修理 Car Repair

 Dialog 對話

A: 嗨,我的車好像有問題。

A: Hi. My car seems to have a problem.

B: 怎麼了?

B: What's wrong?

A: 我開上高速公路時,引擎不順。

A: When I drive it on the freeway, the engine does not run smoothly.

B: 你在有那問題之前開多快?

B: How fast do you have to be going before you have the problem?

A: 大約時速60哩。

A: I think about 60 miles per hour [mph].

B: 我知道了,我們要把車子放到診斷機上面。

B: I see. We'll have to put it on the diagnostic machine.

A: 那要多久?

A: How long will that take?

B: 很難說,我們現在很忙,可能要幾個小時。

B: It's hard to say. We're pretty busy right now. It might be several hours.

A: 你們今天下午有車子可以借我嗎?

A: Do you have a car I can borrow for this afternoon?

| B: 當然，我去開一臺給你。 | B: Sure, of course. I'll get one for you. |

| A: 太好了，謝謝。 | A: Great. Thanks. |

 Word Bank 字庫

diagnostic machine n. 診斷機

 Useful Phrases 實用語句

1. 我需要換機油。

   I need the oil changed.

2. 我車開來做例行保養。

   I brought it in for scheduled maintenance.

3. 引擎不順。

   The engine is not running right.

4. 車後部有怪聲。

   There is a strange noise in the rear.

5. 雨刷要換新。

   The windshield wipers need to be replaced.

6. 我要買新輪胎。

   I want to buy new tires.

7. 請檢查煞車。

   Please check the brakes.

8. 我何時要把車開來修車廠？

   When should I bring it in to the shop?

9. 何時會修好？

   What time will it be finished?

10. 我想跟技師說話。

    I'd like to talk to the mechanic.

住所

郵電通訊

日常活動

銀行與保險

交通

食品與飲食

購物

社交活動

教育

休閒活動

醫療

緊急情況

11. 我要停在哪裡？

Where should I park it?

12. 你們怎麼計費？

What are your rates?

13. 修理要多少錢？

What will it cost to fix?

14. 更換零件會比較便宜嗎？

Is it cheaper to replace that part?

15. 維修有什麼選擇呢？

What are my options for repair?

Notes 小叮嚀

　　如果你一定要把新車留廠修理，代理商通常會提供一臺代步車 (loaner) 供你使用，如果沒有代步車，許多車廠有交通車服務。如果不需等待太久，修車廠有等待室，可以看電視、上網或讀書報打發時間。

5.4 租車
Renting a Car

5.4a 在租車處 At a Car Rental Company

Dialog 1 對話1

A: 嗨，我們要租車，你們現在有什麼車呢？

A: Hi. We need to rent a car. Do you have anything available now?

B: 你有預訂嗎？

B: Did you reserve one?

A: 沒有，我們今天才決定租一臺車。

A: No. We decided today to try to get one.

B: 好，我們確實還有些車，都是大型房車。

B: OK. We do have some still available. They are all full size sedans.

A: 沒有小一點的嗎？

A: Nothing smaller?

B: 抱歉，所有小車都租出去或被訂走了。

B: Sorry. All the smaller cars are either out or reserved.

A: 租其中一臺房車一星期要多少錢？

A: What's the cost for renting one of the sedans for a week?

B: 我們有一星期收費175元。

B: We have a weekly rate of $175.

Dialog 2　對話2

A: 我要一星期計價的方案。

A: I'll take the weekly rate offer.

B: 好，我需要一張有效的駕照及一張信用卡。

B: Fine. I'll need to see a valid driver's license, and I'll need a credit card, too.

A: 在這裡。

A: Here you go.

住所

郵電通訊

日常活動

銀行與保險

交通

食品與飲食

購物

社交活動

教育

休閒活動

醫療

緊急情況

B: 好，請填這張表，你填表的時候我來處理車子。

B: Great. Please fill out this form. While you do that, I'll process the car for you.

A: 會很久嗎？

A: Will it take long?

B: 一點都不會，幾分鐘就好。

B: No, not at all. It'll be ready in just a few minutes.

Dialog 3 對話3

A: 好了，已經完成了。

A: OK. You are all set to go.

B: 我何時要還車？

B: What time do I have to have the car back?

A: 3月6日星期六中午前。

A: Have it here on Saturday, March 6th, by noon.

B: 如果我晚了會怎樣？

B: What happens if I am late?

A: 我們有兩小時寬限期，之後我們會收一天的費用。

A: We have a two-hour grace period, after that we'll charge you for another day.

B: 可以在另一地點還車嗎？

B: Is it possible to drop it off at another location?

A: 可以，但是你必須至少在兩天前先打電話告訴我們，讓我們知道。

A: Yes, but you'll have to phone us at least two days ahead to let us know.

 Useful Phrases 實用語句

1. 我要租一臺車。

   I want to reserve a car.

2. 我 11 月 5 日要用。

   I need it on the 5th of November.

3. 我要租一星期。

   I want to rent it for a week.

4. 我要租一天。

   I need it for a day.

5. 租金多少錢？

   What is the rate?

6. 你們有任何優惠嗎？

   Do you have any specials?

7. 這是我的信用卡。

   Here is my credit card.

8. 我在哪裡簽名？

   Where do I sign?

9. 我想升級。

   I want to upgrade.

10. 你們有小 [大] 一點的車嗎？

   Do you have any smaller [bigger] cars?

11. 我不需要保險。

   I don't want the insurance.

12. 額外保險方案多少錢？

   How much is the extra insurance coverage?

住所 郵電通訊 日常活動 銀行與保險 交通 食品與飲食 購物 社交活動 教育 休閒活動 醫療 緊急情況

Language Power 字句補給站

租 車 Car Rental

住所
郵電通訊
日常活動
銀行與保險
交通
食品與飲食
購物
社交活動
教育
休閒活動
醫療
緊急情況

- rental agreement[lease] 租約
- daily rate 每日租金
- weekend special 週末優惠
- weekly rate 每週租金
- long term rental 長期租賃
- upgrade 升級
- 4x4 (four wheel drive) 四輪傳動車
- pickup [dropoff] point 取[還]車地點
- liability insurance 第三責任險
- full coverage 全險
- additional coverage 額外保障
- unlimited mileage 不限哩程
- manual/five speed 手排
- automatic 自排
- chauffeur/driver 司機

sedan 轎車

compact 小型車

midsize 中型房車

full size 大型房車

luxury 豪華車

van 箱型車

limousine (limo)
加長型轎車

SUV (Sports Utility Vehicle)
休旅車

jeep 吉普車

hatchback
斜背式汽車

sports car 跑車

truck 貨車

convertible
敞篷車

RV
旅行車（內有床、廚房）

station wagon
旅行車

　　在美國租車需要信用卡，上網先查租車資料，貨比三家，先訂車，較能確定你可以租到你想要的車。大都市比小城鎮租車的選擇多、限制少、價格也較低，因此搭機到小城鎮 (通常費用高昂) 再租車未必划算。網路預訂時可能就要支付車子租金，到租車公司領車時再加保險費。如果租車時想省點保費，可以看看自己本身保險夠不夠或信用卡公司有什麼保障，許多信用卡公司確實提供刷卡租車保險，如果不足，可以在租車時加買保險。

　　取車時，為避免租到較差的車，可以要求先看車或換車，並考慮其他要件後再簽租車同意書。租車公司有不同的租車方案及規定，租車時要依自己的需要，詳問租車代表，如車型、廠牌、價錢 (每日/周)、保險、汽油、哩程數、加第二人以上駕駛是否收費及其保險保障等基本須知。如無法使用自己的導航裝置，可詢問車內是否備有 GPS (為高級車配備)，或需另付租費(每日約 \$12或每周 \$60，遺失的話須付 \$600)。高級車種尚有call out 按鈕，碰到任何問題，可直接按鈕與租車中心聯絡。如行車經常到收費路段 (如伊利諾州、印度安納州、俄亥俄州及東北部數州)，可詢問車內是否備有電子收費裝置 (I-Pass或 E-Z Pass) 及使用方法，直接於租車之信用卡內支付過路費，節省現金繳費時間。長途駕駛者不妨確定所租車輛是否有 audio out 之連接孔或 USB 插槽，可連接 I-pod、MP3、手機、USB 等播放自己喜歡的音樂。

　　其他問題如萬一必須更改還車時間或地點、逾時還車及還車時汽油若不足時如何計價或罰金，通常在租約中訂定甲地租車乙地還車，需額外支付 \$150 以上車輛運輸費(即租車公司將車運回甲地的成本)，租約未定而臨時變動還車地點，還車時必須支付罰金 \$600，不可不慎。所有問題要在簽名前問清楚，再訂租車合約。

　　還車時間要注意不要遲到，否則可能會被加收一天租金。美國不僅有不同時區 (共 6 個時區，某些州有兩個)，絕大多數州 (除夏威夷州及亞利桑那州外) 並實行日光節約時間 (daylight saving time, DST)，在三月第二個週日往前撥快 1 小時 (半夜兩點變三點)，十一月第一個週日往撥後慢一小時 (半夜兩點變一點)。相鄰的兩個城市如果分屬不同時區，即使只有數哩之遙，也可能因未注意時間差異而耽誤了還車或班機時間。

　　取車時與租車人員確認車子狀態正常、汽油滿格，還車時也要加滿汽油，否則會被以較高油價扣錢。有的租車公司以稍低於市面油價推出的「跑光汽油案」，對大多數不精於計算及不想冒險跑光汽油的消費者而言並不划算。在不熟悉或不同的城市租還車時，務必向租車公司拿份地圖請他們標出還車地點確切位置及開車指示。越來越多的租車公司還車地點為整車中心，而非原來的租車地點，顧客必須還車後，另搭接駁車到機場，因此一定要先行了解還車地點，才不會耽誤搭機時間，有些租車公司已將還車地點內建到 GPS 協助顧客。另一點要注意的是有些機場租車公司雖然方便 (也因此可能索價較高)，但營業時間並非 24 小時，早晚班機到達，可能無法取車，這點在訂車時就要知道。

5.4b 租車保險 Rental Car Insurance

Dialog 對話

A: 先生，你的車要投保額外的保險嗎？

A: Sir, would you like to add additional insurance on the car?

B: 我不確定。

B: I'm not sure.

A: 州政府規定至少要保意外責任險。

A: The State requires that you have at least minimum liability.

B: 我要買這個，我要確定我有合法保障。

B: I'll buy it. I want to make sure I'm legally covered.

A: 只要每天多花 7 元。

A: It will only cost an additional $7 a day.

住所
郵電通訊
日常活動
銀行與保險
交通
食品與飲食
購物
社交活動
教育
休閒活動
醫療
緊急情況

B: 它保障什麼呢？ → **B:** What does it cover?

A: 碰撞及傷害。 → **A:** Collision and injury.

Word Bank 字庫

> insurance [ɪnˋʃʊrəns] n. 保險
> minimum [ˋmɪnəməm] n. 至少
> liability [ˏlaɪəˋbɪlətɪ] n. 責任
> collision [kəˋlɪdʒən] n. 碰撞
> injury [ˋɪndʒərɪ] n. 傷害

5.4c 還車 Dropping Off the Rental Car

Dialog 1 對話1

A: (租車公司人員) 嗨，你今天好嗎？ → **A:** (Car Rental Clerk) Hi, how're you doing today?

B: 好。 → **B:** Fine.

A: 你要還車嗎？ → **A:** Are you returning your car?

B: 是的。 → **B:** Yes.

A: 請讓我看你的租約。

A: Please let me see your rental agreement form.

B: 在這裡。

B: Here you go.

A: 好,我檢查一下

A: OK. Let me check it.

B: 好的。

B: Sure.

Dialog 2 （對話2）

A: 汽油是滿的嗎?

A: Is it full of gas?

B: 是的。我還要簽什麼嗎?

B: Yes, it is. Do I need to sign anything else?

A: 不必,但要確定取走你所有的物品。好,這是你的收據,和租約上一樣。

A: No, but make sure you took all your things out of the car. Alright. Here's your receipt, same amount as on your rental agreement.

B: 謝謝。

B: Thank you.

5.5 火車
Train

美國國鐵 Amtrak 是全國性鐵路系統，連接美國各大小城鎮 (要有火車誤點的心理準備)，火車路線各有其名，車內提供與機上類似的服務。乘客可以利用網路訂票，所有列車都禁菸。

 Dialog 1　對話1

A: 早安，我可以為你服務嗎？

A: Good morning. May I help you?

B: 可以，我想知道到波特蘭的票價是多少？

B: Yes. I want to know how much tickets to Portland cost?

A: 我看看，我的電腦顯示普通車廂是105元。

A: Let's see. My computer tells me they cost $105 for coach.

B: 是來回票嗎？

B: Is that round trip?

A: 不是，是單程。

A: No. That's one way.

B: 來回票多少錢？

B: What does round trip cost?

A: 145元。

A: Those cost $145.

住所

郵電通訊

日常活動

銀行與保險

交通

食品與飲食

購物

社交活動

教育

休閒活動

醫療

緊急情況

B: 私人包廂多少錢？

B: What is the cost for a private room?

A: 那列車沒有這種服務。

A: We don't offer that service on that run.

Word Bank 字庫

coach [kotʃ] n. 普通車廂
round trip n. 來回
run [rʌn] n. 班次

Language Power 字句補給站

◆ 火車 Train

ticket window	售票窗口
train station	車站
boarding platform	月臺
conductor	車掌
passenger	乘客
first class	頭等車廂
business class	商務車廂
coach class	普通車廂
lounge cars	休閒車廂
dining car	餐車
sleeper [sleeping] car	臥鋪
departure	離開
arrival	抵達
one-way ticket	單程車票
round-trip ticket	來回車票
reservation	預訂
destination	目的地

住所

郵電通訊

日常活動

銀行與保險

交通

食品與飲食

購物

社交活動

教育

休閒活動

醫療

緊急情況

 Dialog 2 （對話2）

A: 請問餐車在哪裡？

A: Excuse me. Where is the dining car?

B: 兩節車廂後面，只要通過車內兩道門。

B: It is two cars down. Just pass trough the doors of the next two cars.

A: 我們可以買到咖啡嗎？

A: Can we get coffee there?

B: 當然，你可以買到任何你要喝的，包括雞尾酒。

B: Sure. You can get anything you want to drink, even cocktails.

A: 現在有供餐嗎？

A: Are they serving meals now?

B: 有，這列車的餐車都是開放的。

B: Yes. On this run the dining car is open all the time.

Tips （小祕訣）

　　餐車的服務，依照列車路線而有所不同 (但短程的火車沒有餐飲服務)，網路上及車站內可以查到火車上供應的食物選擇，乘客也可以將自己的飲料及食物帶上車。在餐車內可以飲酒，如果有私人包廂，也可以在包廂內飲酒，但是普通車廂內是禁酒的。

Useful Phrases 實用語句

1. 我要兩張到夏普斯堡的票。

   I want to buy two tickets to Sharpsburg.

2. 本地的火車站在哪裡？

   Where is the local train station?

3. 售票口在哪裡？

   Where is the ticket window?

4. 兩張票，謝謝。

   Two tickets, please.

5. 我要一張臥鋪 (的票)。

   I want a sleeper car.

6. 我要普通車廂。

   I want coach.

7. 有餐車嗎？

   Is there a dining car?

8. 上車時間是何時？

   What time does the train board?

9. 何時會抵達？

   When will it arrive?

10. 今天火車準時嗎？

    Is the train on time today?

11. 有幾站？

    How many stops are there?

12. 火車在哪個月臺到站？

    Which platform does it arrive at?

13. 我們要坐哪裡？

    Where can we sit?

14. 坐任何你喜歡的位置。

    Sit anywhere you want.

15. 火車上禁菸。

    There is no smoking on the train.

住所 郵電通訊 日常活動 銀行與保險 交通 食品與飲食 購物 社交活動 教育 休閒活動 醫療 緊急情況

16. 所有乘客上車！(列車長呼叫所有人)

All aboard!

5.6 大眾運輸
Mass Transit Systems

美國一些大城市有地下鐵或輕軌電車 (走地上) 的大眾運輸工具，在治安較好的城市，算是安全且有效率，大眾運輸依照城市不同，各有不同名稱，在舊金山稱為 BART，在奧勒岡州的波特蘭市叫做 MAX，在芝加哥稱為 L。

大眾運輸票可以購買單程或者是有不同日期的票種或月票可以選擇，也可以在網路購買。票或卡都可以儲值，可使用儲值機在插入信用卡或現金後完成儲值，或者售票口人員也可以幫忙儲值，有些系統可以接受某時限內的退票。

Dialog (對話)

A: 嗨，我可以為你服務嗎？

A: Hi. May I help you?

B: 哈囉，我們要買一週券。

B: Hello. We want to buy one-week passes.

A: 好，每張一週券是25元。

A: OK. One-week passes cost \$25 each.

B: 像一般車票一樣使用嗎？

B: Do we use them just like regular tickets?

A: 是的，今天開始你可以無限制搭乘七天，但要確定到站時別忘記你的票。

A: Yes. You can ride as much as you like for seven days starting today. Just be sure you don't forget your pass at your destination.

住所
郵電通訊
日常活動
銀行與保險
交通
食品與飲食
購物
社交活動
教育
休閒活動
醫療
緊急情況

B: 如果我們待超過七天，我們要再買另一張嗎？

B: If we stay more than a week, do we have to buy another one?

A: 不必，你可以以10%的折扣加值。

A: No. You can add value to the one you have at a 10% discount.

B: 好，我們要兩張。

B: OK. We want two of them.

 Useful Phrases 實用語句

1. 最近的地鐵站在哪裡？

   Where is the nearest subway station?

2. 我需要一日票。

   I need a day pass.

3. 通過旋轉門。

   Pass through the turnstiles.

4. 哪裡可以買票？

   Where can I buy a ticket?

5. 搭電扶梯下 [上] 樓。

   Take the escalator down [up].

6. 我們進這車廂吧。

   Let's get on this car.

7. 小心縫隙！

   Mind the gap!

8. 不要倚靠車門。

   Don't lean against the doors.

9. 那是博愛座。

   That's a priority seat.

10. 我們最好坐在別處。

    We'd better sit someplace else.

住所 ｜ 郵電通訊 ｜ 日常活動 ｜ 銀行與保險 ｜ 交通 ｜ 食品與飲食 ｜ 購物 ｜ 社交活動 ｜ 教育 ｜ 休閒活動 ｜ 醫療 ｜ 緊急情況

11. 我們的目的地只有三站距離。

Our destination is only three stops away.

12. 我們下站下車。

We get off at the next stop.

13. 我們的站到了。

Here's our station [stop].

14. 我們要在這裡換車。

We must transfer here.

15. 這是這條路線的終點。

This is the end of the line.

16. 我們要怎樣出車站？

How do we get out of the station?

17. 我們要用哪個出口？

Which exit should we use?

18. 那裡有一個電扶梯。

Over there is an escalator.

Language Power 字句補給站

◆ 大眾運輸 Mass Transit

subway	地鐵
mass transit system	大眾運輸系統
turnstile	旋轉門
pass	通過
gap	縫隙
cable car, light rail car, trolley car, tram, street car	輕軌電車
ticket machine	售票機
stop	小車站
station	大車站
emergency	緊急情況
transfer	轉車

住所
郵電通訊
日常活動
銀行與保險
交通
食品與飲食
購物
社交活動
教育
休閒活動
醫療
緊急情況

5.7 巴士
Bus

在美國因為多數人自己開車，巴士班次並不多。公車是不找零的，因此要準備好零錢，上車時就要付車資，或是在上車前就買好當地的車票或車票卡。

Dialog 1 對話1

A: 對不起，你可以告訴我去南波士頓的巴士是哪一班嗎？

A: Excuse me. Can you tell me which bus to take to South Boston?

B: 你可以搭 65 或 115 路。

B: You can catch either the 65 or the 115.

A: 謝謝，那些巴士有在這裡停嗎？

A: Thank you. Do those buses stop here?

B: 事實上，它們都在前面不遠處停。

B: Actually they both stop down the block a little ways.

A: 我知道了，再次感謝你。

A: I see. Thanks again.

Dialog 2 對話2

A: 對不起，這巴士到傑克遜廣場嗎？

A: Excuse me. Does this bus go to Jackson Square?

B: 是的，你要坐8站。

B: Yes, it does. You need to ride for eight stops.

A: 謝謝。

A: Thanks.

 Useful Phrases 實用語句

1. 我需要一張巴士圖。

   I need a bus map.

2. 那裡有個巴士站。

   There's a bus stop.

3. 是下一站。

   It's the next stop.

4. 我們要坐4站。

   We must ride for four stops.

5. 我們要轉兩次車。

   We'll have to transfer twice.

6. 巴士總站在城裡。

   The main bus station is downtown.

7. 機場巴士在哪裡？

   Where is the airport bus?

8. 巴士多久來一班？

   How often does a bus arrive?

9. 每十分鐘來一班。

   A bus stops here every ten minutes.

10. 哪一班巴士去河邊？

    Which bus goes to Riverside?

11. 277路去那裡。

    The 277 goes there.

12. 277號巴士去你的目的地。

    Bus number 277 goes to your destination.

住所｜郵電通訊｜日常活動｜銀行與保險｜交通｜食品與飲食｜購物｜社交活動｜教育｜休閒活動｜醫療｜緊急情況

住所
郵電通訊
日常活動
銀行與保險
交通
食品與飲食
購物
社交活動
教育
休閒活動
醫療
緊急情況

5.8 灰狗巴士
Greyhound

灰狗巴士有良好的安全紀錄，路線涵蓋全美各大小城鎮 (其他較小的巴士系統路線有限)，可以欣賞各地風光，沿途停靠的車站提供食物及前往其他地區的轉車站，適合有時間但預算有限的人。

Dialog 對話

A: 嗨，歡迎光臨灰狗巴士。

A: Hi. Welcome to Greyhound.

B: 哈囉，我們要買到克里夫蘭的車票。

B: Hello. We want to buy tickets to Cleveland.

A: 好，下一班巴士今天下午2:30出發。

A: Fine. The next bus leaves at 2:30 this afternoon.

B: 好，我們可以用信用卡付款嗎？

B: Good. Can we pay by credit card?

A: 當然，沒問題。

A: Yes, of course. No problem.

B: 票多少錢？

B: How much are the tickets?

A: 單程票嗎？

A: Is this for one way only?

B: 是的。

B: Yes, it is.

A: 每張售價 85 元。

A: The ticket price is $85 each.

B: 好的。

B: Fine.

A: 我需要看你們兩人的照片證件。

A: I'll need to see photo I.D. for both of you.

B: 好，但是為什麼呢？

B: OK, but why?

A: 為了安全理由，最近每個人都需要如此。

A: It's for security reasons. These days it's required of everybody.

B: 即使是美國公民？

B: Even U.S. citizens?

A: 是的，你們現在要托運行李嗎？

A: Yes. Would you like to check your luggage in now?

B: 是的，謝謝。

B: Yes, please.

A: 好，我在這裡收行李，確定你們的行李放上名字標籤。

A: OK. I'll take them here. Be sure to put your name tags on them.

住所

郵電通訊

日常活動

銀行與保險

交通

食品與飲食

購物

社交活動

教育

休閒活動

醫療

緊急情況

B: 謝謝。

B: Thank you.

Useful Phrases 實用語句

1. 一張到聖路易的票，謝謝。

   A ticket to St. Louis, please.

2. 巴士何時抵達？

   When does the bus arrive?

3. 我們需要一些行李標籤。

   We need some luggage tags.

4. 車程要多久？

   How long does it take before it arrives?

5. 車上可以飲食嗎？

   Are food and drinks allowed on the bus?

5.9 計程車
Taxi

Dialog 對話

A: 我有一些行李。

A: I have some luggage.

B: 我打開車廂，幫你把它放進去。

B: I'll open the trunk and put it in for you.

A: 謝謝，我要去公園大道飯店，但是我要先在商業大樓停一下。

A: Thank you. I want to go to the Park Avenue Hotel, but I need to stop at the Commerce Building first.

B: 公園大道東區或南區？

B: Park Avenue East side or South end?

A: 我不知道有兩個。

A: I didn't know there are two.

B: 你有地址嗎？

A: Do you have an address?

A: 有，在這裡。

A: Yes. Here it is.

B: 好，我知道了，是在南區。

B: OK. I see it's on the South end.

A: 可以嗎？

A: Is it OK?

B: 可以，我知道現在去那裡的最佳路線。

B: Yes. I know the best way to go now.

A: 你可以在商業大樓等我幾分鐘嗎？

A: Can you wait for me for a few minutes at the Commerce Building?

B: 當然可以，但是5分鐘後每分鐘會多收費30分錢。

B: Sure. There is a 30¢ per minute surcharge after five minutes though.

A: 沒問題。

A: No problem.

住所 郵電通訊 日常活動 銀行與保險 交通 食品與飲食 購物 社交活動 教育 休閒活動 醫療 緊急情況

住所
郵電通訊
日常活動
銀行與保險
交通
食品與飲食
購物
社交活動
教育
休閒活動
醫療
緊急情況

 Useful Phrases 實用語句

1. 請載我去機場。

   Take me to the airport, please.

2. 我要去這個地址。

   I want to go to this address.

3. 到那裡要多久？

   How long will it take to get there?

4. 我要盡快到那裡。

   I need to get there as fast as possible.

5. 我要把行李放進行李廂。

   I need to put luggage in the trunk.

6. 在這裡等，我兩分鐘後回來。

   Wait here. I'll be back in two minutes.

7. 不用找 (零錢) 了。

   Keep the change.

 Language Power 字句補給站

◆ 計程車 Taxi

taxi, cab	計程車
tip	小費
metered	按表收費的
radio dispatched	無線電派車的
address card	有地址的名片
destination	目的地
pickup point	接載乘客地點

住所

郵電通訊

日常活動

銀行與保險

交通

食品與飲食

購物

社交活動

教育

休閒活動

醫療

緊急情況

Notes 小叮嚀

依照居住城市及乘坐距離，在美國計程車的花費可能所費不貲。在美國通常必須打電話叫計程車，也可以透過叫車 APP，任何時間都可以叫到車，但是較早或較晚時會比較困難。計程車都是按表計費，如果發現不是如此，就直接下車不要搭乘，紐約大都會街上可以隨手招到計程車，但晚上 8 點至早上 6 點會用夜間計價費率。在大都市許多計程車司機是移民，英語並非他們的母語，所以要多注意溝通，如果能寫下你要去的地址、攜帶名片或地圖，都可以避免走丟或走了冤枉路。

有行李時，車資會增加一些，除非隨身提包，行李讓司機服務不要自己拿。給計程車司機的小費通常是 10%-15% 或者是讓司機留下找的零錢。近年寬鬆政策物價攀升，一件小行李的小費約 $3，一到二件大行李約 $5，二到四件以上大行李約 $10 (含小費)，到賭場的小費通常需要多給些。

5.10 問路
Directions

在美國使用地圖是非常普遍的，每個人都必須學會看地圖找路或使用導航設備及 google 地圖，如果是開車前往某地，出發之前就要先查好路線或請教別人怎麼去。

5.10a 開車 Driving

Dialog 對話

A: 對不起，我們試著要去歐琛體育場。

A: Excuse me. We're trying to get to Autzen Stadium.

住所｜郵電通訊｜日常活動｜銀行與保險｜交通｜食品與飲食｜購物｜社交活動｜教育｜休閒活動｜醫療｜緊急情況

B: 你要走另一個方向。

B: You need to go the other direction.

A: 離這裡遠嗎？

A: Is it very far from here?

B: 不會，迴轉往回開大約半哩，你過橋下橋坡後右轉，直走，半哩後你會看到體育場在你右邊，你不會錯過的。

B: No. Make a U-turn and drive back about half a mile. After you cross over the bridge, take the off ramp going right. Stay on that road. After about another half mile, you'll see the stadium on your right. You can't miss it.

A: 好，多謝了。

A: Great. Thanks very much.

  Word Bank 字庫

stadium [`stedɪəm] n. 體育場
U-turn [`ju`tɜm] n. 迴轉
cross [krɔs] v. 穿越
ramp [ræmp] n. 坡道

5.10b 走路 Walking

Dialog 對話

A: 請問古德沙馬力坦醫院在哪裡？

A: Excuse me, where is the Good Samaritan Hospital?

B: 大約六個街區外。

B: It is about six blocks away.

A: 是這個方向嗎？

A: Is it in this direction?

B: 是的，但你要穿過李公園。

B: Yes, but you ought to go through Lee Park.

A: 抱歉，這裡我不熟，公園有多遠？

A: Sorry. I'm not familiar with this area. How far is the park?

B: 直走三個街區，你會看到它在街道的另一邊。

B: It's three blocks up the street. You'll see it on the other side of the street.

A: 穿過公園後，我該怎麼做？

A: What should I do after I go through the park?

B: 你一到公園另一邊，就右轉直走。

B: Once you are on the other side of the park, turn right and go straight.

A: 容易看到(醫院)嗎？

A: Is it easy to see?

B: 是的,那裡有個很有名的地標,只要找一個南北戰爭的大士兵雕像。

B: Yes, there is a famous landmark there. Just look for the big statue of a Civil War soldier.

A: 好,非常謝謝。

A: Great. Thanks a lot.

Word Bank 字庫

landmark [`lænd͵mɑrk] n. 地標
statue [`stætʃʊ] n. 雕像
soldier [`soldʒɚ] n. 士兵

Useful Phrases 實用語句

1. 火車站在哪個方向?

   Which way is the train station?

2. 最近的銀行在哪裡?

   Where is the nearest bank?

3. 你可以告訴我怎麼到圖書館嗎?

   Can you tell me how to get to the library?

4. 這裡有提款機嗎?

   Is there an ATM machine near here?

5. 往前直走。

   Go straight up the street.

6. 沿著街道走。

   Walk down the street.

7. 跟什麼路交叉?

   What's the cross street?

8. 在走路範圍嗎？

   Is it within walking distance?

9. 我想我迷路了。

   I think I'm lost.

10. 走另一邊。

    Go the other way. / It's the opposite direction.

11. 你走錯路了。

    You're going the wrong way.

12. 迴轉並往回走兩個街區。

    Turn around and go back two blocks.

13. 越過公園。

    Walk through the park.

14. 穿越馬路。

    Cross the street.

15. 你會看到它在你左 [右] 手邊。

    You'll see it on your left [right].

16. 它在學校後面。

    It's behind the school.

17. 它在銀行旁邊。

    It's next to [beside] the bank.

18. 走過地下道。

    Walk through the underpass.

19. 走天橋。

    Take the overpass.

20. 右 [左] 轉。

    Turn right [left].

21. 上樓。你會看到你前面。

    Go upstairs. You'll see it in front of you.

22. 它在榆樹街及迪倫街轉角。

    It's on the corner of Elm and Dillon Street.

23. 在一街及威廉路的十字路口。

    At the intersection of First Street and William Road.

住所　郵電通訊　日常活動　銀行與保險　交通　食品與飲食　購物　社交活動　教育　休閒活動　醫療　緊急情況

左 住所
郵電通訊
日常活動
銀行與保險
交通
食品與飲食
購物
社交活動
教育
休閒活動
醫療
緊急情況

24. 過橋。

Go across the bridge.

25. 它是個很有名的地標。

It is a famous landmark.

26. 你不會錯過。

You can't miss it.

27. 抱歉，你可以再說一遍路線嗎？

Excuse me, can you repeat the directions?

28. 你可以幫我寫下來嗎？

Can you write down the directions for me?

29. 你可以指地圖給我看嗎？

Can you show me on the map?

Language Power 字句補給站

◆ 問路 **Directions**

turn left [right]	左 [右] 轉
go straight	直走
go back	走回去
turnaround	迴轉
go up [down] the street	往前直走下去
behind	在後面
next to	隔壁
beside	在旁邊，附近
above	在上面
under	在下面
across from	在對面
go through	穿越
go over [under]	走上 [下]
pass	越過
corner	角落
intersection	十字路口
crosswalk	斑馬線
sidewalk	人行道

road	路
street, avenue	街
boulevard	大道
block	街區
half a block	半個街區
park	公園
bridge	橋
fountain	噴水池
route	路線
overpass	高架橋，天橋
underpass	地下道
skywalk	天橋
tunnel	隧道
wrong way	錯向
lost	走丟
mile	哩
quarter of a mile	四分之一英里
half a mile	半英里
traffic lights	紅綠燈
off [on] ramp	下 [上] 橋坡
(which) direction	(哪個) 方向
(ask for) directions	問路

Notes 小叮嚀

　　如果迷路了，找人問路就好，可以拿出圖片或拿紙寫下目的地的名稱及地址，請問別人怎麼去，多數人會幫忙，但要注意美國大城市中有些區域並不安全；如果路邊無人可問，必須要敲門問當地居民時，注意自己的言行，不要被當成可疑人物，當然不可以在別人屋外探頭探腦，屋內的人可能會報警，敲門或按門鈴就好，裡面的人出來時要說「對不起打擾你了」(Sorry to bother you.)，並往後站一點減輕別人壓力。到一個地區拜訪的時候，要知道哪裡治安不好別去，當然更別提在那裡問路了，雖說大部分地區是安全的，但到外地從事休閒旅遊，諮詢當地旅遊中心相關治安資訊也是必要的。

住所 / 郵電通訊 / 日常活動 / 銀行與保險 / 交通 / 食品與飲食 / 購物 / 社交活動 / 教育 / 休閒活動 / 醫療 / 緊急情況

Unit 6 Food and Eating

食品與飲食

購買食品,在大、中型城鎮有許多超級市場及新鮮的食品雜貨店,使用折價券或購買超市品牌的產品會有優惠,小城鎮較常見新鮮農產店。在飲食方面,傳統美國餐廳及速食店到處都是,在大城市有不同族裔的餐館可選,最普遍的是中國菜、義大利菜及墨西哥菜,小城鎮的餐廳及菜色選擇就簡單多了,雖然食材取得因季節而異,多數餐廳都希望提供令人滿意的服務。顧客對不熟悉的餐廳,可以請服務生描述菜色、做法及推薦佳肴。除了速食店及自助餐外,其他餐廳都是要給小費的。

住所
郵電通訊
日常活動
銀行與保險
交通
食品與飲食
購物
社交活動
教育
休閒活動
醫療
緊急情況

6.1 在超級市場
At the Supermarket

Dialog 1 對話1

A: 對不起，早餐麥片在哪裡？

A: Excuse me. Where are the breakfast cereals?

B: 走到第3排，在左手邊。

B: Go down to Aisle 3. You'll see them on the left side.

A: 紙製品也在那裡嗎？

A: Are paper products down there too?

B: 第2排。

B: Aisle 2.

A: 謝謝。

A: Thanks.

Dialog 2 對話2

A: 我們去結帳櫃臺。

A: Let's go to the checkout counter.

B: 我來推車。

B: OK. I'll push the cart.

A: 等等,我們不能去那裡,那是 10 項商品以下的快速結帳櫃臺。

A: Wait. We can't go there. It's an express line for ten items or less.

B: 喔,我們有幾項?

B: Oh, how many items do we have?

A: 我看看,1,2,3…我們一定超過10項。

A: Let me see. One, two, three… We definitely have more than ten items.

B: 好,我們回去排隊吧。

B: Alright. Let's go back and line up.

Dialog 3 對話3

A: 好,總共是 85.76 元。

A: OK. The total charge comes to $85.76.

B: 我用支票付款。

B: I'll pay by check.

A: 好,我們收本地支票。

A: Fine. We accept local checks.

B: 我可以另外取得現金嗎?

B: Can I get some extra cash?

A: 你可以多寫 20 元或更多。

A: You can write it for $20 more.

B: 好，謝謝。 → **B:** Great. Thanks.

A: 雜貨要用紙袋還是
塑膠袋裝？ → **A:** Would you like your groceries in paper or plastic today?

B: 紙袋，謝謝。 → **B:** Paper, please.

A: 好，我讓一個服務
員來幫你拿到你車
上。 → **A:** OK. I'll have an attendant help you take your things to your car.

Useful Phrases 實用語句

○ 超市 Supermarket

1. 我們必須去超市。

   We need to go to a supermarket.

2. 我要買新鮮的農產品。

   I want to buy fresh produce.

3. 我們每天外送新鮮農產品。

   We have fresh produce delivered everyday.

4. 肉類部門在哪裡？

   Where is the meat department?

5. 你會在第6排後面找到。

   You'll find it behind Aisle 6.

6. 麵包在那邊，在熟食旁邊。

   The bakery is over there next to the deli.

7. 找特價的東西。

   Look for things on sale.

8. 冰淇淋在哪裡？

   Where is the ice cream?

住所 郵電通訊 日常活動 銀行與保險 交通 食品與飲食 購物 社交活動 教育 休閒活動 醫療 緊急情況

9. 在冷凍食品區內找一找。

   Look in the frozen foods section.

10. 我需要買一些家用品。

   I need to buy some household goods.

11. 我們結帳吧。

   Let's check out.

12. 我們去出納員那裡。

   Let's go to the cashier.

13. 我有折價券。

   I have coupons.

14. (你要) 紙袋還是塑膠袋？

   (Do you want) paper or plastic?

● 肉品部門 For the Meat Department

1. 我要精瘦的牛排。

   I want lean steaks.

2. 我要多點脂肪。

   I want more fat.

3. 我要一磅牛絞肉。

   I want a pound of ground beef.

4. 我要兩磅排骨。

   I want two pounds of spareribs.

5. 我要新鮮的香腸。

   I want fresh sausages.

6. 豬排在哪裡？

   Where are the pork chops?

7. 我要一隻放山雞。

   I want a free range chicken.

8. 我要半隻雞。

   I want a half chicken.

9. 我要全雞。

   I want a whole chicken.

10. 我要一隻火雞。

I want a turkey.

● 肉販 Butcher/Meat Cutter

1. 你要肉片多薄？

How thin do you want the slices?

2. 我會切薄片。

I'll slice it thin.

3. 讓我秤重。

Let me weigh it.

4. 我會把它包起來。

I'll wrap it up.

5. 這些是最上等的。

These are the best cuts.

6. 這些切片是最精瘦的。

These cuts are very lean.

7. 這肉很嫩。

This meat is very tender.

● 蔬菜水果 For Fruits and Vegetables

1. 我要一磅四季豆。

I want a pound of green beans.

2. 我要一些洋蔥。

I need a few onions.

3. 番茄在哪裡？

Where are the tomatoes?

4. 這些蔬菜新鮮嗎？

Are these vegetables fresh?

5. 磅秤在哪裡？

Where is the weigh scale?

6. 柳橙多少錢？

How much are oranges?

7. 我要買一串葡萄。

I want to buy a bunch of grapes.

Language Power 字句補給站

◆ 超市 **Supermarket**

aisle	走道
box-boy	裝箱員
attendant	服務員
shopping cart	購物車
cashier	出納員
checkout counter	結帳櫃臺
express line/lane	快速結帳通道
frozen foods section	冷凍區
meat department	肉類部門
cereal	麥片，穀片
produce	農產品
dairy	乳製品
coupons	折價券
bakery	麵包店
on sale	拍賣
bulk sale	大量販賣
items	項目

住所
郵電通訊
日常活動
銀行與保險
交通
食品與飲食
購物
社交活動
教育
休閒活動
醫療
緊急情況

- prime 最高級的
- roast 烤
- free range 野放的
- white meat 白肉(如雞胸肉)
- red meat 紅肉(牛、羊肉)

- choice 選擇
- fryers 油炸肉
- farm raised 養殖場的
- dark meat 深色肉(如雞腿肉)
- fillet 肉排

ham 火腿

hamburger 漢堡肉

ground beef [pork]
碎牛[豬] 肉

bacon 培根

sausage 香腸

salami 義大利香腸

bologna 大紅香腸，
義大利波隆納香腸

patties 肉末餡餅

mutton 羊肉

lamb chops 羊排

ribs 肋排

pork chops 豬排

steak 牛排

liver 肝

chicken breasts [legs/ wings]
雞胸[腿/翅膀]

turkey 火雞

drumstick 雞腿

duck 鴨肉

住所 郵電通訊 日常活動 銀行與保險 交通 食品與飲食 購物 社交活動 教育 休閒活動 醫療 緊急情況

水果 Fruit

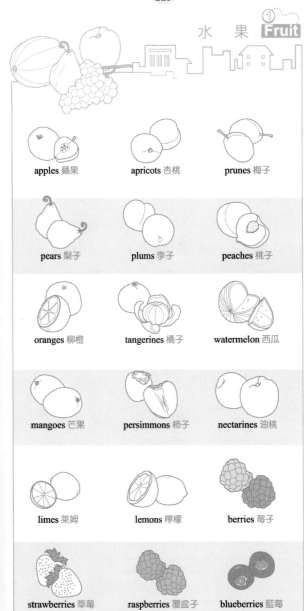

apples 蘋果	apricots 杏桃	prunes 梅子
pears 梨子	plums 李子	peaches 桃子
oranges 柳橙	tangerines 橘子	watermelon 西瓜
mangoes 芒果	persimmons 柿子	nectarines 油桃
limes 萊姆	lemons 檸檬	berries 莓子
strawberries 草莓	raspberries 覆盆子	blueberries 藍莓

住所
郵電通訊
日常活動
銀行與保險
交通
食品與飲食
購物
社交活動
教育
休閒活動
醫療
緊急情況

水 果 ② Fruit

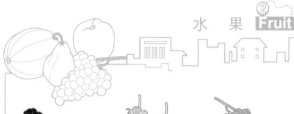

boysenberries 波森莓	blackberries 黑莓	(red/white) grapes (紅/白)葡萄
papayas 木瓜	avocados 酪梨	pineapples 鳳梨
muskmelons (黃皮)蜜瓜	honeydew melons (綠皮)香瓜	cantaloupes (皺皮)哈密瓜
bananas 香蕉	cherries 櫻桃	kiwis 奇異果
grapefruit 葡萄柚	coconuts 椰子	loquats 枇杷

蔬　菜 **Vegetable**

住所

郵電通訊

日常活動

銀行與保險

交通

食品與飲食

購物

社交活動

教育

休閒活動

醫療

緊急情況

tomatoes 番茄

potatoes 馬鈴薯

beans 豆子

corn 玉米

lettuce 萵苣

cabbage
包心菜，高麗菜

carrots 紅蘿蔔

peas 碗豆

sprouts 豆芽

green pepper 青椒

red pepper 紅椒

radish 小紅蘿蔔

artichoke 朝鮮薊

onions 洋蔥

green onion 青蔥

cucumbers 小黃瓜

pickles 泡菜

zucchini squash
綠皮胡瓜

蔬 菜 **Vegetable** ②

mushrooms 香菇

broccoli 綠花椰菜

cauliflower 白花椰菜

asparagus 蘆筍

pumpkins 南瓜

eggplants 茄子

sweet potatoes 番薯

celery 芹菜

spinach 菠菜

chili peppers 辣椒

garlic 蒜頭

堅 果 **Nuts**

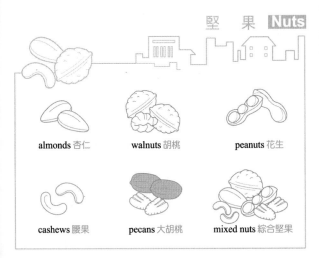

almonds 杏仁   walnuts 胡桃   peanuts 花生

cashews 腰果   pecans 大胡桃   mixed nuts 綜合堅果

住所｜郵電通訊｜日常活動｜銀行與保險｜交通｜食品與飲食｜購物｜社交活動｜教育｜休閒活動｜醫療｜緊急情況

住所
郵電通訊
日常活動
銀行與保險
交通
食品與飲食
購物
社交活動
教育
休閒活動
醫療
緊急情況

230

麵包 Breads

 bakery 麵包店   loaf 條

slice 片   whole wheat 全麥

white 白吐司[麵包]	**rye** 黑麥	**muffins** 馬芬，小圓鬆糕
bagels 貝果	**doughnuts** 甜甜圈	**corn bread** 玉米麵包
garlic bread 大蒜麵包	**bread rolls** (橢)圓形麵包	**hot dog buns** 夾熱狗的麵包
hamburger buns 夾漢堡的麵包	**French bread** 法國麵包	**English muffin** 英式馬芬

飲　料 **Beverages**

soda pop
加味蘇打水，汽水

soft drinks 汽水

juice 果汁

fresh juice
新鮮果汁

milk 牛奶

bottled water
瓶裝水

coffee 咖啡

decaffeinated coffee
無咖啡因咖啡

tea 茶

apple cider 蘋果西打

apple juice 蘋果汁

ginger ale
薑汁汽水

root beer 沙士

beer 啤酒

wine 葡萄酒

liquor 酒

concentrated juice
濃縮果汁

sparkling water
氣泡水

住所　郵電通訊　日常活動　銀行與保險　交通　食品與飲食　購物　社交活動　教育　休閒活動　醫療　緊急情況

雜貨食品 Groceries

- flour 麵粉
- cream cheese 奶油乳酪
- shredded cheese 細碎起司
- low fat milk 低脂牛奶
- no fat milk 零脂牛奶
- spices 香料
- powdered sugar 糖粉
- soy sauce 醬油
- butter 奶油
- syrup 楓糖蜜
- cones 冰淇淋餅筒
- taco chips 玉米餅片
- chip dip 碎餅沾醬
- pancake mix 鬆餅混合淋醬

- cheese 起司
- sliced cheese 片裝起司
- whole milk 全脂牛奶
- skim milk 脫脂牛奶
- cream 奶精
- sugar 糖
- salt and pepper 鹽及胡椒
- cooking oil 料理油
- margarine 人造奶油
- frosting 蛋糕上奶油及糖做成的覆片
- potato chips 薯條
- pretzels 椒鹽捲餅
- pie crust 派皮
- waffle 格狀烘餅

廚房 **Kitchen** ①

refrigerator 冰箱　　oven 爐子，烤箱　　range 爐臺

counter 流理臺　　sink 廚房水槽　　faucet 水龍頭

cabinets 廚櫃　　blender 果汁機　　cookware 廚具

microwave 微波爐　　coffee grinder 咖啡研磨機　　coffee maker 煮咖啡機

rice cooker 煮飯鍋，電鍋　　pan 平底鍋　　pot 鍋子

utensils 食器　　silverware 銀器　　bottle opener 開瓶器

住所｜郵電通訊｜日常活動｜銀行與保險｜交通｜食品與飲食｜購物｜社交活動｜教育｜休閒活動｜醫療｜緊急情況

廚 房 **Kitchen** ②

can opener 開罐器

colander 濾鍋

containers 容器

corkscrew 瓶塞鑽

cutting board 砧板

frying pan 煎鍋

grater 磨碎器

measuring cups[spoons]
量杯[匙]

bowl 碗

hot pad 高溫墊

potholder
隔熱手套

sifter 篩子

spatula 鍋鏟

tea strainer 濾茶器

cups 杯子

saucers 杯碟

COOKBOOK
cookbook 食譜

mixer 攪拌器

住所 郵電通訊 日常活動 銀行與保險 交通 食品與飲食 購物 社交活動 教育 休閒活動 醫療 緊急情況

glasses 玻璃杯

plates 盤子

dishes 盤子；菜肴

knife 刀子

paring knife 削皮刀

fork 叉子

spoon 湯匙

wine glass 酒杯

beer glass 啤酒杯

goblet 高腳杯

stein 有柄啤酒杯

mug 馬克杯

dishwasher 洗碗機

dishwashing soap 洗碗精

aluminum foil 錫箔紙

plastic wrap 保鮮膜

住所｜郵電通訊｜日常活動｜銀行與保險｜交通｜食品與飲食｜購物｜社交活動｜教育｜休閒活動｜醫療｜緊急情況

6.2 在咖啡廳
At a Coffee Shop

Dialog 1 對話1

A: 我要一杯拿鐵，謝謝。

A: I'd like a *latte*, please.

B: 你要什麼大小？

B: What size do you want?

A: 你們有幾種？

A: What sizes do you have?

B: 我們有小、中、大，請看這邊。

B: We have short, tall, and *grande*. Look here.

A: 中杯就好了。

A: Tall is fine.

B: 這邊用還是帶走？

B: Is it for here or to go?

A: 這邊用。

A: For here.

住所
郵電通訊
日常活動
銀行與保險
交通
食品與飲食
購物
社交活動
教育
休閒活動
醫療
緊急情況

Word Bank 字庫

latte [`latɛ] n. 拿鐵 (義大利文)

tall [tɔl] adj. 中杯的

grande [`grandɛ] n. 大杯的 (義大利文)

Useful Phrases 實用語句

1. 這邊用還是帶走？

   (Is it) for here or to go?

2. 請給我冰咖啡。

   Ice coffee, please.

3. 請給我糖球。

   Liquid sugar, please.

4. 奶精在哪裡？

   Where is the cream?

5. 我喝黑咖啡。

   I drink it black.

Dialog 2 對話2

A: 你們有無線網路嗎？	A: Do you have wireless access here?
B: 有。	B: Yes, we do.
A: 要多少錢呢？	A: How much does it cost?

住所

郵電通訊

日常活動

銀行與保險

交通

食品與飲食

購物

社交活動

教育

休閒活動

醫療

緊急情況

B: 免費,但是我要給你連線密碼。

B: It's free, but I'll have to give you the access code.

Word Bank 字庫

wireless [`waɪrlɪs] adj. 無線的
access [`æksɛs] n. 連線
code [kod] n. 密碼

Tips 小祕訣

在許多國家,咖啡是極受歡迎的飲料,在美國,普通咖啡 (regular coffee) 既普遍又廉價,許多地方都可以免費續杯。一般而言,美國人習慣喝熱咖啡,冰咖啡在餐廳或速食店並不是那麼普遍;在餐廳裡,服務生會過來問是否再來些咖啡,或咖啡喝一半冷掉了,是否要再倒一些熱咖啡進去「Do you want to warm it up?」。

近年有些美國連鎖咖啡盛行義大利風,以商業手法或義大利文為杯子尺寸命名,short/small, tall/medium, *grende*/large, *venti*/extra large。商業命名是經營手法,但有時名不符實,如 medium 稱為 tall (比short高),*grande* 給消費者覺得大 (*grande* 義法西葡文皆同),而 *venti* [`vɛntɪ] 超大杯,意為「20」盎司,但義大利並不用盎司為單位。

6.3 選擇餐廳
Choosing a Restaurant

美國餐廳種類繁多,除了傳統美國餐廳還有各色民族菜肴,當然速食店也到處都是,在大城市人行道會有飲食攤販 (vendor),賣貝果、冰淇淋、熱狗等等;有些高級餐廳需要先預訂,有些則需要正式衣著才可進入用餐。

Dialog 1 (對話1)

A: 你知道有什麼好餐廳嗎？

A: Do you know of any good restaurants?

B: 直走有一家不錯。

B: There is a good one down the street.

A: 是什麼名字呢？

A: What is its name?

B: 我不記得，但是它的義大利菜很好。

B: I don't remember, but it has great Italian food.

Word Bank (字庫)

restaurant [`rɛstərənt] n. 餐廳
Italian [ɪ`tæljən] adj. 義大利的

Useful Phrases (實用語句)

1. 你有何建議嗎？

   Do you have any suggestions?

2. 我知道有家不錯的墨西哥餐廳。

   I know of a good Mexican restaurant.

3. 我可以看菜單嗎？

   May I see the menu?

4. 我想為明天訂位。

   I want to make a reservation for tomorrow.

5. 這裡有吸菸區嗎？

   Is there a smoking section here?

住所
郵電通訊
日常活動
銀行與保險
交通
食品與飲食
購物
社交活動
教育
休閒活動
醫療
緊急情況

6. 我們要等多久呢？

How long will we have to wait?

7. 我們會晚點回來。

We'll come back later.

 Dialog 2 對話2

A: 你們這裡有中國菜嗎？

A: Do you serve Chinese food here?

B: 有，我們有西式及中式菜肴。

B: Yes, we have both Western and Chinese dishes.

A: 我可以先看菜單嗎？

A: May I see the menu first?

B: 當然，請等一下。

B: Sure, just a minute.

 Word Bank 字庫

serve [sɜv] v. 提供服務
western [ˋwɛstən] adj. 西方的
dish [dɪʃ] n. 菜肴

 Useful Phrases 實用語句

1. 我的叉子掉了，請再給我一支。

I dropped my fork. I need another one, please.

2. 你們有筷子嗎？

Do you have chopsticks?

3. 我想看甜點單。

   I'd like to see the dessert menu.

4. 我需要一根吸管,謝謝。

   I need a straw, please.

Notes 小叮嚀

　　判斷中國餐館是否道地只要看上門的客人就知道了。除了華人聚集的大城市,海外的中國餐館多數已加入當地人的口味,因此感覺不中不西。這類中國餐廳經常菜肴都是酸甜 (sweet and sour) 口味以迎合老外,在國外的白米飯也幾乎都是乾硬的泰國米,廚師也不一定是華人,但人在國外,將就些吧!如果帶老外到中國餐館用餐,可以告訴餐廳不要放味精 (MSG),許多老外對味精過敏。在美國的中國餐館用餐後要結帳時,服務生會送來幸運餅 (fortune cookies),內有處事格言或運勢預測,後又加入樂透明牌。許多老外到中國大陸或臺灣才知道原來這只是海外中國餐館吸引顧客的手法,中國餐廳並沒有這樣的花招,對到美國去住的華人也很新鮮。另一個特點是海外的中國餐館皆在戶外懸掛紅燈籠,很好辨識。

6.4 餐廳內──帶位
Getting Seated

到餐廳用餐要等帶位,不要逕自入內,想坐在哪個區 (侍者不同) 坐下前就表明,不要自己隨便換位,引起原侍者可能因失去桌位服務之小費收入而不悅。餐廳禁菸已漸成趨勢,許多地區的餐廳全面禁菸 (smoke free)。西方文化裡把喝湯擺第一,且習慣上點菜前會先點個冷飲或咖啡。

Dialog 1 對話1

A: 歡迎光臨,幾位?

A: Welcome. How many?

住所
郵電通訊
日常活動
銀行與保險
交通
食品與飲食
購物
社交活動
教育
休閒活動
醫療
緊急情況

B: 兩位，謝謝。　　　　**B:** Table for two, please.

A: 好，吸菸還是不吸菸呢？　　**A:** Very good. Smoking or non-smoking?

B: 不吸菸。　　　　**B:** Non-smoking.

A: 您要靠窗嗎？　　　**A:** Would you like a window seat?

B: 好，謝謝。　　　　**B:** Yes, please.

 Useful Phrases　實用語句

1. 我們想要坐在外面陽臺。

   We'd like to sit out on the terrace.

2. 我們想要在外面平臺用餐。

   We'd like to eat out on the deck, please.

3. 我們要先去吧檯。

   We'll go to the bar first.

Dialog 2　對話2

A: (服務生) 您坐在這裡舒適嗎？　　**A:** (waiter) Are you comfortable?

B: 舒服，這裡很好。　　**B:** Yes, this is nice.

A: 菜單在這裡。	A: Here are your menus.
B: 謝謝。	B: Thank you.
A: 您要先點個飲料嗎？	A: Would you like to order a drink first?
B: 我要點瑪格麗塔。	B: I'd like a *margarita*.

 Word Bank 字庫

comfortable [ˋkʌmfətəbl] adj. 舒適的
menu [ˋmɛnju] n. 菜單
margarita [ˏmɑrgəˋritə] n.瑪格麗塔 (一種墨西哥雞尾酒，含有龍舌蘭 *tequida*、碎冰、萊姆汁 lime juice、杯口有一圈鹽巴)

 Useful Phrases 實用語句

1. 我們可以先看飲料單嗎？
   May we see your drink list?
2. 我們想先喝飲料。
   We'd like our drinks first.
3. 我們想要邊用晚餐邊喝飲料。
   We want our drinks with our dinner.
4. 我們要晚點喝飲料。
   We'll have drinks later.

住所｜郵電通訊｜日常活動｜銀行與保險｜交通｜食品與飲食｜購物｜社交活動｜教育｜休閒活動｜醫療｜緊急情況

5. 我們今晚不想喝飲料 [雞尾酒] 。

We don't want any drinks [cocktails] tonight.

 Language Power　字句補給站

◆ 食物及餐廳 Food and Restaurants

waiter	服務生
waitress	女服務生
terrace	陽臺
juice	果汁
appetizers	開胃菜
side order	附加餐點
to go	帶走
for here	這裡用
refill	續杯
entrée	主菜
sauce	醬汁
fillet	牛排
fish fillet	魚排
cocktail	雞尾酒
chowder	濃湯
salad dressing	沙拉醬
MSG	味精
jelly	果凍
jam	果醬
dessert	甜點

◆ 常見西餐烹調方式 Common Cooking Methods

baked	烤
broiled	燒烤
fried	油煎，炸
deep fried	油炸
boiled	煮
sautéed	於少許熱油中嫩煎的 (尤指肉或魚)

6.5 點餐
Ordering Meals (and Drinks)

 Dialog 1 對話1

A: 這是您的飲料，您準備點餐了嗎？

A: Here are your drinks. Are you ready to order?

B: 今日特餐是什麼呢？

B: What is today's special?

A: 雞肉袋餅加摩雷醬汁。

A: Chicken *fajitas*, with *mole* sauce.

B: 包含什麼其他的呢？

B: What else is included?

A: 這餐點包含湯或沙拉及一杯飲料。

A: The meal includes soup or salad and a drink.

Word Bank 字庫

fajita [fəˋhitə] n. (墨西哥)袋餅(內有生菜、番茄、紅蘿蔔絲、洋蔥絲、起司及肉條)

mole sauce n. 摩雷醬(一種墨西哥沾醬由豆子、薑、巧克力、辛香料做成)

soup [sup] n. 湯

salad [ˋsæləd] n. 沙拉

住所｜郵電通訊｜日常活動｜銀行與保險｜交通｜食品與飲食｜購物｜社交活動｜教育｜休閒活動｜醫療｜緊急情況

Useful Phrases 實用語句

1. 您準備點餐了嗎？

   Are you ready to order?

2. 請再多給我們一分鐘。

   Please give us another minute.

3. 今日特餐是什麼呢？

   What is today's special?

4. 你建議我們試什麼呢？

   What do you recommend we try?

5. 本店特餐是什麼呢？

   What is the house special?

6. 這裡什麼受歡迎呢？

   What's popular here?

7. 你們有兩人套餐嗎？

   Do you have set meals for two?

Dialog 2 對話2

A: 我要點牛排。

A: I would like to order a steak.

B: 你要幾分熟？

B: How do you want it cooked?

A: 五分熟。

A: I'd like it medium rare.

B: 你要牛排醬嗎？

B: Do you want steak sauce?

247

A: 要。

A: Yes, I do.

B: 你要馬鈴薯泥還是烤馬鈴薯？

B: Do you want mashed or baked potato with that?

A: 烤的。

A: Baked.

 Dialog 3 （對話3）

A: 我要菜單上的6號餐，但不要太辣。

A: I want number 6 on the menu, but not very spicy.

B: 好的，要不要來個開胃菜？

B: Certainly. Would you like an appetizer?

A: 好，我點(炸)烏賊。

A: Yes. I'll have the *calamari*.

B: 很好，要喝什麼嗎？

B: Very well. Anything to drink?

A: 你們有啤酒嗎？

A: Do you have beer?

B: 有的，我們有微釀(啤酒)系列。

B: Yes, we have a selection of micro brews.

住所｜郵電通訊｜日常活動｜銀行與保險｜交通｜食品與飲食｜購物｜社交活動｜教育｜休閒活動｜醫療｜緊急情況

A: 你們有啤酒單嗎？

A: Do you have a list of your beers?

B: 有，我去拿給你。

B: Yes, I'll get it for you.

Word Bank 字庫

spicy [`spaɪsɪ] adj. 辣的
calamari [ˌkælə`marɪ] n. 烏賊 (通常是炸的，義大利文，即
　　英文的 squid)
selection [sə`lɛkʃən] n. 選擇
micro [`maɪkro] adj. 微小的
brew [bru] n., v. 釀造 (微釀啤酒為小酒廠所製少量的啤酒)
list [lɪst] n. 清單

Useful Phrases 實用語句

1. 你們有供應雞尾酒嗎？
   Do you serve cocktails?
2. 我可以看一下飲料單嗎？
   May I see the drink list?
3. 請描述這種啤酒。
   Please describe this beer.
4. 我想再來一杯這個。
   I'd like another one of these.
5. 這是免費招待的脆餅及莎莎醬。
   Here is your complimentary chips and salsa.

住所

郵電通訊

日常活動

銀行與保險

交通

食品與飲食

購物

社交活動

教育

休閒活動

醫療

緊急情況

Tips 小祕訣

煎牛排的說法

在臺灣常點五分熟牛排的人，如果到美國點牛排說「Medium, Please.」端上來的多半已是七分熟了，所以要說「Medium rare, please.」才能享受到所要的口感。這或許與美國人比我們少接觸生食有關，換言之，我們的3、5、7分熟到美國可能是5、7、9分的熟度。每個人對幾分熟感受不同，每個廚師拿捏的熟度也不同，下面列出煎熟的顏色程度做大致的標準參考，可能比感覺幾分熟還準一些：

I'd like my steak rare, please. 我想要我的牛排三分熟。

或直接說

Blue rare [very rare], please. 二分熟(外層快炙，內層紅色為溫肉)

Rare, please. 三分熟(外層灰咖啡色，最內層紅色，其餘粉紅色)

Medium rare, please. 五、六分熟(外層咖啡色，最內層粉紅色，其餘粉紅至咖啡色)

Medium, please. 七分熟(外層咖啡色，最內層有些粉紅色，其餘少數粉紅至咖啡色)

Medium well, please. 八至九分熟(全部幾乎是咖啡色，肉汁已收乾)

Well-done, please. 全熟(全部是咖啡色，味道乾澀)

可以囑咐：

Please have it cooked just right. 請煎得剛好。

Please don't overcook [undercook] it. 請勿煎太熟 [生]。

Notes 小叮嚀

餐桌禮儀

基本餐桌禮儀不可忽略，美國雖是平權社會，男士的紳士風度仍然存在，為女士開門，為最鄰近自己的女士拉椅子都是被期待的行為。有些人用餐前要先祈禱 (say grace)，別急著開動。喝湯勿低頭就碗，吃麵包要先撕成小片，要有「公筷母匙」的概念。用餐時不要先聞食物，否則美國人會感到受冒犯。

用餐時有刺或骨頭，千萬不要直接從嘴裡吐在盤子上，要用叉子接著，放到盤子旁邊，不可放在餐桌上，也不可以打嗝，在美國這都是失禮的。萬一打嗝，要道歉說「Excuse me.」再加上解釋「I ate too much.」，在人前打哈欠、伸懶腰、打噴嚏、打嗝這些動作都要表示抱歉及解釋。

要擤鼻涕、剔牙、補妝都要去洗手間，才不會無禮。別人道歉時可以說沒關係 (It's OK.)，(上帝) 保佑你 (God) B/bless you.或保重 (Take care.) 另外，要拿遠處的食物或調味料，必須請別人傳過來 (例如 Please pass the salt.) 而不是自己伸長手臂去拿。要拿餐盤上最後一片食物時，必須先問別人是否需要，才不會失禮。

刀叉擺放也要注意，如將刀叉各擺在 5 及 7 點鐘位置，表示仍在進食。兩者擺在 5 點鐘位置為用餐完畢，兩者都在 7 點鐘位置表示食物不合胃口或不好吃，可能會讓廚師很難過。

對外國餐飲文化或社交禮儀 (social etiquette) 不了解，可請教當地人或宴請餐聚之主人、賓客，有助於拉近距離，是實用又有趣的話題。

6.6 點酒
Ordering Wine

Dialog 對話

A: 服務生，我們要一瓶酒。

A: Waiter. We would like a bottle of wine.

B: 好的，你要什麼呢？	**B:** Certainly, what would you like?
A: 你有任何推薦嗎？	**A:** Do you have any recommendations?
B: 我們有一種不錯的本店酒，一紅一白。	**B:** We have a good house wine. A red and a white.
A: 我們試試白酒，還有請給兩個冰酒杯。	**A:** We'll try the white. Two chilled glasses, too, please.
B: 馬上來，先生。	**B:** Right away, Sir.

 Word Bank 字庫

recommendation [ˌrɛkəmɛnˋdeʃən] n. 推薦
chilled [tʃɪld] adj. (冰)冷的

Tips 小祕訣

　　葡萄酒類分紅酒 (red wine)、白酒 (white wine)、甜 (sweet) 及不甜 (dry) 等種類。

住所

郵電通訊

日常活動

銀行與保險

交通

食品與飲食

購物

社交活動

教育

休閒活動

醫療

緊急情況

6.7 滿意服務
Service Satisfaction

Dialog　對話

A: (服務生) 您喜歡您的餐點嗎？

A: (waiter) Are you enjoying your meal?

B: 喜歡，不錯。

B: Yes, it's good.

A: 要來份甜點嗎？

A: How about dessert?

B: 你們有什麼呢？

B: What do you have?

A: 讓我拿甜點單給你看。

A: Let me show you the dessert menu.

Word Bank　字庫

meal [mil] n. 餐點
dessert [dɪˋzɜt] n. 甜點

Useful Phrases　實用語句

1. 服務生，我打翻了我的飲料。
   Waiter, I spilled my drink.
2. 你可以收走這個嗎？
   Would you take this, please?

3. 請加點水。

   More water, please.

4. 請多點沾醬。

   More dipping sauce, please.

5. 我還需要一份紙巾。

   I need another napkin.

6. 你還要什麼嗎？

   Do you want anything else?

7. 不了，謝謝，我飽了。

   No thanks. I'm full.

8. 請多給點脆餅。

   More chips, please.

9. 我們要一份點心帶走。

   We want a dessert to go.

10. 我們的帳單，謝謝。

    Our bill, please.

Language Power 字句補給站

◆ 醬料 Sauces

salt	鹽巴
pepper	胡椒
ketchup	番茄醬
sugar	糖
Thousand Island	千島醬
Italian	義大利醬
oil and vinegar	油醋醬
steak sauce	牛排醬
mustard	芥末醬
Tabasco sauce	辣醬
sweet and sour sauce	甜酸醬
barbecue sauce	烤肉醬
satay sauce	沙嗲醬
salsa	莎莎醬

guacamole	酪梨醬
mole sauce	摩雷醬 (巧克力辛辣醬)
buffalo sauce	水牛辣醬
tartar sauce	塔塔醬
Hollandaise sauce	蛋黃醬/荷蘭醬

6.8 點甜點
Ordering Desserts

 Dialog 對話

A: 你們有什麼派呢？

A: What kind of pie do you have?

B: 我們有蘋果、草莓、水蜜桃、藍莓、檸檬及巧克力鮮奶油。

B: We have apple, strawberry, peach, blueberry, lemon, and chocolate cream.

A: 我要一片藍莓派。

A: I'd like a piece of blueberry pie.

B: 你要加冰淇淋嗎？

B: Do you want it *à la mode*?

A: 要。

A: Yes.

住所
郵電通訊
日常活動
銀行與保險
交通
食品與飲食
購物
社交活動
教育
休閒活動
醫療
緊急情況

Word Bank 字庫

strawberry [ˋstrɔˏbɛrɪ] n. 草莓
peach [pitʃ] n. 水蜜桃
blueberry [ˋbluˏbɛrɪ] n. 藍莓
à la mode [ˏɑləˋmod] adj. (法文)加冰淇淋的

6.9 買單
Paying the Bill

Dialog 對話

A: 我們要帳單，謝謝。

A: I would like the bill, please.

B: 我去拿給你。

B: I'll get it for you.

A: (帳單來了) 我們看一下，總共54元，我們應該留10%小費。

A: (bill arrives) Let's see. It comes to $54. We should leave a 10% tip.

C: 我認為服務生的服務特別好，我們該多給點小費。

C: I think the waiter's service was especially good. I think we ought to tip more.

A: 好，我留15%，那是多少錢呢？

A: OK, I'll leave 15%. How much is that?

C: 大約8元。

C: About $8.

住所
郵電通訊
日常活動
銀行與保險
交通
食品與飲食
購物
社交活動
教育
休閒活動
醫療
緊急情況

A: 我有 5 元紙鈔，你有1元的紙鈔嗎？

A: I've got a five dollar bill. Do you have any ones?

C: 有，這裡有3元。

C: Yes, here is three bucks.

A: 好，我們搞定了。

A: Good. We got it covered.

✎ Word Bank 字庫

bill [bɪll], check [tʃɛk] n. 帳單
tip [tɪp] n. 小費

📖 Useful Phrases 實用語句

1. 這裡有收服務費嗎？

   Is there a service charge here?

2. 服務費是多少呢？

   How much is the service charge?

3. (這是小費，) 謝謝。 (給小費時說謝謝就可以)

   (Here's your tip.) Thank you.

4. 我們來分攤帳單 [小費]。

   Let's split the bill [tip].

5. 我們各付各的。

   Let's go Dutch.

6. 這次我請客。/這次我來付。

   It's my treat this time. / I'll cover it this time.

7. 好吧，我們輪流。

   OK. Let's take turns.

　　除了特別時候請客，搶著付帳可不是美國文化 (真的不必搶，一來奇怪，二來沒人會跟你爭)，點餐金額外尚有稅金及小費才是支出總數。與朋友吃飯通常是各付各的或分攤費用，也可以輪流付帳，這次我付，下次朋友付。

　　服務員必須靠小費補貼過低的薪資，因此小費這部分最好不要刷卡而是給現金，只要將小費留在桌上就可以，但記得不要給過於零碎的小費。有些服務員因為希望拿到較好的小費而頻獻殷勤，不必因此受影響，按自己感受給小費就好。若是餐廳為隨你吃的自助式 buffet，有提供少許服務如倒咖啡、收盤子等就酌量給小費。至於機場、學校等自己拿餐盤點餐結帳的自助式 cafeteria 及速食店，因為服務都是自己來，就不必給小費了。

　　2008 年金融風暴前，在一般的美國餐廳用餐，小費約為消費額百分之 10%-15%，若是在較高檔優質服務的餐廳晚餐則為 15%-20% 的小費。如果帳單已含 10% 的服務費 (service charge)，就不必再給小費，但似乎不太多見。

　　金融風暴後，美國大量印鈔的結果使得小費支出也被迫攀升，現今在一般的美國餐廳用餐，服務普通之午餐小費行情 (tips) 約為消費額的15%，較高檔 (upscale) 或優質服務的餐廳晚餐約為 20% 的小費。同桌人數較多的話，要多給一些，許多餐廳註明 6 人以上帳單直接加收服務費 18%-23%。如果帳單已包含某百分比的服務費 (service charge)，則視情況酌量再給一些或不給也可以。然而卻有越來越多的美國餐廳口徑一致，不管消費者感受如何，直接在菜單上註明餐點加稅收外，另加收 18% 之服務費 (18% gratuity added)，用餐時碰到大多數餐廳皆如此，消費者也只能無奈接受。

6.10 剩餘食物打包
Taking Extra Food Home

Dialog 對話

A: 我們要打包剩餘的食物回家。

A: We'd like to take the leftover food home.

B: 好的，先生。

B: Yes, Sir.

A: 可以要多一些醬料嗎？

A: Is it possible to get some extra sauce?

B: 稍等一下，我去問。

B: Just a moment, I'll go ask.

Word Bank 字庫

leftover [`lɛf͵tovɚ] n. 剩餘食物
extra [`ɛkstrə] adj. 多餘的

Useful Phrases 實用語句

1. 我想另外點餐帶走。

   I'd like to place an extra order to go.

2. 請用盒子裝起來。

   Please box these up.

Tips 小祕訣

　　將多餘食物帶回家，也可以問可否給一個 bag 或 doggy bag，意指剩菜是要給小狗吃的。 如果要外帶的話直接說食物加 to go 就可以，例如：「A chicken salad to go. 」「A cheeseburger to go. 」「A coffee to go. 」。

6.11 速食
Fast Food

Dialog 1 對話1

A: 我可以為你服務嗎？

A: May I help you?

B: 我要一份漢堡、薯條及可樂。

B: I want a hamburger, fries, and a coke.

A: 你的漢堡要什麼大小呢？

A: What size hamburger do you want?

B: 大的。

B: Large.

A: 這裡用還是帶走？

A: Is this for here or to go?

B: 帶走。

B: To go.

A: 好的，你的餐點馬上就好。

A: OK. Your order will be ready soon.

Word Bank 字庫

hamburger [`hæmbɝgɚ] n. 漢堡
fries (French fries) [fraɪz] n. 薯條

Dialog 2 對話2

A: 不好意思，我需要些紙巾。

A: Excuse me. May I have more napkins?

B: 它們在調味料那邊。

B: They are over there with the condiments.

A: 那要多點番茄醬呢？

A: What about some more ketchup?

B: 也在那邊。

B: It's over there, too.

Word Bank 字庫

condiment [`kɑndəmənt] n. 調味料
ketchup [`kɛtʃəp] n. 番茄醬

Useful Phrases 實用語句

1. 我要多點些薯條。

   I want to order more fries.

2. 我要再點一個漢堡。

   I want to order another burger.

3. 我要的是套餐，不是單點漢堡。

   I'd like a meal, not just a hamburger.

4. 請不要放洋蔥。

   No onions, please.

5. 你們有什麼口味的冰淇淋？

   What flavor of ice cream do you have?

6.12 餐廳訂位
Making a Reservation at a Restaurant

 Dialog 對話

A: 哈囉，豐月餐廳。

A: Hello. Harvest Moon restaurant.

B: 哈囉，我要預訂今晚 (的位子)。

B: Hello. I'd like to make a reservation for tonight.

A: 好，你們有幾位？

A: Very well. How many will be in your party?

B: 將會有七位。

B: There will be seven of us.

A: 何時會到呢？

A: And what time will you arrive?

B: 大約7點。

B: Around seven.

住所　郵電通訊　日常活動　銀行與保險　交通　食品與飲食　購物　社交活動　教育　休閒活動　醫療　緊急情況

A: 好的，我們期待見到你們。

A: All right. We look forward to seeing you.

Word Bank 字庫

party [`pɑrtɪ] n. 一夥人
look forward to 期待

Useful Phrases 實用語句

1. 你們今晚有任何位子嗎？

   Do you have any tables available for tonight?

2. 我想訂位。

   I'd like to make a reservation.

3. 今晚有現場演奏嗎？

   Is there live music tonight?

4. 今晚有收娛樂費嗎？

   Is there a cover charge for tonight?

Tips 小祕訣

　　cover charge 通常是在有表演的餐廳或夜店對每人在餐點服務之外多收取的費用，可以稱為表演費、節目費或娛樂費。如果在夜店只有飲料或點心的服務，並無太多餐點可供應時，此收費可能包含了免費的飲料及小點心。

Unit 7 Shopping

購物

購物是美國人重要的生活方式，到處都有各式各樣的購物機會，大型購物中心、(名牌)暢貨中心、特殊貨品商店、特別訂製商店、二手商店、跳蚤市場等；大城市提供流行及設計的貨品，小城鎮就有些當地的貨品及手工藝品。購物通常有包裝服務(多免費)及運送服務(多要收費)。在美國購買衣物要多注意尺寸的問題，對一般身材的東方人而言，衣服可能要小一號，要找合身衣物當然要試穿才準。

住所

郵電通訊

日常活動

銀行與保險

交通

食品與飲食

購物

社交活動

教育

休閒活動

醫療

緊急情況

264

7.1 超級市場 / 大賣場
Supermarkets/ Bulk Stores

7.1a 尋找物品 Looking for Something

Dialog 對話

A: 農產品區在哪裡？

A: Where is the produce department?

B: 在 1 號走道。

B: It's on Aisle 1.

A: 你們這裡也有熟食區嗎？

A: Do you have a deli here, too?

B: 有，在後面，10 號走道後面。

B: Yes, we do. It's located in the back, at the end of Aisle 10.

A: 我有折價券，我要把折價券給誰？

A: I have a coupon book. Who do I give the coupons to?

B: 給你的收銀員。

B: Give them to your cashier.

A: 謝謝。

A: Thanks.

7.1b 結帳 Checkout

Dialog 對話

A: 先生,你可以來這裡結帳。

A: Sir. You can come here to check out.

B: 真的嗎?這裡沒人排隊。

B: Really? There is nobody in this line.

A: 這是快速結帳櫃臺。

A: This is the express lane.

B: 那是什麼意思?

B: What does that mean?

A: 如果你買9項以下商品且付現,你可以使用快速結帳櫃臺。

A: If you have nine items or less, and are paying cash, you can use the express lane.

B: 很方便呢。

B: Very convenient.

A: 你要紙袋還是塑膠袋?

A: Do you want a paper or plastic bag today?

B: 塑膠袋,謝謝。

B: Plastic, please.

住所 郵電通訊 日常活動 銀行與保險 交通 食品與飲食 購物 社交活動 教育 休閒活動 醫療 緊急情況

7.1c 折價券 Coupons

Dialog 對話

A: 我有這些物品的折價券。

A: I have coupons for some of these items.

B: 好,交給我,我來核對。

B: OK. Give them to me. I'll check them.

A: 好,謝謝。

A: OK, thank you.

B: 沒什麼。你要我們裝箱員幫你提這些東西嗎?

B: Sure, no problem. Would you like one of our box boys to help you carry these things out for you?

A: 不,沒關係,我自己提。

A: No, that's OK. I'll carry them.

B: 祝你有愉快一天。

B: Have a nice day.

A: 你也是,再見。

A: You too. Bye.

住所

郵電通訊

日常活動

銀行與保險

交通

食品與飲食

購物

社交活動

教育

休閒活動

醫療

緊急情況

Notes 小叮嚀

　　農產品秤重貼上標價結帳或在櫃臺結帳時再秤重，(熱門的) 熟食外帶經常要抽號碼牌等候服務。如果購買少數幾項物品，可以走快速結帳 (express lane / line) 櫃臺，有些賣場甚至設有少樣物品自己刷卡結帳的櫃臺 (self check-out)，替顧客省去大排長龍的不便。

　　通常推車都是推到外面停車場放東西後再歸位。有些超市有貼心的裝箱員幫忙裝箱並且幫忙老人、婦女或購買大量物品的人推物品或提東西。

Language Power 字句補給站

◆ 超市 Supermarket

produce	農產品
dairy	乳製品
meat department	肉類區
canned goods	罐頭
instant foods	速食
frozen foods	冷凍食品
breakfast cereal	早餐麥片
household items	家用品
cashier	收銀員
home pharmacy	家用藥品區
beverages	飲料
beers and wines	啤酒及葡萄酒
snacks	零食
deli	熟食
grocery cart	超市購物推車
checkout counter	結帳櫃臺
baked goods	烘焙食品
candy and sweets	糖果類

住所
郵電通訊
日常活動
銀行與保險
交通
食品與飲食
購物
社交活動
教育
休閒活動
醫療
緊急情況

住所
郵電通訊
日常活動
銀行與保險
交通
食品與飲食
購物
社交活動
教育
休閒活動
醫療
緊急情況

7.2 五金行購物
Hardware Store Shopping

當你需要整修、油漆房屋、整理花圃或庭院時，可以到大小城鎮都有的五金行，大型五金店常是許多區域的集中點，交通方便，顧客匯集。消費者在較小的商店可以得到較快速的服務及諮詢，但是大型商店的價錢較便宜。

7.2a 買油漆 Buying Paint

Dialog 對話

A: 嗨，我需要買些油漆。

A: Hi. I need to buy some paint.

B: 室內或室外用的？

B: Interior or exterior?

A: 室外用。

A: For the outside.

B: 好，室外用油漆在後面，走道的最盡頭。

B: OK. Exterior paint is located in the back at the far end of the aisle.

A: 謝謝。

A: Thanks.

B: 如果你需要什麼，就問吧。

B: If you need help, just ask.

A: 再次謝謝你，油漆前我需要先攪拌嗎？

A: Thanks again. Do I need to stir it before I paint?

B: 我們會在你走前搖勻。

B: We'll shake it up for you before you go.

A: 還有，油漆多少錢？

A: By the way, how much is your paint?

B: 價格標在架子上，大多是1加侖罐裝，但如果你買5加侖裝，可以打9折。

B: The prices are on the shelves. Most are in one gallon cans, but if you buy the five gallon size, you'll get a 10% discount.

A: 你們有混色漆嗎？

A: Do you mix paint for color too?

B: 有，你需要一個顏色樣品，我們才能調出來。

B: Yes, we do. You'll need a color swatch, so we can create the color you want.

A: 好。

A: Great.

Word Bank 字庫

stir [stɜ] v. 攪拌
color swatch n. 顏色樣品

7.2b 油漆工具 Painting Tools

Dialog 對話

A: 我有所有需要的油漆了，我要用什麼刷子？

A: I have all the paint I want. Which brushes should I use?

B: 我建議你買兩至三支寬的油漆刷及兩支窄刷用來刷狹窄的地方。

B: I suggest you buy two or three wide brushes, and a couple of narrow ones for tight spots.

A: 你們有刮漆板嗎？

A: Do you have any paint scrapers?

B: 有，在這裡。

B: Sure. They're over here.

Useful Phrases 實用語句

1. 我需要買一些工具。

   I need to buy some tools.

2. 油漆區在哪裡？

   Where is the paint section?

3. 我可以用什麼阻止屋頂漏水？

   What can I use to stop leaks in my roof?

4. 我需要一條花園水管。

   I need a garden hose.

5. 我必須封一條漏水的水管。

   I need to seal a leaky pipe.

6. 我需要修理抽屜的建議。

   I need some advice about fixing a drawer.

7. 有人可以幫我將這些裝上車嗎？

   Can someone help me load these into my car?

8. 當然，我可以幫你。

   Sure, I'll help you.

住所 | 郵電通訊 | 日常活動 | 銀行與保險 | 交通 | 食品與飲食 | 購物 | 社交活動 | 教育 | 休閒活動 | 醫療 | 緊急情況

Language Power 字句補給站

五金工具 Hardware

- roofing material 屋頂材料
- lighting 燈光
- lawn and gardening supplies 草皮及花圃設備
- electrical supplies 電氣設備
- lumber 木材
- plumbing supplies 修水管設備
- tools 工具
- fertilizer 肥料
- fasteners 固定物

nails 鐵釘

paint 油漆

paint brushes 油漆刷

spray paint 噴漆

patio furniture 庭院家具

rake 耙子

shovel 鏟子

chainsaw 鏈鋸

handsaw 手鋸

files 銼刀

pliers 鉗子

hammer 鐵鎚

住所　郵電通訊　日常活動　銀行與保險　交通　食品與飲食　購物　社交活動　教育　休閒活動　醫療　緊急情況

273

五金工具 **Hardware** ②

 screws 螺絲釘

 screwdriver 螺絲起子

 hose 水管

 nozzle 噴嘴

 sprinkler 灑水器

 wheelbarrow 獨輪手推車

 spade 鍬

 crescent wrench 可調整開口大小的扳手

 tape measure 捲尺

 electrical tape 絕緣膠帶

 duct tape 膠布

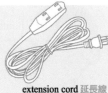 extension cord 延長線

 caulking gun 填縫料

 toilet plunger 馬桶通管器

 screws and washers 螺帽及螺絲釘

住所｜郵電通訊｜日常活動｜銀行與保險｜交通｜食品與飲食｜購物｜社交活動｜教育｜休閒活動｜醫療｜緊急情況

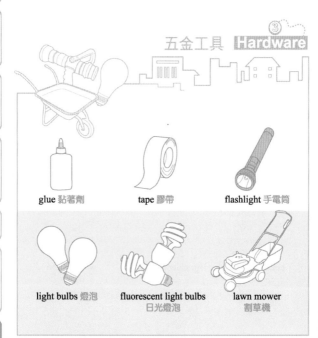

glue 黏著劑

tape 膠帶

flashlight 手電筒

light bulbs 燈泡

fluorescent light bulbs
日光燈泡

lawn mower
割草機

> Can someone help me load these into my car?

住所｜郵電通訊｜日常活動｜銀行與保險｜交通｜食品與飲食｜購物｜社交活動｜教育｜休閒活動｜醫療｜緊急情況

7.3 藥局
Pharmacies/Drugstores

美國的藥局提供專業配藥及用藥諮詢，拿醫師的處方箋配藥約需等候5-10分鐘。藥房也提供許多不需處方的藥品，需要諮詢也可到配藥部門詢問藥劑師，此外還有各式各樣的個人清潔相關用品。

7.3a 配藥 Filling Up a Prescription

Dialog （對話）

A: 嗨，我可以為您效勞嗎？

A: Hi. May I help you?

B: 可以，我有醫師的處方箋。

B: Yes. I have a prescription from my doctor.

A: 好，我看一下。

A: OK. Let me have a look at it.

B: 在這裡。

B: Here you are.

A: 我知道了，大約需要十分鐘配藥。

A: I see. It will take about ten minutes to fill this.

B: 我該十分鐘後回來嗎？

B: Shall I come back in ten minutes?

住所
郵電通訊
日常活動
銀行與保險
交通
食品與飲食
購物
社交活動
教育
休閒活動
醫療
緊急情況

A: 你也可以晚點回來，如果這樣更方便的話。

A: You can come back later than that if it's more convenient.

B: 我有些東西要買，大約半小時後回來。

B: I have some other shopping to do. I'll be back in about half an hour.

A: 好，拿著這個號碼牌，你回來時藥就配好了。

A: Fine. Take this number slip. When you return, your prescription will be waiting for you.

B: 謝謝。

B: Thanks.

7.3b 領藥 Picking Up Medicine

Dialog （對話）

A: 嗨，我的藥配好了嗎？這是我的號碼牌。

A: Hi. Is my prescription ready? Here's my slip.

B: 好了，在這裡。

B: Yes. Here it is.

A: 我該怎樣服藥？

A: How do I take the medicine?

B: 三餐飯後，標籤上有說明。

B: Take it three times a day after a meal. You can find the directions right here on the label.

A: 服用後會嗜睡嗎？ → **A:** Will I feel drowsy?

B: 不會。 → **B:** No, you won't.

A: 在這裡付錢嗎？ → **A:** Do I pay here?

B: 請到後面櫃臺結帳處。 → **B:** Please go over to the cashier at the end of the counter.

Word Bank 字庫

prescription [prɪ`skrɪpʃən] n. 處方
direction [də`rɛkʃən] n. 指示
drowsy [`draʊzɪ] adj. 嗜睡的

Useful Phrases 實用語句

1. 最近的藥局在哪裡？

   Where is the nearest pharmacy [drugstore]?

2. 我有醫生開的處方。

   I have a prescription from a doctor.

3. 我需要配這個處方。

   I need this prescription filled.

4. 你的藥配好了。

   Your prescription is ready.

5. 我需要一些過敏藥。

   I need some allergy medicine.

住所｜郵電通訊｜日常活動｜銀行與保險｜交通｜食品與飲食｜購物｜社交活動｜教育｜休閒活動｜醫療｜緊急情況

住所

郵電通訊

日常活動

銀行與保險

交通

食品與飲食

購物

社交活動

教育

休閒活動

醫療

緊急情況

6. 我需要繼續配這個處方。

   I need this prescription refilled.

7. 藥房什麼時候關門？

   What time does the pharmacy close?

8. 我還需要注意什麼嗎？

   Do I need to know anything else?

9. 避免喝酒。

   Avoid alcohol.

10. 多休息。

    Rest well.

11. 我會變得嗜睡嗎？

    Will I feel drowsy?

12. 服藥後可以開車嗎？

    Can I drive after taking the medicine?

13. 如果覺得好了，要停止服藥嗎？

    Should I stop taking the medicine when I feel recovered?

14. 我可以在哪裡找到OK繃？

    Where can I find band aids?

 Language Power 字句補給站

◆ 藥局 **Pharmacies / Drugstores**

pharmacist	藥劑師
drugs	藥；毒品
medicine	藥品
over the counter	不需處方的
fill a prescription	配藥
refill	連續處方
pills	藥丸
capsules	膠囊
tablets	藥錠
powder	藥粉
liquid	液狀
band aids	OK繃

allergy medicine	過敏藥
ointments	軟膏
creams	乳霜
lotions	乳液
bandages	繃帶
aspirin	阿斯匹靈
throat lozenges	喉糖
cough syrup	咳嗽糖漿
cold medicine	感冒藥
vitamins	維他命
calcium	鈣
painkiller	止痛藥
sleeping pills	安眠藥

7.4 購物中心
Shopping Malls

購物中心是消費重地，有些購物中心很大，以小禮品店及大百貨公司為號召，還有餐廳、電玩店、電影院及其他活動和服務，有些甚至要花上一整天來逛。購物中心有位置圖，告知你所在位置，來此購物與其他地方無異，只是大多了，當然這也意味著有許多令人眼花撩亂的貨品可選購。

7.4a 集合處 Meeting Point

Dialog 對話

A: 我們停在靠近入口處。

A: Let's park close to the entrance.

B: 好主意，這樣我們容易找車。

B: Good idea; that way we'll be able to find our car easily.

A: 你想我們會在這裡待多久？

A: How long do you think we'll be here?

B: 我想我需要四或五個小時。

B: I think I'll need four or five hours.

A: 我也是(要這麼久)。

A: Sounds about right for me, too.

B: 我們要從哪裡開始？

B: Where should we start?

A: 我們一起進去看店面位置圖。

A: Let's go in together and look at the store locator.

B: 好主意，之後我們解散，午飯再碰面。

B: Good idea. After that maybe we can split up and meet for lunch.

A: 好。

A: Right.

Useful Phrases 實用語句

1. 我們該在哪個入口碰面？

   Which entrance shall we meet at?

2. 三點我會在西北入口與你會面。

   I'll meet you at the northwest entrance at 3:00.

3. 我們來看看店面位置。

   Let's look at the store locator.

4. 我們到美食區。

   Let's go to the food court.

5. 我們坐電扶梯。

   Let's take the escalator.

6. 我想找飲水機。

   I want to find a drinking fountain.

7. 我想從那部販賣機弄點東西喝。

   I'm going to get something to drink from that vending machine.

8. 我們在這些長椅上坐一下。

   Let's sit on these benches for a while.

9. 你跟我們買的東西在這裡等,我去開車。

   You wait here with our purchases. I'll go get the car.

7.4b 挑選衣物 Looking for an Article of Clothing

Dialog 對話

A: 嗨,我能為你效勞嗎?

A: Hi. May I help you?

B: 我想買件皮夾克。

B: I would like to buy a leather jacket.

A: 我們這裡有一些,我拿給你看。

A: We have some over here. Let me show you.

B: 這些是什麼皮做的?

B: What kind of leather are they made of?

A: 是牛皮做的。

A: They're all made of cowhide.

B: 我想要一件及腰的。　→　**B:** I want one that is waist length.

A: 在這裡，你要試穿一件看看嗎？　→　**A:** They are here. Would you like to try one on?

B: 好，這裡有鏡子嗎？　→　**B:** Yes. Is there a mirror here?

A: 在那邊，如果你要幫忙或有問題就叫我。　→　**A:** Over there. Call me if you need help or have questions.

B: 謝謝。　→　**B:** Thanks.

 Tips 小祕訣

　　在美國的商場購物，如果售貨員不忙碌，會主動招呼你，問你要找什麼或是否需要幫忙「Hi, how are you?」「How can I help you?」「Are you looking for anything today?」，如果有需要幫忙就可以直接問。如果只是逛逛就說「Thank you. I'm just looking.」或簡單地說「Just looking.」就好。

7.4c 試穿 Trying On

 Dialog 對話

A: 我喜歡這件夾克，但是不太合身。　→　**A:** I like this jacket, but it doesn't fit right.

B: 我看看，太大了，是吧？

B: Let me see. It is too big, isn't it?

A: 是的，你有小一點的嗎？

A: Yes. Do you have one that is a little smaller?

B: 我看一下存貨間。

B: Let me check our stockroom.

A: 好，謝謝。

A: OK. Thanks.

(一會兒後 A little later)

B: 試試這一件吧。

B: We have one. Try this on.

A: 很好，剛剛好。

A: Very good. It fits perfectly.

B: 這是你要的嗎？

B: Is it what you want?

A: 對，我要買這件。

A: Yes, it is. I'll take it.

B: 好，你要直接穿嗎？

B: OK. Do you want to wear it now?

住所
郵電通訊
日常活動
銀行與保險
交通
食品與飲食
購物
社交活動
教育
休閒活動
醫療
緊急情況

A: 是的，你可以幫我把舊衣放到袋子裡嗎？	**A:** Yes, I do. Can you put my old one in a bag for me?
B: 當然，一點都不麻煩。刷卡或付現？	**B:** Sure, no trouble at all. Will this be cash or credit?
A: 我付現。	**A:** I'll pay cash.

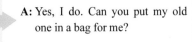 Useful Phrases 實用語句

1. 這是什麼材質做的呢？

   What material is this made of?

2. 我可以試穿嗎？

   May I try it on?

3. 更衣室在哪裡？

   Where is the change room?

4. 它太小 [大] 了。

   It's too small [big].

5. 我想試另一件。

   I want to try another one.

6. 我要買這兩件。

   I'll take these two.

7. 我考慮看看。

   I'll think about it.

8. 這個超過我的預算。

   It's beyond my budget.

9. 會縮水嗎？

   Will it shrink?

10. 會褪色嗎？

    Will the color fade?

11. 可以烘乾嗎？

Can I put it in a dryer?

12. 這要乾洗嗎？

Should this be dry cleaned?

13. 我可以寄放在這裡，晚點回來拿嗎？

Can I leave it here, and pick it up later?

7.4d 銷售稅 Sales Tax

Dialog 對話

A: 總共是 16.48 元，謝謝。

A: That will be $16.48, thank you.

B: 真的嗎？價錢標示是 14.99 元。

B: Really? The price on it says $14.99.

A: 那是因為本州的銷售稅。

A: It's because of the sales tax in this state.

B: 稅要多少呢？

B: How much is the tax?

A: 10%。

A: 10%

B: 每州都一樣嗎？

B: Is it the same in every state?

住所

郵電通訊

日常活動

銀行與保險

交通

食品與飲食

購物

社交活動

教育

休閒活動

醫療

緊急情況

A: 不是，各州不同，某些州沒有銷售稅。

A: No. It varies from state to state, and some don't have a sales tax.

B: 謝謝你告訴我這個。

B: Thanks for telling me about this.

Notes 小叮嚀

美國大部分的州都課銷售稅，但每州稅率不同，且哪些物品課多少稅也不同。有些州食品免稅。所以購物時的標示金額，在結帳時都要在消費金額外，加上一筆銷售稅。若不明白帳單的金額，可以請問結帳人員。有些大城市除了州稅外，還有另外的市稅。阿拉斯加、德拉威、蒙大拿、新罕布夏及奧勒岡等五個州都免課銷售稅。

7.4e 會員卡 Membership Card

Dialog 對話

A: 你今天有帶會員卡嗎？

A: Do you have your membership card today?

B: 我沒有會員卡。

B: I don't have a membership card.

A: 你要今天成為會員嗎？

A: Would you like to become a member today?

住所 郵電通訊 日常活動 銀行與保險 交通 食品與飲食 **購物** 社交活動 教育 休閒活動 醫療 緊急情況

住所

郵電通訊

日常活動

銀行與保險

交通

食品與飲食

購物

社交活動

教育

休閒活動

醫療

緊急情況

B: 當會員有優惠嗎？ → **B:** Is it useful to be a member?

A: 你所有的購物都有10%的折扣，而且可以累積點數換贈品。 → **A:** You get 10% off on all purchases, plus points towards free gifts.

B: 我要怎樣成為會員？ → **B:** How do I become a member?

A: 很簡單，只要填這張申請表然後交回給我。 → **A:** It's easy. Just fill out this application and give it back to me.

B: 我什麼時候拿到卡呢？ → **B:** When will I get the card?

A: 只要幾分鐘處理你的申請，之後就可以拿到卡了。 → **A:** It takes just a few minutes to process your application. Afterwards you'll get your card.

 Useful Phrases 實用語句

1. 可以打折嗎？

   Is it possible to get a discount?

2. 如果買兩份，可以打折嗎？

   If I buy two of them, is it possible to get a discount?

住所
郵電通訊
日常活動
銀行與保險
交通
食品與飲食
購物
社交活動
教育
休閒活動
醫療
緊急情況

Notes 小叮嚀

　　在美國的購物中心或商店買東西是不殺價的，殺價可能會招來異樣眼光，因為那不是美國人的消費習慣，除非是在跳蚤市場或車庫拍賣；某些場所如果辦了會員卡就有10%的折扣，但是辦卡可能要等一下子。

7.5 百貨公司
Department Stores

百貨公司內的商品雖然令人眼花撩亂，但是詢問想購買商品的基本問題如價錢、顏色、保固期限、款式、尺寸、維修、退換都是必要的，如果沒有貨了，還有何時進貨的問題。除非特別指定包裝材料及樣式，否則多數美國商家提供免費包裝服務。

Dialog 對話

A: 請問廚具在哪一樓？

A: Excuse me. Which floor are kitchen appliances on?

B: 在六樓。

B: They are on the sixth floor.

A: 你可以告訴我果汁機在哪裡嗎？

A: Can you tell me where the blenders are?

B: 我來告訴你，跟我來。

B: Let me show you. Follow me.

A: 謝謝。

A: Thanks.

B: 在這裡，我們今天這組特價。

B: Here they are. We have this model on sale today.

A: 我沒聽過這牌子。

A: I've never heard of this brand.

B: 是新廠牌。

B: They are new to the market.

A: 我想找知名的廠牌。

A: I prefer a more famous brand.

B: 當然，我們有不同廠牌的貨品。

B: Sure. We stock several more brands.

A: 這個有什麼功能？

A: Please tell me about this one.

B: 它有五段變速及快速清潔的易拆系統。

B: It has five speeds and an easy removal system for fast cleaning.

A: 耐用嗎？

A: Is it very durable?

B: 是的，它獲得消費者報告高度好評。

B: Yes. It got a high rating from Consumer Reports.

A: 保固如何？

A: What about its warranty?

B: 三年全部更換保固。

B: It has a three-year full replacement guarantee.

 Word Bank 字庫

> blender [`blɛndɚ] n. 果汁機
> removal [rɪ`muvl] n. 拆除
> replacement [rɪ`plɛsmənt] n. 更換
> guarantee [͵gærən`ti] n. 保證

 Useful Phrases 實用語句

1. 多少錢？

   How much does it cost?

2. 多少錢？

   What is the price?

3. 有打折嗎？

   Is there a discount?

4. 有什麼顏色？

   What colors does it come in?

5. 有藍色的嗎？

   Do you have a blue one?

6. 有什麼機型 [式樣]？

   What models [styles] do you carry?

7. 存貨有什麼尺寸？

   What sizes do you have in stock?

8. 有小 [大] 一點的嗎？

   Do you have a smaller [larger] one?

9. 這個要包裝。

   I'd like this wrapped.

10. 這要小心包裝。

   This needs to be carefully wrapped.

11. 告訴我維修的條件。

Tell me about the maintenance plan.

12. 有延長保固合約嗎？

Is there an extended maintenance contract available?

13. 我怎麼修理它？

How do I get it fixed [repaired]?

14. 下次到貨什麼時候？

When will the next shipment come in?

15. 什麼時候再有存貨？

When will you have them in stock again?

16. 告訴我保固的事。

Tell me about the warranty [guarantee].

7.6 (名牌) 暢貨中心
Outlet Centers

美國的(名牌)暢貨中心規模相當龐大，雖多設在城外交通不便，但折扣多，在週末還是吸引很多人潮。美國及加拿大的衣服尺寸比亞洲標準尺寸要大，買衣服最好要試穿，一般尺寸標示有 XXL (double extra large) 超超大，XL (extra large) 超大，L (large) 大，M (medium) 中，S (small) 小，XS (extra small), Petité 超小，F (free size/one size fits all) 單一尺寸；一個在亞洲穿大號衣服的人，在美國可能買中號才合身。折扣標示若為 30% off，就是臺灣的七折，別搞混了。

Dialog 對話

A: 我們去這間暢貨中心吧。

A: Let's go to this outlet center.

B: 我沒去過暢貨中心，那裡真的好嗎？

B: I've never been to an outlet. Is it any good?

A: 暢貨中心可以用很好的價錢買名牌商品。

A: Outlet stores have very good prices on famous name brand items.

B: 有什麼樣的東西呢?

B: What sorts of things do they have?

A: 應有盡有,鞋子、衣服、禮品、高爾夫球具等等。

A: Almost everything. Shoes, clothing, gift items, golf equipment, whatever.

B: 我想我們要在那兒待好一陣子。

B: I think we'll be there a long time.

A: 也許吧,我知道有些複合商場很大,而且有用餐區。

A: Maybe. I know some of these complexes are pretty big, and even have places to eat.

Word Bank 字庫

brand [brænd] n. 牌子,名牌
sort [sɔrt] n. 種類
equipment [ɪˋkwɪpmənt] n. 裝備
complex [ˋkɑmplɛks] n. 複合式建築

Language Power 字句補給站

◆ 衣服質料種類 Clothing Materials

wool	羊毛
cotton	棉
silk	絲
leather	皮革
angora	安哥拉羊毛
cashmere	喀什米爾羊毛織品

denim	丹寧布(牛仔褲布料)
flannel	法蘭絨
velvet	絲絨
polyester	聚酯纖維
nylon	尼龍
rayon	嫘縈
acetate	醋酸纖維
acrylic	亞克力纖維
Lycra	萊卡

住所｜郵電通訊｜日常活動｜銀行與保險｜交通｜食品與飲食｜購物｜社交活動｜教育｜休閒活動｜醫療｜緊急情況

衣服 Clothing 1

sweater 毛衣

jacket 夾克

coat 外套

slacks
寬鬆休閒長褲

jeans 牛仔褲

pants 長褲

shorts 短褲

(hooded) sweatshirt
(有兜帽的)運動衫

shirt 襯衫

gloves 手套

mittens 連指手套

scarf 圍巾

socks 短襪

hat 帽子

sneakers 運動鞋

boots 靴子

belt 皮帶

tie 領帶

衣　服　**Clothing** ②

skirt 裙子

blouse 女上衣

tank top 男女背心

stockings 襪

swimsuit 泳衣

nightwear 睡衣

pajamas
睡衣（上衣及長褲）

dress 洋裝

T-shirt T恤

sandals 涼鞋

high heels 高跟鞋

flip flops 人字拖鞋

stocking cap
無帽緣軟帽

baseball cap 棒球帽

bandana 頭巾

住所｜郵電通訊｜日常活動｜銀行與保險｜交通｜食品與飲食｜購物｜社交活動｜教育｜休閒活動｜醫療｜緊急情況

7.7 其他購物場所
Other Shopping Places

7.7a 車庫拍賣 Garage Sale

 Dialog 對話

A: 我們停一下，他們正在舉辦車庫拍賣。

A: Let's stop here. They're having a garage sale.

A: 我想買這臺咖啡機，還可以用嗎？

A: I'd like to buy this coffee maker. Does it work?

B: 可以的，讓我展示給你看。

B: Yes, it does. Here, let me show you.

A: 看來還可以使用。

A: It looks like it works fine.

B: 是的，它還很好，只是我在比賽時贏到一個新的。

B: Yes, it's very good. I'm selling it because I won a new one in a contest.

A: 你很幸運，這個你要賣多少錢？

A: You are lucky. How much do you want for this one?

B: 價錢應該在上面，在這裡。

B: The price should be on it. There it is.

住所 | 郵電通訊 | 日常活動 | 銀行與保險 | 交通 | 食品與飲食 | 購物 | 社交活動 | 教育 | 休閒活動 | 醫療 | 緊急情況

A: 12元，我有10元，你接受嗎？	**A:** \$12. I've got ten on me. Will you accept that?
B: 當然，快要收攤了，我只想趕快賣掉。	**B:** Sure. It's almost time to stop the sale for the day, and I want to get rid of it.
A: 好的，謝謝。	**A:** Great. Thanks.

Word Bank 字庫

> contest [`kɑntɛst] n. 比賽
> get rid of 處理掉

Tips 小祕訣

　　車庫拍賣及庭院拍賣在美國是一樣的，都是把家裡不用的東西 (常擺在車庫內) 拿出來放在車庫或庭院便宜賣，時間通常都是在週末，這類拍賣可以殺價，要收的時候去最便宜，如果你識貨的話，還可能找到寶藏或收藏品，網路搜尋附近地區或查看當地報紙可找到這類拍賣的消息。

7.7b 跳蚤市場 Flea Markets

Dialog 對話

A: 我看到明天遊樂園有跳蚤市場的消息。	**A:** I read about a flea market going on at the fairgrounds tomorrow.

B: 我不知道那是什麼。

B: I don't know what that is.

A: 就是比庭院拍賣還大的拍賣。

A: It's like a yard sale, but it's much bigger.

B: 多大呢？

B: How big?

A: 大概超過上百個攤位吧。

A: There might be as many as one hundred sellers there.

B: 真的嗎？ 那一定有很多要賣的東西。

B: Really? There must be a lot of stuff there for sale.

A: 是啊，上千個新的和舊的東西。

A: Yes. Thousands of things new and used.

B: 東西便宜嗎？

B: Are things cheap?

A: 是的，就像車庫或庭院拍賣。

A: Yes, just like a garage or yard sale.

Word Bank 字庫

fairground n. 遊樂園

Useful Phrases 實用語句

1. 這可以用嗎？
   Does this work?

2. 你有另一個嗎？
   Do you have another one of these?

3. 這怎麼使用呢？
   How does this work?

4. 這個用多久了？
   How old is this?

5. 這個我願意付你15元。
   I'll give you $15 for it.

6. 你願意少收點錢嗎？
   Will you take less?

7. 你願意算我便宜點嗎？
   Will you give me a better [lower] price?

8. 我想想看。
   Let me think about it.

9. 我晚點再來。
   I'll come back later.

Tips 小祕訣

　　跳蚤市場是美國文化的一部分，有些跳蚤市場有上百個攤位，新舊貨都有，大部分的人去找好的二手貨，和車庫或庭院拍賣一樣，跳蚤市場多半在週末才有，當地報紙或布告欄會有這類拍賣的地點、時間等消息。

　　除了跳蚤市場外，喜好收集者可以在古董及收集品雜誌「Antiques & Collectables」或網站得知何處、何時、有何主題的收藏品可購買或拍賣 (auction)，如果購買物品需要郵寄，先付郵資，店家也多半願意幫忙寄出商品。

住所｜郵電通訊｜日常活動｜銀行與保險｜交通｜食品與飲食｜購物｜社交活動｜教育｜休閒活動｜醫療｜緊急情況

住所 | 郵電通訊 | 日常活動 | 銀行與保險 | 交通 | 食品與飲食 | 購物 | 社交活動 | 教育 | 休閒活動 | 醫療 | 緊急情況

7.8 家具選購
Furniture Shopping

在美國挑家具可能是件樂事，也可能極為昂貴。大小型家具店有各式各樣來自全世界及美國製的家具，許多地區性的設計師或工廠有自己的展示間，消費者可以直接在該處購買或訂製。家具體積大且運送困難，所以運送家具多由家具店提供，如果是在當地家具公司購買家具，運送多是免費。

7.8a 選購 Shopping

Dialog 1 對話1

A: 我可以幫你找什麼嗎？

A: May I help you find something?

B: 我們在找新家的家具。

B: We are looking for some new furniture for our home.

A: 好，請隨意看。

A: OK. Please feel free to look a-round.

B: 謝謝。

B: Thanks.

A: 如果需要幫忙，讓我們知道。

A: If you need help, just let us know.

Dialog 2 對話2

A: 對不起，這是什麼？

A: Excuse me. What is this?

B: 這是常溫控制。

B: That is the thermostat control.

A: 你是說這躺椅是加溫的？

A: You mean this recliner is heated?

B: 是的，這種椅子在寒冷的地區很受歡迎。

B: Right. This kind of chair is popular in cold regions.

A: 我知道了，事實上我們在找有按摩功能的躺椅。

A: I see. Actually, we were looking for a recliner with massage functions.

B: 跟我來，我告訴你們在哪裡。

B: Follow me. I'll show you where they are.

A: 謝謝。

A: Thanks.

Word Bank 字庫

thermostat control **n.** 常溫控制
recliner [rɪˋklaɪnɚ] **n.** 躺椅

7.8b 運送 Delivering

Dialog 對話

A: 好，所有的事都弄好了，你要我們何時運送？

A: OK, everything is all set. When do you want us to deliver?

B: 你可以週末送來嗎？

B: Can you come this weekend?

A: 當然，你幾點方便？

A: Sure. What time is convenient for you?

B: 星期六下午3點好嗎？

B: How about 3:00 in the afternoon on Saturday?

A: 我會寫在運送日誌上。

A: I'll write it down in our delivery schedule book.

B: 好，我告訴你地址及電話。

B: Great. Let me tell you our address and phone number.

A: 請說，如果有問題的話，我們會打電話給你。

A: Please. We'll call you if there are any problems.

住所
郵電通訊
日常活動
銀行與保險
交通
食品與飲食
購物
社交活動
教育
休閒活動
醫療
緊急情況

7.8c 刮損 Damaged Furniture

Dialog (對話)

A: 木神家具，我能為你效勞嗎？

A: Wood Master Furniture. May I help you?

B: 嗨，我是史丹陳，我上週向你們買了些家具。

B: Hi. I'm Stan Chen. I bought some furniture from you last week.

A: 喔，陳先生，我記得你。

A: Oh, Mr. Chen. I remember you.

B: 我打來是因為我在你們昨天送來的其中一件家具中發現一道又大又深的刮痕。

B: I'm calling because I have found a very big, deep scratch in one of the pieces you delivered yesterday.

A: 我知道了，別擔心。我們今天會去看一下。

A: I see. Don't worry. We'll come out today and look at it.

B: 你們會換貨嗎？

B: Will you replace it?

A: 是的，如果我們無法修復到像新的一樣的話。

A: Yes, if we can't repair it so it's just like new.

B: 謝謝，那我放心了。

B: Thanks. It's good to know that.

住所

郵電通訊

日常活動

銀行與保險

交通

食品與飲食

購物

社交活動

教育

休閒活動

醫療

緊急情況

住所
郵電通訊
日常活動
銀行與保險
交通
食品與飲食
購物
社交活動
教育
休閒活動
醫療
緊急情況

✏️ Word Bank 字庫

scratch [skrætʃ] n. 刮傷
replace [rɪˋples] v. 更換

 Useful Phrases 實用語句

1. 我想看沙發。

   I'd like to look at some sofas.

2. 我想買燈。

   I'm interested in buying a lamp.

3. 我需要餐桌及椅子。

   I need a dining table and chairs.

4. 躺椅在哪裡？

   Where are the recliners?

5. 我想看茶几。

   I want to look at your coffee tables.

6. 你們送貨嗎？

   Do you deliver?

7. 你們何時運送？

   When will you deliver it?

8. 這是皮革嗎？

   Is this leather?

9. 有其他顏色嗎？

   What other colors does it come in?

10. 它是何種木頭做的？

    What type of wood is it made of?

Language Power 字句補給站

家具 **Furniture** 1

- wood 木頭
- leather 皮革
- entertainment center 娛樂區
- contemporary style 當代的款式
- modern style 摩登款式
- classic 古典的
- traditional 傳統的
- colonial 殖民地風格的
- custom built 顧客訂製的

sofa 沙發

couch 長椅，躺椅

recliner 躺椅

armchair 有扶手的椅子

chair 椅子

coffee table 咖啡桌；茶几

ottoman 有墊褥的矮凳；墊腳凳

magazine rack 雜誌架

desk 書桌

dresser 梳妝臺

bed 床

lamp 燈

家具 **Furniture** ②

住所
郵電通訊
日常活動
銀行與保險
交通
食品與飲食
購物
社交活動
教育
休閒活動
醫療
緊急情況

desk lamp 檯燈　　table lamp 桌燈　　floor lamp 落地燈

rug 小地毯　　chest 五斗櫃　　dining table 餐桌

cushions 靠墊　　bookshelf 書架　　mirror 鏡子

end table 茶几　　shelf 架子　　drawer 抽屜

captain's chair
將軍椅

office chair
辦公椅

7.9 電腦及電子產品
Computers and Electronics

在美國購買電腦及其他電子產品很方便，許多商店專門販售此類產品，工作人員多半很快就能找到你所需的產品並解說產品功能。

7.9a 選購手提電腦 Buying a Laptop Computer

Dialog 對話

A: 哈囉，我想請人幫忙解說，我考慮購買一臺手提電腦。

A: Hello. I'd like to talk to somebody about buying a notebook computer.

B: 沒問題，我可以回答你任何問題。

B: No problem. I can answer any of your questions.

A: 我要一臺輕的，但電池耐久的。

A: I want one that is light, but has long battery life.

B: 好，讓我向你解說這一臺，三磅重，電力持續四小時。

B: OK. Let me tell you about this one. It weighs three pounds, and its battery will last four hours.

A: 螢幕夠大，但解析度如何？

A: The screen is big enough. What about the resolution?

B: 很高，它的畫素是個中翹楚之一。

B: Very high. Its pixel count is one of the best.

住所　郵電通訊　日常活動　銀行與保險　交通　食品與飲食　購物　社交活動　教育　休閒活動　醫療　緊急情況

住所

郵電通訊

日常活動

銀行與保險

交通

食品與飲食

購物

社交活動

教育

休閒活動

醫療

緊急情況

A: 跑得快嗎？

A: Is it fast?

B: 它有市面上最快速的晶片之一。

B: It has one of the fastest chips on the market.

A: 多少錢呢？

A: What does it cost?

B: 2,900元。

B: $2,900.

A: 很貴呢！

A: It's pretty expensive!

B: 它有 300 元郵寄退費、另外送一個電池及一個有質感的提袋。

B: It comes with a $300 mail in rebate, an extra battery, and a quality carrying bag.

A: 這樣聽起來好多了。

A: That makes it sound better.

🖊 Word Bank 字庫

resolution [ˌrɛzəˋluʃən] n. 解析度
pixel [ˋpɪksḷ] n. 畫素
chip [tʃɪp] n. 晶片
rebate [ˋribet] n. 退費，折讓

住所｜郵電通訊｜日常活動｜銀行與保險｜交通｜食品與飲食｜購物｜社交活動｜教育｜休閒活動｜醫療｜緊急情況

Language Power 字句補給站

電腦 **Computers**

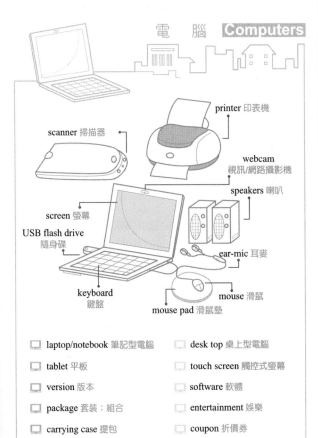

printer 印表機

scanner 掃描器

webcam 視訊/網路攝影機

speakers 喇叭

screen 螢幕

USB flash drive 隨身碟

ear-mic 耳麥

keyboard 鍵盤

mouse 滑鼠

mouse pad 滑鼠墊

- [ ] laptop/notebook 筆記型電腦
- [ ] tablet 平板
- [ ] version 版本
- [ ] package 套裝；組合
- [ ] carrying case 提包

- [ ] desk top 桌上型電腦
- [ ] touch screen 觸控式螢幕
- [ ] software 軟體
- [ ] entertainment 娛樂
- [ ] coupon 折價券

7.9b 數位相機 Digital Camera

Dialog 對話

A: 嗨，我能為你效勞嗎？

A: Hi. May I help you?

B: 是的，我想買數位相機。

B: Yes. I want to buy a digital camera.

A: 我們有幾臺，你要找特定的牌子嗎？

A: We have several. Do you know what brand you want?

B: 沒有，我想先了解一些資訊。

B: No. I would like to get some information first.

A: 我來告訴你。

A: Let me tell you about them.

Useful Phrases 實用語句

● **顧客 Customer**

1. 電池可維持多久？

   How good is the battery life?

2. 電池充電要多久？

   How long does it take to charge the battery?

3. 電力不足的時候我可以充電嗎？

   Can I charge the battery while there is little power in it?

4. 電池有充電記憶功能嗎？

   Does the battery have recharge memory?

5. 我何時要買新電池？

   When do I need to buy a new battery?

住所 / 郵電通訊 / 日常活動 / 銀行與保險 / 交通 / 食品與飲食 / 購物 / 社交活動 / 教育 / 休閒活動 / 醫療 / 緊急情況

6. 另外買一顆電池要多少錢？

   How much is an extra battery?

7. 有伸縮鏡頭嗎？

   Does it have zoom?

8. 也可以錄影嗎？

   Can it record motion, too?

9. 我可以照幾張照片？

   How many shots can I take?

10. 相機可以編輯照片嗎？

    Can it edit pictures?

11. 我需要什麼來下載照片？

    What do I need to download the pictures?

12. 有多少畫素設定？

    What pixel settings does it have?

13. 請告訴我保固的事。

    Tell me about the warranty please.

14. 有附攜帶盒嗎？

    Does it come with a carrying case?

15. 多買一張(記憶)卡要多少錢？

    How much is an extra card?

16. 我可以有中文的顧客手冊嗎？

    Can I get an owner's manual in Chinese?

售貨員 Salesperson

1. 電池壽命是三個小時。

   The battery life is three hours.

2. 伸縮鏡頭在這裡。

   The zoom is here.

3. 也有攝影功能。

   It has a movie function, too.

4. 它有許多編輯功能。

   It has many editing functions.

住所
郵電通訊
日常活動
銀行與保險
交通
食品與飲食
購物
社交活動
教育
休閒活動
醫療
緊急情況

5. 它有三種畫素設定。

It has three different pixel settings.

6. 它有兩年保固。

It has a two-year warranty.

7. 你可以用這條USB線下載。

You can download with this USB cord.

8. 你可以用讀卡機下載。

You can download with a card reader.

9. 這相機有藍芽。

This camera has Bluetooth.

10. 它附有攜帶盒。

It comes with a carrying case.

 Language Power 字句補給站

◆ 相機及電子產品 Cameras and Electronic Products

DVD player	DVD 放映機
USB cord	USB線
USB port	USB插座
memory card	記憶卡
Bluetooth	藍芽
charger	充電器
digital	數位的
flat screen	平面螢幕
LCD	液晶顯示
card reader	讀卡機
hardware	硬體
carrying case	攜帶盒
speakers	喇叭
video camera	攝影機
digital camera	數位相機
digital alarm clock	電子鬧鐘
owner's manual	顧客手冊

7.10 購買手錶
Buying a Watch

7.10a 選購手錶 Choosing a Watch

Dialog 1 對話 1

A: 嗨！我想看一些手錶。

A: Hi. I'd like to look at some watches.

B: 好的，你喜歡哪一種？

B: Certainly. What type do you like?

A: 我偏好刻度錶。

A: I prefer analog watches.

B: 我知道了：我們這邊有一組很好的那種錶。

B: I see. We have a nice group of those over here.

A: 我可以看看嗎？

A: May I see that one?

B: 當然，在這裡。

B: Yes, of course. Here you are.

A: 我可以試戴嗎？

A: May I try it on?

B: 可以，請。

B: Yes, please do.

A: 錶帶太鬆了。

A: The band is too loose.

B: 別擔心，我們可以調整到適合你。

A: Don't worry; we can adjust it to fit you.

Word Bank　字庫

analog watch **n.** 刻度錶
band [bænd] **n.** (錶)帶

Dialog 2　對話2

A: 我很喜歡這隻錶，但不喜歡它的錶帶。

A: I like this watch a lot, but I don't like its band.

B: 你喜歡什麼款式的錶帶？

B: What type of band do you like?

A: 皮帶。

A: Leather.

B: 我了解了，我們有幾款皮錶帶可以選。

B: I see. We have several leather bands to choose from.

A: 多少錢呢？

A: What do they cost?

B: 我們只是掉換過來，所以價錢一樣。

B: We'll simply exchange it, so it's the same price.

A: 好，我想要一款窄的、黑色的皮錶帶。

A: Great. I'd like a narrow, black leather band.

7.10b 維修 Maintenance

 Dialog 1 對話1

A: 我的手錶電池沒電了。

A: The battery is dead in my watch.

B: 沒問題，我們會換一個新的。

B: No problem. We'll put a new one in.

A: 要多久呢？

A: How long will it take?

B: 只要幾分鐘。

B: Only a few minutes.

A: 我十分鐘後回來。

A: I'll be back in ten minutes.

B: 可以。

B: It will be ready.

住所　郵電通訊　日常活動　銀行與保險　交通　食品與飲食　購物　社交活動　教育　休閒活動　醫療　緊急情況

A: 謝謝。

A: Thanks.

Dialog 2 (對話2)

A: 我的手錶不動了。

A: My watch has stopped working.

B: 讓我看一下。

B: Let me have a look at it.

A: 在這裡。

A: Here it is.

B: 我今天必須要把它留下來。

B: I'll have to keep it for the day.

A: 好，你想可能是什麼問題？

A: OK. What do you think might be wrong?

B: 可能是電池沒電或需要清洗了。

B: It might have a dead battery, or perhaps it needs cleaning.

A: 我明天下午來拿。

A: I'll come back tomorrow afternoon.

B: 好。

A: OK.

住所 郵電通訊 日常活動 銀行與保險 交通 食品與飲食 購物 社交活動 教育 休閒活動 醫療 緊急情況

 Useful Phrases 實用語句

1. 我喜歡刻度錶。

   I like analog watches.

2. 我想要買隻電子錶。

   I want to buy a digital watch.

3. 我需要一個新錶帶。

   I need a new watchband.

4. 我想要小一點的。

   I'd like something smaller.

5. 我想要一隻粗獷的手錶。

   I want a rugged watch.

6. 它防水嗎？

   Is it waterproof?

7. 我需要一款顯示時間及日期的。

   I need one that tells time and date.

8. 錶帶太大了。

   The band is too big.

9. 錶帶需要調整。

   The band needs to be adjusted.

10. 我要一個有扣環的錶帶。

    I want a band with a buckle.

11. 我要一個皮錶帶。

    I want a leather band.

12. 我要一個不鏽鋼錶帶。

    I want a stainless steel watchband.

13. 你們有男女對錶嗎？

    Do you have a matching men and women's set?

14. 它有附盒子嗎？

    Does it come in a box?

15. 你可以包裝嗎？

    Can you gift-wrap it?

住所
郵電通訊
日常活動
銀行與保險
交通
食品與飲食
購物
社交活動
教育
休閒活動
醫療
緊急情況

Language Power 字句補給站

◆ 手錶 Watches

wristwatch	腕錶
wristband, watchband	錶帶
band	帶子
analog	指針的
buckle	扣環
latch	閂
time, date, and year display	時間、日期、年份顯示
waterproof, water resistant	防水
shock resistant	防震
face	錶面
battery	電池
replace battery	更換電池
alarm	鬧鐘

7.11 購買眼鏡
Buying Glasses

7.11a 量度數 Getting a Prescription

Dialog 對話

A: 哈囉，我想買副新眼鏡。

A: Hello. I would like to buy new glasses.

B: 你以前有來過我們的店嗎？

B: Have you been to our shop before?

A: 沒有。

A: No.

B: 你知道度數(處方)嗎？

B: Do you know your prescription?

A: 不，我不知道。

A: No, I don't.

B: 那我們要先量你的視力。

B: Then first we need to check your eyesight.

A: 好。

A: OK.

B: 請過來這邊坐。

B: Please come over here and sit down.

A: 好。

A: OK.

B: 請看這個探視器。

B: Look into the viewer please.

A: 好。

A: Alright.

B: 好，就這樣，完成了。

B: Good. That's it. Done.

住所　郵電通訊　日常活動　銀行與保險　交通　食品與飲食　購物　社交活動　教育　休閒活動　醫療　緊急情況

住所
郵電通訊
日常活動
銀行與保險
交通
食品與飲食
購物
社交活動
教育
休閒活動
醫療
緊急情況

prescription [prɪˋkrɪpʃən] n. 處方
eyesight [ˋaɪ͵saɪt] n. 視力

7.11b 選鏡框 Choosing the Frame

Dialog 對話

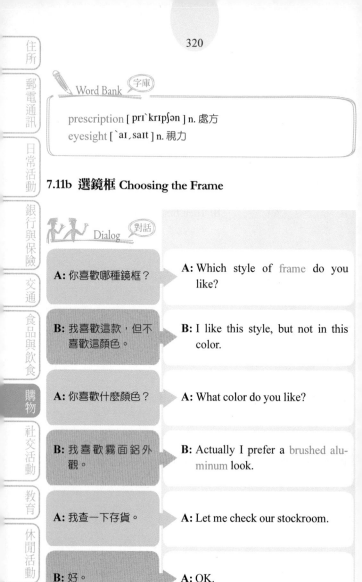

A: 你喜歡哪種鏡框？

A: Which style of frame do you like?

B: 我喜歡這款，但不喜歡這顏色。

B: I like this style, but not in this color.

A: 你喜歡什麼顏色？

A: What color do you like?

B: 我喜歡霧面鋁外觀。

B: Actually I prefer a brushed aluminum look.

A: 我查一下存貨。

A: Let me check our stockroom.

B: 好。

A: OK.

(稍後 Later)

A: 我們有你要找的。

A: We have what you are looking for.

B: 太好了。

B: Great.

A: 試戴看看,照照鏡子。

A: Try them on, and look in this mirror.

B: 我喜歡,很輕,但很緊。

B: I like them; they're light, but they are very tight.

A: 我們會處理那個問題。

A: We'll take care of that problem.

B: 好,我要這副。

B: Good. I want this frame.

A: 我今天會訂貨,星期一會好。

A: I'll place the order today. They should be ready on Monday.

B: 你有名片嗎?

B: Do you have a name card?

A: 有,在這裡。

A: Yes, here you are.

B: 我星期一要打電話過來嗎？

B: Should I call on Monday?

A: 我們會打給你。

A: We'll call you.

B: 謝謝。

B: Thank you very much.

Word Bank 字庫

frame [frem] n. 鏡框
brushed [brʌʃt] adj. 霧狀的
aluminum [əˋlumɪnəm] n. 鋁

7.11c 拿眼鏡 Picking Up Glasses

Dialog 對話

A: 我來拿新眼鏡。

A: I'm here to pick up my new glasses.

B: 好的，請稍坐一下。

B: Certainly. Please sit down and wait a moment.

A: 謝謝。

A: Thanks.

B: 在這裡，試戴看看。　**B:** Here they are. Try them on.

A: 看來很好，而且剛剛好。　**A:** They look good. They fit well, too.

B: 你覺得該調整時就帶過來。　**B:** Bring them in anytime you think they need adjusting.

A: 好，我會，有保護盒嗎？　**A:** OK, I will. Do they have a protective case?

B: 有，在這裡。　**B:** Yes. Here it is.

A: 好，謝謝。　**A:** Great, thanks.

Word Bank 字庫

adjust [əˋdjʌst] v. 調整
protective case n. 保護盒

7.11d 隱形眼鏡 Contact Lenses

Dialog 對話

A: 我想買隱形眼鏡。　**A:** I'd like to buy contact lenses.

住所
郵電通訊
日常活動
銀行與保險
交通
食品與飲食
購物
社交活動
教育
休閒活動
醫療
緊急情況

B: 你以前有戴過嗎？

B: Have you worn contacts before?

A: 沒有。

A: No.

B: 你有處方嗎？

B: Do you have your prescription?

A: 有。

A: Yes, I do.

B: 好，除非你戴拋棄式，否則記住你要清洗隱形眼鏡。

B: Good. Remember that you must wash contacts, unless you buy disposables.

A: 好，配好隱形眼鏡要多久？

A: OK. How long will it take to make the contacts?

B: 要看你買哪一種。

B: It depends on what you buy.

Word Bank 字庫

contact lenses, contacts [`kɑntækts] n. 隱形眼鏡
disposable [dɪ`spozəbḷ] n., adj. 拋棄式(的)

Useful Phrases 實用語句

○ **顧客 Customer**

1. 我要配隱形眼鏡。

   I'd like to get contact lenses.

2. 它們可以改變我眼睛的顏色嗎？

Can they change my eye color?

3. 我可以戴多久？

How long can I wear them?

4. 我可以戴它們過夜嗎？

Can I wear them overnight?

5. 我需要每天用手清洗它們嗎？

Do I need to wash them by hand everyday?

6. 那拋棄式呢？

What about disposable contacts?

7. 我有什麼可選擇的？

What are my options?

● 眼鏡店 Eye Glass Shop

1. 你戴隱形眼鏡多久了？

How long have you been wearing contacts?

2. 你以前有戴過隱形眼鏡嗎？

Have you had contacts before?

3. 它們幾天就會配好。

They'll be ready in a few days.

4. 你要哪種隱形眼鏡？

What type of contacts do you want?

5. 我要檢查你的視力。

I'll need to check your eyesight.

6. 你知道你的度數嗎？

Do you know your prescription?

Language Power 字句補給站

◆ 隱形眼鏡 Contact Lenses

soft [rigid] contact lenses	軟 [硬] 式隱形眼鏡
gas permeable	透氣
extended wear	長戴型

daily disposables	(每日) 拋棄式
UV [ultra violet] protection	防紫外線
tinted, colored	有顏色的
moisture	溼潤
eye moisturizer	人工淚液
solutions	消毒液
saline solution	生理食鹽水
cleaning solution	清潔液
shortsighted/nearsighted	近視
farsighted	遠視
super thin	超薄
measure visual acuity	測量視力

7.11e 太陽眼鏡 Sunglasses

 Dialog 對話

A: 我在找太陽眼鏡。

A: I'm looking for some sunglasses.

B: 我們有一些名牌，請看看。

B: We have some famous brands. Please look.

A: 很好看。

A: These are nice.

B: 戴戴看，鏡子在這裡。

B: Put them on. Here is a mirror.

A: 我看它們對我的臉而言太大了。

A: I see they are too big for my face.

B: 試試這些。

B: Try these on.

A: 很好看，很酷，但太暗。

A: Very nice looking. Very cool, but they're too dark.

B: 我們可以替你換鏡片。

B: We can change the lenses for you.

A: 我需要付鏡片的錢嗎？

A: Do I need to pay for the cost of the lenses?

B: 不，不需額外的費用。

B: No. No extra charge.

A: 是防紫外線400的鏡片嗎？

A: Are they UV400 lenses?

B: 是的，我們用這裡的機器測試 (測試及顯示)。

B: Yes, they are. Let's test them with the machine here. (test and display)

A: 好，如果你找到我要的顏色，我就買了。

A: Good. I'll take them if you can get the right color.

Useful Phrases 實用語句

1. 我需要量視力。

   I need to have my eyes checked.

2. 我需要新眼鏡。

   I need new glasses.

3. 我的眼鏡需要調整。

   My glasses need to be adjusted.

4. 我眼鏡需要調緊。

   My glasses need to be tightened.

5. 太緊了。

   They're too tight.

6. 我要買太陽眼鏡。

   I want to buy sunglasses.

7. 我的眼鏡需要一個盒子。

   I need a case for my glasses.

8. 我要看一下你們的鏡框。

   I want to look at your frames.

9. 我的眼鏡何時會好？

   When will my glasses be ready?

Language Power 字句補給站

◆ 眼鏡 Glasses

eye clinics	眼科診所
optometrist	驗光師
eye doctor, ophthalmologist	眼科醫師
sunglasses	太陽眼鏡
lenses	鏡片
plastic	塑膠
metal	金屬
14K gold	14K金
case	盒子

住所
郵電通訊
日常活動
銀行與保險
交通
食品與飲食
購物
社交活動
教育
休閒活動
醫療
緊急情況

tighten	調緊
loosen	調鬆
nose pads	鼻墊片

Notes 小叮嚀

　　許多美國民眾對自己的視力並不清楚，美國沒有大量戴眼鏡的人口，即使戴眼鏡也多半度數輕微，民眾談到視力多半只說「我有點近視/遠視」(I'm a little nearsighted/farsighted.)，「我要戴老花眼鏡」(I need my reading glasses.)，「我視力模糊」(I have blurry vision./My vision is blurry.)。除非是驗光師之間的談話才會以精確度數表達。民眾通常依照他們眼科醫師或驗光師決定的處方 (prescription) 配眼鏡，醫療診斷屬於個人隱私，民眾除非與醫師、家人或特殊情形下才會提到視力問題外，在臺灣習以為常問人視力幾度 (What's the prescription of your glasses?) 或什麼血型 (What's your blood type?)，在美國是很唐突的，他們可能自己都不知道，為何別人想知道? 臺灣所稱之 100 度為 1 diopter，但 diopter (屈光度)、myopia (近視)、hyperopia (遠視)、astigmatism (散光)、presbyopia (老花眼) 等字屬於醫療用語，多數民眾可能不知道也不會用，醫護人員如果聽到民眾用醫療術語反而會覺得詫異。最佳視力在美國是 20/20 (在 20 呎或 6 公尺距離可看清楚)，歐洲標示為 6/6，即我們所說的 1.0。測量視力的方法與其他國家類似，都是看字母或圖表。

7.12 購物問題
Shopping Problems

7.12a 更換 Exchanges

Dialog 1 對話1

A: 我昨天買了這個，但我需要更換。

A: I bought this yesterday, but I need to exchange it.

住所

郵電通訊

日常活動

銀行與保險

交通

食品與飲食

購物

社交活動

教育

休閒活動

醫療

緊急情況

B: 你有收據嗎？

B: Do you have the receipt?

A: 是的，我有。

A: Yes, I do.

B: 哪裡有問題嗎？

B: What is wrong with it?

A: 太小了。

A: It's too small.

B: 好，我換一個大一點的給你。

B: OK. I'll find a bigger one for you.

Dialog 2 對話2

A: 嗨，我幾天前買這隻腕錶，但現在它壞了。

A: Hi. I bought this wristwatch here a few days ago, but now it's not working.

B: 是的，我記得你，讓我看一下手錶。

B: Yes, I remember you. Let me have a look at the watch.

A: 在這裡。

A: Here you are.

B: 我看一下什麼問題。

B: I'll check it to see what the problem is.

A: 要多久呢？	A: How long will that take?
B: 喔，別擔心這隻錶，我現在馬上換別隻給你。	B: Oh, don't worry about this watch. I'll give you a different one right now.
A: 我可以要相同款式及顏色的嗎？	A: Can I have the same style and color?
B: 好的，沒問題。	B: Yes, no problem.

 Word Bank 字庫

exchange [ɪksˋtʃendʒ] v. 替換
receipt [rɪˋsit] n. 收據
wristwatch [ˋrɪst͵watʃ] n. 腕錶

 Useful Phrases 實用語句

1. 它損壞了。

   It's damaged.

2. 我不喜歡這個顏色。

   I don't like the color.

3. 它的尺寸不對。

   It's the wrong size.

4. 這是收據。

   Here's the receipt.

5. 我要個換一個不一樣的。

   I want to exchange this for a different one.

住所
郵電通訊
日常活動
銀行與保險
交通
食品與飲食
購物
社交活動
教育
休閒活動
醫療
緊急情況

7.12b 退錢 Refunds

Dialog 對話

A: 我要退錢，我買的這隻錶不準。

A: I want to get a refund. This watch I bought does not keep time.

B: 你有收據嗎？

B: Do you have the receipt?

A: 在這裡。

A: Yes. Here it is.

B: 通常像這種情形我們提供更換。

B: Usually we offer an exchange in cases like this.

A: 知道了，你們有另一隻完全像這隻的錶嗎？

A: I see. Do you have another watch exactly like this one?

B: 我們好像沒有了，那我現在退錢給你吧。

B: It looks like we don't, so I'll give you a refund right now.

A: 謝謝。

A: Thank you.

B: 不客氣。

B: Yes, no problem.

Word Bank　字庫

refund v. [rɪˈfʌnd], n. [ˈrɪˌfʌnd] 退錢

Useful Phrases　實用語句

1. 這商品壞了。

   This product is broken.

2. 這衣服有瑕疵。

   This clothing is flawed.

3. 我這個要退錢。

   I want a refund for this.

4. 這是收據，你可以查看購買日期。

   Here is the receipt. You can check the date of purchase.

Notes　小叮嚀

　　每個州政府對商店及貨品的退換規定不一，顧客不一定每樣商品都可退換，最好在購買前就問清楚，尤其是如果購買貴重的東西，越要注意收據上有關更換或退錢的規定，一般而言，美國商店多願意協助顧客解決購物問題。

　　美國的夏季拍賣 (summer sale) 是在勞動節週末做最後「Labor Day Sale」，冬季大拍賣 (winter sale) 是在耶誕節過後做「Christmas Sale」。若是在季末特價時，購買買一送一的物品 (Buy one get one free) 恐怕難以更換或退貨，而標有「恕不退貨」(All sales are final!) 聲明的拍賣品，就不可能更換或退貨了。

住所
郵電通訊
日常活動
銀行與保險
交通
食品與飲食
購物
社交活動
教育
休閒活動
醫療
緊急情況

Unit 8 Social Activities

社交活動

美國多數的社交活動包含飲食及聊天,有些則有禮物餽贈,如耶誕節、喬遷、畢業、準新娘禮物會及婚禮等,還有一些是需要特別打扮的活動,如萬聖節及扮裝派對等;多數的邀約為非正式的場合,少數的場合要求較正式的穿著,例如退休歡送會、婚禮、公司開幕、畢業典禮等。到朋友家並不一定需要帶禮物,但是禮多人不怪,帶些飲料或點心都好。

8.1 邀約朋友到郊外
Setting Up an Outing

8.1a 計畫 Planning

 Dialog 對話

A: 我想我們這個週末該找幾個朋友出來玩。

A: I think we should get some people together this weekend and have some fun.

B: 好啊,聽起來是個好主意,但我們該做什麼?

B: Sure. It sounds like a good idea, but what should we do?

A: 我想我們該去銀瀑州立公園。

A: I think we should go to Silver Falls State Park.

B: 我聽說那是個很好的地方。

B: I hear that's a nice place.

A: 是的,我們可以健行、野餐、玩樂以及看看美麗的瀑布。

A: Yes, it is. We can hike, picnic, play around, and see beautiful waterfalls, too.

B: 你要邀多少人?

B: How many people do you want to invite?

A: 我不確定,我們打電話給認識的每個人並邀請他們。

A: I'm not sure. Let's just call everybody we know and invite them.

B: 好，就這麼做吧。	B: OK. Let's do it.

8.1b 打電話邀請 Calling Some Friends and Inviting Them

Dialog 對話

A: 哈囉。	A: Hello.

B: 哈囉，傑瑞嗎？	B: Hello. Is this Jerry?

A: 是的。	A: Yes, it is.

B: 嗨，傑瑞，我是馬丁施。	B: Hi, Jerry. This is Martin Shih.

A: 嗨，馬丁，什麼事？	A: Hi, Martin. What's up?

B: 我打電話來邀請大家這個週末去銀瀑布郊遊。	B: I'm calling people to invite them to an outing at Silver Falls this coming weekend.

A: 酷，什麼時候？	A: Cool. What time?

住所
郵電通訊
日常活動
銀行與保險
交通
食品與飲食
購物
社交活動
教育
休閒活動
醫療
緊急情況

B: 星期六早上十點左右。

B: Saturday, in the morning around ten.

A: 誰會去？

A: Who'll be there?

B: 目前聽來好像滿多人的，大約 15 個人說他們會去。

B: So far it sounds like a lot of people. About fifteen have said they want to go.

A: 哇，聽起來很棒，我們該在哪裡碰面呢？

A: Wow! Sounds great. Where should we meet exactly?

B: 公園南側入口，你有辦法到那裡嗎？

B: The south entrance of the park. Do you have a way to get there?

A: 喔，我正在想我能搭誰的便車？

A: Well, I was wondering if I could catch a ride with someone.

B: 我想沒問題，我會告訴你誰願意載人。

B: I think it's no problem. Let me tell you who said they'd be willing to give rides.

A: 謝謝。

A: Thanks.

住所
郵電通訊
日常活動
銀行與保險
交通
食品與飲食
購物
社交活動
教育
休閒活動
醫療
緊急情況

8.1c 郊外聚會 At the Outing

Dialog 對話

A: 真棒,結果真好。

A: This is great. What a turn out.

B: 是啊,今天超過30個人來這裡。

B: Yes. More than thirty people here today.

A: 希望我們帶來野餐的東西夠吃。

A: I hope we brought enough food for the picnic.

B: 沒問題,每個人都帶了一、兩樣東西來跟大家分享。

B: No problem. Everybody brought one or two things for everyone to share.

A: 好,就算我們需要更多,公園內有間商店,雖然那裡的東西很貴。

A: Yes, and even if we need more, there is a store here at the park, although things there are pretty expensive.

B: 對,可以的話,我們最好不要在那裡買東西。

B: Right. We'd better avoid buying things there if possible.

A: 我們在瀑布旁走走之後,或許可以打棒球。

A: After we do some hiking around the waterfalls, maybe we can play baseball.

B: 山姆帶了球網及排球。

B: Sam brought a volleyball net and ball.

A: 好,那更好,不需要太多空間。

A: Good. That's probably better. It won't use up so much room.

B: 對,而且每個人都會打排球。

B: Right, and anyone can play volleyball.

A: 好,只要好玩就行了。

A: Sure. We just want to play for fun anyway.

B: 我們也可以在旁邊煮東西。

B: We can cook close to the game, too.

8.1d 照相 Photo Taking

Dialog 1 對話1

A: 我們來拍團體照。

A: Let's have a group photo.

B: 大家過來這裡。

B: Everybody come over here.

A: (這是) 拍照的好地點,大樹是好背景。

A: Good spot for a photo. The big trees make a nice background.

B: 每個人靠近點好嗎?

B: Everybody get closer together?

A: 嘿，你呢？傑瑞，你不在照片裡。	**A:** Hey! What about you, Jerry? You won't be in the photo.
B: 我要找個人幫我們照相。	**B:** I'm going to ask someone to help us take the picture.

 Dialog 2 （對話2）

A: 對不起，先生，你可以幫我們照張相嗎？	**A:** Excuse me, sir. Would you please help us take a photo of our group?
B: 當然，沒問題。	**B:** Certainly. No problem.
A: 請按這裡，相機已準備好了。	**A:** Just press here. The camera is ready to shoot.
B: 好，大家想開心的事，準備好了嗎？說「cheese」！	**B:** OK. Everybody think happy thoughts. Ready? Say cheese!

 Useful Phrases （實用語句）

1. 我們選個地方見面。

   Let's choose a place to meet.

2. 我們該何時聚會呢？

   What time should we get together?

3. 音樂會何時開始？

   What time does the concert start?

4. 我到底要在哪裡和你見面呢？

   Where exactly should I meet you?

住所
郵電通訊
日常活動
銀行與保險
交通
食品與飲食
購物
社交活動
教育
休閒活動
醫療
緊急情況

5. 你今天想做什麼？

   What do you want to do today?

6. 我們早點去，避開人群。

   Let's go early and beat the crowd.

7. 我們要怎麼到那裡？

   How are we going to get there?

8. 我們搭火車。

   We'll take the train.

9. 巴士會是最便宜、最簡單的。

   The bus would be the cheapest and easiest.

10. 到那裡要多久？

    How long will it take to get there?

11. 我們會在一個小時後到。

    We'll be there in an hour.

12. 到那裡要四個小時。

    It will take about four hours to get there.

13. 我們要住在哪裡？

    Where are we going to stay?

14. 我們要預訂飯店。

    We need to get hotel reservations.

15. 我們可以住我朋友家。

    We can stay at my friend's house.

16. 我們最好看天氣穿衣服。

    We'd better dress for the weather.

17. 明天天氣會如何？

    What's the weather going to be like tomorrow?

18. 明天會又熱又陽光普照。

    It will be hot and sunny tomorrow.

19. 今晚會冷，風也會很大。

    The weather will be cold and windy tonight.

20. 帶把傘。

    Bring an umbrella.

住所 郵電通訊 日常活動 銀行與保險 交通 食品與飲食 購物 社交活動 教育 休閒活動 醫療 緊急情況

8.2 電話用語
Telephone Expressions

8.2a 平時閒談 On the Phone for Casual Talk

Dialog 對話

A: 哈囉。

A: Hello.

B: 嗨，瑪麗在嗎？

B: Hi, is Mary there?

A: 我就是。

A: This is she.

B: 嗨，我是巴瑞。

B: Hi, Mary, this is Barry.

A: 嗨，巴瑞，什麼事？

A: Hi, Barry. What's up?

B: 我要問你邀我參加晚宴的事。

B: I want to ask you about the dinner party you invited me to.

A: 好啊，什麼問題？

A: Sure. What's your question?

住所
郵電通訊
日常活動
銀行與保險
交通
食品與飲食
購物
社交活動
教育
休閒活動
醫療
緊急情況

B: 我要帶什麼？

B: What should I bring?

A: 其實你什麼都不用帶。

A: Actually, you don't need to bring anything.

B: 真的？我以為大家都要帶些吃的或喝的。

B: Really? I thought people were supposed to bring something to eat or drink.

A: 這類晚宴不必，你可能以為是 (大家各帶一道菜的) 便飯聚餐。

A: Not to this type of dinner party. You're probably thinking of a potluck.

B: 好，那我只需要到就好，對嗎？

B: OK. Then I only need to show up, right?

A: 這樣就夠好了。

A: That's good enough.

B: 我可以帶女朋友參加嗎？

B: Is it OK to bring my girlfriend?

A: 可以呀！請帶她來。

A: That would be great. Please do.

B: 好，我們星期六晚上見。

B: OK. We'll see you on Saturday night.

A: 到時候見，再見。 → **A:** See you then. Bye.

B: 再見。 → **B:** Bye.

 Word Bank 字庫

be supposed to 應該
show up 出現

 Useful Phrases 實用語句

1. 哈囉，我是傑瑞王。

   Hello. This is Jerry Wong.

2. 我要找卡爾傑克森。

   I'm calling for Carl Jackson.

3. 卡爾傑克森在嗎？

   Is Carl Jackson in?

4. 他何時回來？

   When will he return?

5. 你可以打他手機。

   You can call his cell phone.

6. 你有他的手機號碼嗎？

   Do you have his cell phone number?

7. 他何時會回來？

   What time will he be back?

8. 我可以留言嗎？

   Can I leave a message?

9. 請留話給他。

   Please give him a message.

10. 請告訴他我打電話來過。

Please tell him I called.

11. 我的(手機)號碼是 (717)387-6768。

My (cell phone) number is (717)387-6768.

12. 我會晚點再打。

I'll call back later.

13. 麻煩請他回電給我

Please ask him to call me.

14. 任何時間都可以打來。

Call anytime.

15. 謝謝你的幫忙,再見。

Thanks for your help. Good-bye.

16. 謝謝,再見。

Thank you. Good-bye.

8.2b 邀請及受邀 Invitation

Dialog 1 對話1

A: 哈囉,蘇珊,我想邀請你和你先生星期日過來吃中國菜。

A: Hello, Susan. I'd like to invite you and your husband over for Chinese food on Sunday.

B: 聽來很棒,你要煮嗎?

B: That sounds good. Are you going to cook?

A: 是的,我想讓大家嚐嚐我會做的幾道菜。

A: Yes. I want everybody to taste some of the dishes I know how to make.

B: 我們該幾點到？

B: What time should we arrive?

A: 大概5點就可以，我們會在6點左右用餐。

A: Around five will be fine. We'll eat at about six.

B: 我們該穿什麼呢？

B: How should we dress?

A: 輕鬆就可以，有6－8個人，人來就好，輕鬆一下。

A: Casual is fine. There will be six to eight people. Just come and have fun.

B: 聽起來很棒，星期天見。

B: Sounds great. See you on Sunday.

Dialog 2 對話2

A: 嗨，約翰，我想邀請你去星期六晚上的派對。

A: Hi, John. I want to invite you to a party on Saturday night.

B: 在哪裡？什麼樣的派對？

B: Where is it, and what's it for?

A: 大約晚上8點開始，好玩而已。在我家辦。

A: It will start around eight in the evening. It's just for fun. It's at my house.

B: 我該帶什麼嗎？

B: Should I bring something?

住所

郵電通訊

日常活動

銀行與保險

交通

食品與飲食

購物

社交活動

教育

休閒活動

醫療

緊急情況

A: 你不必帶任何東西，但是帶些點心或飲料也好。

A: You don't have to bring anything, but some snack foods or something to drink would be nice.

B: 好的，沒問題，我會帶些東西來分享。

B: OK. No problem. I'll bring something to share.

A: 你記得怎麼來我家嗎？

A: Do you remember how to get to my place?

B: 我想我記得，也許你該再給我地址。

B: I think so. Maybe you should give me the address again.

A: 好的，也確認一下你有我的電話。

A: Sure. Let's make sure you have my phone number, too.

Let's have a group photo.

Everybody come over here.

住所 郵電通訊 日常活動 銀行與保險 交通 食品與飲食 購物 社交活動 教育 休閒活動 醫療 緊急情況

8.2c 邀請卡樣本 Invitation Card Sample

(a) 正式邀請卡樣本 Formal Invitation Sample

Alexander E. Gaston （邀請人）

President （頭銜）

requests the pleasure of your company （榮幸邀請您的參與）

at dinner （晚餐）

in honor of Margaret Tanmal （貴賓）

Friday, the tenth of March （日期）

at seven o'clock （時間）

in the Kyle Ballroom （地點）

The Ellsinore （地址）

Collins Hills Drive

Southmeadows

map enclosed （附地圖）

R.S.V.P. Office of University Relations （請回覆聯絡辦公室）

(345) 926-3407 （聯絡電話）

Hi, John. I want to invite you to a party on Saturday night.

(b) 半正式邀請卡樣本 Semiformal Invitation Sampel

> Dr. and Mrs. Alex E. Corts （邀請人）
>
> cordially invite you （誠摯邀請您）
>
> to dinner （來晚餐）
>
> to welcome the University's new Dean （歡迎新院長）
>
> Friday, February 27 （日期）
>
> at 7 p.m. （時間）
>
> in the Canyon Room （地點）
>
> Moss Ashey University Center
>
> Response card enclosed （附上回覆卡）

8.2d 回覆：接受及拒絕邀請

Reply: Accepting and Declining the Invitation

Useful Phrases 實用語句

● **口頭接受 Accepting (verbal)**

1. 感謝你邀請我，我一定會到。

   Thanks for inviting me. I'll be there for sure.

2. 聽來很棒，我們到時候見。

   Sounds wonderful. We'll see you then.

● **口頭拒絕 Declining (verbal)**

1. 感謝你邀請我，但我有另外的約會要參加。(正式)

   Thanks for inviting me, but I have another engagement to attend. (FORMAL)

2. 聽起來很棒，但我那天晚上不行。

   That sounds great, but I can't make it that night.

351

◎ 書面接受 Accepting (written)

1. 謝謝，我們在那裡見。(簽名)

   Thanks. We'll see you there. (sign your name)

2. 期待見到你們大家。(簽名)

   Looking forward to seeing you all. (sign your name)

◎ 書面拒絕 Declining (written)

1. 謝謝你的邀請，我們那晚不能參加，希望很快在另一個聚會再見。(正式)

   Thank you for the invitation. We cannot attend that night. Hope to see you again soon on another date. (FORMAL)

2. 謝謝，但是恐怕我們沒辦法到。抱歉，以後見了。

   Thanks, but I'm afraid we can't make it. Sorry. See you later though.

 Language Power 字句補給站

◆ 晚餐派對 Dinner Parties

formal	正式的
casual	非正式的
potluck	一人帶一道菜的便飯派對
dish	一道菜肴
deli	熟食
soda	汽水
juice	果汁
orange	柳橙
grape	葡萄
grapefruit	葡萄柚
apple	蘋果
cranberry	小紅莓
wine	葡萄酒
brandy	白蘭地
champagne	香檳
cup	杯子(裝熱飲)

住所

郵電通訊

glass	玻璃杯(裝冷飲及酒)
goblet	高腳杯
cocktails	雞尾酒
whiskey	威士忌
beer	啤酒
knife	刀子
steak knife	牛排刀
fork	叉子
salad fork	沙拉叉
spoon, soup spoon	湯匙
utensils	餐具
plate	盤子
napkin	餐巾
placemat	桌墊
salt	鹽
pepper	胡椒
sugar	糖
coffee	咖啡
cream	奶精
creamer	奶精罐
salad	沙拉
salad dressing	沙拉醬
ice	冰
ice cube	冰塊
refill	續(杯)
pass the...	傳…

日常活動

銀行與保險

交通

食品與飲食

購物

社交活動

教育

休閒活動

醫療

緊急情況

8.3 接待賓客
Receiving Guests (and Gifts)

賓客到家裡時，先為他們倒飲料並請他們坐下來，如果賓客彼此不熟識，要介紹每個人給彼此認識，家裡要安排好地方，讓賓客可以自己倒飲料且有合適的空間坐下來聊天。

 Dialog 1 　對話1

A: 嗨，傑瑞，請進。

A: Hi, Jerry. Come on in.

B: 謝謝，我來的太早嗎？

B: Thanks. I'm not too early, am I?

A: 不會，已經有幾個人來了。

A: No. Several people are here already.

B: 我帶了一份禮物給新房。

B: I brought a gift for the house.

A: 太好了，謝謝，我把它跟其他的放在一起。

A: Great. Thanks. I'll put it over here with the others.

B: 好。

B: OK.

A: 我幫你把外套掛起來。

A: Let me take your coat. I'll hang it up for you.

住所

郵電通訊

日常活動

銀行與保險

交通

食品與飲食

購物

社交活動

教育

休閒活動

醫療

緊急情況

住所
郵電通訊
日常活動
銀行與保險
交通
食品與飲食
購物
社交活動
教育
休閒活動
醫療
緊急情況

B: 謝謝。

B: Good. Thank you.

A: 那邊有些食物及飲料，請自行取用。

A: There are some food and drinks over there. Please help yourself.

B: 好的，我會。

B: OK. I will.

A: 我來介紹你給一些人認識。

A: Let me introduce you to some people, too.

B: 好，謝謝。

B: Great. Thanks.

Dialog 2 （對話2）

A: 傑瑞，我來向你介紹傑克王。

A: Jerry. I'd like to introduce Jack Wong to you.

B: 嗨，很高興見到你，我是傑瑞克拉克。

B: Hi. Pleased to meet you. I'm Jerry Clark.

C: 哈囉，我是傑克王，我也很高興認識你。

C: Hello. I'm Jack Wong. I'm glad to meet you, too.

A: 我要看看其他客人，你們倆聊聊。

A: I'm going to check on some other guests. I'll leave you two to chat.

C: 沒問題，我想晚點和你多聊一些。

C: No problem. I hope to talk to you more later.

A: 喔，當然，我很快就過來，我想把你介紹給大家。

A: Oh, for sure. I'll be back soon. I want to introduce you to every-one.

B: 別擔心，我會讓他覺得自在。

B: Don't worry. I'll make him feel at home.

Useful Phrases 實用語句

1. 謝謝你邀請我。

   Thanks for inviting me.

2. 很高興你能來。

   Glad you could make it.

3. 我帶了這個(禮物)給你。

   I brought this (gift) for you.

4. 我該坐在哪裡？

   Where should I sit?

5. 請坐這裡。

   Please sit here.

6. 我來帶你看看(我家)。

   Let me show you around (the house).

7. 讓我來介紹你給大家認識。

   Let me introduce you to everyone.

8. 我來自我介紹。

   Let me introduce myself.

9. 嗨，我是班，你的大名是？

   Hi, my name's Ben. What's yours?

10. 當作在自己家(別拘束)。

    Make yourself at home.

11. 喝點東西。

Have something to drink.

12. 自行取用。

Help yourself.

13. 你要喝點東西嗎？

Would you like something to drink?

14. 洗手間在哪裡？

Where is the bathroom?

15. 我可以在哪裡掛大衣？

Where can I hang my coat?

16. 我來幫你拿夾克。

Let me take your jacket.

17. 這個我該放哪裡？

Where should I put this?

18. 放在廚房垃圾筒。

Put it in the sink [garbage can].

19. 拿給我，我會替你處理。

Give it to me. I'll take care of it for you.

Notes 小叮嚀

　　受邀參加派對，禮物通常不是必要的，除非是生日派對、準新生兒禮物派對或準新娘禮物派對；如果想送個禮物也是可以的，人們通常帶飲料或酒，主人會道謝並收下，如果主人在開門時收到禮物，會謝謝對方表示待會再拆開。如果要送主人禮物，必須知道對方的喜好並且不要買太昂貴的物品，否則主人會很困擾，糖果、玻璃製品及其他特別食品都是很好的選擇，花可以當做禮物，但是要避免送整束玫瑰這種有特別意涵的花，選花時可以請教花店的人。

　　在聚會時如果沒見過某人，通常男士們會彼此握手，如果要與人握手，在說話前就先伸出手，握緊對方的手並微笑，握手時介紹自己，不要握太久並讓他們口頭回應你的介紹；女士們也漸漸習慣握手，特別是某些專業人士，女士若認識對方或彼此是親戚還會擁抱，男士們彼此間通常不擁抱，但這要看他們之間的交情而定。談話時要保持個人及對方該有的空間，彼此相距大約為一個手臂的距離，美國人通常與對方談話時頗為輕鬆，所以在社交場合輕鬆自然就可以。

8.4 聊天
Chatting

8.4a 輕鬆的晚宴 At a Casual Dinner Party

Dialog 對話

A: 每道菜都看起來很好吃。

A: Everything looks delicious.

B: 請自行取用。

B: Please help yourself to every-thing.

住所

郵電通訊

日常活動

銀行與保險

交通

食品與飲食

購物

社交活動

教育

休閒活動

醫療

緊急情況

A: 那是什麼？

A: What is that?

B: 是肉條，我用我媽媽的食譜。

B: That's meatloaf. I used my mom's recipe.

A: 我沒吃過。

A: I've never tried it before.

B: 請拿一些，我會傳給你。

B: Please take some. I'll pass it to you.

A: 謝謝。

A: Thanks.

B: 你要喝什麼？

B: What would you like to drink?

A: 你們有果汁嗎？

A: Do you have any fruit juice?

B: 有，我們有柳橙汁及葡萄汁。

B: Yes. We have orange and grape.

A: 我要葡萄汁。

A: I'd like grape.

B: 好，也請拿些馬鈴薯泥。

B: Sure. Be sure to take some mashed potatoes, too.

 Word Bank 字庫

recipe [ˋrɛsəpɪ] n. 食譜

 Useful Phrases 實用語句

1. 嗨，怎麼樣啊？
   Hi, how's it going?
2. 有什麼事嗎？
   What's up?
3. 有新鮮事嗎？
   What's new?
4. 你好嗎？
   Hi, how are you doing?
5. 好久不見。
   Long time no see!
6. 最近好嗎？
   How have you been?
7. 你看起來很好。
   You look well.
8. 你看來很棒。
   You look great!
9. 你的家人好嗎？
   How is your family?
10. 很開心又看到你。
    Great to see you again.
11. 你打扮得真好。
    You're dressed well.
12. 你的洋裝很可愛。
    Your dress is lovely.
13. 你的衣服很好。
    Your clothing is very nice.

住所｜郵電通訊｜日常活動｜銀行與保險｜交通｜食品與飲食｜購物｜社交活動｜教育｜休閒活動｜醫療｜緊急情況

14. 我覺得還不錯。

I feel OK.

15. 你的身體還好嗎？

How's your health?

16. 不賴。

Not bad.

17. 最近不怎麼好。

Not so good lately.

18. 很糟。

Pretty bad.

19. 我想很好。

Pretty good I think.

20. 我 (健康) 夠好了，謝謝。

I'm well enough, thanks.

8.4b 正式晚宴 At a Formal Dinner Party

Dialog 對話

A: 大家晚安！

A: Good evening, everyone!

B: 晚安，連先生。

B: Good evening, Mr. Lien.

A: 我可以坐這裡嗎？

A: May I sit here?

B: 當然，請便。

B: Yes, of course. Please do.

A: 我看大家已經到這裡了，我好像有點遲到。

A: I see everyone is here already. I'm afraid I'm a little late.

B: 不盡然，我們正為大家倒酒，要不要來一點？

B: No, not really. We were just pouring wine for everyone. Would you like some?

A: 好的，謝謝。

A: Yes, please.

B: 我們在喝紅酒，你可以喝嗎？

B: We're having a red right now. Is it alright for you?

A: 可以，謝謝。

A: That will be fine, thank you.

B: 你公司最近如何？

B: How are things going at the company these days?

A: 事實上不錯。我該告訴你明年的計畫。

A: Not bad actually. I should tell you about our plans for next year.

B: 我想知道，請說。

B: I'd like to know. Please go on.

住所
郵電通訊
日常活動
銀行與保險
交通
食品與飲食
購物
社交活動
教育
休閒活動
醫療
緊急情況

Notes 小叮嚀

　　餐桌禮儀在美國並不難理解，尤其在輕鬆的場合，人們不會在滿口食物時交談，但在餐桌上與他人談話是應該的；餐巾通常是拿來擺在腿上而不是放在桌上使用，拿遠的食物時要讓別人幫你傳過來，而不是自己伸長手去拿以免失禮。

　　參加較正式場合，必須穿著得體、坐姿合宜並說些禮貌性的對話，如果有敬酒祝賀及外燴服務，別給小費，說聲「謝謝」即可。正式場合可能有演講，這時要避免用餐，但可以繼續喝東西，正式場合需要禮貌及保守的言談舉止，與其他人共同創造出愉悅的交誼環境。

 Useful Phrases 實用語句

● **聊天話題──天氣 Topics for Chatting － Weather**

1. 今天天氣很好。

   The weather is good today.

2. 你覺得今天天氣如何？

   What do you think of the weather today?

3. 天氣如何？

   How's the weather?

4. 今天多雲。

   It's cloudy today.

5. 我希望雨停。

   I hope the rain stops.

6. 我希望別下雨了。

   I hope it stops raining.

7. 我希望不要下雨。

   I hope it doesn't rain.

8. 這裡的天氣通常如何？

   What's the weather like around here usually?

9. 今天真熱。

   It's really hot today.

10. 今天有點涼。

It's a little cool today.

11. 你想今天會下雪嗎？

Do you think it will snow today?

12. 今天天氣真棒。

The weather is great today.

Tips 小祕訣

　　美國人談論天氣多為談話的開場白，其實真正談論天氣並不多。

● 工作 Jobs

1. 你從事什麼職業？

What do you do?

2. 你在哪裡工作？

Where do you work?

3. 你在那裡工作多久了？

How long have you worked there?

4. 你喜歡那裡嗎？

Do you like it there?

5. 你打算住在那裡嗎？

Do you plan to stay there?

6. 那工作有趣嗎？

Is it an interesting job?

7. 你公司有多少人？

How many people are there in the company?

8. 我喜歡我的工作。

I like my job.

9. 我的工作普通。

My job is so so.

住所

郵電通訊

日常活動

銀行與保險

交通

食品與飲食

購物

社交活動

教育

休閒活動

醫療

緊急情況

364

10. 我想換工作。

I'd like to change my job.

11. 我必須加班。

I have to work overtime.

12. 你加班工作多嗎？

Do you work much overtime?

13. 你的老闆如何？

How's your boss?

14. 有升遷的機會。

There are chances for promotion.

15. 你可以升遷嗎？

Can you get promotions?

16. 它是一個很好的工作場所。

It's a pretty good place to work.

● 關於房子 About a House

1. 你有個可愛的家。

You have a lovely home.

2. 這桌子很漂亮。

This is a beautiful table.

3. 你一定喜歡住在這裡。

You must like living here.

4. 誰漆這些油漆？

Who did these paintings?

5. 你自己布置的嗎？

Did you decorate yourself?

6. 你家很舒適。

Your home is so comfortable.

7. 你的庭院看起來很棒。

Your yard looks great.

8. 你的後院很好。

Your backyard is very nice.

9. 裡面有很多空間。

You have a lot of room inside.

10. 我喜歡你布置的方式。

I like the way you have decorated.

● 家庭照片 Family Pictures

1. 看一下我的家庭相簿。

Have a look at my family photo album.

2. 這些相片很好。

These photos are nice.

3. 這些人是誰？

Who are these people?

4. 他們是你的小孩嗎？

Are those your children?

5. 你有很多好照片。

You have a lot of nice pictures.

6. 還有嗎？

Do you have any more?

 Notes 小叮嚀

　　不管是正式或輕鬆的社交活動，談話內容不要牽涉到個人隱私，在與對方不熟的情況下，有關婚姻或政治話題，尤其要避免；可以交談的話題如運動、工作，娛樂方面像電影、戲劇、音樂活動、歌手、演員等，其他如值得一去的好地方、個人嗜好、慶典活動等都是好話題。

住所
郵電通訊
日常活動
銀行與保險
交通
食品與飲食
購物
社交活動
教育
休閒活動
醫療
緊急情況

8.5 祝賀及拜訪
Congratulating and Visiting

Dialog 對話

A: 我要謝謝你今天來這裡。

A: I want to thank you for being here today.

B: 我的榮幸，我很高興你今天邀我來拜訪。

B: My pleasure. I'm very glad you invited me to visit today.

A: 你來我公司的升遷活動，對我意義重大。

A: It means a lot to me that you have come to my company's promotional event.

B: 真的，我很高興來參加，還有要恭喜你的升遷。

B: Really, I'm happy to attend. By the way, congratulations on your promotion.

A: 謝謝，我對這件事感到很興奮。

A: Thank you. I'm very excited about it.

B: 你會繼續留在這辦公室工作嗎？

B: Will you continue to work out of this office?

A: 會，再六個月，然後就搬到城的另一邊。

A: Yes, for the next six months, then I'll move across town.

8.6 派對種類及習俗說明
Kinds of Parties and Explanation of Traditions

8.6a 生日派對 At a Birthday Party

 Dialog 對話

A: 嗨,傑瑞,生日快樂!

A: Hi, Jerry. Happy birthday!

B: 謝謝,貝蒂。

B: Thanks, Betty.

A: 我買了個禮物給你。

A: I brought you a gift.

B: 謝謝,我會等會再拆。

B: Thanks. I'll open it later.

B: 進來認識我其他的朋友。

B: Come in and meet some of my other friends.

A: 好。

A: OK.

B: 等一下,他們正把蛋糕拿出來。

B: Wait, they're bringing out the cake.

住所
郵電通訊
日常活動
銀行與保險
交通
食品與飲食
購物
社交活動
教育
休閒活動
醫療
緊急情況

A: 看那些蠟燭！你幾歲了？

A: Look at all those candles! How old are you?

B: 很(不)好笑，來吧，我來吹熄它們。

B: Very funny. Come on. I'll blow them out.

A: 你得先許願。

A: You have to make a wish first.

B: 我知道。

B: I know that.

A: 還有你得一次吹掉所有蠟燭。

A: And you have to blow out all the candles on the first try.

B: 為什麼？

B: Why?

A: 不然願望不會實現。

A: Otherwise the wish won't come true.

B: 我不知道還有這回事。

B: I didn't know that.

Useful Phrases 實用語句

1. 我需要為派對買些東西。

   I need to buy some things for the party.

2. 我要弄些裝飾。

   I want to get some decorations.

3. 最近的派對用品專賣店在哪裡？

   Where is the nearest party store?

4. 請來參加我的生日派對。

   Please come to my birthday party.

5. 你的生日派對在什麼時候？

   When is your birthday party?

6. 我想邀請你的小孩來我兒子的生日派對。

   I want to invite your kids to my son's birthday party.

7. 我買了個禮物。

   I brought a gift.

8. 吃些蛋糕。

   Have some cake.

9. 這裡是一些派對小禮物 (道別時送給客人)。

   Here are some party favors.

10. 我們狂歡吧！

    Let's party!

 Language Power 字句補給站

◆ 歡樂派對 Fun Parties

birthday boy [girl]	壽星 (男[女])
birthday, b-day	生日
birthday cake	生日蛋糕
birthday card	生日卡
invitation	邀請
candles	蠟燭
present, gift	禮物
party favors	(道別時送給客人之)派對小禮物
noisemaker	發出聲響的物品
party [funny] hat	派對帽
balloon	氣球
ribbon	彩帶，緞帶
confetti	碎紙片
glow light	螢光

住所

郵電通訊

日常活動

銀行與保險

交通

食品與飲食

購物

社交活動

教育

休閒活動

醫療

緊急情況

370

| surprise party | 驚喜派對 |
| gift wrapping paper | 包裝紙 |

Tips 小祕訣

美國壽星不分年紀大小，通稱「birthday boy [girl]」。

Cultural Tips 文化祕笈

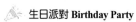 聚會派對須知

除了一般的聚會派對之外，不同主題的派對，人們有不同的期待。

生日派對 Birthday Party

如果是小孩的生日，帶份禮物並準備唱歌和玩遊戲；如果是 21 歲生日，通常會喝很多酒，因為在美國 21 歲是可以合法喝酒的開始。雖說每個人慶祝生日有差異，一般而言，快到 30 歲時，生日派對就會平靜許多。

準新娘派對及準新生兒派對 Bridal Shower & Baby Shower

準新娘派對及準新生兒派對都是女士的派對，送禮物給準新娘和準新生兒、吃簡單的點心並聊很多女士們的話題，通常都是很輕鬆隨性的派對。

單身派對 Bachelor's Party

單身派對是準新郎單身的最後一個派對，喝酒、進食、限制級的笑話及男士間的話題，隨意穿著即可，會有一些很活躍或較瘋狂的活動。

週年派對 Anniversary Party

通常是在一些好餐廳舉辦的平靜晚餐，因此需要合宜的穿著打扮，飲酒及舉杯祝福是很平常的。

餞行派對 Farewell Party

類似週年派對，但多與公司有關，飲酒及舉杯祝福升遷而必須搬

住所
郵電通訊
日常活動
銀行與保險
交通
食品與飲食
購物
社交活動
教育
休閒活動
醫療
緊急情況

到另一城市或州的人 (們)，需要正式的穿著打扮。

開放參觀及親師會 Open House & Parent-Teacher Events

這類的聚會都是較安靜的活動，人們藉此機會在友善的氣氛裡碰面並詢問學校、教會或其他場所的情況，可以穿著舒適衣著前往，會場備有飲料及點心。

喬遷之喜派對 House Warming Party

這是參觀某人新房子或新鄰居家裡的聚會，習慣上要帶份禮物，且是新房子或新家用得到的東西。

畢業派對 Graduation Party

這是家裡有人畢業或畢業生們舉辦的派對，不管是哪一種都少不了香檳及狂歡，為畢業生準備小禮物，穿舒適的衣著並準備照相吧！此派對和 21 歲生日頗為類似。

萬聖節及化裝派對 Halloween and Costume Parties

這些是有趣的派對，可以打扮成任何你想要的樣子，萬聖節時的巫婆、骷髏、鬼及其他怪物相當受歡迎，但也可以打扮成其他你喜歡的樣子；除了奇怪的飲料、食物及糖果外，如果是成年人的派對，有時也會有酒精飲料。

感恩節晚餐 [派對]

這是家庭成員聚在一起用餐團圓的日子，如果受邀參加感恩節晚餐，穿著乾淨、舒適、輕便的衣著，享受家庭氣氛的用餐及談話，不需帶禮物。

耶誕節晚餐 [派對]

像感恩節一樣，耶誕節也是家庭團聚的日子，但是要交換禮物，因此受邀參加耶誕節晚餐時，要準備一份給邀請者全家的禮物並帶著開心和善的態度，享用耶誕晚餐。

新年派對 New Year Party

這是狂歡慶祝新年到來的時刻，暢飲、跳舞、祝賀、聊天及從事任何可以讓你開心的活動，對一年最後一晚而言都是合適的，有

些派對是正式的，但大多數不是，享受美好時光就對了。

街坊聚會 Block Party

這是大型的鄰居聚會，大夥兒到一戶或幾戶人家拜訪，大部分是在戶外舉辦，每個人帶些食物來與大家分享，通常會有啤酒及其他冷飲，鄰居們聊天、用餐及照相，穿著完全以舒服輕便為原則。

聚餐派對 Potluck Party

通常美國人會辦聚餐派對及烤肉活動，參加這類活動，每個人要準備一道菜或買些飲料或從熟食店帶來的食物、點心，聚餐派對類似街坊派對，但是規模比較小一點。

 Language Power 字句補給站

◆ 舉杯祝賀 Toasting

舉杯祝賀在社交活動是很平常的，常說的祝賀內容及場合如下：

1.	祝你健康！(退休時)	To your health!
2.	好好享用美食！(法文，晚餐活動時)	Bon Appétit! [ˌbɔnapeˋti]
3.	旅途平安！	Safe voyage!
4.	旅途愉快！	Bon voyage! (Have a nice trip!)
5.	恭喜！(畢業、升遷、婚禮時)	Congratulations!
6.	敬好友！(朋友聚會時)	Here's to good friends!
7.	乾杯！(任何活動)	Cheers!

8.6b 離開時道別及感謝 Leave Taking and Thanking

 Useful Phrases 實用語句

1. 我得走了。

I have to go now.

2. 謝謝你來。

   Thank you for coming.

3. 我很享受這個派對。

   I've enjoyed the party.

4. 別忘了你的東西。

   Don't forget your things.

5. 請問我的大衣在哪裡？

   Where is my coat, please?

6. 等一下，我來拿你的大衣。

   Just a moment, I'll get your coat.

7. 請再來。

   Please come again.

8. 我希望很快看到你。

   I hope to see you again soon.

9. 晚點見。

   See you later.

10. 很快再見到你。

    See you again soon.

11. 放輕鬆。

    Take it easy.

12. 替我向大家說哈囉 [再見]。

    Say hello [goodbye] to everyone for me.

13. 保重。

    Take care.

14. 再見 [回頭見]。

    See you around.

15. 祝你有個美好一天。

    Have a nice day!

16. 晚點見。

    Later.

17. 再見。

    See ya.

住所
郵電通訊
日常活動
銀行與保險
交通
食品與飲食
購物
社交活動
教育
休閒活動
醫療
緊急情況

18. 再見(西班牙語)。

Adiós.

8.6c 感謝卡 Thank-You Card

在接受別人幫忙或受邀參加了某類活動後，美國人通常會寄出感謝卡向對方致意。

Useful Phrases 實用語句

1. 謝謝你上星期幫我。

Thanks for helping me out last week.

2. 謝謝你做的一切。

Thanks for everything.

3. 謝謝你邀請我，聚會很棒。

Thanks for inviting me. It was great.

4. 聚會很棒，謝謝你到場。

The event was great. Thanks for being there.

5. 謝謝你，希望很快再看到你。

Thank you and hope to see you again soon.

6. 謝謝你的光臨，如有任何需要請來電。

Thank you for attending. Please call if you have any needs.

Unit 9 Education

教育

美國的學校是個開放的學習環境,強調引導下的創造性,測驗評量確定學習成效,透過課堂表現及其他形式的評量,教師得以了解學生學習情形。家長期望學校提供一個使子女發展潛力、養成獨立人格的學習環境,在完成十二年基礎教育後,具備解決問題的基本能力。大學是高等教育場所,提供學生研讀專門科系的環境、設備、知識及挑戰。

教育

9.1 美國學制說明
Educational System in America

美國擁有頂尖大學及學院,基礎教育也很好,但每個社區學校品質不同,公立學校免費入學,私立學校收費昂貴。小孩從五歲開始就學,進入K-12系統,即幼稚園 (kindergarten) 一年 (為進入小學準備,許多小學也附設幼稚園)、小學 (grade [elementary] school) 六年、國中 (junior high [middle] school) 兩年、高中 (high school) 四年,總共十二年基礎教育結束;大學及學院對外州生收費較高,對外國學生收費更高。

歲 數	學 校	年 級/年 數
3-4	托兒所 (nursery school)	
K-12 開始		
5	幼稚園 (kindergarten)	
6-11	小學 (elementary school)	1到6年級 (first-sixth grades)
12-13	國中 (middle school)	7到8年級 (seventh-eighth grades)
14-17	高中 (high school)	9到12年級 (ninth-twelfth grades)
基礎教育結束		
18 and over	大學 (college, university)	4年
	研究所 (graduate school)	

Language Power　字句補給站

◆ 學校 Schools

day care center	托兒中心
nursery school	托兒所
kindergarten	幼稚園
elementary [primary, grade] school	小學
junior high [middle] school	國中
high school	高中
register	註冊
enroll	入學

住所 郵電通訊 日常活動 銀行與保險 交通 食品與飲食 購物 社交活動 教育 休閒活動 醫療 緊急情況

teacher, instructor	老師
classrooms	教室
textbooks	教科書
admin [administrations] office	教務處
class schedule	課表
lab class	實習課
tuition	學費
professor	教授
audit	旁聽
credits	學分
diploma	學位
required [elective] class	必[選]修
Bachelor's Degree	大學學位
B.S.	理學士
B.A.	文學士
undergraduate program	大學課程
graduate program	研究所課程
Master's [Graduate] Degree	碩士學位
M.S.	理學碩士
M.A.	文學碩士
MBA	企管碩士
Doctorate	博士學位
PhD.	博士
lecture	講課
seminar	討論會
workshop	工作坊
presentation	介紹，報告
speech	演講
oral report	口頭報告
written report	書面報告
placement test	分級測驗
interview	面談
take notes	做筆記
group discussion	小組討論
team [group] project	團體作業

住所
郵電通訊
日常活動
銀行與保險
交通
食品與飲食
購物
社交活動
教育
休閒活動
醫療
緊急情況

9.2 托兒所
Nursery School/Day Care Center

 Dialog 對話

A: 早安，我在為我的小孩找日間托育。

A: Good morning. I'm looking for day care for my child.

B: 請坐，讓我告訴你我們提供什麼。

B: Please sit down, and let me tell you about what we offer.

A: 謝謝。

A: Thank you.

B: 我們是有執照的托兒中心，我們的設備已通過政府的健康及安全檢查。

B: We are a licensed day care center. Our facility has passed all government inspections for health and safety.

A: 你們有多少員工？

A: How many staff do you have?

B: 我們有四位員工，但只有兩位實際上是托兒中心的負責人。

B: We have four staff, but only two of us are actual daycare providers.

A: 你們要照顧多少小孩？

A: How many children do you take care of?

B: 我們每天只能照顧14位小孩。

B: We are only allowed to take in fourteen children a day.

住所 郵電通訊 日常活動 銀行與保險 交通 食品與飲食 購物 社交活動 教育 休閒活動 醫療 緊急情況

A: 有名額給我的小孩嗎？	**A:** Is there enough room for my child?
B: 目前我們還可以多收三個小孩。	**B:** Currently we are able to accept three more children.
A: 這裡收費多少？	**A:** How much does it cost here?
B: 我們每個月收費350元。	**B:** We charge \$350 a month.

 Word Bank 字庫

staff [stæf] n. (一組)工作人員
inspection [ɪn`spɛkʃən] n. 檢查

Useful Phrases 實用語句

○ 父 / 母 Parent

1. 我的小孩很害羞。

   My child is shy.

2. 我的小孩很活潑。

   My child is active.

3. 我的小孩脾氣暴躁。

   My child has a temper.

4. 我的寶貝在長牙。

   My baby is teething.

5. 我的小孩還在用奶瓶。

   My child is still using a bottle.

6. 我的寶貝喜歡人抱。

   My baby likes to be held.

7. 她要 (拍背) 打嗝。

She needs to be burped.

8. 她牙牙學語。

She babbles.

9. 他喜歡爬來爬去。

He likes to crawl around a lot.

10. 他會用馬桶。

He uses the toilet.

11. 他會尿床。

He wets the bed.

12. 他會尿褲子。

He wets his pants.

13. 我不准他吃甜食。

I don't let him eat sweets.

14. 她仍吸吮拇指。

She still sucks her thumb.

◎ 負責人 Provider

1. 他整天哭。

He cried all day.

2. 他跟其他小孩玩得開心。

He plays well with the others.

3. 他好像有點生病。

He seems a little sick.

4. 他沒睡午覺。

He did not take a nap.

5. 她跟一個小孩打架。

She fought with one of the other kids.

6. 她跌倒擦傷膝蓋了。

She fell and scraped her knees.

7. 護士處理了她的傷。

The nurse took care of her injury.

住所 郵電通訊 日常活動 銀行與保險 交通 食品與飲食 購物 社交活動 教育 休閒活動 醫療 緊急情況

◆ 照顧幼兒 Child Care

breast feeding	哺乳
formula	配方奶粉
baby food	嬰兒食物
burp	打嗝
diaper	尿布
cradle	搖籃
high chair	孩童高腳椅
toddler	剛學步的小孩
infant	嬰兒
pacifier	奶嘴

Notes 小叮嚀

　　托兒中心 (day care center) 或家庭托兒 (home day care) 不難找，但品質及收費各有不同，選擇托兒中心時要注意負責人是否有好聲望，是否有基本準則，是否提供啟發性的活動，是否具備體貼又有素質的老師及員工，是否有執照，是否可以讓家長接送小孩有彈性，以及是否從開關門時間到緊急應變都有妥善規範及執行能力。

9.3 幼稚園
Kindergarten

Dialog 1 對話1

A: 哈囉，我小孩要上課，我想了解這裡的課程。

A: Hello. I'd like to know about classes for my child here.

B: 請坐，讓我告訴你我們的課程。

B: Please sit down. Let me tell you about our program.

住所
郵電通訊
日常活動
銀行與保險
交通
食品與飲食
購物
社交活動
教育
休閒活動
醫療
緊急情況

A: 謝謝。

A: Thanks.

B: 我們有星期一到星期五的課程，但也有週末的課程。

B: We have a Monday through Friday schedule, but offer weekend classes, too.

A: 我知道了，週末課程比較貴嗎？

A: I see. Are the weekend classes more expensive?

B: 如果你一次付全年費用的話就不會。

B: Not if you pay the full year fee at once.

A: 你們還有其他付款選擇嗎？

A: What other payment options do you have?

B: 你可以月付、每三個月或每半年付一次。

B: You can pay by the month, every three months or six months.

A: 都是一樣費用嗎？

A: Is it all the same rate?

B: 不一樣，你報越久的課程並繳清，全部費用越少。

B: No. The longer you sign up and pay for, the less it costs overall.

Word Bank 字庫

kindergarten [`kɪndə‚ˌgɑrtn̩] n. 幼稚園
option [`ɑpʃən] n. 選擇
fee [fi] n. 費用

Dialog 2 對話2

A: 每個老師要帶幾個小孩？

A: How many children per teacher are there?

B: 我們一個老師帶七個小孩。

B: We have one teacher for each seven students.

A: 有遊樂場嗎？

A: Is there a playground?

B: 有，我們有經常維修、設備完整的遊樂場。

B: Yes. We have a fully equipped playground constantly monitored.

A: 老師的資格呢？

A: What are your teacher's qualifications?

B: 我們的老師都是大學畢業。

B: All our teachers are university graduates.

A: 幾點開始上課？

A: What time does the school start?

B: 早上7:30開始，7:30以後你可以載小孩到這裡。

B: It opens at 7:30 a.m. You can drop your child off anytime after that.

A: 幾點要來接他呢？

A: What time do I have to pick him up?

B: 下午3點放學，但我們到5點都有人在這裡。

B: Classes end by 3:00 p.m., but we have people here until 5:00.

Word Bank 字庫

fully equipped adj. 完整設備的
playground [ˋpleˏɡraʊnd] n. 遊樂場
constantly [ˋkɑnstəntlɪ] adv. 經常地
monitor [ˋmɑnətɚ] v., n. 維護，看管
qualification [ˏkwɑləfəˋkeʃən] n. 資格
graduate [ˋɡrædʒʊɪt] n. 大學畢業
drop off 卸下，下(車)
pick up 接

Notes 小叮嚀

托兒所 (day care center) 提供0-3或5歲小孩的照顧及活動，幼兒所 (nursery school) 提供2-3或5歲，幼稚園 (kindergarten) 提供5歲左右小孩學習的課程，家長當然必須對設備及人員有所了解，才能將小孩放心託付照顧。

住所 郵電通訊 日常活動 銀行與保險 交通 食品與飲食 購物 社交活動 教育 休閒活動 醫療 緊急情況

 Useful Phrases 實用語句

1. 請告訴我你們的課程。

   Please tell me about your curriculum.

2. 我想看你們的設備。

   I'd like to see your facilities.

3. 你們提供午餐嗎？

   Do you provide lunches?

4. 你們有育兒訓練嗎？

   Do you have nursing training?

5. 你們有什麼規定？

   What are your rules?

6. 你們開業多久了？

   How long have you been in business?

7. 你們提供什麼玩具？

   What toys do you provide?

8. 遊樂場安全嗎？

   Is the playground safe?

9. 我什麼時候可以接送小孩？

   What time can I drop off and pick up my child?

10. 你們怎麼訓練小孩守紀律？

    How do you discipline the children?

住所　郵電通訊　日常活動　銀行與保險　交通　食品與飲食　購物　社交活動　教育　休閒活動　醫療　緊急情況

9.4 小學及高中
Grade School and High School

美國合法居民的小孩可以免費上公立學校，學校依稅基、州及當地規範、社區需求及其他條件決定品質。公立學校都是男女合校 (co-ed)，平均師生比約為 1:20，學生必須達到課程最基本要求才能畢業。

私立學校收費至少 \$25,000 以上，私校有的是男女分校，有的是合校；有的私立學校是教會學校，有些是預備學校(prep school)，學生以進入名校為目標，私立學校師生比約為 1:18。

中小學並不算學期制，而是學年制，中小學九月初開學一直上到六月中結束，學生上課時間通常為週一到週五早上 8:00 到下午 3:00，之後是體育活動或其他課外活動，休假時間為耶誕節及新年一週(不像大學有三至四週寒假)，春假一週，暑假從六月中到八月約兩個半月；需要補救教學的學生，可能有輔導課要上。如果學校財力允許，可能提供有規劃的夏季活動。

9.4a 為小孩上學註冊 Registering a Child for School

Dialog 對話

A: 嗨，我是傑生胡，我需要為小孩上學註冊。

A: Hi. My name is Jason Hu. I need to register my children for school.

B: 好的，胡先生，你是新來這地區的嗎？

B: Certainly, Mr. Hu. Are you new to the area?

A: 是的，我們約兩個月前搬到這裡。

A: Yes. We moved here about two months ago.

B: 好,你要先填一些表格。

B: Alright. First you will need to fill out some forms.

A: 我帶了身分證明及居住身分資料。

A: I brought identification and residency status information with me.

B: 很好。

B: Great.

A: 我知道學校已經開學了,那會有問題嗎?

A: I know school started already. Is that a problem?

B: 你的小孩會有一點落後,但我們有為像你們這種情況所設的補救課程。

B: Your children will be a little behind, but we have make up programs for families in situations like yours.

A: 那樣很好。

A: That's good.

B: 我們將需要測驗你小孩的英語能力。

B: We'll have to test your children's English ability.

A: 我們有在母國的測驗結果。

A: We have test results from our home country.

B: 好,我們可以用那些結果決定他們能力表現的程度。

B: Good. We can use those results to determine their level of performance capability.

B: 他們仍然需要經過我們幾個教外籍生英語的老師面談。

B: They'll still have to go through an interview process with a couple of our ESL instructors.

A: 好。

A: OK.

Word Bank 字庫

register [`rɛdʒɪstə] v. 註冊
residency [`rɛzədənsɪ] n. 居住
status [`stetəs] n. 身分
ESL(English as a Second Language) 英語為第二語，即外籍人士學習英語

Useful Phrases 實用語句

1. 我要如何註冊學校？

   How do I register for school?

2. 我要如何為小孩上學註冊？

   How do I register my children for school?

3. 填這些表。

   Fill out these forms.

4. 這是我的身分證明。

   Here is my identification.

5. 我的小孩該上幾年級？

   Which grade will my child be in?

6. 他會上五年級。

   He will be in the fifth grade.

7. 我要出示什麼？

   What do I need to show?

8. 學校何時開學？

   When does school start?

住所
郵電通訊
日常活動
銀行與保險
交通
食品與飲食
購物
社交活動
教育
休閒活動
醫療
緊急情況

9. 緊急時候我要聯絡誰？

Who can I contact in case of emergency?

10. 我何時可以和他的老師們談話？

When can I talk to his teachers?

9.4b 找老師談話 Talking to a Teacher about the Child

Dialog 對話

A: 嗨，李太太，請坐。

A: Hi, Mrs. Lee. Please sit down.

B: 謝謝，我想告訴你關於我兒子的幾件事。

B: Thanks. I'd like to tell you a few things about my son.

A: 好，請說。

A: Certainly, please.

B: 我兒子用功讀書，但不太跟其他人一起玩。

B: My son studies hard, but doesn't play with others much.

A: 這是個問題嗎？

A: Is it a problem?

B: 我想他因為語言隔閡而害羞。

B: I think he is shy because of the language barrier.

A: 是的，我知道他的母語是中文。

A: Yes. I know he is a native Chinese speaker.

住所
郵電通訊
日常活動
銀行與保險
交通
食品與飲食
購物
社交活動
教育
休閒活動
醫療
緊急情況

B: 我可以幫他什麼忙嗎？

B: Is there anything I can do to help him?

A: 我想我們要確定他會參加英語活動營。

A: I think we should make sure he is going to the ESL activity club.

B: 聽起來很好，有什麼樣的活動呢？

B: That sounds very good. What kinds of activity does it have?

A: 有很多有趣的活動給外籍學生，讓他們交朋友、練習英語及純粹玩樂。

A: The club has many fun activities for foreign students that allow them to make friends, practice English, and just have fun.

✎ Word Bank 字庫

language barrier n. 語言隔閡
native [`netɪv] adj. 道地的

9.4c 聯絡老師為子女請假
Contacting a Teacher for Taking Leave

Dialog 對話

A: 嗨，你是安德森先生嗎？

A: Hi. Are you Mr. Anderson?

B: 是的，我是。

B: Yes, I am.

住所

郵電通訊

日常活動

銀行與保險

交通

食品與飲食

購物

社交活動

教育

休閒活動

醫療

緊急情況

A: 我是潘蜜拉許。

A: I'm Pamela Hsu.

B: 喔，是啊，你是珊蒂的媽媽。

B: Oh, yes. You are Sandy's mom.

A: 是的，我女兒下週一必須缺課。

A: Yes, that's right. My daughter must miss class on Monday, next week.

B: 我知道了，希望沒有什麼問題才好。

B: I see. I hope there is no problem.

A: 她必須為了牙套去看牙醫。

A: She must go to a dentist because of her braces.

B: 我知道了，我會給你她那天的作業，她可以在家準備。

B: I see. I'll give you that day's assignment, so she can prepare at home.

A: 非常謝謝你。

A: Thank you very much.

✎ Word Bank 字庫

dentist [`dɛntɪst] n. 牙醫
braces [`bresɪz] n. 牙套

9.4d 校車 School Bus

Dialog 對話

A: 哈囉,我的名字是約翰謝,我想知道校車何時會從我們家經過。

A: Hello. My name is John Hsieh. I'd like to know what time the school bus comes by our house.

B: 你的地址是?

B: What is your address?

A: 南聖街564號。

A: 564 South Holly Street.

B: 你一定是凱莉謝的父親。

B: You must be Kelly Hsieh's dad.

A: 是啊,沒錯。

A: Yes, that's right.

B: 校車大約早上7:30及下午5:30經過你家。

B: The bus should come by your home around 7:30 a.m., and 5:30 p.m.

A: 謝謝,我的小孩要在哪裡上車?

A: Thank you. Where should my child go to get on the bus?

B: 校車在南聖街及格蘭街口停車接幾個小孩。

B: The bus stops to pick up several children at the corner of South Holly and Grant Street.

住所 郵電通訊 日常活動 銀行與保險 交通 食品與飲食 購物 社交活動 教育 休閒活動 醫療 緊急情況

A: 我知道了，那離我們家很近，再次謝謝你。

A: I see. That's very close to our home. Thanks again.

9.4e 午餐 Lunch

Dialog 對話

A: 我想買午餐卡。

A: I want to buy a lunch card.

B: 好的，你可以在這裡的總辦公室買。

B: Sure. You can buy it here in the main office.

A: 多少錢？

A: How much is it?

B: 你要買一年嗎？

B: Do you want to buy it for the whole year?

A: 是的。

A: Yes.

B: 50元。

B: It costs $50.

A: 自助餐何時開門？

A: What time does the cafeteria open?

B: 中午12點到1點開門。

B: It's open from 12:00 noon to 1:00.

A: 有菜單嗎?

A: Is there a menu?

B: 菜色是固定的,但每天換,你可以在學校網站看到。

B: The serving is set, but it changes every day. You can check it out on the school's website.

A: 學校有其他的用餐地方嗎?

A: Are there any other food outlets available in the school?

B: 有,學校兩邊有兩個全天開的福利社,還有販賣機。

B: Yes. There are two snack bars open all day at both ends of the school, and there are vending machines, too.

A: 謝謝你的幫忙。

A: Thanks for your help.

 Word Bank 字庫

cafeteria [kæfə`tırıə] n. 自助餐
vending machine n. 販賣機

9.4f 外籍學生英語課程 ESL Program

 Dialog 對話

A: 我想了解學校的英語課程。

A: I'd like to find out some information about the school's ESL program.

B: 你想知道什麼呢？

B: What would you like to know?

A: 我想知道是誰教的。

A: I'd like to know who teaches it.

B: 我們有許多優秀老師，如果你想，可以和他們見面。

B: We have several well-qualified teachers. You can meet them if you'd like.

A: 我知道了，謝謝，班級大嗎？

A: I see. Thanks. Are the classes large?

B: 不大，事實上有些才三、四個學生，絕不會超過八個。

B: No. Actually some only have three or four students. There is never more than eight.

A: 每天都有課嗎？

A: Are the classes everyday?

B: 是的，每堂兩小時。

B: Yes, and each class lasts two hours.

A: 你們有其他英語課程嗎？

A: Do you have other ESL programs?

住所 郵電通訊 日常活動 銀行與保險 交通 食品跟飲食 購物 社交活動 教育 休閒活動 醫療 緊急情況

B: 有，我們也有密集班，每天四小時，週一到週五。

B: Yes. We have an intensive program, too. It lasts four hours every day, Monday through Friday.

Word Bank 字庫

well-qualified [`wɛl`kwɑləfaɪd] adj. 資格好的

intensive [ɪn`tɛnsɪv] adj. 密集的

9.4g 關於在美國上學身分規定
Status Regarding Attending School in America

因為愛國法案及反恐規定，簽證申請規定經常修正，以下是打算長住美國的外國人要了解的最新簽證規定：

1. 到美國讀書需要 F1 簽證，配偶及子女可以申請 F2 簽證赴美同住，小孩可以在美就讀，但配偶不得在美就讀或工作。
2. 到美國讀書當交換學生需要 J1 簽證，配偶及子女可以申請 J2 簽證赴美同住，小孩可以在美就讀，但配偶不得在美就讀或工作。
3. 如果在美工作或訓練需要 H 簽證，配偶及子女可以申請 H4 簽證赴美同住，小孩可以就讀，但配偶不得工作。

以上所指子女必須是 21 歲以下。只要就讀或工作的簽證合法，且合法申請配偶及子女的簽證，其簽證及身分就受到合法保護，子女可以和當地居民的子女一樣免費就讀中小學；但有些美國公民才享有的權利，例如社會安全福利，並不包含在內，這是在成為美國公民 5 年後 (或更久，要看規定) 才有的福利，相關問題可以請教移民局 (USCIS, U.S. Citizenship and Immigration Service)。

9.4h 關於學校規定 School Regulations

每州對於學校的規定不同，但都包含對出缺席、考試、評分、師生衣著、禁藥和槍械，以及校內的行為規範。

住所
郵電通訊
日常活動
銀行與保險
交通
食品與飲食
購物
社交活動
教育
休閒活動
醫療
緊急情況

出缺席 (Attendance)

國、高中學生出席是強制的，除非生病、喪假或其他合理的理由，如果學生缺席，學校會通知家長，所以子女無法到校時，最好先聯絡學校。

考試及評分標準 (Testing and Grading Standards)

是由州及聯邦政府規定的，小考、大型的紙筆測驗、全面學科考試、作業、演講及報告和其他課堂活動都是經常性且強制的，當然這些都是作為學科評分的依據。也有一些定期的標準測驗檢驗每個學生每學科的表現，如果請假核准，通常可以補考；評分經常以100分為基準，100-90是A，89-80是B，79-70是C，69-60是D，60以下是F不及格。

穿著規定 (Dress Codes)

對學生的規定通常十分寬鬆，但是整潔及樸素端莊是必要的，對師生而言都是如此；美國的學校不穿制服，除非是貴族學校，學校的穿著規定每個社區不盡相同，但從小學到中學，學生穿著都是以輕便為主。

毒品及槍械 (Illegal Substances and Ammunition)

學生的櫃子或校園內其他可能藏有毒品或槍械的地方可能會被搜索，如有必要，執法人員可持搜索狀(search warrants)搜索可疑之處並查扣毒品槍械。大城市的學校常有這類嚴重的問題，所以校園的守衛或校警肩負校園安全把關之責，有些學校使用其他設備，如金屬探測器(metal detectors)，來維護校園安全。

校園內行為 (Behavior on Campus)

不是硬性規定，但學生要能以社會公民的方式對待他人，即不可打架、吵鬧及挑釁他人或學校附近居民，總而言之，學生可以做他們自己，但要遵守有禮貌、不破壞公物的基本原則。

修習科目 (Subjects)

國、高中科目包含數學、歷史、社會、科學、健康與體育、音樂、英文、藝術、外語及其他因地理因素而必須修習的課程，如南方各州必須修習美國南北戰爭；在西北各州修習如何在山野裡求生就很受歡迎，成績單依照學校制度不同，每年寄發 2-3 次。高中生在最

後一年若課業表現良好並已修習大多數必修科目,可以在校時間少一些,表現優異的高中生也可以選修科目。

但每個學校能提供的選修課程依學校資源而異,公立學校依賴稅收資助,較富裕地區的公立高中能提供較多課程資源,高中體育課包含游泳課,但如果中小學有游泳設備及師資,就會安排游泳課,駕駛課則是高中選修課程。學校歡迎並樂於解答家長對學校、教育制度、學校設備或學生表現所提出的任何疑問。

學校課外活動 (Extracurricular Activities)

學校為各年齡的學生提供課外活動,社團成員們聚在一起發展他們的興趣,如藝術、健行、彈奏樂器及其他的嗜好;課外活動可能需要收費,但因為學生付不起高昂的費用,所以必須維持低收費的原則。

親師會 PTA (Parent Teacher Association)

親師會是為了讓家長與學校緊密合作,為學生提供更好的教育環境而存在;親師會定期招開座談,讓老師及家長們公開及私下對學校課程、管理、校務基金、評分標準、師資及其他相關問題交換意見。

夏令營 (Summer Camp)

夏令營是美國許多夏季活動場所的通稱,讓孩童享受戶外活動的樂趣,也學習當地的歷史及自然環境,像水上活動、健行、歌唱及藝術活動等,讓小孩感受到樂趣的活動;有些夏令營有特殊的目的,如讀書會、舞蹈、高爾夫、登山、音樂、戲劇,有些夏令營只有1-2週,有的為期一個月,收費從幾百到幾千美元都有。

Language Power 字句補給站

◆ 中小學校園 Grade [Junior-High, High] School

gym	體育館
tennis court	網球場
basketball court	籃球場
playing field	運動場
track	跑道

football field	足球場
baseball field	棒球場
auditorium	禮堂
principal	校長
principal's office	校長室
extracurricular activities	課外活動
coaches	教練
students	學生
teachers	教師
staff	教職員
custodians, janitors	守衛，工友
classes	課程
textbook	教科書
report card	成績單
parent teacher conference	親師會
lockers	櫃子
gym lockers	體育館的櫃子
P.E. (physical education)	體育課
swimming lessons	游泳課
driver training class	駕駛課
clubs	社團
yearbook	畢業紀念冊
lab	實驗室
curriculum	課程
sports	運動
homework	家庭作業
assignments	作業
roll call	點名
absent [present]	缺 [出] 席
detention	留校輔導
make up	彌補
pass [fail]	及格 [不及格]
incomplete	未完成
credits	學分
diploma	學位
graduation	畢業

住所
郵電通訊
日常活動
銀行與保險
交通
食品與飲食
購物
社交活動
教育
休閒活動
醫療
緊急情況

住所
郵電通訊
日常活動
銀行與保險
交通
食品與飲食
購物
社交活動
教育
休閒活動
醫療
緊急情況

school grounds [campus]	校園
assembly	集合
prom	畢業舞會
advisor	指導老師

9.5 大學
College/University

9.5a 各類學院名稱 Names of Schools [Colleges, Institutes]

✤ School of art and design 藝術及設計學院

✤ College of business 商業學院

✤ College of education 教育學院

✤ College of engineering 工程學院

✤ School of journalism and mass communications 大眾傳播學院

✤ College of science (biology, chemistry, computer science, meteorology, physics...) 自然科學學院 (生物、化學、電腦、氣象、物理……)

✤ College of social sciences (history, psychology, anthropology, geography, political science, environmental studies, urban and regional planning, economics...) 社會科學院(歷史、心理、人類學、地理、政治、環保、都市計畫、經濟……)

✤ School of music and dance 音樂及舞蹈學院

✤ School of nursing 護理學院

✤ School of humanities and arts (English, linguistics, philosophy, theater...) 人文藝術學院 (英語、語言學、哲學、戲劇……)

9.5b 申請入學 Applying for School

College 是學院，university 是大學，由不同學院組成，但這兩字經常交替使用。雖然每個學校的申請要求不同，但多數學校的入學許可至少是三要件審查結果。

1. 標準測驗成績：大學部需要托福 TOEFL (Test of English as a Foreign Language) 及學業評量測驗 SAT I and II (Scholastic Assessment Tests)，研究所需要托福 TOEFL 及研究所入學測驗 GRE (Graduate Record Exam)

成績，商業研究所需要托福 TOEFL 及 GMAT (Graduate Management Admission Test) 成績

2. 在校平均成績 GPA (Grade Point Average) 及工作經驗

3. 個人自傳、研究領域自述及教授推薦信或雇主推薦信

臺灣的大學生每班學生年紀幾乎相同，許多學生上大學選科系多還是聽父母師長意見，許多學生不諱言不知自己志向及人生目標為何。美國的大學生則不是如此，他們可能年紀稍長，在上大學前許多人都有些工作經驗，體會到自己要什麼及為什麼上大學，另一方面也要存錢或自食其力上大學；外籍學生的學費比美籍學生貴上許多，美籍生若是外州學生也比本州生貴一些。

美國大學依照各學校所定的優先順序決定發給入學許可，申請人須在 12 到 24 個月之前就開始作業，除了準備考試之外，許多文件必須翻譯成英文或經過公證手續(notarized)。通常學年是在秋季的 8 月下旬或 9 月開始，但許多學校也發給一月開始就學的春季入學許可，申請人可以選擇要在何時就讀，但拿到入學許可後至多可延後報到入學一年。

美國大學一年分為兩學期(semester)或四學期制(quarter)都有，兩學期制每學期 15 週，四學期制 10 週為一期，暑期課程不分學制通常都較短。大學部(undergraduate)及研究所(graduate school)排課時間可能在晚上，社區學院 (community college)也有夜間課程，但一般而言，全部上夜間課程完成學業的情形並不多見。

所有課程以英文授課，所以外籍學生必須有一定的英文能力才能勝任，所以學校將此列為入學要件；如果是條件式入學，即學校先允許入學，但英文未達到要求標準的外籍生，學校會要求他們去上密集英文課程，並重複考托福或其他標準測驗直到通過標準，除了英文能力之外，當然必須會使用電腦，學校提供各種電腦課程，包含為從沒碰過電腦的人開課，美國大學電腦室(computer labs)多為 24 小時開放。

如果你調查並計畫妥當，在美國上大學可以簡單一些，最好在抵達當地之前就了解學校及其課程狀況；當然了解天氣及地理狀況才知道到那裡該準備什麼衣物，及抵達當地可以從事什麼活動。此外，當地對於學生有何支援系統也需要了解，例如健康服務及任何對國際學生提供服務的特別機構。

住所
郵電通訊
日常活動
銀行與保險
交通
食品與飲食
購物
社交活動
教育
休閒活動
醫療
緊急情況

9.5c 新生說明 Orientation

Dialog 對話

A: 對不起，我要找新生說明處。

A: Excuse me. I need to find out where orientation is.

B: 你是國際學生嗎？

B: Are you an international student?

A: 是的。

A: Yes, I am.

B: 嗯，一般說明會在康納廳開始，但是國際學生可能晚點要到凱爾廳做進一步說明。

B: Well, general orientation will start at Conner Hall, but international students may want to go to Kyle Hall later in the day for further orientation.

A: 謝謝，請問何時開始註冊？

A: Thanks. Can you tell me when class registration will start?

B: 研究生從星期一開始。

B: That will begin on Monday for graduate students.

A: 那大學部呢？

A: What about four-year students?

住所 郵電通訊 日常活動 銀行與保險 交通 食品與飲食 購物 社交活動 教育 休閒活動 醫療 緊急情況

住所 ｜ 郵電通訊 ｜ 日常活動 ｜ 銀行與保險 ｜ 交通 ｜ 食品與飲食 ｜ 購物 ｜ 社交活動 ｜ 教育 ｜ 休閒活動 ｜ 醫療 ｜ 緊急情況

B: 你現在可以在線上註冊。

B: You can register online now.

A: 我可以在哪用電腦？

A: Where can I get access to a computer?

B: 學生中心有電腦可以用。

B: There are computers available for students at the Student Union.

 Word Bank 字庫

> orientation [ˌorɪenˈteʃən] n. 新生說明
> graduate [ˈgredʒuɪt] adj. 研究所的
> access [ˈæksɛs] n. 管道，入口

 Useful Phrases 實用語句

1. 我到哪裡註冊上課？

   Where do I go to register for classes?

2. 你要到行政大樓。

   You must go to the administration building.

3. 你可以線上註冊。

   You can register online.

4. 我需要一個課程目錄。

   I need a course catalog.

5. 我在哪裡付課程費用？

   Where do I pay for classes?

6. 一個學分多少錢？

   How much does a credit cost?

7. 每個課程幾個學分？

   How many credits per class are there?

8. 我需要住校的資料。

I need information about housing on campus.

9. 我需要在校外住宿的資料。

I need to find out about off-campus housing.

10. 我需要國際學生社團的資料。

I need some information about international student groups.

11. 我需要約個時間見格林教授。

I want to make an appointment to see Professor Green.

12. 我要去校園書店。

I want to go to the campus bookstore.

13. 這堂課在哪一棟大樓？

Which Hall [building] is this class in?

14. 這堂課要繳額外費用嗎？

Are there any additional fees for this class?

15. 這堂課實習要多付費嗎？

Does this class's lab cost extra?

16. 這堂課也有實習嗎？

Does this class have a lab class, too?

17. 視聽室在哪裡？

Where is the audio-visual room?

18. 讀書小組通常在哪裡碰面？

Where do the study groups usually meet?

19. 學生中心大廳是最常碰面的地方。

The Student Union Hall is the most popular place to meet.

20. 我需要一張學生證。

I need to get a student I.D. card.

Language Power 字句補給站

◆ 學院 / 大學校園 College/University

campus	校園
professor	教授
university president	大學校長
hall	走廊
campus bookstore	校園書店
dormitory	宿舍
off-campus housing	校園外住宿
married student housing	已婚學生住宿
administration(s) office	行政辦公室
campus health center	校園健康中心
campus security	校園安全
student card	學生證
registration	註冊
tuition	學費
add [drop]	加 [退]
waiting list	候補名單
deadline	截止日
mid-terms	期中考
finals	期末考
blue book	答案本(考試時用來寫問答題的小本子，封面為藍色)
lectures	講課
assignments	作業
research	研究
credits	學分
audit	旁聽
school symbol	校徽
school mascot	學校吉祥物
school colors	學校顏色(校隊制服、紀念品的顏色等)
international students office	國際學生辦公室
overseas students club	海外學生社團

住所
郵電通訊
日常活動
銀行與保險
交通
食品與飲食
購物
社交活動
教育
休閒活動

醫療

緊急情況

Tips 小祕訣

　　美國大學裡的希臘系統(the Greek system)是眾所皆知的，也就是兄弟會(Fraternities)或姊妹會(Sororities)，因這兩個字源自拉丁文，且兄弟會或姊妹會除少數特例之外，都以兩到三個希臘字母命名，兄弟會及姊妹會通稱為希臘系統，會員為「希臘人」(the Greeks)；青年學子聚在一起為共同目標努力(如社交、領導能力、社區服務、專業學習及榮譽等)，並做一輩子如同兄弟、姊妹般情誼的朋友，會員必須經過面試及通過入會過程，雖然這些社團立意良善，但美國各地大學的兄弟會卻經常傳出酗酒鬧事，有些大學已對兄弟會開出禁酒令。

Cultural Tips 文化祕笈

課堂學習與互動

　　在美國讀書的學習態度要主動積極，在各級學校都一樣，課前預習(preview)，課後複習(review)，在課堂上必須適時表達意見，這些都需要足夠的語言能力才能漸入佳境，除了了解教材及課外書籍內容之外，美國人強調創新及批判性的見解(creative and critical thinking [feedback])而不是重複或抄襲教材或課外書裡的意見，抄襲交出去的報告可是會被退學的。另外，可以和同學討論上課內容，但同學的筆記是不可能借來影印的。

　　除了語言能力外，某些人可能要克服個性問題，美國文化欣賞主動積極具有高度競爭力的個人，因此害羞、內向、安靜、扭捏的個性在美國是行不通的，不了解亞洲文化的人還會以為這樣的人心裡有問題。人在國外本來就是少數族裔，有時老美不見得知道如何與你互動，主動與人結交朋友(當然選擇友善溫和的人)即使語言能力尚待加強又何妨，要交朋友就要自己主動，能獲得友誼並提升語言能力及了解國外生活，何樂不為？

9.5d 網路選課 Choosing Classes on the Net

Dialog （對話）

A: 嗨，我是這裡的新生，你可以教我怎麼在網路上選課嗎？

A: Hi, I'm a new student here. Can you show me how I can choose classes on the net?

B: 當然，很簡單，到註冊頁後，點選課表直到找到你要的課程。

B: Sure. It's pretty easy. Just go to the registration page and click through the class lists until you find the ones you want.

A: 如果我選課之前，這門課已經滿了，它會告訴我嗎？

A: Does it tell me if a class is full before I select it?

B: 會的，你也可以把自己排在候補名單。

B: Yes. You can add yourself to a waiting list, too.

A: 我選完該怎麼做？

A: What should I do when I finish choosing?

B: 你確定選好了，要按「送出」鍵。

B: You have to click on the "send" button when you are sure you're ready.

A: 我了解了，謝謝。

A: I see. Thanks.

9.5e 加退選 Adding and Dropping Classes

Dialog 1 對話1

A: 請問這是註冊組嗎?

A: Excuse me. Is this the registrar's office?

B: 是的,我可以為你效勞嗎?

B: Yes, it is. May I help you?

A: 我要加退選幾門科目。

A: I want to add and drop some classes.

B: 好,你要填這個表,包括科目代號,我也要確定你可以加選其他課程,課可能滿了。

B: Fine. You'll need to fill out this form including the number of the class. I'll also have to check to make sure you can add the other class. The class might be full.

A: 謝謝。

A: Thanks.

Dialog 2 對話2

A: 我填好表格了。

A: I've finished filling out the form.

B: 好，我看一下。 ▶ **B:** OK, let me see it.

A: 我什麼時候知道更 正完成？ ▶ **A:** When will I know if the changes are accepted?

B: 等幾分鐘，我在電腦裡改一下，電腦會顯示是否一切都沒問題。

B: Wait just a couple of minutes. I'll put the changes into my computer. It will tell us if everything is OK.

A: 好。 ▶ **A:** OK.

B: 退選沒問題，但你要加選的已經滿了，但你可以問教授是否可以讓你加選。

B: Well, dropping this class is no problem, but the class you want to add is full. You can ask the professor if it's OK for you to join, though.

A: 我要怎麼做？ ▶ **A:** How do I do that?

B: 你要和他約時間並 且讓他簽這張加選 表。 ▶ **B:** You'll have to make an appointment with him and have him sign this add form.

A: 我知道了，我今天就做。

A: I see. I'll do it today.

B: 你最好先打電話給那個系的祕書，看你何時可以和他談，如果他說好，請他簽名，然後把表格拿回來這裡。

B: You'd better call the secretary of that department first to see when you can talk to him. If he says yes, have him sign the form. Then bring it back here.

A: 謝謝你的幫忙。

A: Thanks for your help.

Dialog 3 　對話3

A: 哈囉，安德森教授，我是林蘇，我和你約好要和你談話。

A: Hello, Professor Anderson. I'm Sue Lin. I have an appointment to speak with you.

B: 是的，當然，請進，請坐，有什麼問題嗎？

B: Yes, of course. Please come in and sit down. What is your question?

A: 我想加選您的企業倫理課，但已經滿了。

A: I'd like to join your business ethics class, but it's full.

住所

郵電通訊

日常活動

銀行與保險

交通

食品與飲食

購物

社交活動

教育

休閒活動

醫療

緊急情況

住所

郵電通訊

日常活動

銀行與保險

交通

食品與飲食

購物

社交活動

教育

休閒活動

醫療

緊急情況

B: 喔，我知道了，我查一下有多少學生在我加選名單上。(幾秒鐘後) 看來我已加收兩名了，我問你一個問題。

B: Oh. I see. Let me check to see how many students are on my add list. (a few seconds later) It appears that I've accepted two more already. Let me ask you a question.

A: 好。

A: Sure.

B: 你主修企管碩士課程嗎？

B: Are you majoring in the MBA program?

A: 是的。

A: Yes.

B: 好，我最多多收六名學生，如果他們是修那個課程。

B: Good. I accept up to six more students if they are in that program.

A: 太好了，請簽這張表格。

A: That's great for me. Please sign this form.

B: 沒問題。

B: No problem.

Word Bank 字庫

business ethics n. 企業倫理

Notes 小叮嚀

現在學校選課多透過網路進行，加退選截止日多在開課後第五週左右，加退選當然也會影響到學費的多寡，退選是否會留下成績單上退選 (W) 註記或退回部分學分費要看各校規定。

Useful Phrases 實用語句

1. 我要加 [退] 選。

   I want to add [drop] a class.

2. 這更正將會影響我的學費嗎？

   Will this change affect my tuition?

3. 加 [退] 選截止日是何時？

   What is the add [drop] deadline?

4. 有候補名單嗎？

   Is there a waiting list?

5. 多少學生可以加入？

   How many students can be in that class?

6. 課滿了嗎？

   Is the class full?

9.5f 付學費 Paying Tuition

Dialog 對話

A: 這裡是我繳學費的地方嗎？

A: Is this where I pay tuition?

B: 是的，你可以在這裡或者可以在線上付。

B: Yes, you can pay here, or you can pay online.

A: 我知道，但我還無法用電腦。

A: I know, but I don't have access to a computer yet.

B: 沒問題，你要付現金還是支票？

B: No problem. Will you pay cash or check?

A: 我可以用信用卡嗎？

A: May I use a credit card?

B: 可以。

B: Yes, you may.

A: 我是外籍學生，我不確定我需要付的總額是多少。

A: I'm a foreign student. I'm not sure what the total amount I need to pay is.

B: 我可以幫你算。

B: I'll calculate it for you.

A: 你知道這些課要不要付額外費用？

A: Do you know if any of these classes have extra fees?

B: 我把它們輸入電腦，馬上就會知道。

B: We'll know right now as I enter them in the computer.

A: 謝謝。

A: Thanks.

Word Bank 字庫

tuition [tju`ɪʃən] n. 學費
online [`ɑn‚laɪn] adv. 線上
calculate [`kælkjə‚let] v. 計算
amount [ə`maʊnt] n. 總金額

9.5g 認識室友 Meeting a New Roommate

Dialog 對話

A: 嗨，我是你的室友，法蘭克王。

A: Hi. I'm Frank Wong, your dorm room partner.

B: 很高興認識你，我是史丹泰爾包。

B: Pleased to meet you. I'm Stan Talbo.

A: 我看你已準備好要用房間左側。

A: I see you are set up for using the left side of the room.

B: 是的，我希望可以這樣。

B: Yes. I hope that's OK.

A: 當然，沒問題。

A: Sure, no problem.

B: 我們有電話嗎？

B: Do we have a phone?

A: 沒有，我們要用外面走廊的電話。

A: No. We have to use the phones out in the hallway.

B: 我知道了，那淋浴間或浴室呢？

B: I see. What about showers or a bathroom?

A: 走廊盡頭有共用的。

A: There are communal ones at the end of the hall.

Word Bank 字庫

hallway [`hɔl͵we] n. 走廊
shower [`ʃauɚ] n. 淋浴
communal [`kɑmjʊn̩] adj. 共用的

Notes 小叮嚀

　　各家大學宿舍設備不同，學費是個因素，男女宿舍通常有某個程度的區隔，例如男女舍在不同樓層或在不同棟，宿舍可能設有門禁。

住所

郵電通訊

日常活動

銀行與保險

交通

食品與飲食

購物

社交活動

教育

休閒活動

醫療

緊急情況

9.5h 尋找校外租屋資訊
Looking for Off-Campus Housing Information

Dialog 對話

A: 你在看什麼？

A: What are you looking at?

B: 我在看校外租屋的公布欄。

B: I'm checking the bulletin board for off-campus housing.

A: 你要什麼樣的房子？

A: What kind of place do you want?

B: 我想要有我自己的房間，但不需要太大。

B: I'd like to have my own room, but I don't need anything very big.

A: 或許你要考慮一間四房屋。

A: Maybe you should consider a quad.

B: 我聽過，與另外三間房間共用廚房，對嗎？

B: I've heard of those. They share a kitchen with three other rooms, right?

A: 對，你有自己的房間及浴室。

A: That's right. You have your own room and bathroom.

B: 便宜嗎？

B: Are they cheap?

住所｜郵電通訊｜日常活動｜銀行與保險｜交通｜食品與飲食｜購物｜社交活動｜教育｜休閒活動｜醫療｜緊急情況

A: 通常比宿舍便宜，而且還有停車位。	**A:** Usually they cost less than a dorm room, and have parking for your car.

Word Bank 字庫

bulletin board n. 公布欄
campus [`kæmpəs] n. 校園
quad [kwɑd] n. 四房屋

9.5i 約見學業諮詢教授
Making an Appointment with an Academic Advisor

 Dialog 對話

A: 我想約見學業諮詢教授。	**A:** I'd like to make an appointment to see an academic advisor.
B: 你有系上分配的指導教授嗎？	**B:** Have you been assigned an advisor from your department yet?
A: 我不確定。	**A:** I'm not sure.
B: 我先查一下登記冊，如果你有被指定，你應該先見那位。	**B:** Let me check the registry first. If you have been assigned one, you should see that person first.
A: 我知道了，謝謝。	**A:** I understand. Thanks.

住所 郵電通訊 日常活動 銀行與保險 交通 食品與飲食 購物 社交活動 教育 休閒活動 醫療 緊急情況

Word Bank 字庫

academic [ˌækəˋdɛmɪk] adj. 學業的
advisor [ədˋvaɪzə] n. 諮詢師
registry [ˋrɛdʒɪstrɪ] n. 登記冊

Notes 小叮嚀

　　大學裡有許多事要了解，因此知道自己的學業諮詢教授及外籍學生服務等事項都是必要的，重要事項學校也會通知你；至於租屋、健康服務、學生保險、社團活動和娛樂活動、學業諮詢等，都有各類部門可以幫忙。

　　美國文化裡，每個人都是平等的，因此沒有亞洲人長幼尊卑的概念，也沒有對無親屬關係之他人使用親屬稱謂的情形。「平等」反映在每個層面 (家庭、工作) 及人際關係上。因此，大學裡沒有學長姊、學弟妹的稱呼，實際上也沒有這樣的機制或連結 (除講紀律的軍校外)。

9.5j 在學校書店 At the Campus Bookstore

Dialog 對話

A: 嗨，歷史類在哪裡？

A: Hi. Where is the history section?

B: 你要一般歷史區或是歷史教科書區？

B: Do you want the general history section or the history textbook section?

A: 歷史教科書。

A: History textbooks.

B: 到樓上那一區，所有的教科書都在那上面。

B: Go to the section upstairs. All the textbooks are up there.

A: 謝謝。

A: Thanks.

B: 你準備要買時，一定要出示學生證。

B: When you are ready to buy, be sure to present your student I.D. card.

A: 我還沒有學生證。

A: I don't have mine yet.

B: 你有付學費的證明嗎？

B: Do you have any proof that you paid tuition?

A: 有，我有收據。

A: Yes, I have a receipt.

B: 出示給收銀員看，你可以打八折。

B: Present that to the cashier; you'll get a 20% discount.

A: 謝謝你告訴我。

A: Thank you for telling me.

✎ Word Bank 字庫

textbook [`tɛkst,bʊk] n. 教科書
section [`sɛkʃən] n. 部門
present [prɪ`zɛnt] v. 出示

住所
郵電通訊
日常活動
銀行與保險
交通
食品與飲食
購物
社交活動
教育
休閒活動
醫療
緊急情況

 Notes 小叮嚀

　　學生證可以讓你在校園或附近不同種類的商店，如電影院、書店、餐飲店等，享受八或九折優惠。

9.5k　在圖書館 At the Library

Dialog 對話

A: 嗨，我要借這本書。

A: Hi. I want to check out this book.

B: 你有學生證嗎？

B: Do you have your student card?

A: 有。

A: Yes, I do.

B: 好，我看一下，然後我會幫你借出這本書。

B: OK. Let me see it, and then I'll sign the book out to you.

A: 我可以借多久？

A: How long can I keep it?

B: 兩個星期。

B: Two weeks.

A: 好，我也預借了一本書。

A: Great. I also reserved a book.

B: 你有收到通知說現在在這裡了嗎？

B: Did you receive a notice saying it's here now?

A: 沒有，我只是想問問看。

A: No. I just thought I'd ask.

B: 書名是什麼？我看一下是否已在這裡。

B: What is the book's title? I'll see if it's here now.

A: 書名是《Running Back》。

A: The title is *Running Back*.

B: 沒有，還沒進來，但已經逾期了，我會聯絡借走的人。

B: No. It's not in yet. It's overdue though. I'll contact the person that has it.

A: 這倒提醒我，逾期要罰多少錢？

A: That reminds me. What is the fine for overdue books?

B: 每天50分。

B: 50¢ a day.

 Useful Phrases　實用語句

● 學生 / 圖書館使用人 Student / Library User

1. 我要借這本書。

   I want to check out this book.

2. 我要預借一本書。

   I want to reserve a book.

3. 我有一本逾期的書。

   I have an overdue book.

4. 你有一本叫做《Running Back》的書嗎？

Do you have a book called *Running Back*?

5. 期刊區在哪裡？

Where is the periodical section?

6. 我想知道參考書區在哪裡。

I want to know where the reference section is.

7. 請幫我找這本書。

Please help me locate this book.

8. 這裡有個人的研讀區嗎？

Are there any private study rooms here?

9. 視聽室在哪裡？

Where is the audio-visual room?

10. 這裡有影印機嗎？

Is there a copying machine here?

11. 我需要用網路。

I need Internet access.

○ **圖書館員 Librarian**

1. 我需要看你的圖書館證或學生證。

I need to see your library or student card.

2. 我會替你保留那本書。

I'll reserve the book for you.

3. 請在此簽名。

Please sign here.

4. 你可以借兩個星期。

You can have it for two weeks.

5. 你可以延長借閱期限。

You may extend the lending period.

6. 期刊區在那邊。

The periodical section is over there.

7. 我告訴你那區在哪裡。

I'll show you where that section is.

8. 你要的書還回來時，我會通知你。

I'll notify you when the book you want is returned.

9.51 學校健康中心 At the School Health Center

Dialog 對話

A: 我覺得不舒服。

A: I don't feel well.

B: 請進來躺下，我是校護。

B: Come in and lie down. I'm the school nurse.

A: 我整個早上都覺得不舒服。

A: I have felt sick all morning.

B: 我看看，你應該回家。

B: I'll check you out, but it sounds like you ought to go home.

A: 我媽媽在家，我打電話給她。

A: My mom is home. I'll call her.

B: 別擔心，我來打。

B: Don't worry. I'll do it.

住所 郵電通訊 日常活動 銀行與保險 交通 食品與飲食 購物 社交活動 教育 休閒活動 醫療 緊急情況

住所 郵電通訊 日常活動 銀行與保險 交通 食品與飲食 購物 社交活動 教育 休閒活動 醫療 緊急情況

Notes 小叮嚀

　　中小學生在校的健康服務資源有限，大學就好些，通常校園的健康中心有如診所一般，大多數大學生的健康保險已包含在學費裡，所以學生完成註冊繳費，保險就已經啟動，外籍學生可以加入外籍學生保險。在大學健康中心的就醫過程與一般相同，請參見第 11 章醫療。

Unit 10 Leisure Activities

休閒活動

美國面積廣大,可以享受到各式各樣的休閒娛樂,不同的地區及氣候狀況提供不同種類的休閒活動。本章列出需要多問多說才能盡情享受的休閒活動對話,一般來說較複雜的休閒活動多有訓練課程。

住所 郵電通訊 日常活動 銀行與保險 交通 食品與飲食 購物 社交活動 教育 休閒活動 醫療 緊急情況

10.1 靜態展覽（美術館及博物館）
Exhibitions (Art Museums and Museums)

 Dialog 對話

A: 我們每一區都要買票嗎？

A: Do we have to buy a ticket for each part of the museum?

B: 不必，你只要在入口買一張票就可以。

B: No, you don't. You just buy one ticket at the entrance.

A: 那柯威爾收藏區呢？

A: What about the Caldwell collection?

B: 喔，抱歉，我忘了。你要另外買一張票。

B: Oh, sorry, I forgot. There is a special ticket you have to buy for that.

A: 去哪兒買呢？

A: Where do I get it?

B: 收藏室入口旁，我指給你看。

B: Next to the entrance of the collections' room. Let me show you there.

 Word Bank 字庫

collection [kə`lɛkʃən] n. 收藏
entrance [`ɛntrəns] n. 入口

Tips 小祕訣

博物館通常都要收門票，票價依名氣及規模大小而定，多數博物館會有紀念品可買，如明信片或複製藝術品等。有些人則是逆向操作，先買明信片給工作人員看，再詢問怎麼找到該藝術品，這在時間有限而博物館超大的情形下，確不失為妙招。

10.1a 租用導覽設備 Renting Audio Guides

Dialog 1 對話1

A: 這裡有語音導覽可以用嗎？

A: Is there any audio guide information available for this place?

B: 有，我們有收費的語音導覽。

B: Yes, you can rent an audio guide for a fee.

A: 費用多少呢？

A: How much is the fee?

B: 3元。

B: $3.

A: 操作簡單嗎？

A: Is it easy to use?

B: 是的，就像遙控器一樣，只要看展示品上的編號，然後按下號碼。

B: Yes, it's just like a remote control. Just look at the number of the display. Then press the number.

住所
郵電通訊
日常活動
銀行與保險
交通
食品與飲食
購物
社交活動
教育
休閒活動
醫療
緊急情況

A: 聽起來不錯，謝謝。

A: Sounds good. Thanks.

Word Bank 字庫

audio [`ɔdɪˌo] n., adj. 聲頻(的)，音頻(的)
fee [fi] n. 費用
remote control n. 遙控器
display [dɪ`sple] n. 展示品

Useful Phrases 實用語句

1. 我需要語音導覽機。

   I need an audio guide.

2. 怎樣開機呢？

   How do you turn it on?

3. 也有樓層圖嗎？

   Is there a floor map, too?

 Dialog 2 對話2

A: 這個導覽機壞了。

A: This player does not work.

B: 怎麼了？

B: What's wrong?

A: 我不知道，剛才還好好的，然後就壞了。

A: I don't know. It was OK, but then it quit working.

B: 沒問題，我拿另一個給你。

B: No problem. Let me get you another one.

A: 你們也有此地的書面介紹嗎？

A: Do you also have a written guide for here?

B: 我們有一份2元的 (書面介紹)。

B: We have one you can buy for \$2.

A: 有一些照片嗎？

A: Does it have some pictures?

B: 有，有一些很棒的照片。

B: Yes, it has some excellent photos.

✎ Word Bank 〈字庫〉

quit [kwɪt] v. 停止，放棄
guide [gaɪd] n. 導引

Tips 〈小祕訣〉

　　許多觀光地區及博物館備有小型地圖及簡介，另有錄音導覽可供租借，費用通常為 \$3-\$5 元。有些博物館出租 iPod (約 5 元) 導覽或提供 APP 下載到手機導覽 (須考量網路費)。除了會員外，有些博物館會給學生及教師折扣，如有這些身分，不妨出國前申請國際學生證或教師證備用。在美國免費出租採取押金，而非押證件的方式，因為抵押證件有侵犯個資之嫌。

10.1b 博物館捐款 Donations at Museums

 Dialog 對話

A: 歡迎光臨廉威爾博物館。

A: Welcome to the Lanwell Museum.

B: 謝謝,這裡是售票窗口嗎?

B: Thank you. Is the ticket window here?

A: 進入本博物館不用收費。

A: There is no charge to enter our museum.

B: 真好!

B: How nice!

A: 我們會問訪客是否考慮捐款。

A: We do ask people to consider giving a donation.

B: 多少呢?

B: How much?

A: 任何金額都可以。

A: Any amount is fine.

Word Bank 字庫

ticket window n. 售票口
consider [kən`sɪdɚ] v. 考慮
donation [do`neʃən] n. 捐款
amount [ə`maʊnt] n. 金額

住所 郵電通訊 日常活動 銀行與保險 交通 食品與飲食 購物 社交活動 教育 休閒活動 醫療 緊急情況

Tips 小祕訣

　　多數博物館收取門票，有些則是要求參觀者捐款，金額不拘，多數人的捐款在$1-$5之間。別忘記，許多博物館在星期一休館。

10.2 表演活動
Performance Activities

10.2a 百老匯表演 Broadway Shows

Dialog 1 對話1

A: 我們今晚要看什麼表演呢？

A: What show do we want to see tonight?

B: 我不知道，有這麼多可以選。

B: I don't know. There are so many to choose from.

A: 是啊， 我們或許該看些評論。

A: Yes, there are. Maybe we should look at some reviews.

B: 好主意，我們也該打電話查一下有沒有票及價錢。

B: Good idea. We need to call and check on ticket availability and prices, too.

A: 對，受歡迎的秀很快就賣完了，我們可能來不及買某些票了。

A: Yes. Popular shows sell out quickly. We might be too late for some.

B: 還有很棒的非百老匯秀。

B: There are great off-Broadway shows also.

A: 是，那倒是真的，這想法很讚！

A: Yes, that's true. Good thinking!

Word Bank 字庫

review [rɪ`vju] n. 評論
sell out 賣完
off-Broadway [`ɔf͵brɔd͵we] adj. 非百老匯的
Good thinking! 這想法很讚！

Dialog 2 對話2

A: 現在是中場時間，我們到外面劇院大廳喝一杯吧！

A: It's intermission time. Let's go out into the theater lobby and get a drink.

B: 聽起來不錯，我也有點餓。

B: That sounds good. I'm hungry, too.

A: 我確定他們也有些點心可吃。

A: I'm sure they'll have something to snack on also.

B: 你覺得這場表演到目前如何呢？

B: What do you think of the show so far?

A: 很有娛樂性，我很喜歡。

A: It's really entertaining. I'm enjoying it very much.

B: 演得好而且燈光很特別。

B: The acting is good and the lighting is very special.

A: 你以前有看過百老匯表演嗎？

A: Have you seen any Broadway shows before?

B: 有，但每次來好像都是新上演的。

B: Yes, but every time I go, it seems new.

Word Bank 字庫

intermission [ˌɪntəˋmɪʃən] n. 中場
snack on 吃點心
entertaining [ˌɛntəˋtenɪŋ] adj. 娛樂的
lighting [ˋlaɪtɪŋ] n. 燈光

Notes 小叮嚀

　　不管英文程度如何，在紐約不可錯過百老匯現場歌舞劇表演，另外還有非百老匯表演，可以換個口味。只要在街頭或旅館拿到表演節目單 (playbill)，就可以依據節目資訊及劇評知道如何選擇這些表演，當然出發前就做功課是最好的；訂票方式有電話及網路訂票，但會有手續費，如果人已在紐約，不妨到購票處現場或上網找低價的「清倉票」(last minute ticket)。去看表演時衣著要注意，不要太休閒隨便，適當的衣著是對現場表演的尊重。

住所｜郵電通訊｜日常活動｜銀行與保險｜交通｜食品與飲食｜購物｜社交活動｜教育｜休閒活動｜醫療｜緊急情況

10.2b 電影 Movies

Dialog 對話

A: 嗨，雪莉，你今晚要看電影嗎？

A: Hi, Shirley. Would you like to see a movie tonight?

B: 好啊，在演什麼？

B: Sure. What's on?

A: 我查過報紙，我看到今年得最佳影片的電影在上演。

A: I checked in the newspaper. I see the movie that won best picture this year is on.

B: 好，我想看，幾點在哪裡碰面？

B: Good. I'd love to see it. Where and when shall we meet?

A: 電影7:15開始，我們6點在戲院見，這樣就可以先吃飯。

A: The movie starts at 7:15 tonight. Let's meet at the theater at six o'clock so we can eat first.

B: 好。

B: OK.

10.2c 歌劇 Operas

Dialog 對話1

A: 我們看場歌劇吧。

A: Let's see an opera performance.

B: 好主意,我們如何買票?

B: Good idea. How do we get tickets?

A: 我們要打電話或上網看是否有票。

A: We'll have to call or surf the net to see if any tickets are available.

B: 我們要在哪裡找售票中心?

B: Where do we find ticket outlets?

A: 我們可以上網查。

A: We can surf the net.

Dialog 2 (對話2)

A: 貝爾斯門票公司,我能為你效勞嗎?

A: Bells Tickets Office. May I help you?

B: 嗨,我想買歌劇的門票。

B: Hi. I'd like to buy tickets for the opera.

A: 恐怕今晚的票都賣完了。

A: I'm afraid tonight's performance is sold out.

B: 明天晚上呢?

B: What about tomorrow night?

A: 有剩幾張。

A: We have a few left.

B: 座位是哪裡的？

B: Where are the seats located?

A: 五個在左邊看臺，三個在第二排。

A: There are five located in the balcony on the left, and three in the second row.

B: 有兩個一起的座位嗎？

B: Are there two seats together?

A: 有，第二排的是。

A: Yes, two in the second row are.

B: 多少錢？

B: How much are they?

A: 一張85元。

A: They are $85 a piece.

B: 我想預訂那兩張，謝謝。

B: I'd like to reserve those two seats, please.

A: 好，麻煩你現在在電話上用信用卡付款。

A: Fine. You'll have to pay now over the phone by credit card.

B: 沒問題，我要怎樣取票？

B: No problem. How do I get the tickets?

A: 你可以在歌劇院或來我們辦公室取票，我們為你寄送票收費6元。

A: They'll be waiting for you at the opera house, or you can come to our office and get them. We'll deliver them to you for a $6 fee.

10.2d 音樂會 Music Concerts

 Dialog 對話

A: 嘿，鮑伯，殺手馬芬樂團下週來城裡。

A: Hey, Bob. The Killer Muffins are going to be in town next week.

B: 酷，我們買票吧，音樂會票價多少？

B: Cool! Let's get tickets. How much are tickets for the concert?

A: 廣播說每張20元。

A: The radio said they're $20 each.

B: 音樂會何時開始？

B: What time does the concert start?

A: 8點。

A: 8:00.

B: 在哪裡？

B: Where is it?

住所｜郵電通訊｜日常活動｜銀行與保險｜交通｜食品與飲食｜購物｜社交活動｜教育｜休閒活動｜醫療｜緊急情況

438

A: 在牛宮。	**A:** At the Cow Palace.
B: 那裡有很多停車位嗎？	**B:** Is there plenty of parking there?
A: 有，但是我們可以搭接駁車去那裡。	**A:** Yes, but we can take the shuttle bus out to there.
B: 好主意，這樣方便多了。	**B:** Good idea, it's much more convenient.

 Useful Phrases 實用語句

● **顧客 Customer**

1. 我要兩張票，謝謝。

   I'd like two tickets, please.

2. 我要訂兩張票。

   I want to reserve two tickets.

3. 音樂會何時開始？

   What time does the concert start?

4. 有什麼座位？

   What seats are available?

5. 戲院地址是？

   What's the address of the theater?

6. 今晚有什麼電影？

   What movies are on tonight?

7. 這週有什麼上演？

   What's showing this week?

8. 這週誰在表演？

   Who's performing this week?

● 售票代理員 Ticket Agent

1. 你要坐哪裡？

   Where do you want to sit?

2. 你要如何付款？

   How would you pay?

3. 付現還是刷卡？

   Will this be cash or credit?

4. 你的票幾分鐘就好。

   Your tickets will be ready in a few minutes.

5. 看螢幕顯示有什麼位置。

   Look at the monitor to see what seats are available.

6. 如果你上我們的網站，你會看到有什麼座位可選。

   You'll see what seats are available if you visit our website.

7. 你的票要用郵寄的嗎？

   Would you like your tickets delivered?

 Language Power 字句補給站

◆ 表演活動 Performance Activities

theater	戲院
opening night	開幕
scalped tickets	黃牛票
reservations	預訂
musical	音樂劇
movie premiere	首映會
opera house	歌劇院
box office	售票室，票房
ticket booth	售票亭
balcony	看臺
live performance	現場表演
cabaret	夜總會 (娛樂表演)
vaudeville	雜耍娛樂表演
variety	綜藝節目
dance performance	舞蹈表演

住所 郵電通訊 日常活動 銀行與保險 交通 食品與飲食 購物 社交活動 教育 休閒活動 醫療 緊急情況

stage play	舞臺劇
concert	音樂會
symphony	交響樂
orchestra	交響樂團
backstage pass	後臺通行證

Tips 小祕訣

　　歌劇、音樂會、現場表演等在大型場地演出的表演，可以透過電話或網路購票，以信用卡付費，消費者亦可直接到市內售票據點購買，若為觀眾超過千人的大型表演，常有交通車負責接觀眾到表演地點。

10.3 球賽
Sporting Events

在美國，人們喜歡去看球賽，如棒球、足球、籃球、曲棍球等等。在許多大城市有職業球隊，職業球賽的門票可能很貴，但是少年聯盟隊伍及大學校隊也提供精彩的觀賽機會，而且票價也便宜許多。

Dialog 1 對話1

A: 兩張票，謝謝，我們想要本壘區後面的上層座位。

A: Two tickets, please. We'd like the upper deck **behind** home plate.

B: 好，共50元。

B: OK. That's $50.

A: 比賽何時開始？

A: What time does the game begin?

住所

郵電通訊

日常活動

銀行與保險

交通

食品與飲食

購物

社交活動

教育

休閒活動

醫療

緊急情況

B: 晚上7點。

B: 7 p.m.

A: 我可以在這裡買節目單嗎?

A: Can I buy a program here?

B: 先進場,你會看到賣節目單及其他紀念品的攤位。

B: Go inside first, you'll see a stand selling them and other souvenirs.

 Word Bank 字庫

upper deck n. 上層座位
home plate n. 本壘區
program [`progræm] n. 節目單
souvenir [ˌsuvə`nɪr] n. 紀念品
stand [stænd] n. 攤位

 Dialog 2 對話2

A: 我們的座位在這裡。

A: Here are our seats.

B: 座位很好。

B: They're pretty good.

A: 我又餓又渴。

A: I'm hungry and thirsty.

B: 沒問題,小販來了。

B: No problem. Here comes a vendor.

| 住所 | 郵電通訊 | 日常活動 | 銀行與保險 | 交通 | 食品與飲食 | 購物 | 社交活動 | 教育 | 休閒活動 | 醫療 | 緊急情況 |

A: 好，我來買點熱狗和飲料。 → **A:** Great. I'll get us some hotdogs and drinks.

Useful Phrases 實用語句

1. 兩張票，謝謝。

   Two tickets please.

2. 你們要坐哪裡？

   Where do you want to sit?

3. 我們坐在體育館的上 [下] 方。

   Let's sit in the upper [lower] decks of the stadium.

4. 我要找販賣區。

   I want to find the concession stand.

5. 兩份熱狗，謝謝。

   Two hot dogs please.

6. 調味料在哪？

   Where are the condiments?

7. 調味料在那裡。

   The condiments are there.

8. 我要買節目單。

   I want to buy a program.

9. 我們去找座位吧。

   Let's find our seats.

Language Power 字句補給站

◆ 球類活動 Sporting Events

umpire, referee	裁判
stadium	體育館
vendor	小販
foul	壞球
court	球場
scoreboard	計分板

timeout	暫停，休息時間
half time	半場
innings	局

Tips 小祕訣

運動比賽都有各自的比賽規則，但也有雷同處。所有比賽都要讓觀賽者愉快並讓球隊老闆賺錢，因此食物、飲料跟紀念品一樣都很昂貴；大的聯盟比賽允許觀眾花許多時間進入座位，球賽結束時，因為交通都堵塞，所以也不需要急著離開。

10.4 夜生活
Nightlife

晚上外出最好結伴，並且走在燈光明亮的地方，在美國除了少數大都市有精采的夜生活外，許多中小型城市在市區的商業中心下班後，可能像空城一樣。有些城市有住在市區的貧窮人口或少數無家可歸的流浪漢徘徊在便利商店門口，因此夜晚在市區要格外當心。

10.4a 外出 Going Out

Dialog 對話

A: 晚上有什麼地方好去呢？

A: Where is a good place to go at night?

B: 你是說外出進城嗎？

B: You mean go out on the town?

A: 是的。

A: Yes.

住所
郵電通訊
日常活動
銀行與保險
交通
食品與飲食
購物
社交活動
教育
休閒活動
醫療
緊急情況

B: 那要看你想做什麼。

B: It depends on what you want to do.

A: 這附近有沒有好的爵士夜店呢？

A: Are there any good jazz bars around here?

B: 當然，而且它們幾乎整晚都開著。

B: Sure, and they stay open almost all night.

A: 要收節目費嗎？

A: Any cover charge?

B: 有，但不貴。

B: Yes, but it's not high.

 Useful Phrases 實用語句

1. 這裡的夜生活怎樣？

   What's the nightlife like here?

2. 你可以推薦一間俱樂部嗎？

   Can you recommend a club to us?

3. 節目費是多少呢？

   What's the cover charge?

4. 快樂時光是什麼時候呢？

   When's happy hour?

Tips 小祕訣

　　有表演的餐廳可能在餐點費用外，外加節目費。快樂時光 (happy hour) 指的是下班後 4 點到 8 點的時段，店家為商業促銷，啤酒可能特別便宜或買一送一 (two for one)，並贈送爆米花或脆餅等小點心 (finger food)。星期五的 happy hour 較其他日子熱絡，人們說 TGIF (Thank God It's Friday) 感謝上帝，隔天是週末不必上班。

10.4b 爵士夜店 At the Jazz Club

Dialog 對話

A: 歡迎光臨「來享薩 (克斯風)吧」，娛樂費是每人5元。

A: Welcome to "Let's Have Sax." There's a $5 cover charge per person.

B: 這裡是10元。

B: Here's $10.

A: 拿著這個 (入場券)，你可以免費喝兩杯飲料。

A: Take this (entry coupon). You can get two free drinks with it.

B: 這裡可以跳舞嗎？

B: Is there dancing here?

A: 可以，9點以後。

A: Yes, there is, after nine o'clock.

住所
郵電通訊
日常活動
銀行與保險
交通
食品與飲食
購物
社交活動
教育
休閒活動
醫療
緊急情況

10.4c 夜店內 Inside the Club

A: 我們可以坐哪兒呢？

A: Where can we sit?

B: 哪裡都可以，先來先坐。

B: Anywhere you like. It's first come, first serve.

A: 可以吸菸嗎？

A: Can we smoke here?

B: 吸菸區在那邊。

B: We have a smoking section over there.

A: 好。

A: Good.

B: 我們這裡也賣各種牌子的香菸。

B: We sell all brands of cigarettes here, too.

10.4d 點飲料 Ordering a Drink

A: 我們想 (拿入場券) 換兩杯飲料。

A: We'd like to exchange this (entry coupon) for two drinks.

B: 好，你們要喝什麼呢？ → **B:** OK. What do you want to have?

A: 你們有飲料單嗎？ → **A:** Do you have a drink list?

B: 有，但是憑入場券只能點啤酒或汽水。 → **B:** Yes, but actually these coupons are only good for beer or soft drinks.

A: 了解了，好，兩杯啤酒，但是請給我們飲料單。 → **A:** I see. OK, two beers, please, but please bring a drink list.

B: 沒問題，我會連飲料一起送過來。 → **B:** No problem. I'll be right back with your drinks.

 Useful Phrases 實用語句

1. 我們想點食物及飲料。

   We'd like some food and drinks.

2. 請多加點飲料 [再來一杯]。

   More drinks, please.

3. 我要續杯。

   I'd like a refill.

4. 這裡有公共電話嗎？

   Is there a pay phone here?

5. 你有火柴嗎？

   Do you have any matches?

6. 我需要火柴。

   I need matches.

7. 我需要打火機。

   I need a lighter.

住所　郵電通訊　日常活動　銀行與保險　交通　食品與飲食　購物　社交活動　教育　休閒活動　醫療　緊急情況

8. 洗手間在哪裡？

Where is the restroom?

Notes 小叮嚀

在美國，因現實需求，多數地方沒車等於沒腿，所以 16 歲可以考照開車，要購買香菸、投票、當兵必須年滿 18 歲，買酒需年滿 21 歲。要進入酒吧 (pub, tavern)、俱樂部 (club)、賭場 (casino) 等場所，要帶證件備查，證明已超過合法年紀 21 歲。如果沒帶證件是進不去的。除非是很明顯的情形，西方人通常很難猜到東方人年紀。事實上，供應酒精飲料的場所幾乎要查看每位顧客的證件，不論他們看來年紀如何。在美國，商家或其他場所要求查看證件是常有的事，所以不必多猜疑。

喝酒後絕不可駕車，在美國酒駕的處罰是非常嚴重的。這也是為什麼美國為了減少青少年喝酒開車事故，而在 1980 年代將全國最低買酒年紀從 18 歲延到 21 歲的緣故，事實也證明這是有效的手段。在美國租車必須年滿 21 歲，許多租車公司對 25 歲 (被視為駕駛漸趨安全之年齡) 以下駕駛每日加收昂貴的未足齡費用 (underage surcharge)，並限制可租車種。25 歲以下駕駛人的租車條件因此相較其他成年人嚴苛。

至於投票年紀從 21 歲改為 18 歲則剛好相反，因為美國越戰 (Vietnam War) 期間 18 歲可上戰場為國犧牲，卻須等到 21 歲才有投票權，在學生抗議下，美國才將投票權從 21 歲改為 18 歲。所以美國人在 18 歲擁有多數成年人的權利義務，但要到 21 歲才算是完全的成年人，所以 21 歲生日是個重要里程，壽星多會喝酒慶祝。諷刺的是在外作戰的傷兵回到國內，卻可能因為未足齡而無法買酒。

10.4e 跳舞 Dancing

Dialog 對話

A: 我們來跳舞吧。　　　　　A: Let's dance.

B: 我不會跳舞。 → **B:** I'm not a good dancer.

A: 沒關係，你隨便怎麼跳都行。 → **A:** It doesn't matter, you just move anyway you want.

B: 希望我不會踩到別人。 → **B:** I hope I don't step on anybody.

A: 如果這樣，只要微笑說抱歉。 → **A:** If you do, just smile and say sorry.

B: 好，走吧。 → **B:** OK, let's go.

Tips 小祕訣

　　大都市的夜生活提供另一個了解當地生活及文化的管道，例如在紐約夜生活各式各樣、多采多姿，中型城市也有不錯的選擇；在熱鬧的場所排隊，或到看來不錯的地方逛逛，每個人覺得有趣好玩的想法不盡相同，讓自己嘗試接受不同的體驗。有些夜店 (像臺灣也是) 會推出淑女之夜及快樂時光，提供各式的音樂、舞步，若對跳舞沒興趣的人，來此坐坐、喝東西、聊天，也是輕鬆的夜晚娛樂方式。

　　小城鎮的夜生活當然比不上大城市的五光十色，但大多有一些酒吧可以喝點東西，有些地方可以聽當地樂團現場演奏或有舞池可以跳舞，這些地方多在9點或10點打烊。此外有一些較晚打烊的電影院或影片出租店、保齡球館 (bowling alley)、撞球場 (billiard / billiards, pool or snooker hall [或 parlor, room or club]) 及 24 小時的便利商店，最後就是汽車旅館內的電影頻道了。比起來美加人民比我們要早睡早起的多。

住所｜郵電通訊｜日常活動｜銀行與保險｜交通｜食品與飲食｜購物｜社交活動｜教育｜休閒活動｜醫療｜緊急情況

10.4f 脫口秀俱樂部 Going to a Comedy Club

Dialog 對話

A: 你今晚想去脫口秀俱樂部嗎？

A: Do you want to go to a comedy club tonight?

B: 我很喜歡喜劇，笑一笑很好玩。

B: I like comedy a lot. It's fun to laugh.

A: 我也是，但我想可能有個問題。

A: Me too, but I think there might be a problem.

B: 什麼呢？

B: What's that?

A: 很多笑話都跟他們本身的文化有關。

A: A lot of the jokes are based in the culture they come from.

B: 是啊，我們可能不懂哪裡好笑。

B: Yes. Right. We may not understand what is funny about them.

A: 好吧，我們晚餐時再想一想。

A: Well, we can think it over during dinner.

Tips 小祕訣

　　大都市夜生活較常見脫口秀俱樂部，詼諧的脫口秀輪番上臺之餘，可能也有些好笑的短劇穿插。

10.5 運動及旅遊休閒
Sporting and Leisure Activities

10.5a 騎馬 Horse Rides

Dialog 對話

A: 我們這裡可以在海邊騎馬。

A: We have rides available here on the beach.

B: 我們從沒騎過馬。

B: We've never ridden horses before.

A: 那沒問題，我們的馬很溫馴。

A: That's no problem. Our horses are very tame.

B: 我了解，要多少錢呢？

B: I see. How much does it cost?

A: 騎4小時25元。

A: We have a four hour beach ride for $25.

Word Bank 字庫

ride [raɪd] n., v. 騎乘
tame [tem] adj. 溫馴的

住所

郵電通訊

日常活動

銀行與保險

交通

食品與飲食

購物

社交活動

教育

休閒活動

醫療

緊急情況

Useful Phrases 實用語句

1. 我要一匹溫馴的馬。

   I want a tame horse.

2. 我以前從未騎過馬。

   I've never ridden a horse before.

3. 我的馬鞍有點鬆。

   My saddle feels loose.

4. 請查看我的馬鞍。

   Please check my saddle.

10.5b 拜訪國家公園 Visiting National Parks

美國有非常棒的國家公園,例如優勝美地、大峽谷及黃石公園,這些都是體驗大自然鬼斧神工的絕佳地點。國家公園提供露營、健行及其他的設施,進入國家公園需要買票,但是票價合理,且公園警察能提供許多訊息及協助,廣大的公園內已開發區可能有商店、餐廳及其他使旅程更舒適便利的設備。

Dialog 1 對話1

A: 嗨,歡迎來到雷尼爾山國家公園。

A: Hi. Welcome to the entrance to Mt. Rainier National Park.

B: 謝謝,我們要付多少錢?

B: Thanks. How much do we need to pay?

A: 每輛車15元可以待一星期,或50元待整個夏天。

A: $15 per car for one week or $50 for the whole summer.

B: 但我們只要待兩天。

B: But we only want to stay two days.

A: 你們可以徒步走入公園，待一星期5元，但是除此之外沒有更低的價錢。

A: You can enter on foot for \$5 a week, but other than that there is no lower price.

B: 好，我們付汽車的價錢。

B: OK. We'll pay the car price.

Dialog 2 對話2

A: 我看到在那邊有好的露營地。

A: I see a nice camping spot over there.

B: 我們到那停車紮營。

B: Let's park there and set up camp.

A: 我晚點去買些柴火。

A: I'll go buy some firewood later.

B: 好，我們今晚可以享受烤火及烤棉花糖。

B: Good. We can enjoy a nice fire and roast marshmallows tonight.

A: 時間還早，所以我想我們還可以健行幾個小時。

A: It's early, so I think we can go hiking for a couple of hours, too.

住所

郵電通訊

日常活動

銀行與保險

交通

食品與飲食

購物

社交活動

教育

休閒活動

醫療

緊急情況

Word Bank 字庫

firewood [`faɪr,wʊd] n. 柴木
roast [rost] v. 烤
marshmallow [`marʃ,mælo] n. 棉花糖

 Dialog 3 對話3

A: 去健行前，確定食物都收在車內。

A: Before we go hiking, be sure all the food is put away inside the car.

B: 好，我知道熊及其他動物可能聞到味道會跑過來。

B: OK. I know bears and other wild animals might smell it and come close.

A: 對，我們要小心。

A: That's right. We have to be careful.

B: 如果我們健行時看到任何野生動物，我們也要離遠點。

B: If we see any wild animals while hiking, we need to stay clear of them too.

A: 又說對了，他們沒有被馴服，如果是帶著幼子的動物，更要離遠點。

A: Right again. They are not tame. Especially stay away from them if they have young with them.

B: 我們健行時最好邊說話邊弄點聲響，那樣動物會遠離我們，不會被嚇到。

B: It's best if we talk and make some noise as we hike, that way animals will hear us and not be startled.

A: 嘿，別忘記帶水及地圖。

A: Hey! Don't forget to bring water and the map.

住所 | 郵電通訊 | 日常活動 | 銀行與保險 | 交通 | 食品與飲食 | 購物 | 社交活動 | 教育 | 休閒活動 | 醫療 | 緊急情況

Word Bank 字庫

tame [tem] adj. 馴服的
startle [`startl] v. 吃驚，驚跳

Useful Phrases 實用語句

1. 我可以在哪裡拿到露營地的地圖？
   Where can I get a map of the campground?
2. 你可以在訪客中心拿到地圖。
   You can get a map at the visitor's center.
3. 公園[國家公園]警察介紹何時開始？
   What time does the Park Ranger's presentation begin?
4. 我們需要預訂一個露營地點。
   We need to reserve a camping spot.
5. 小木屋還有房間嗎？
   Are there any rooms available at the lodge?
6. 我們哪裡可以買到柴木？
   Where can we buy firewood?
7. 我們來升營火吧。
   Let's start a campfire.

Language Power 字句補給站

◆ 國家公園 National Parks

entrance fee	入園費
campground	露營地
trail	路徑
compass	羅盤
map	地圖
tent	帳篷
sleeping bag	睡袋
camping spot	露營地點

campfire	營火
matches	火柴
cooking stove	爐子

10.5c 在海邊 At the Beach

  Dialog 對話

A: 嗨，關於這裡的規則我有個問題。

A: Hi. I have a question about the rules here.

B: 你有什麼問題呢？

B: What is your question?

A: 可以撿拾海邊的貝殼嗎？

A: Is it all right to collect seashells from the beach?

B: 可以的，還可以在指定的區域挖蛤。

B: Yes, it is. It's also OK to dig for clams in designated areas.

A: 撿拾漂流木呢？

A: What about picking up driftwood?

B: 不，這個海灘不行，也不可以生火。

B: No, not at this beach. No fires allowed, either.

A: 其他海邊可以嗎？

A: Is it OK at any other beach?

B: 可以，我在地圖上指一些給你看。

B: Yes, let me show you some on a map.

Word Bank 字庫

collect [kə`lɛkt] v. 收集
seashell [`si,ʃɛl] n. 貝殼
dig [dɪg] v. 挖
clam [klæm] n. 蚌，蛤
designated [`dɛzɪg,netɪd] adj. 指定的
driftwood [`drɪft,wʊd] n. 漂流木

Notes 小叮嚀

　　在美國休閒旅行，多數地區是對大眾開放的，但是能先確定一下總是較保險。有時遊客可能必須穿越私人道路或土地才能到達某個海邊或河岸，如果看到「私人土地，不可侵入」(Private property. Don't Trespass.) 的標誌時，必須獲得許可才能通過，侵入私人土地的結果，可能讓主人覺得安全受威脅而拿槍以對或是報警處理。

10.5d 觀光船 Bay Cruises

Dialog 對話

A: 我們可以在這裡買遊海船票嗎？

A: Can we buy tickets for a cruise on the bay here?

B: 可以。

B: Yes, you can.

A: 有晚上的遊船嗎？

A: Are there any evening cruises?

B: 有，我們在 7 點登船，7:30 出發。

B: Yes. We board at 7:00 p.m., and set sail at 7:30.

A: 船上有晚餐嗎？

A: Is dinner available on board?

B: 當然有，船票包含五道精緻美食。

B: Certainly. A fine five-course meal is included in the price.

Word Bank 字庫

cruise [kruz] n. 悠遊
bay [be] n. 海灣
set sail 出發
fine [faɪn] adj. 精緻的

Notes 小叮嚀

許多水上活動價格不低，從事水上活動首重天氣條件，許多地區氣溫變化較大，即使夏季遊河或出海到附近小島一遊，都必須要帶件外套備用，晚上看夜景風大，氣溫若降到60°F/16°C左右，甚至要厚外套、帽子、圍巾才足夠保暖。

左側邊欄（由上而下）：住所、郵電通訊、日常活動、銀行與保險、交通、食品與飲食、購物、社交活動、教育、休閒活動、醫療、緊急情況

10.5e 租水上摩托車 Jet Ski Rental

Dialog 對話

A: 我們想要租水上摩托車。

A: We want to rent some jet skis.

B: 我們有很多，看這邊。

B: We have many. Look over here.

A: 太好了，多少錢呢？

A: Great. How much does it cost?

B: 4小時30元或整天50元。

B: $30 for four hours, or $50 for the day.

A: 我們以前沒騎過，會有問題嗎？

A: We've never used one before. Is that a big problem?

B: 一點也不會，我們可以給你免費上一堂課。

B: Not at all. We'll give you a lesson free.

A: 要多久呢？

A: How long will that take?

B: 只要10-15分鐘。

B: Only 10-15 minutes.

10.5f 海邊游泳 Swimming at the Beach

Dialog 對話

A: 嗨，這裡游泳安全嗎？

A: Hi. Is it safe to swim here?

B: 你要小心暗流。

B: You must be careful of the undertow.

A: 會很危險嗎？

A: Is it very dangerous?

B: 可能會。

B: It can be.

A: 我會游泳，但游得不是很好。

A: I can swim, but not great.

B: 這裡有很多救生員，你就待在標示區域內。

B: There are many lifeguards here. Just stay in the marked areas.

A: 那些區域安全嗎？

A: Are those areas safe?

B: 比在海邊其他地方游泳安全多了。

B: They are much safer than other parts of the beach for swimming.

Word Bank 字庫

undertow [`ʌndə͵to] n. 暗流
lifeguard [`laɪf͵gɑrd] n. 救生員
marked [mɑrkt] adj. 標示出的

Useful Phrases 實用語句

1. 這裡可以游泳嗎？

   Is it OK to swim here?

2. 我需要救生衣。

   I need a life vest.

3. 我們需要一些救生圈及浮板。

   We need some rubber tubes and kick boards.

4. 我們需要蛙鞋。

   We need some fins.

5. 我們來找一些浮潛用具吧。

   Let's get some snorkeling equipment.

6. 這裡有救生員嗎？

   Is there a lifeguard here?

Notes 小叮嚀

　　海邊游泳在許多地方是安全的，但你必須小心強浪，並避免到許多海水溫度低的地方游泳。在颶風季節，到美東佛羅里達大西洋沿岸或墨西哥灣的颶風好發帶 (hurricane alley)，要特別注意氣象報告。即使颶風還在數百哩外，已悄然帶來強烈海邊暗流。要到海邊游泳最好先問旅館及查看當地氣象及水域狀況，且選擇有救生員的海邊。

住所
郵電通訊
日常活動
銀行與保險
交通
食品與飲食
購物
社交活動
教育
休閒活動
醫療
緊急情況

10.5g 滑水 Water Skiing

Dialog 1 對話1

A: 好，抓住繩尾走到側邊。

A: OK. Grab the end of the rope and go over the side.

A: 繩子變緊時，我會打信號讓你開始。

A: When the rope becomes tight, I'll signal you to hit it.

B: 好，我會看你的信號。

B: Right. I'll be watching for your signal.

B: 如果我倒下去，我會等你回來，我才可以再次抓住繩子。

B: If I fall, I'll wait for you to come back around so I can grab the rope again.

A: 如果你倒下去，我們會升起安全旗。

A: We'll be sure to raise the safety flag if you fall.

Word Bank 字庫

grab [græb] v. 抓住
signal [`sɪgn̩] n. 信號
raise [rez] v. 升起
safety flag n. 安全旗

Dialog 2 對話2

A: 我累了，你現在要滑水嗎？

A: I'm tired. Do you want to ski now?

B: 不了，我今天夠了。 → **B:** No. I've had enough for today.

A: 那我們去碼頭。 → **A:** Let's head for the docks then.

B: 好主意，我們去那裡綁船。 → **B:** Good idea. We'll tie up the boat there.

A: 好，我們無論如何都需要替船加油。 → **A:** Yes. We need to refuel the boat anyway.

B: 是的，然後我們可以開始烤肉。 → **B:** Yeah. Then we can start the barbeque.

 Word Bank 字庫

dock [dɑk] n. 碼頭
refuel [riˋfjuəl] v. 加油

Useful Phrases 實用語句

1. 我需要救生衣。
   I need a life jacket.
2. 握緊拖繩。
   Hold the tow rope tightly.
3. 拉！(開始滑水！)
   Hit it!
4. 繫緊船。
   Tie up the boat.

Language Power 字句補給站

◆ 滑水 Water Skiing

life vest [jacket]	救生衣
towrope	拖繩
ski boat	滑水拖船
slalom	障礙滑水 [雪] 比賽
spotter	快艇上的看守員
skier down	滑水者落水

10.5h 釣魚 Fishing

在美國湖邊、河裡、小溪及海域釣魚都很受歡迎，但釣魚需要執照並且要遵守規定；釣魚器具及執照在戶外運動用品店可以購買得到。

Dialog 1 對話1

A: 我們在這間戶外運動用品店買釣魚執照吧。

A: Let's stop at this sporting goods store and buy fishing licenses.

B: 好，我們也要買一本釣魚法規。

B: Alright. We need to get a fishing regulation book, too.

A: 我們可以買一份特別的兩天執照。

A: We can buy a special two-day license.

B: 那樣我們可以省點錢。

B: We'll save money that way.

Word Bank 字庫

sporting goods store n. 戶外運動用品店
license [`laɪsn̩s] n. 執照
regulation [ˌrɛɡjəˈleʃən] n. 規則

Dialog 2 對話2

A: 嗨,我們要買兩天的釣魚許可。

A: Hi. We want to buy two-day fishing permits.

B: 好,一份18元。

B: Sure. They cost $18 each.

A: 好,你也賣釣魚用具嗎?

A: OK. Do you sell fishing tackle here, too?

B: 是的,我們店裡的釣魚區有你會需要的物品。

B: Yes. We have everything you'll need in the fishing section of the store.

Word Bank 字庫

fishing permits n. 釣魚許可
fishing tackle n. 釣魚用具
section [`sɛkʃən] n. 區

Dialog 3 對話3

A: 我們要很早開始。

A: We need to get started very early.

B: 對，一大早釣魚最好。

B: Right. Fishing is best in the early morning.

A: 確定帶餌了。

A: Be sure to bring the bait.

B: 我有帶餌還有釣魚盒子。

B: I've got it and our tackle box.

A: 好，我們今天也要嘗試一些誘餌。

A: Good. We'll want to try some lures today, too.

Word Bank 字庫

bait [bet] n. 魚餌
tackle box n. 釣魚盒子
lure [lʊr] n. 誘餌

10.5i 海釣 Ocean Sport Fishing

Dialog 1 對話1

A: 我要買釣魚執照。

A: I want to buy a fishing license.

B: 你要從事哪種釣魚活動呢？

B: What type of fishing are you going to do?

A: 我要搭鮭魚船出海。

A: I want to go out on a salmon boat.

住所
郵電通訊
日常活動
銀行與保險
交通
食品與飲食
購物
社交活動
教育
休閒活動
醫療
緊急情況

B: 這樣的話你應該去碼頭。	**B:** In that case you should go to the docks.
A: 為什麼？	**A:** Why?
B: 你可以向運動用品店買執照。	**B:** You can buy the license from the outfitter.
A: 那我需要其他的裝備嗎？	**A:** What about the other equipment I need?
B: 他們會有你所需的裝備。	**B:** They'll have everything you need.

Word Bank 字庫

salmon [`sæmən] n. 鮭魚
outfitter [`aʊt‚fɪtə] n. 運動用品店 [商]
equipment [ɪ`kwɪpmənt] n. 設備，裝備

Useful Phrases 實用語句

1. 我想買一張釣魚證。

   I'd like to buy a fishing license.

2. 我需要一些釣魚設備。

   I need some fishing equipment.

3. 我需要一些魚餌。

   I need some bait.

4. 這張釣魚證可以用多久？

   How long will this license last?

住所 郵電通訊 日常活動 銀行與保險 交通 食品跟飲食 購物 社交活動 教育 休閒活動 醫療 緊急情況

住所
郵電通訊
日常活動
銀行與保險
交通
食品與飲食
購物
社交活動
教育
休閒活動
醫療
緊急情況

Dialog 2　對話2

A: 哈囉，我們想要海釣鮭魚。

A: Hello. We're interested in going ocean fishing for salmon.

B: 我們每天早上有包船出海。

B: We have charter boats going out every morning.

A: 多少錢？

A: What does it cost?

B: 每位成人5小時75元。

B: $75 per adult for a five-hour trip.

A: 何時開船？

A: What time does the boat leave?

B: 早上6點。

B: 6 a.m.

A: 我們要帶任何器具嗎？

A: Do we need to bring any gear?

B: 不用，價錢裡每樣都包了。

B: No. Everything is included in the price.

Word Bank　字庫

charter boat n. 包船

住所

郵電通訊

日常活動

銀行與保險

交通

食品與飲食

購物

社交活動

教育

休閒活動

醫療

緊急情況

 Useful Phrases 實用語句

1. 我們可以在那裡買魚餌。

   We can buy bait over there.

2. 我需要一支較大的魚鉤。

   I need a bigger hook.

3. 這是一支較大的魚鉤。

   Here is a larger hook.

4. 裝好魚鉤。

   Set the hook.

5. 漁網拿好。

   Get the net.

6. 拉魚上岸。

   Land the fish.

7. 我來清理魚。

   I'll clean the fish.

 Tips 小祕訣

在美國，釣魚及打獵不僅要看季節，準備裝備，也需要證件。如果是生手，專門的教練可以提供資料及裝備，並給你所需要的指導。

Fishing is best in the early morning.

10.5j 滑雪 Snow Skiing

滑雪對許多人而言是個好玩的運動，科羅拉多州、華盛頓州、奧勒岡州、猶他州及其他州都有滑雪場及滑雪設備，其中奧勒岡州的 Mt. Hood，整年都有世界聞名的山坡滑雪道；下坡及越野滑雪在開發完整的區域都有，你可以買或租用滑雪設備，但滑雪其實是頗昂貴的活動，滑雪設備和纜車票都不便宜，光是纜車票從每日 $10 到專屬某些特定人士造訪的昂貴滑雪區的 $100 都有，因此喜愛滑雪活動者可以先去電詢問，選擇價格較低時再造訪；週末滑雪活動常包含滑雪課程，記得穿著一定要保暖。

Dialog 1　對話1

A: 明天我需要早早開始。

A: I want to get started early tomorrow.

B: 我也是，纜車早上7點開始。

B: Me, too. The lift starts working at 7:00 am.

A: 那不太重要，因為我們要先上課。

A: That's not important to us because we have to take lessons first.

B: 對，我想我們不必用到纜車。

B: True. I guess we won't have to use the lift.

A: 幾堂課後我們可以去初學者緩坡。

A: After a couple of lessons, we can go to the bunny lift.

B: 對，像我們這種初學者，我們可以試試那裡的小山坡。

B: Right. It's for beginners like us. We can try a little hill there.

住所
郵電通訊
日常活動
銀行與保險
交通
食品與飲食
購物
社交活動
教育
休閒活動
醫療
緊急情況

 Word Bank 字庫

lift [lɪft] n. 纜車
bunny lift n. 初學者緩坡

Dialog 2 對話2

A: 確定你的靴子綁緊了，不然會扭到腳。

A: Check to make sure your boots are fastened tightly; otherwise you may sprain an ankle.

B: 滑雪危險嗎？

B: Is snow skiing dangerous?

A: 可能，確定你的裝備良好，還有你只在指定地區滑雪是很重要的。

A: It can be. It's important to make sure your equipment is in good condition, and that you ski only in designated areas.

B: 如果我受傷呢？

B: What if I get injured?

A: 滑雪巡邏員會來幫你，他們總在滑雪坡道巡邏，看是否有人有麻煩。

A: The ski patrol people will come to help you. They are always around on the slopes looking to see if someone is in trouble.

 Word Bank 字庫

fasten [`fæsn̩] v. 綁緊
sprain [spren] v. 扭到
designated area n. 指定地區
slope [slop] n. 坡道

Dialog 3 (對話3)

A: 我們去小木屋一會兒暖暖身體。

A: Let's go into the lodge for a while and warm up.

B: 好,去休息一下喝杯熱咖啡也好。

B: OK. It would be nice to hang out and have a cup of hot coffee.

A: 是的,我們也可以看看其他滑雪者。

A: Yes. And we can watch the other skiers, too.

B: 他們也有東西吃,還有滑雪設備及其他服務。

B: They also have things to eat, ski equipment and other services as well.

A: 是啊,那倒提醒我要查看綁帶了。

A: Yeah. That reminds me. I need to have my binders checked.

B: 小木屋內有個地方可以讓你把那弄好。

B: There is a place you can get that done in the lodge.

Word Bank (字庫)

lodge [lɑdʒ] n. 小木屋
remind [rɪ`maɪnd] v. 提醒
binder [`baɪndɚ] n. 綁帶

Dialog 4 (對話4)

A: 今天我們要去越野滑雪。

A: Today we are going cross-country skiing.

B: 好，那比下坡滑雪便宜多了。

B: Great. It's much cheaper than downhill skiing.

A: 是的，而且也簡單多了。

A: Yes. It's a lot simpler to do, too.

B: 設備一樣，但是雪橇長多了。

B: The equipment is the same, but the skis are much longer.

A: 這是很休閒的滑雪方式。

A: It's a much more leisurely way to snow ski.

B: 你也可以多看看鄉村。

B: You get to see much more of the countryside, too.

 Useful Phrases 實用語句

1. 我要在哪裡買纜車券？

   Where can I buy lift tickets?

2. 我們去排隊坐纜車。

   Let's get in line for the lift.

3. 我們去租小木屋。

   Let's rent a room at the lodge.

4. 我們去滑坡吧！

   Let's hit the slopes.

5. 我的滑雪板需要上蠟。

   I need to have my skis waxed.

6. 我要上一些滑雪課程。

   I want some skiing lessons.

7. 我要學怎麼滑下坡道。

   I want to learn how to downhill.

住所

郵電通訊

日常活動

銀行與保險

交通

食品與飲食

購物

社交活動

教育

休閒活動

醫療

緊急情況

474

8. 我需要學怎麼越野滑雪。

I want to learn how to cross-country ski.

9. 我需要租滑雪設備。

We need to rent some equipment.

 Language Power 字句補給站

◆ 滑雪 Snow Skiing

skis	雪橇
ski poles	滑雪杖
goggles	護眼罩
ski wax	雪蠟
chair lift	椅子纜車
lift-ticket	纜車票
ski patrol	滑雪巡邏
ski mask	滑雪面罩
bunny slope	緩坡道
downhill	下坡
cross-country	越野
ski conditions	雪況

10.5k 美國印地安原住民保留區
Native American Indian Reservations

 Dialog 對話

A: 哈囉，我有一個關於溫泉地印地安保留區的問題。

A: Hello. I have a question about the Warm Springs Indian Reservation.

B: 什麼問題呢？

B: What is your question?

A: 進入保留區需要任何許可證或特別許可嗎？

A: Do I need any permits or special permission to go into the reservation?

B: 不用，保留區是開放給大眾的，不過某些地方有時並不開放。

B: No, you don't. The reservations are open to the public, although there are some parts of the reservation that are restricted at times.

A: 為什麼呢？

A: Why?

B: 住在那裡的族人認為有些地區是特別的，有時候舉行特別的活動只有當地族人能參加。

B: Some places are considered very special by the tribe that lives there, and sometimes special events take place that only the tribe members can attend.

A: 我知道了，謝謝你的資訊。

A: I see. Thanks for the information.

住所
郵電通訊
日常活動
銀行與保險
交通
食品與飲食
購物
社交活動
教育
休閒活動
醫療
緊急情況

 Word Bank 字庫

permit [`pɜmɪt] n. 許可證
permission [pə`mɪʃən] n. 許可
reservation [ˌrɛzə`veʃən] n. 保留區
restrict [rɪ`strɪkt] v. 限制
tribe [traɪb] n. 部落
attend [ə`tɛnd] v. 參加，出席

Tips 小祕訣

　　印地安原住民保留區在美國各地都有，在許多保留區可以看到他們開設的賭場，有些保留區是休閒度假區，任何人都可以去打高爾夫、游泳、騎馬及從事其他休閒活動，有的地方標榜體驗部落生活，遊客可以買到許多原住民的食物及別緻的手工藝品。

10.51 賭城 Gambling (Las Vegas or Other Places)

 Dialog 1 對話1

A: 我們該去哪個賭場呢？

A: Which casino should we go to?

B: 很難講，拉斯維加斯有很多賭場。

B: Hard to say. There are so many in Las Vegas.

A: 我也想看場秀。

A: I want to see a show, too.

B: 嗯，大的賭場都有秀。

B: Well, all the major casinos have shows.

A: 真好，飲料也是免費。

A: Right, and drinks are free.

B: 只有在賭博時才免費。

B: Only while you are gambling.

Word Bank 字庫

casino [kə`sɪno] n. 賭場
show [ʃo] n. 秀，表演
gamble [`gæmbl̩] v. 賭博

Dialog 2 對話2

A: 對不起，我們需要拉霸 [吃角子老虎] 的代幣。

A: Excuse me. We need some tokens for the slot machines.

B: 你要多少？

B: How many do you want?

A: 200元等值。

A: $200 worth.

B: 好，把你的錢放在盤子上然後滑入窗戶下。

B: OK. Just put your money in the tray and slide it under the window.

A: 在這裡。

A: Here you are.

住所
郵電通訊
日常活動
銀行與保險
交通
食品與飲食
購物
社交活動
教育
休閒活動
醫療
緊急情況

住所
郵電通訊
日常活動
銀行與保險
交通
食品與飲食
購物
社交活動
教育
休閒活動
醫療
緊急情況

B: 這裡是你的代幣，祝你好運。

B: And here are your tokens. Good luck.

A: 謝謝。

A: Thanks.

Word Bank 字庫

token [`tokən] n. 代幣
slot machine n. 拉霸，吃角子老虎
worth [wɜθ] adj. 等值的
tray [tre] n. 盤子
slide [slaɪd] v. 滑動

Useful Phrases 實用語句

1. 我們來賭博。
   Let's gamble.

2. 我們去賭城的大街 (拉斯維加斯賭場林立的大街)。
   Let's go to the Strip.

3. 我們去黃金峽谷 (拉斯維加斯市內)。
   Let's go to Glitter Gulch.

4. 你喜歡玩 21 點嗎?
   Do you like to play Black Jack?

Language Power 字句補給站

◆ **賭博 Gambling**

deck (of cards)	一副紙牌
shuffle	洗牌
cut the deck	切牌
deal	發牌
dealer	發牌員

Black Jack	21點
Keno	一種類似樂透賭博遊戲，使用號碼彩球及紙牌
Roulette Table	輪盤桌
poker	撲克牌
chips	圓形籌碼

Notes 小叮嚀

多數州規定禁止在公共空間喝酒 (Open Container Laws) 以避免酒駕，法律規定酒瓶打開即違法。公共空間如街道、公園、移動的公共或私人車輛上等處禁止喝酒，但「公共空間」的定義未明，有些人拿紙袋遮住酒瓶，他人從外觀無從得知是否喝酒，有時不一定會被取締。禁止公開飲酒也有例外，如大學校園或球賽前在停車場打開後車廂的野餐聚會 (tailgate party)。

賭城拉斯維加斯 (Las Vegas) 與紐奧良 (New Orleans) 是美國極少數可以在街上喝酒的城市，街道販售特別造型的酒精飲料供觀光客體驗公開飲酒，可說是城市特色。因此標價僅 $1 的路邊攤位酒精飲料，多數觀光客還樂於附上 $1-$2 的小費。

10.6 烤肉聚餐
Barbeque Parties

Dialog 對話

A: 我們要辦一個七月四日 (國慶日) 烤肉會。

A: We're going to have a 4th of July barbeque.

B: 我要帶什麼呢？

B: What should I bring?

A: 一道沙拉或洋芋片都好。

A: A salad or potato chips would be fine.

住所

郵電通訊

B: 那喝的呢？ 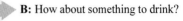 **B:** How about something to drink?

日常活動

A: 我們已有啤酒及汽水。 **A:** We have beer and soft drinks already.

銀行與保險

B: 我會多帶一些。 **B:** I'll bring more anyway.

交通

A: 好主意。 **A:** Good idea.

食品與飲食

 Word Bank 字庫

barbeque [`barbɪˌkju] n. 烤肉
soft drinks n. 汽水

購物

社交活動

Useful Phrases 實用語句

1. 我們要看煙火秀。

   We want to see the fireworks show.

教育

2. 我們可以在哪裡買到煙火呢？

   Where can we buy some fireworks?

休閒活動

3. 我們來烤肉吧。

   Let's have a barbeque.

 Notes 小叮嚀

醫療

如果要放煙火 (fireworks)，應該先了解當地州政府對煙火類型的規定。

緊急情況

10.7 小鎮嘉年華
The County Fair

Dialog 對話

A: 我們去小鎮嘉年華吧。

A: Let's go to the county fair.

B: 那是什麼？

B: What's that?

A: 小鎮嘉年華是為期一週的市集，有很多東西可看。

A: County fairs are big weeklong fairs with lots of things to see.

B: 像什麼呢？

B: Like what?

A: 動物、藝術、歌唱及舞蹈表演、產品展示、競賽等等。

A: Animals, art, singing and dancing performances, product demonstrations, competitions, etc.

B: 好像有很多看頭。

B: It sounds like there are a lot to see.

A: 很多事可做，可以玩遊戲、贏獎品及乘坐大嘉年華(遊樂設施)。

A: A lot to do. There are games to play, prizes to win, and big carnival rides.

B: 會很貴嗎？

B: Is it expensive?

住所　郵電通訊　日常活動　銀行與保險　交通　食品與飲食　購物　社交活動　教育　休閒活動　醫療　緊急情況

A: 不算貴，每人大約 5-6元，但遊樂區內你要多付些。

A: No, not really. It usually costs five or six dollars per person, but you have to pay extra for some things inside the fairgrounds.

Language Power 字句補給站

◆ 小鎮嘉年華 The County Fair

farm animals	農場動物
art show	藝術表演
singing performance	歌唱表演
carnival rides	乘坐嘉年華 (遊樂設施)
Rodeo	牛仔競技表演
growers competition	農產品競賽
product show	產品展示
cotton candy	棉花糖
corn dogs	脆皮熱狗 (熱狗裹麵糊後油炸)
carnival games	嘉年華遊戲

Tips 小祕訣

　　美國夏天到處可見小鎮嘉年華，這是美國傳統的一部分，每個小鎮都會舉辦。有錢點的大城鎮嘉年華規模較大，提供人們食物及多樣娛樂，是全家的好去處，州嘉年華的規模更大，也是在夏天舉辦，吸引更多的人潮，嘉年華的收費看規模大小及地點而定。

10.8 動物園
The Zoo

 Dialog 對話

A: 嗨，動物園開到很晚嗎？

A: Hi. Is the zoo open very late?

B: 今天開到下午6點。

B: It's open until 6 p.m. today.

A: 有可愛動物區嗎？

A: Is there a petting zoo, too?

B: 有，在西區。

B: Yes, there is. It's on the west side.

A: 要多收費嗎？

A: Is there an extra charge?

B: 平時不必。

B: Not on weekdays.

A: 我們可以在那裡拍照嗎？

A: Can we take pictures there?

B: 可以，但不要用閃光燈。

B: Yes, but please don't use flash.

住所 郵電通訊 日常活動 銀行與保險 交通 食品與飲食 購物 社交活動 教育 休閒活動 醫療 緊急情況

住所

郵電通訊

日常活動

銀行與保險

交通

食品與飲食

購物

社交活動

教育

休閒活動

醫療

緊急情況

Word Bank 字庫

petting zoo n. 可愛動物區(可以撫摸擁抱動物之區域)
flash [flæʃ] n. 閃光燈

10.9 遊樂園
Amusement Parks

Dialog 1 對話1

A: 嗨，我們要四張票。

A: Hi. We want tickets for four.

B: 我們有半日通行證及全日通行證。

B: We have half-day and full-day passes.

A: 全日票可以讓我們做什麼？

A: What does the all-day pass allow us to do?

B: 跟半日票一樣，但你可以待到關門時間。

B: It's the same as the half-day pass, but you can stay until closing time.

A: 你們什麼時候關閉園區呢？

A: What time do you close the park?

B: 園區在晚上11:30關。

B: The park closes at 11:30 p.m.

A: 通行證可以乘坐每樣東西和進入園區所有地方嗎？

A: Does the pass allow us to ride and enter everything in the park?

B: 可以,除了明日世界,每個人要多花2.5元。

B: Yes, except Future Land. It costs $2.50 per person more.

 Dialog 2 對話2

A: 票務員告訴我,我們應該詳閱這些警語。

A: The ticket agent told me we should read these warnings.

B: 警語說些什麼呢?

B: What do the warnings say?

A: 大部分是關於健康考量。

A: Mostly they are about health considerations.

B: 好的,我知道了。我的健康沒問題。

B: Oh, OK, I see. I have no problem with my health.

Word Bank 字庫

warning [`wɔrnɪŋ] n. 警告
consideration [kən͵sɪdə`reʃən] n. 考量

Useful Phrases 實用語句

1. 這是乘坐那個設施的隊伍嗎?
   Is this the line for that ride?
2. 從哪裡開始排隊?
   Where does the line start?
3. 小孩可以坐這個嗎?
   Can children ride this one?

住所 郵電通訊 日常活動 銀行與保險 交通 食品與飲食 購物 社交活動 教育 休閒活動 醫療 緊急情況

4. 一日券可以做什麼？

What does a day pass allow us to do?

5. 入場券包含乘坐遊樂設施嗎？

Does the pass include the rides?

Unit 11 Health Care

醫療

美國醫療服務佳，但是費用昂貴，因此要住在美國，醫療保險是必要的。雖然醫院及診所到處林立，但是如果能有了解你病史的家庭醫師可以請教健康問題是最好不過了，當然分門別類的各科醫師也提供各科別的專門醫療服務。和各類服務一樣，移民們或許在居住的城鎮可以找到適合的同族裔醫師就診，溝通會容易多了；但要到國外長住，自己的健康問題，像是藥物過敏或過敏源，還是要先查好英文怎麼說，尤其如果有特別的情形，要準備自己的病歷影印帶出國，在當地看病時可以讓醫師很快了解你的狀況，最好也帶著醫藥專業中英字典備用。

11.1 預約及更改預約
Reservation and Changing an Appointment Time

11.1a 預約 Making an Appointment

 Dialog 對話

A: 我要掛號。

A: I want to make an appointment to see a doctor.

B: 好,你有常看的醫師嗎?

B: Alright. Do you have a regular physician?

A: 沒有。

A: No, I don't.

B: 沒關係。我幫你安排看亞當斯醫師。

B: That's OK. I'll make an appointment for you to see Doctor Adams.

A: 謝謝,他是什麼醫師?

A: Thank you. What kind of doctor is he?

B: 他是一般醫師,如果你需要專門醫師,他會推薦一個給你。

B: He's a general practitioner. If you need a specialist, he'll recommend one to you.

A: 我懂了,我何時可以過去?

A: I see. Thank you. What time is my appointment?

住所
郵電通訊
日常活動
銀行與保險
交通
食品與飲食
購物
社交活動
教育
休閒活動
醫療
緊急情況

B: 明天下午2點可以嗎？

B: Is 2:00 tomorrow good for you?

A: 可以。

A: Yes, that is fine.

 Useful Phrases 實用語句

1. 我需要預約掛號。

   I need to make an appointment to see a doctor.

2. 我何時可以見醫師？

   When can I see the doctor?

11.1b 更改預約 Changing an Appointment Time

Dialog 對話

A: 哈囉，亞當斯醫師辦公室。

A: Hello. Doctor Adams office.

B: 哈囉，我的名字是唐納王，我需要改約時間。

B: Hello. My name is Donald Wong. I need to change the time of my appointment.

A: 你排什麼時候看醫師？

A: What time are you scheduled to see the doctor?

B: 明天下午2點。

B: Tomorrow at 2 p.m.

住所

郵電通訊

日常活動

銀行與保險

交通

食品與飲食

購物

社交活動

教育

休閒活動

醫療

緊急情況

A: 你要改成幾點？

A: What time would you like to re-schedule for?

B: 後天早上。

B: The day after tomorrow, some time in the morning.

A: 抱歉，早上約滿了，下午早一點呢？

A: I'm sorry, but his schedule is full in the morning. What about early afternoon?

B: 1點可以嗎？

B: Is 1:00 available?

A: 可以。

A: Yes, it is.

B: 好，我那時會到。

B: Good. I'll be there then.

A: 我現在寫下來，謝謝你打來。

A: I'll write it down now. Thank you for calling.

B: 不客氣，也謝謝你。

B: You're welcome. Thank you, too.

📖 Language Power 字句補給站

◆ 醫院標示及常用字 Hospital Signs and Common Words

hospital	醫院
clinic	診所
specialist	專門醫師
general practitioner	一般醫師

physician	內科醫師
family doctor	家庭醫師
temperature	體溫
pulse	脈搏
blood pressure	血壓
nurse	護士
medicine	藥
prescription	處方
pharmacy	藥局
x-ray	X光
examination	檢查
stethoscope	聽診器
ambulance	救護車
appointment	預約
emergency room	急診室
tests	檢驗
waiting room	等待室，候診室
wheel chair	輪椅
shot	打針

◆ 專門科別及醫師 Medical Areas and Specialists

pediatrician/pediatrics	小兒科醫師/小兒科
internal medicine	內科
surgeons/surgery	外科醫師/外科
gynecologists/gynecology	婦產科醫師/婦產科
urologist/urology	泌尿科醫師/泌尿科
otolaryngology/ear nose and throat (ENT)	耳鼻喉科
dentist/dentistry	牙科醫師/牙科
dermatologist/dermatology	皮膚科醫師/皮膚科
ophthalmologist/ophthalmology	眼科醫師/眼科
neurologist/neurology	神經科醫師/神經科
psychologist	心理醫師
psychiatrist/psychiatry	精神科醫師/精神科
physical therapists/ physical therapy	復健師/物理治療

住所
郵電通訊
日常活動
銀行與保險
交通
食品與飲食
購物
社交活動
教育
休閒活動
醫療
緊急情況

11.2 內科
Internal Medicine

11.2a 報到 Informing Arrival

Dialog 對話

A: 我與亞當斯醫師有約。

A: I have an appointment to see Dr. Adams.

B: 請問你的名字？

B: Your name, please?

A: 唐納王。

A: Donald Wong.

B: 是的，王先生，我看到你有1點的約，請坐下稍等，醫師馬上來看你。

B: Yes, Mr. Wong. I see you have a 1:00 appointment. Please sit down and wait. The doctor will see you soon.

A: 謝謝。

A: Thanks.

B: (護士) 王先生，我先來量脈搏及體溫。

B: (nurse) Let me take your pulse and temperature first, Mr. Wong.

A: 好。

A: OK.

B: 我也要量你的血壓。

B: I'll check your blood pressure, too.

11.2b 症狀說明 Describing Symptoms

Dialog 1 （對話1）

A: 哈囉，王先生，請進來坐下。

A: Hello, Mr. Wong. Please come in and sit down.

B: 謝謝。

B: Thank you.

A: 怎麼了？

A: What is wrong?

B: 我有時候覺得頭昏，胃也不舒服。

B: I feel dizzy and sick to my stomach sometimes.

A: 你有這種感覺多久了？

A: How long have you felt this way?

B: 斷斷續續約三週了。

B: On and off for about three weeks.

A: 我知道了。

A: I see.

Word Bank 字庫

dizzy [ˋdɪzɪ] adj. 暈眩的

on and off 斷斷續續

Dialog 2 對話2

A: 我要做一些血液檢查。

A: I'm going to have some blood tests done.

B: 我可以很快回家嗎？

B: Can I go home soon?

A: 我想你可以離開，但是我首先得要得到檢查結果。

A: I think you can go, but first I want to get the results of the test.

B: 那要多久？

B: How long will that take?

A: 約一個小時。

A: About an hour.

B: 我要在哪裡等？

B: Where should I wait?

A: 在候診室，那裡有雜誌及報紙。

A: In the waiting room. There are magazines and newspapers there.

B: 我可以在附近吃點東西嗎？

B: Can I get anything to eat close to here?

住所

郵電通訊

日常活動

銀行與保險

交通

食品與飲食

購物

社交活動

教育

休閒活動

醫療

緊急情況

A: 可以，走廊過去有自助餐廳及點心吧。

A: Yes. There is a cafeteria and snack bar down the hall.

B: 很好，謝謝。

B: Great. Thanks.

 Useful Phrases 實用語句

1. 我覺得不舒服。

   I don't feel well.

2. 這裡痛。

   It hurts here.

3. 我覺得暈眩。

   I feel faint.

4. 我想吐。

   I feel like throwing up [vomiting].

5. 我可以在哪裡配處方？

   Where can I fill this prescription?

6. 我需要配這個處方。

   I need this prescription filled.

7. 我今晚需要住院嗎？

   Will I need to spend the night in the hospital?

8. 我胃痛。

   I have a stomachache.

9. 痛得很厲害。

   The pain is severe.

10. 我最近胃抽筋。

    I have stomach cramps lately.

11. 我消化不良。

    I have indigestion.

12. 我一直吐。

    I keep throwing up.

住所
郵電通訊
日常活動
銀行與保險
交通
食品與飲食
購物
社交活動
教育
休閒活動
醫療
緊急情況

13. 我無法吞下食物。

I can't keep food down.

14. 我腹瀉。

I have diarrhea.

15. 我血尿 [便]。

There's blood in my urine [stool].

16. 我喉嚨痛。

My throat is soar.

17. 我鼻塞 [流鼻水]。

I have a stuffy [runny] nose.

18. 我一直咳不停。

I can't stop coughing.

19. 我感冒好不了。

I can't stop this cold.

20. 我一直頭痛。

I keep getting headaches.

21. 我頭很痛。

I have a bad headache.

22. 我偏頭痛。

I have a migraine.

23. 我的頭強烈抽痛。

I have a powerful, throbbing headache.

24. 我胸痛。

There is a pain in my chest.

25. 我胸痛。

My chest hurts.

26. 我呼吸不順。

I can't breathe well.

27. 我便祕。

I'm constipated.

28. 我發冷。

I often feel chilly.

29. 我虛弱及頭昏。

I feel weak and dizzy.

30. 我想我發燒了。

I think I have a fever.

31. 我全身痠痛。

I feel soar all over.

 Language Power 字句補給站

◆ 疼痛及症狀敘述 Describing Pain and Symptoms

pain	疼痛
soar	痠痛
ache	痛
sore throat	喉嚨痛
aching muscles	肌肉痛
headache	頭痛
migraine	偏頭痛
slight	輕微的
mild	溫和的
sharp	劇烈的
intense	密集的
severe	嚴重的
burning	灼熱的
throbbing	抽痛的
prickling, stinging	刺痛的
crampy	抽筋似的
splitting	撕裂般的
swollen	腫脹的
feeling faint	感覺暈眩
sick, ill	生病的
throw up, vomit	嘔吐
allergic	過敏的
allergy	過敏
flu	流行感冒
heartburn	胃酸逆流
dull, numb	麻木的

住所 郵電通訊 日常活動 銀行與保險 交通 食品與飲食 購物 社交活動 教育 休閒活動 醫療 緊急情況

住所
郵電通訊
日常活動
銀行與保險
交通
食品與飲食
購物
社交活動
教育
休閒活動
醫療
緊急情況

11.2c 診斷說明 Explaining a Diagnosis

Dialog 對話

A: 你的檢查報告回來了。

A: Your test results are back.

B: 報告怎麼說？

B: What do they tell you?

A: 我想你很好，看來你只是疲倦。

A: I believe you are fine. It just looks like you are fatigued.

B: 我搬到這個新地方以後一直很忙。

B: I have been very busy after moving to this new place.

A: 你可能太忙了，而且不適應新環境。

A: Yes, you have been too busy probably and not used to your new environment.

B: 我該怎麼辦？

B: What should I do?

A: 慢下來，並且讓你的身體習慣住在這裡。

A: Slow down and let your body get used to living here.

B: 我需要吃藥嗎？

B: Do I need any medicine?

A: 我會開一些藥給你。

A: I'm going to prescribe some medicine for you.

B: 好，我需要回診嗎？

B: OK. Will I need to return to the hospital?

A: 三四天後若持續感覺不舒服再回來，要多休息。

A: Only if you continue to feel poorly after three or four days. Be sure to rest more.

Word Bank 字庫

fatigue [fə`tig] n., v. 疲累
get used to 習慣

Useful Phrases 實用語句

1. 請坐這裡。

   Please sit down here.

2. 我要量你脈搏。

   I'm going to check your pulse.

3. 你覺得如何？

   How do you feel?

4. 哪裡痛？

   Where does it hurt?

5. 我要量你的體溫。

   I'll take your temperature.

6. 請躺下。

   Please lay down.

7. 張嘴說「啊」。

   Open your mouth and say ah.

8. 我要安排你做一些檢查。

   I'm going to schedule you for some tests.

9. 我想你最好待在醫院過夜。

   I think you'd better stay in the hospital overnight.

住所
郵電通訊
日常活動
銀行與保險
交通
食品跟飲食
購物
社交活動
教育
休閒活動
醫療
緊急情況

住所

郵電通訊

日常活動

銀行與保險

交通

食品與飲食

購物

社交活動

教育

休閒活動

醫療

緊急情況

10. 預約下週。

Make another appointment for next week.

11. 我需要照X光。

I'll need some x-rays.

11.2d 申請診斷證明(保險給付用) Applying for a Diagnostic Report for Claiming Insurance

Dialog 對話

A: 我需要一些資料來申請保險理賠。

A: I need some information, so I can claim this on my insurance.

B: 好，我會給你收據及已填表格的影印本。

B: Sure. I'll give you the receipts and copies of forms that were filled out.

A: 謝謝。

A: Thank you.

Tips 小祕訣

　　保險公司各家規定不同，所以要了解保障內容，需要保險理賠時才能保障自己的權益，聯絡你的保險公司申請理賠時，告知他們發生什麼事並詢問他們需要什麼文件才能申請成功。

11.3 藥房領藥
Filling Up the Prescription at the Pharmacy

Dialog 對話

A: 哈囉，我需要配這個處方。

A: Hello. I need to have this prescription filled.

B: 好的，先生，請讓我看一下。

B: Alright, sir. Let me see it please.

A: 在這裡。

A: Here you go.

B: 幾分鐘就好。

B: It will be ready in a few minutes.

A: 我需要在店裡買一些東西。

A: I need to shop for a few other things in the store.

B: 沒問題，你回來時你的處方就好了。

B: No problem. Your prescription will be ready when you return.

A: 謝謝。

A: Thanks.

Tips 小祕訣

　　如果藥吃完了仍需連續處方 (refill)，必須再看醫師拿到新處方單；許多醫院有附設藥局，可以在看完病後直接到該藥房配藥，不需到外面藥房。

住所
郵電通訊
日常活動
銀行與保險
交通
食品與飲食
購物
社交活動
教育
休閒活動
醫療
緊急情況

11.4 小兒科
Pediatrics

Dialog 1 對話1

A: 請進。

A: Please come in.

B: 謝謝，我的小男孩生病了。

B: Thank you. My boy is sick.

A: 我看看，有什麼症狀？

A: Let's have a look. What are his symptoms?

B: 他發燒和胃不舒服。

B: He has a fever, and his stomach is upset.

A: 有吐嗎？

A: Is he vomiting?

B: 沒有。

B: No.

A: 我先做一些基本的檢查。

A: I'll check his vital signs first.

Dialog 2 對話2

A: 嗨，你叫什麼名字？

A: Hi, what is your name?

B: 吉米。

B: Jimmy.

A: 嗨，吉米，我是席姆斯醫師，我要看一下你的嘴好嗎？

A: Hi, Jimmy. I'm Doctor Sims. I'm going to have a look inside your mouth, OK?

B: 好。

B: OK.

A: 請張嘴說「啊」。

A: Please open your mouth and say ah.

B: 啊。

B: Ahhhh.

A: 好，現在量你的體溫，我要把這個輕輕地放到你耳朵裡。

A: Fine. Now let's check your temperature. I'm going to put this lightly in your ear.

B: 好。

B: OK.

A: 別擔心，不會痛。看來你有點發燒，吉米。

A: Don't worry. It won't hurt. It looks like you have a fever, Jimmy.

B: 我知道了。

B: I see.

A: 我要量你的脈搏。

A: I'm going to check your pulse now.

B: 好。

B: OK

Dialog 3 （對話3）

A: 他的脈搏還好，我想他輕微感染到某種型態的流行感冒病毒，我要給他打一針。

A: His pulse is fine. I think he has caught some type of slight flu virus. I'm going to give him a shot.

B: 會痛嗎？

B: Will it hurt?

A: 不，不太會，護士會很小心，打完針後我會給你處方，你可以在醫院藥房或其他地方配藥，按照瓶子上的指示服藥，並確定他喝很多流質及充分休息。如果兩天後沒改善的話，打電話給我。

A: No, not really. The nurse will be very careful. After she gives you the shot, I'll give you a prescription. You can get it filled at the pharmacy here at the hospital, or elsewhere. Follow the instructions on the bottle, and make sure he gets plenty of fluids and rest. Call me if he has not improved after two days.

B: 謝謝你，醫師。

B: Thank you, Doctor.

Word Bank 字庫

vital sign n. 活力徵兆
fever [`fivə] n. 發燒
virus [`vaɪrəs] n. 病毒
instruction [ɪn`strʌkʃən] n. 指示
fluid [`fluɪd] n. 流質
improve [ɪm`pruv] v. 改善

Useful Phrases 實用語句

● 爸 / 媽 Parent

1. 我帶小孩來看醫生。

   I'm here with my child to see the doctor.

2. 我已為我的小孩預約。

   I made an appointment for my child.

3. 我小孩生病了。

   My child is ill [sick].

住所 郵電通訊 日常活動 銀行與保險 交通 食品與飲食 購物 社交活動 教育 休閒活動 醫療 緊急情況

4. 他不想吃東西。

   He doesn't want to eat.

5. 她皮膚起疹子。

   Her skin has a rash.

6. 他軟 [水，血] 便。

   His stool is loose [watery, bloody].

7. 我小孩需要預防注射。

   My child needs some immunization shots.

8. 我小孩一直吐。

   My baby keeps vomiting.

9. 她暈車。

   She has motion sickness.

10. 她根本不睡。

    She won't sleep at all.

11. 我小孩聽起來一直都在痛。

    My baby sounds like he is in pain all the time.

醫師 Doctor

1. 有什麼問題？

   What seems to be the problem?

2. 請敘述他的症狀。

   Please describe his symptoms.

3. 他生病多久了？

   How long has he been sick?

4. 我會檢查他的基本健康。

   I'll check his basic health.

5. 你覺得怎樣？

   How do you feel?

6. 哪裡痛？

   Where does it hurt?

7. 這樣痛嗎？

   Does this hurt?

8. 說「啊」。

   Say ah.

9. 我要給他打針。

   I'm going to give him a shot.

10. 我需要做些測試。

   I'll need to do some tests.

11. 我要檢查他的體溫 [脈搏，血壓，喉嚨]。

   I'll check his temperature [pulse, blood pressure, throat] .

12. 確定他有足夠休息及攝取很多流質。

   Make sure he gets plenty of rest and fluids.

13. 確定他吃藥。

   Be sure to give him the medicine.

14. 如果問題持續，打電話給我。

   Call me if the problem continues.

15. 預約下星期。

   Make another appointment for next week.

 Language Power 字句補給站

◆ 小兒科 Pediatrician

child, kid	小孩
baby	嬰兒，幼童
infant	嬰兒
boy	男孩
girl	女孩
son	兒子
daughter	女兒
sneeze	打噴嚏
vomit, throw up	嘔吐
immunization	免疫
medicine	藥品
dose	劑量
diarrhea	下痢
stool sample	大便樣本
urine sample	尿液樣本

11.5 外科
Surgery

 Dialog 1 對話1

A: 哈囉，陳先生，檢驗回來了，報告顯示手術是必要的，為了治療問題，我們必須盡快為你開刀。

A: Hello, Mr. Chen. The tests have come back, and the results show that surgery is necessary. We must operate on you soon in order to cure the problem.

B: 我知道了，很糟嗎？

B: I see. Is it bad?

A: 倒不是，如果我們現在動手術，你很快就會恢復健康。

A: Not really. If we operate now, you'll be back in good health very soon.

B: 我知道了，我何時要開刀？

B: I see. When should I get the surgery done?

A: 越快越好，我建議明天。

A: The sooner, the better. I suggest tomorrow.

B: 明天太快了。

B: Tomorrow is very soon.

A: 是的，我知道，但馬上開刀是很重要的。

A: Yes, I know, but it is very important that we operate right away.

住所
郵電通訊
日常活動
銀行與保險
交通
食品與飲食
購物
社交活動
教育
休閒活動
醫療
緊急情況

B: 我了解了,那就做吧。

B: I understand. Let's do it.

A: 我會做必須的安排,護士待會兒會請你填另外的資料。

A: I'll make the necessary arrangements, and a nurse will be with you in a few minutes to get additional information from you.

B: 好,謝謝。

B: Very good. Thank you.

Dialog 2 (對話2)

A: 我安排今天開刀。

A: I'm scheduled for surgery today.

B: 是的,陳先生,我們已準備好。

B: Yes, Mr. Chen. We are ready for you.

B: 請進來坐下,護士很快就來。

B: Please come in and sit. Nurses will be with you shortly.

Dialog 3 (對話3)

A: 哈囉,陳先生,我們來幫你,請把衣服脫下穿上這件罩衫。

A: Hello, Mr. Chen. We're here to assist you. Please remove your clothing and put on this smock.

B: 好。

B: OK.

A: 我們會用輪椅帶你去手術室。你有任何問題嗎？

A: We'll take you by wheel chair to the operating room. Do you have any questions?

B: 沒有，我都了解了。

B: No. I think I understand everything.

A: 好，手術約三小時，你會在你的病房裡醒來。

A: OK. The operation will take about three hours. You'll wake up in your room.

B: 好，我了解了。

B: Yes, I see.

A: 當然你會由麻醉科醫師麻醉，所以手術中你不會有感覺。

A: Of course you will be put under by an anesthesiologist, so you'll feel nothing during the operation.

B: 我知道了，我準備好了。

B: I understand. I'm ready.

A: 好，放輕鬆，一切都會順利的。

A: OK. Just relax. Everything will be fine.

Word Bank 字庫

surgery [ˋsɝdʒərɪ] n. 手術
smock [smɑk] n. 罩衫
anesthesiologist [ˏænəsˏθizɪˋɑlədʒɪst] n. 麻醉科醫師

Useful Phrases 實用語句

1. 我的手臂有一道很深的傷口。

   I have a deep cut on my arm.

2. 需要縫起來。

   It will need stitches.

3. 我要打石膏。

   I'm going to put on a cast.

4. 你要用枴杖。

   You'll need to use crutches.

5. 你有腦震盪。

   You have a concussion.

6. 你韌帶拉傷。

   Your ligament is torn.

7. 不要把水泡弄破。

   Don't open the blisters.

8. 我會把你肩膀回復原位。

   I'll relocate your shoulder.

9. 痛的很劇烈。

   The pain is sharp.

Language Power 字句補給站

◆ 外傷及醫療用品 External Injuries and Medical Supplies

fall off	跌落
trip	絆倒
fall	跌倒
bump	腫塊，鼓起
cut	刀傷
bruises	瘀傷
scrape	刮傷
gash	深切傷口
fracture	骨折
burn	燒燙傷

住所
郵電通訊
日常活動
銀行與保險
交通
食品與飲食
購物
社交活動
教育
休閒活動
醫療
緊急情況

住所

郵電通訊

日常活動

銀行與保險

交通

食品與飲食

購物

社交活動

教育

休閒活動

醫療

緊急情況

broken	折斷的
sprained	扭傷的
concussion	震盪
dislocated (shoulder)	脫臼 (肩膀)
blisters	水泡
snake [dog] bite	蛇 [狗] 咬
bee sting	蜂螫
sore	痛處
strained	拉傷的
twisted (ankle)	扭傷 (腳踝)
torn ligament	韌帶拉傷
antibiotics	抗生素
gauze	紗布
bandage	繃帶
sling	三角巾，吊腕帶
crutches	枴杖
cast	石膏
stitches	縫
ointment, balm	藥膏
operation, surgery	手術
anesthesia	麻醉
recovery	恢復
operating room	手術室
gurney	有輪子的床或擔架

11.6 婦產科
Gynecology - Obstetrics (OBGYN's)

 Dialog 對話

A: 午安,林小姐 [女士]。

A: Good afternoon, Ms. Lin.

B: 午安。

B: Good afternoon.

A: 我看到你來這裡做一般健檢。

A: I see you are here for a general health check.

B: 是的。

B: Yes. That's right.

A: 最近覺得如何?

A: How have you been feeling lately?

B: 不錯,但我覺得很累。

B: Not bad, but I seem too tired.

A: 好,我們先討論你的健康,等一下再做幾個檢查。

A: OK. Let's discuss your health first, and we'll run some tests later.

B: 好,要多久?

B: Alright. How long will it take?

A: 大約一個小時。 ▷ **A:** About an hour.

B: 檢查會痛嗎？ ▷ **B:** Will any of the tests hurt?

A: 不會，首先我們先談你的病史。 ▷ **A:** No. First let's talk about your health history.

B: 好，我從國外帶了病歷。 ▷ **B:** OK. I brought my health records from overseas.

A: 很好。 ▷ **A:** Great.

 Useful Phrases 實用語句

● 病人 Patient

1. 我想驗孕。

   I'd like to have a pregnancy test.

2. 我可能懷孕了。

   I might be pregnant.

3. 我生理期晚了。

   My period is very late.

4. 我經期不規則。

   My periods are not regular.

5. 我經痛嚴重。

   I have severe menstrual pain.

6. 我現在不是經期，卻在出血。

   I'm not having my period now, but I'm bleeding.

7. 預產期何時？

   When is the baby due?

8. 我要注意什麼？

   What should I be aware of?

9. 我會有什麼感覺？

   How should I expect to feel?

10. 我早上害喜。

    I have morning sickness.

11. 我以前流產過。

    I've had a miscarriage before.

12. 我以前墮胎過一次。

    I've had an abortion in the past.

13. 我現在陣痛。

    I'm having labor pains.

14. 我需要抹片檢查。

    I need a pap test.

15. 我沒有精力。

    I lack energy.

● 其他問題 Other Problems

1. 我乳房有硬塊。

   I feel a lump in my breast.

2. 我需要做乳癌檢查。

   I want to be examined for breast cancer.

3. 我要做全身健康檢查。

   I want a complete health checkup.

● 醫師 Doctor

1. 你最後一次經期是何時？

   When was your last period?

2. 我來為你驗孕。

   I'll test you for pregnancy.

住所 郵電通訊 日常活動 銀行與保險 交通 食品與飲食 購物 社交活動 教育 休閒活動 醫療 緊急情況

3. 恭喜你，你有兩個月身孕。

Congratulations. You're two months pregnant.

4. 你的驗孕是陽性 [陰性]。

Your pregnancy test is positive [negative].

5. 你的小孩八月中出生。

Your baby is due in mid-August.

6. 我們用超音波來檢查胎兒。

We'll check the baby with ultrasound.

7. 我檢查你的一般健康跡象。

I'll check your general health signs.

8. 你最近覺得如何？

How have you been feeling lately?

9. 你生理期正常嗎？

Has your period been regular?

10. 你的精神好嗎？

Is your energy level good?

11. 你懷孕多久了？

How long have you been pregnant?

12. 你墮過胎嗎？

Have you had an abortion before?

13. 我可以建議一些避孕方法及裝置。

I can recommend some birth control methods and controls.

14. 你要照X光。

You need to have an X-ray.

15. 我要為你做乳房檢查。

I'm going to give you a breast examination.

16. 你家族有癌症史嗎？

Is there a history of cancer in your family?

17. 我要建議你做一些飲食改變。

I want to recommend some changes in your diet.

18. 你需要多運動。

You need to get more exercise.

19. 我要跟你談關於維他命及補給品的事。

I'd like to talk to you about vitamins and supplements.

20. 定期回來做產檢。

Come back regularly for pregnancy checkups.

Language Power 字句補給站

◆ **婦產科 OBGYN's**

menstruation, period	月經，生理期
pregnancy	懷孕
pregnant	懷孕的
fetus	胎兒
miscarriage	流產
abortion	墮胎
blood sample	血液樣本
breast cancer	乳癌
menstrual pain	經痛
cramps	(如腹部、胃部) 絞痛，痙攣
discharge	分泌物
virginities	陰道炎
menopause	更年期
menopause symptoms	更年期症狀
hot flashes	潮紅
night sweats	盜汗
depression	心情低落
mood swings	情緒不穩定
hormone treatments	荷爾蒙治療

右側標籤：住所／郵電通訊／日常活動／銀行與保險／交通／食品與飲食／購物／社交活動／教育／休閒活動／醫療／緊急情況

住所
郵電通訊
日常活動
銀行與保險
交通
食品與飲食
購物
社交活動
教育
休閒活動
醫療
緊急情況

11.7 泌尿科
Urology

 Dialog （對話）

A: 嗨，請進來我的辦公室。

A: Hi. Please come into my office.

B: 謝謝。

B: Thank you.

A: 怎麼了？

A: What is wrong?

B: 我小便時有強烈灼熱感而且持續疼痛。

B: There is a strong burning sensation when I urinate, and the pain is continuous.

A: 我了解了，這樣多久了？

A: I see. How long has this been going on?

B: 三天了。

B: For three days.

A: 好，我需要尿液樣本及抽血，我現在幫你打一針減少疼痛。

A: OK. I'll need a urine sample, and I'll need to take your blood, too. I'll give you a shot now to help relieve the pain.

B: 好，謝謝。

B: OK. Thanks.

Word Bank 字庫

sensation [sɛn`seʃən] n. (因外在事物引起的)感覺
urinate [`jurə͵net] v. 排尿

Useful Phrases 實用語句

◎ 病人 Patient

1. 我有灼熱感。

   I have a burning sensation.

2. 我小便不順。

   I can't urinate well.

3. 我尿液帶血。

   There is blood in my urine.

4. 我經常上廁所。

   I go to the toilet very often.

5. 有抽痛、灼熱感。

   There is a throbbing, burning pain.

6. 你可以減少疼痛嗎？

   Can you relieve the pain?

7. 我要吃藥嗎？

   Do I need to take medicine?

◎ 醫師 Doctor

1. 你一天排尿幾次？

   How many times do you urinate a day?

2. 你晚上起來上廁所嗎？

   Do you get up at night to go to the toilet?

3. 我會給你打針。

   I'll give you a shot.

4. 我要抽血。

   I'll take some blood.

住所
郵電通訊
日常活動
銀行與保險
交通
食品與飲食
購物
社交活動
教育
休閒活動
醫療
緊急情況

住所

郵電通訊

日常活動

銀行與保險

交通

食品與飲食

購物

社交活動

教育

休閒活動

醫療

緊急情況

5. 我要做些檢查。

   I need to do some tests.

6. 我需要尿液樣本。

   I need a urine sample.

7. 躺在這裡。

   Lie down here.

8. 深呼吸。

   Breathe deeply.

 Language Power　字句補給站

◆ 泌尿科 Urology

burning sensation	灼熱感
urinalysis	尿液分析
throbbing pain	抽痛
kidney	腎臟
kidney stones	腎結石
penis	陰莖
urinary organ	泌尿器官
prostrate gland	攝護腺
testis	睪丸
venereal disease (VD)	性病
cystitis	膀胱炎
urethritis	尿道炎
gall bladder	膀胱
gall stone	膀胱結石

11.8 耳鼻喉科
Otolaryngology (ENT)

Dialog 對話

A: 醫師，我耳朵很痛。

A: Doctor. I have a terrible earache.

B: 我看看。

B: Let me look.

A: 已經痛三天了。

A: It has been aching for three days.

B: 你有放東西進去嗎？

B: Did you put anything in your ear?

A: 沒有。

A: No.

B: 看來是感染了。

B: It appears to be infected.

A: 我知道了。

A: I see.

B: 我給你一些抗生素。

B: I'll give you some antibiotics.

住所
郵電通訊
日常活動
銀行與保險
交通
食品與飲食
購物
社交活動
教育
休閒活動
醫療
緊急情況

A: 耳朵也不通。 ➤ **A:** It is plugged up, too.

B: 消腫後就通了。 ➤ **B:** It should unplug after the swelling goes down.

 Word Bank 字庫

terrible [`tɛrəbl̩] adj. 可怕的
infect [ɪn`fɛkt] v. 感染
antibiotics [ˌæntɪbaɪ`ɑtɪks] n. 抗生素
plug [plʌg] v. 堵塞 .
swell [swɛl] v., n. 腫脹

Useful Phrases 實用語句

● 病人 Patient

1. 我耳朵痛。

   I have an earache.

2. 我耳朵不通。

   My ears are plugged up.

3. 我耳鳴。

   My ears are ringing.

4. 我的耳朵要清。

   I need my ears cleaned.

5. 我耳垢太多。

   There's too much earwax in my ears.

6. 有流質從我耳朵流出來。

   There is fluid coming out of my ears.

7. 我鼻子不通。

   My nose is stuffed up.

8. 我流鼻水。

I have a runny nose.

9. 我流鼻血。

My nose keeps bleeding.

10. 我不停打噴嚏。

I can't stop sneezing.

11. 我鼻子一直癢。

My nose always tickles.

12. 我現在有過敏問題。

I'm having troubles with allergies.

13. 我沒法嚐或聞東西。

I can't taste or smell anything.

14. 我喉嚨痛。

My throat is sore.

15. 我聲音沙啞。

I have hoarse voice.

16. 我不停咳嗽。

I can't stop coughing.

醫師 Doctor

1. 你的耳朵 [喉嚨，鼻子] 感染了。

Your ear [throat, nose] is infected.

2. 我給你一些抗生素。

I'll give you some antibiotics.

3. 我會清掉耳垢。

I'll remove the earwax.

4. 你有過敏症狀。

You have an allergy.

5. 你要用噴鼻劑。

You need to use a nasal spray.

6. 你喉嚨腫起來。

Your throat is swollen.

住所
郵電通訊
日常活動
銀行與保險
交通
食品與飲食
購物
社交活動
教育
休閒活動
醫療
緊急情況

7. 你扁桃腺發炎。

You have tonsillitis.

Language Power 字句補給站

◆ **耳鼻喉科 ENT (Eear Nose Throat)**

earache	耳痛
ear canal	耳道
earwax	耳垢
hearing problem	聽障
ringing	耳鳴
plugged up	塞住
stuffy nose	鼻塞
bloody nose	流鼻血
hay fever	花粉熱
tonsils	扁桃腺
tonsillitis	扁桃腺炎
cough	咳嗽
sinus	鼻竇

11.9 皮膚科
Dermatology

Dialog 對話

A: 哈囉，你有什麼問題？

A: Hello. What is your problem?

B: 我起紅疹。

B: I have a skin rash.

A: 我看看，看起來像是對什麼過敏。

A: Let's look.—It looks like you are allergic to something.

B: 我不知道，以前沒發生過。

B: I don't know. It's never happened before.

A: 你住在這裡多久了？

A: How long have you been living here?

B: 大約三個月。

B: About three months.

A: 你可能皮膚沾到什麼。

A: You probably got something on your skin.

B: 我該怎麼做？

B: What should I do about it?

A: 我來為你做些檢驗，再做建議。

A: I'll do some tests for you. Then make a recommendation.

B: 嚴重嗎？

B: Is it anything serious?

A: 我不認為。

A: I don't think so.

住所

郵電通訊

日常活動

銀行與保險

交通

食品與飲食

購物

社交活動

教育

休閒活動

醫療

緊急情況

Word Bank 字庫

allergic [əˋlɜdʒɪk] adj. 過敏的

Useful Phrases 實用語句

● 病人 **Patient**

1. 我的皮膚有狀況。

   I have a skin condition.

2. 我的皮膚對某種東西過敏。

   My skin is allergic to something.

3. 我皮膚癢。

   My skin itches.

4. 我皮膚有灼熱感。

   My skin has a burning feeling.

5. 我被嚴重燒傷。

   I got burned badly.

6. 我嚴重晒傷。

   I have a terrible sunburn.

7. 我的皮膚太乾。

   My skin is too dry.

8. 我的皮膚太油。

   My skin is too oily.

9. 我有很嚴重的切傷並且關心復原後不會留下傷疤。

   I have a bad cut and am concerned about it healing without a scar.

10. 我擔心這些痣。

    I'm worried about these moles.

11. 我皮膚有屑片。

    My skin is very flaky.

12. 我有嚴重的粉刺問題。

    I have a terrible acne problem.

◐ **醫師 Doctor**

1. 你有皮膚過敏。

   Your have skin allergies.

2. 你碰到某種毒藤 [橡樹]。

   You got into some poison ivy [oak].

3. 我會在你的皮膚做些測試。

   I'll do some tests on your skin.

4. 你要塗這藥膏。

   You need to apply this ointment.

5. 我會給你治療它的一些藥。

   I'll give you some medicine that will cure it.

6. 你要服藥幾星期。

   You'll need to take this for several weeks.

7. 你暫時要每個星期來看我。

   You'll need to see me every week for a while.

8. 你要改變飲食。

   You need to change your diet.

9. 這藥會讓你的皮膚變乾。

   This medicine will help dry up your skin.

Language Power 字句補給站

◆ **皮膚問題 Skin Problems**

skin	皮膚
dry	乾的
oily	油的
flaky	有皮屑的
burned	燒傷的
itchy	發癢的
acne	粉刺
cut	切割 [傷]
bruised	淤血的
condition	情況

住所
郵電通訊
日常活動
銀行與保險
交通
食品與飲食
購物
社交活動
教育
休閒活動
醫療
緊急情況

moles	痣
wrinkled	有皺紋的
ointment	藥膏
skin conditioners	潤膚品
skin care products	護膚產品
rash	紅疹
insect bite	昆蟲咬傷
athlete's foot	香港腳
chapped lips	嘴唇乾裂
lip balm	護唇膏
tissue (paper)/Kleenex	面紙
warts	疣
corns	繭
scab	斑點，結痂 [疤]
scar	疤
infection	感染

11.10 牙科
Dentistry

11.10a 預約及敘述需求
Making an Appointment and Describing Needs

Dialog 對話

A: 哈囉，這裡是克拉克牙科診所，我能為你服務嗎？

A: Hello. This is Clark Dental Clinic. How may I help you?

B: 哈囉，我的名字是茉蒂蔡，我要看牙醫。

B: Hello. My name is Judy Tsai. I'd like to see a dentist.

A: 好，你有來過我們診所嗎？

A: Very well. Have you been to our clinic before?

B: 沒有,這是我第一次來。

B: No, I haven't. This will be my first visit.

A: 好,你需要什麼?

A: OK. What do you need?

B: 我要洗牙。

B: My teeth need to be cleaned.

A: 好,你要哪一天來。

A: Fine. What day would you like to come in?

B: 星期一下午。

B: Monday, in the afternoon.

A: 預約有一個名額,3點好嗎?

A: The appointment book has an opening. Is 3:00 fine?

B: 好。

B: Yes, it is.

A: 好,蔡小姐,我們星期一見。

A: OK. Miss Tsai, we'll see you on Monday.

B: 謝謝。

B: Thank you.

11.10b 在牙科 At the Dental Clinic

Dialog 對話

A: 嗨，我是你的牙醫，卡爾克拉克。

A: Hi. I'm your dentist, Carl Clark.

B: 哈囉。

B: Hello.

A: 請在牙科椅坐下，我看到你安排今天要洗牙。

A: Please sit down here in the dental chair. I see that you are scheduled for teeth cleaning today.

B: 是的。

B: That's right.

A: 好。我的助理會幫我，請往後躺並張開嘴。

A: OK. My assistant will help me. Please lie back and open your mouth.

B: 好。

B: OK.

A: 我要將這小牙墊放入你口中，請咬下去。如果過程中任何時候你覺得痛，舉手讓我們知道。

A: I'm going to put this small tooth pad in your mouth. Please bite down on it. If at any time during the procedure you feel pain, raise your hand and let us know.

住所 郵電通訊 日常活動 銀行與保險 交通 食品與飲食 購物 社交活動 教育 休閒活動 醫療 緊急情況

Word Bank 字庫

pad [pæd] n. 墊子

Useful Phrases 實用語句

○ **病人 Patient**

1. 我需要洗牙。

   I need my teeth cleaned.

2. 我需要檢查牙齒。

   I need my teeth checked.

3. 我牙痛。

   I have a toothache.

4. 我想我有蛀牙。

   I think I have a cavity.

5. 我要填蛀牙。

   I need a cavity filled.

6. 我要補牙。

   I need a filling.

7. 我喝冷熱飲時，牙齒痛。

   My teeth hurt when I drink something cold or hot.

8. 昨天我的一顆牙斷掉。

   One of my teeth broke yesterday.

9. 我要裝齒冠。

   I need a crown.

10. 我的齒冠要檢查[修理]。

    I need my crown checked [repaired].

11. 我要檢查齒橋 (假牙的架子)。

    I need my bridge checked.

12. 我要調整牙套。

    I need to have my braces adjusted.

13. 我要美白牙齒。

I want my teeth whitened.

14. 我要拔智齒。

I need to have my wisdom teeth pulled.

15. 我要拔牙。

I need a tooth removed.

16. 我可以用信用卡支付嗎？

Can I pay by credit card?

● 牙醫 Dentist

1. 嘴張大。

Open your mouth wide.

2. 放輕鬆。如果你感到任何疼痛，舉起手。

Relax. Raise your hand if you feel any pain.

3. 你需要補牙。

You need a filling.

4. 你需要裝齒冠。

You need a crown.

5. 你需要裝齒橋。

You need a bridge.

6. 我必須拔牙。

I'll have to remove the tooth.

7. 我必須拔出牙齒。

I'll have to pull the tooth.

8. 你的智齒要拔掉。

Your wisdom teeth need to be removed.

9. 你要洗牙。

You need to have your teeth cleaned.

10. 你有牙周病。

You have gum disease.

Language Power 字句補給站

◆ 牙科診所 Dental Clinic

dentist's office	牙醫室
filling	補牙
cavity	蛀牙
crown	齒冠
bridge	齒橋
wisdom teeth	智齒
dental assistant	牙醫助理
braces	牙套
cleaning	清潔
Novocain	局部麻醉劑
gums	牙齦
plaque	牙垢
bacteria	細菌
dental floss	牙線
tartar	牙結石
root canal	牙根管
dentures	假牙
nerve	神經

11.11 眼科
Ophthalmology

Dialog 對話

A: 嗨,瓊斯醫生。

A: Hi, Doctor Jones.

B: 哈囉,你今天有什麼問題?

B: Hello. What is your problem to-day?

住所 郵電通訊 日常活動 銀行與保險 交通 食品跟飲食 購物 社交活動 教育 休閒活動 醫療 緊急情況

A: 我的眼睛痠痛而且充血。

A: My eyes are sore and bloodshot.

B: 我來檢查，張大眼睛。

B: Let me examine you. Open your eyes wide.

A: 好。

A: OK.

B: 我要將光線照進去你的眼睛，不會痛。

B: I'm going to shine a light into your eyes. It won't hurt.

A: 我了解。

A: I understand.

B: 看來我也要浸潤你的眼睛。

B: It looks like I'll need to irrigate your eyes, too.

Word Bank 字庫

bloodshot [`blʌd‚ʃɑt] adj. 充血的
irrigate [`ɪrə‚get] v. 浸潤

Useful Phrases 實用語句

○ **病人 Patient**

1. 我的眼睛痠痛。

   My eyes are sore.

2. 我的眼睛痛而且灼熱。

   My eyes hurt and burn.

3. 我的眼睛充血。

   My eyes are bloodshot.

4. 我的眼睛腫脹。

   My eyes are swollen.

5. 我一直流眼淚。

   My eyes keep watering.

6. 我的眼睛一直覺得癢。

   My eyes always feel itchy.

7. 我一直想流淚。

   My eyes always tear up.

8. 我的眼睛有分泌物。

   I have mucus in my eyes.

9. 我的眼睛裡有東西。

   I have something in my eye.

10. 東西模糊不清。

    Things are blurry.

11. 每件東西看來都扭曲。

    Everything looks distorted.

12. 東西不清楚。

    Things are not clear.

13. 我隨時要瞇眼睛。

    I have to squint all the time.

14. 我眼睛又累又重。

    My eyes feel tired and heavy.

◎ 醫師 Doctor

1. 我要浸潤你的眼睛。

   I'll irrigate your eyes.

2. 你要點眼藥水。

   You need to use eye drops.

3. 你近 [遠] 視。

   You are near [far] sighted.

4. 我要幫你檢查視力。

I'll give you an eye test.

5. 看圖表。

Look at the chart.

6. 你要改眼鏡處方。

You need to change your eyeglass prescription.

Language Power 字句補給站

◆ 眼睛問題 Eye Problems

eyes	眼睛
eyelid	眼皮
eyelash	眼睫毛
far sighted	遠視
near sighted	近視
optic nerve	視神經
blink	眨眼
eye chart	視力檢查表
pupils	瞳孔
iris	虹膜
retina	視網膜
mucus	分泌物，黏液
eye drops	眼藥水
blurry	模糊
squint	瞇眼
conjunctiva	結膜
trachoma	結膜炎
retinitis	視網膜炎
astigmatism	散光
discharge	分泌，流出

11.12 神經科及精神科
Neurology and Psychiatry

Dialog 對話

A: 請進。

A: Please come in.

B: 醫師，謝謝。

B: Thank you, Doctor.

A: 你有什麼問題？

A: What is your problem?

B: 我常覺得頭暈、困惑及顫抖。

B: I feel dizzy, confused, and tremble a lot.

A: 這樣多久了？

A: How long has this been going on?

B: 兩週了。

B: A couple of weeks.

A: 你有其他症狀嗎？

A: Do you have any other symptoms?

B: 我也覺得沒安全感。

B: I feel insecure, too.

住所
郵電通訊
日常活動
銀行與保險
交通
食品與飲食
購物
社交活動
教育
休閒活動
醫療
緊急情況

A: 我會開始做些檢查，我們要找出你體內是否有任何化學不平衡。

A: I'll start by doing some testing. We need to find out if there are any chemical imbalances in your body.

B: 你想我腦內有什麼不對嗎？

B: Do you think there's something wrong with my brain?

A: 現在很難說，我們要先評估你的情形。

A: It's impossible to say right now. We must evaluate your situation first.

✎ Word Bank 字庫

tremble [`trɛmbl] v. 顫抖
symptom [`sɪmptəm] n. 症狀
insecure [ˌɪnsɪ`kjʊr] adj. 沒安全感的
chemical [`kɛmɪkl] adj. 化學的
imbalance [ɪm`bæləns] n. 不平衡
evaluate [ɪ`væljʊˌet] v. 評估

 Useful Phrases 實用語句

● 病人 Patient

1. 我常昏倒。

   I faint often.

2. 我的手常發抖。

   My hands tremble a lot.

3. 每件東西我看來都模糊。

   Everything seems fuzzy to me.

4. 我不記得事情。

   I can't remember things.

5. 我記憶力不如以前。

   My memory is not as good as before.

6. 我覺得麻痺一會兒。

   I felt paralyzed for a while.

7. 我以前中過風。

   I've had a stroke before.

8. 我老是生氣。

   I feel irritated all the time.

9. 我經常覺得憂鬱。

   I often feel depressed.

10. 我不能入睡。

    I can't sleep.

11. 我夜裡醒來滿身汗。

    I wake up all sweaty at night.

12. 我常覺得憂慮。

    I often feel anxious.

◎ 醫師 Doctor

1. 你要做磁核共振掃描。

   You need to take a MRI.

2. 我們會做一系列檢查。

   We'll do a series of tests.

3. 你需要多些睡眠。

   You need more sleep.

4. 你需要一週來一次。

   You need to come in once a week.

5. 你需要一週來見我一次，並且服這個藥。

   You need to see me once a week and take this medicine.

6. 你下週來見我。

   Please come in next week to see me.

住所 郵電通訊 日常活動 銀行與保險 交通 食品與飲食 購物 社交活動 教育 休閒活動 醫療 緊急情況

Language Power　字句補給站

◆ 神經及精神問題 Problems with Nerves and the Mind

MRI (magnetic resonance imaging)	磁核共振掃描
neurosis	精神官能症
paralyzed	麻痺，癱瘓
stroke	中風
stress	壓力
depressed	憂鬱的
depression, melancholia	憂鬱症
tranquilizer	鎮定劑
Prozac	百憂解 (藥名)
insomnia	失眠
nervous breakdown	崩潰
sleepwalking	夢遊
nightmare	惡夢
psychosis	精神病，精神失常
therapist	治療師
culture shock	文化衝擊

Notes　小叮嚀

　　精神及神經方面的問題複雜，需要專業醫藥協助才能診斷出結果。到一個新國度開始新生活產生文化衝擊是很正常的，因此在心理及生理上要有足夠準備，保持健康並閱讀新文化的資訊是很重要的，任何新移民在開始新生活不久若有精神或神經不適，都會想到是文化衝擊造成的，如果擔心自己的精神狀況，務必諮詢醫師。

11.13 急診室
Emergency Room

 Useful Phrases 實用語句

1. 我手斷了。

   I broke my arm.

2. 她嚴重燒傷。

   She is badly burned.

3. 她被刺傷了。

   She has been stabbed.

4. 她要縫針。

   She'll have to have stitches.

5. 我要給他局部注射。

   I'll give him a local.

6. 她需要麻醉劑麻醉。

   She'll need anesthesia to put her out.

7. 血流不止。

   It won't stop bleeding.

8. 很痛。

   It hurts a lot.

9. 我受不了疼痛！

   I can't stand the pain!

10. 我不能移動脖子。

    I can't move my neck.

11. 我們要給你照X光。

    We'll have to x-ray you.

12. 我想你的肩膀脫臼了。

    I think your shoulder is dislocated.

13. 我們要看是否有內出血。

    We'll see if there is internal bleeding.

14. 保持靜止，不要動。

    Stay still. Don't move.

Unit 12 Emergencies

緊急情況

緊急情況指的是警局、火災及救護車服務。除了比較小的社區資源較少或必須從較遠地區調派支援,所有地區都有這些服務。緊急事故的電話為 911;平時就將可能用到的緊急電話查好 (如當地派出所、當地醫院、保險公司電話、駐美辦事處等) 放在電話旁,另備份出門時帶在身上備用 (可下載APP)。遇有重大或緊急事件,也可以向我駐美辦事處求援,打電話時說中文即可;各地辦事處的緊急聯絡電話請見附錄。

12.1 交通事故
Traffic Accidents

12.1a 車禍：叫救護車
Car Accident: Calling for an Ambulance

Dialog 對話

A: 911救援中心

A: 911 dispatcher.

B: 哈囉，這是緊急事件，有一起意外，我們需要救護車。

B: Hello. This is an emergency. There has been an accident. We need an ambulance.

A: 請告訴我你的名字及位置。

A: Please tell me your name and location.

B: 我的名字是貝蒂徐，我在山丘路234號。

B: My name is Betty Hsu. I'm at 234 Hill Drive Way.

A: 是什麼意外？

A: What kind of accident is it?

B: 一個小男孩被車撞，他不動了。

B: A little boy has been hit by a car. He is not moving.

A: 我馬上派一部警車及救護車，請留在線上。

A: I'll dispatch a police car and ambulance immediately. Please stay on the line.

B: 好。 ➤ **B:** OK.

Useful Phrases 實用語句

● 打緊急電話 **Making Emergency Calls**

1. 這裡是警察局嗎？

   Is this the police?

2. 這是緊急事件。

   This is an emergency.

3. 我有一個緊急事件。

   I have an emergency.

4. 我要報告一個意外。

   I want to report an accident.

5. 我要報案。

   I want to report a crime.

6. 我要報告火災。

   I want to report a fire.

7. 警員會很快過來嗎？

   Will an officer come soon?

8. 派一輛救護車來。

   Send an ambulance.

9. 我需要一輛救護車。

   I need an ambulance.

10. 我需要一位員警。

    I need a policeman.

11. 你可以告訴我駐芝加哥臺北經濟文化代表處的電話嗎？

    Could you give me the phone number of the Taipei Economic and Cultural Representative Office in Chicago?

住所
郵電通訊
日常活動
銀行與保險
交通
食品與飲食
購物
社交活動
教育
休閒活動
醫療
緊急情況

● **緊急服務回應 Responses from Emergency Services**

1. 警察在路上了。

   Police are on the way.

2. 消防員很快就來。

   Fire fighters will be there soon.

3. 救護車馬上來。

   An ambulance will arrive shortly.

4. 留在線上。

   Stay on the line.

5. 你傷到什麼？

   What are your injuries?

6. 有人受傷嗎？

   Is anyone injured?

7. 冷靜下來，不要離開現場。

   Stay calm and don't leave the scene.

8. 他沒呼吸多久了？

   How long has he not been breathing?

 Tips 小祕訣

別掛電話，緊急服務可以追蹤正確地址或需要更多資料，並在電話上給予需要的急救指示，在緊急救護人員抵達前幫助傷患，緊急救護服務需要來電者準備回答下列問題：

緊急事故確定地點在哪裡？ What is the exact location of the emergency?

回覆電話號碼？ What is your call back phone number?

什麼問題 [發生什麼事]？ What is the problem? [What exactly happened?]

多少人受傷？ How many people are hurt?

傷者年齡？ How old is the person?

傷者是否清醒？ Is the person conscious?

傷者是否有呼吸？ Is the person breathing?

12.1b 出車禍叫警察

Calling the Police for a Car Accident

Dialog 對話

A: 州警局。

A: State Police.

B: 我需要一位警員來 (處理) 車禍。

B: I need a policeman to come to a car accident.

A: 你在哪裡?

A: Where are you?

B: 格蘭及華盛頓街交 叉路口。

B: The intersection of Grant and Washington Street.

A: 有人受傷嗎?

A: Is anyone injured?

B: 沒有。

B: No.

A: 車在路邊嗎?

A: Are the cars off the road?

B: 不是。

B: No.

A: 車輛可以移動嗎？

A: Can they be moved?

B: 可以。

B: Yes.

A: 把車輛移到路邊，警車很快就到那裡。

A: Move them to the side of the street. A squad car will be there shortly.

B: 好，謝謝。

B: OK. Thank you.

(稍後 Later)

A: (警察) 我有你們及對方駕駛的所有資料。

A: (police officer) I have all the information I need from both you and the other driver.

B: 我需要到警局嗎？

B: Do I need to go to the police station?

A: 不必，但你必須馬上聯絡你的保險公司，並在十天內向機動車輛部門提出意外報告。

A: No, but you do need to contact your insurance company immediately, and you must file an accident report with the DMV within ten days.

B: 我了解了，謝謝你。

B: I understand, thanks.

緊急情況

Word Bank 字庫

squad car n. 警車巡邏車
accident report n. (車禍)意外報告

Useful Phrases 實用語句

● **告訴警察發生什麼事 [車禍] Telling the police what happened [car accident]**

1. 這是我的保險單。

   Here is my proof of insurance.

2. 這是我的駕照。

   Here is my driver's license.

3. 我有打方向燈。

   My indicators were on.

4. 我正在換車道。

   I was changing lanes.

5. 我在等紅綠燈。

   I was waiting for the light to change.

6. 我在等待左轉。

   I was waiting to turn left.

7. 我不確定。

   I'm not sure.

8. 我不知道。

   I don't know.

9. 我開的很慢。

   I was going very slow.

10. 無人受傷。

    No one is injured.

Cultural Tips 文化祕笈

你不能不知，車禍處理及如何保護自己！

在車內放紙筆、急救箱 (first aid kit)、信號閃光 (flares)、反光三角板 (reflective triangle)、手機對車禍事故都會有幫助。當你駕車發生車禍時，立即駛向路旁，熄火，開閃光燈，查看每個人是否無恙，如果有人受傷或任何緊急情形，打911，在施以標準急救方法前，不要移動傷者，在事故地點幾百呎前放信號閃光及反光三角板，警告來車前方有事故。

打電話給警方告知是否有人受傷，如果是在高速公路上而身上沒有電話，沿路有公路電話可使用。

和所有與事故有關的人交換資料，確認交換以下資料：

1. 所有駕駛人的姓名、地址、電話
2. 所有乘客 (passengers) 及目擊者 (witnesses) 的姓名、地址、電話
3. 駕照號碼及車牌號碼 (license plate number)
4. 所有駕駛人的保險公司資料
5. 所有車輛的登記擁有人 (registered owner)
6. 所有車輛的年份 (year)、廠牌 (make)、車型 (model)
7. 如果有目擊者，請他留下姓名與電話。

保留行車紀錄器 (vehical/car video recorder/dashboard camera，簡稱 dash cam) 記錄，除了警察，不要與任何人討論發生什麼事，不要承認自己過錯，也不要做任何指控，這些言論之後可能反而對你不利。如果有時間及情況允許，用手機拍照，並把自己經歷事故的過程及感受做筆記寫下來，用手機錄下來。如果受了傷或懷疑自己受傷，要盡速就醫。

如果自己是目擊者，見到事故發生，應停車給予協助，例如叫救護車及警察，並告訴警察目睹經過，協助警察做更正確的車禍報告。

如果是無人受傷的小車禍，可以不必找警察，和對方交換資料、或許照幾張相片及聯絡保險公司即可，保險公司會處理接下來的事，但是如果對方不合作、生氣或其他情形，仍然需要警察到現場處理。

此外，在加州車禍損失超過金額$500，必須在十天內報告機動車輛部門 (DMV)，在奧勒岡州超過 $1,500 才要向DMV報告，每個州有各自規定的金額。

Language Power 字句補給站

◆ **交通違規及事故 Traffic Offenses and Accidents**

crash	衝撞
hit and run	肇事逃逸
speeding	超速
drunk driving	酒駕
rear-ended	追被撞
injury	受傷
emergency services	緊急服務
swerve	突然轉向
skid	打滑
overturn	翻覆
head-on collision	迎面對撞
fender-bender	(車身刮傷凹陷的) 小車禍
run through a stop light	闖紅燈
car chase	車輛追逐
reckless driving	魯莽駕駛
illegal lane change	違規變換車道

12.1c 申請車禍證明(保險給付用) Applying for Proof of a Car Accident (for Insurance Company)

Dialog 對話

A: 我需要給我保險公司一份車禍報告。

A: I need to get a copy of an accident report for my insurance company.

B: 你的名字及車禍時間？

B: What is your name and when was the accident?

住所
郵電通訊
日常活動
銀行與保險
交通
食品與飲食
購物
社交活動
教育
休閒活動
醫療
緊急情況

A: 約翰胡，車禍是10月29日。

A: John Hu. The accident was on October 29th.

B: 好，我在電腦裡查一下。

B: OK. I'll look it up in our computer.

A: 我要付費嗎？

A: Do I have to pay for it?

B: 要5元處理費。

B: There is a $5 processing fee.

12.1d 聯絡保險公司 Contacting Insurance Company

Dialog 對話

A: 米勒保險，我可以為你服務嗎？

A: Miller's Insurance. May I help you?

B: 我是約翰胡，我今天出了車禍，我要通知車禍並開始理賠程序。

B: I'm John Hu. I was in a car accident today. I want to report it and start the claims process.

A: 好，胡先生，你知道保險號碼嗎？

A: Ok, Mr. Hu. Do you know your policy number?

B: 知道，號碼是5312-9956-7418。

B: Yes. It's 5312-9956-7418.

A: 好，有人受傷嗎？

A: OK. Was anyone injured?

B: 我不認為。

B: I don't think so.

A: 你最好確定，如果有疑問去看個醫生，不然你以後可能理賠會有問題。

A: You'd better make sure. See a doctor if there is any doubt at all. Otherwise you may have trouble with your claim later.

B: 我知道了。

B: I see.

A: 車子現在在哪裡？

A: Where is the car now?

B: 在貝瑞修車廠。

B: At Barry's Auto Body Shop.

A: 好，理賠鑑定師會去那裡查看判定損失。

A: Alright. A claims adjuster will go there and look at it to determine damages.

B: 我還需要做什麼嗎？

B: Is there anything else I need to do?

A: 你想修理會超過1,000元嗎？

A: Do you think the repairs will cost more than $1,000?

住所
郵電通訊
日常活動
銀行與保險
交通
食品與飲食
購物
社交活動
教育
休閒活動
醫療
緊急情況

住所
郵電通訊
日常活動
銀行與保險
交通
食品與飲食
購物
社交活動
教育
休閒活動
醫療
緊急情況

B: 會。

B: Yes, I do.

A: 那你要在十天內去機動車輛部門做報告建檔。

A: Then you also must file an accident report at the Department of Motor Vehicles within ten days.

B: 我了解了，謝謝你告訴我。

B: I understand. Thank you for telling me.

Word Bank 字庫

adjuster [əˋdʒʌstə] n. 鑑定師
file [faɪl] v. 建檔

12.1e 警察命令停車 (交通違規)
Stopped by Police (Breaking Traffic Laws)

Dialog 1 對話 1

A: 有輛警車在我們後面閃紅藍燈。

A: There is a police car behind us with its red and blue lights flashing.

B: 真的嗎？那表示我們必須停車。

B: Really? That means we have to stop the car.

A: 好，我要在這寬點的地方靠邊停車 (等待警察走到車子)。

A: OK. I'll pull over here where it's wider. (Waits for the officer to come up to the car)

C: 午安，我可以看你的駕照嗎？

C: Good afternoon. May I see your driver's license please?

A: 在這裡，警察先生。

A: Here it is, Officer.

C: 你有行照嗎？

C: Do you have the registration for this car?

A: 沒有，這是租來的車。

A: I don't think so. It's a rental car.

C: 知道了，我可以看一下你的租賃契約嗎？

C: I see. May I see your rental agreement?

A: 好的，在這邊。

A: Sure. Here it is.

 Dialog 2 對話2

A: 我做錯什麼嗎？警察先生。

A: Did I do something wrong, Officer?

B: 你在過橋時超車。

B: You passed a car while crossing the bridge.

A: 那是違法的嗎？

A: Is that illegal?

B: 在本州是的，對那個(規定)你要小心點。

B: It is in this State. You have to be careful about that.

A: 我不知道那樣不行。

A: I didn't know it's not all right.

B: 好，這一次我只給你口頭警告。

B: OK, I'm only going to give you a verbal warning this time.

A: 真感謝你。

A: Thank you very much.

B: 小心開車，還有我建議你查看本地的開車規定。

B: Drive carefully, and I suggest you check out the local driving regulations.

 Word Bank 字庫

illegal [ɪˋligl] adj. 違法的
verbal [ˋvɝbl] adj. 口頭的
warning [ˋwɔrnɪŋ] n. 警告
suggest [səˋdʒɛst] v. 建議
regulation [ˏrɛgjəˋleʃən] n. 規定

 Useful Phrases 實用語句

1. 哈囉，警察先生。

   Hello, Officer.

2. 這是我的駕照。

   Here's my license.

3. 我可以知道是什麼問題嗎？

   May I ask what the problem is?

4. 你可以說慢點嗎？

   Could you speak more slowly?

5. 我從外國來，拜訪這城市一週。

   I'm from another country. I'm visiting the city for a week.

6. 抱歉，警察先生，從現在起我會更小心。

   Sorry, Officer, I'll be more careful from now on.

7. 我要怎樣繳罰款？

   How do I pay the fine?

12.2 火災
Fire

Dialog 對話

A: 911接線生，你有什麼緊急事件？

A: 911 operator. What is your emergency?

B: 隔壁失火了。

B: The house next door is on fire.

A: 你的地址是？

A: What is your address?

B: 諾頓街556號。

B: 556 Norton Way.

A: 留在線上，緊急救援上路了。

A: Stay on the line. Emergency services are on the way.

住所
郵電通訊
日常活動
銀行與保險
交通
食品與飲食
購物
社交活動
教育
休閒活動
醫療
緊急情況

Language Power 字句補給站

◆ 火災 Fire

on fire	著火
flames	火焰
smoke	煙霧
fire detector	火災警報器
burning	燃燒的
toxic fumes	毒煙
firefighters	消防員
fire truck	消防車
fire station	消防站
hydrant	消防栓
hose	水管
ladder	梯子
burns	燙傷
ambulance	救護車
ambulance paramedics	緊急救護 (員)
paramedic skills	急救技術
first aid	急救

12.3 緊急救護事故
Medical Emergencies

 Dialog 對話

A: 911救援中心。

A: 911 dispatch.

B: 我需要一輛救護車。

B: I need an ambulance.

A: 是什麼問題？

A: What's the problem?

B: 我朋友在抽搐。

B: My friend is having convulsions.

A: 你在哪裡？

A: Where are you?

B: 西金恩街548號。

B: 548 West King Street.

A: 我現在派救護車去，留在線上，等待下一個指示。

A: I'm sending an ambulance now. Stay on the line for further instructions.

B: 好，請快一點。

B: OK. Please hurry.

A: 保持鎮靜，他們馬上到。

A: Keep calm. They'll be there very soon.

B: 我該怎麼辦？

B: What should I do?

A: 看你的朋友有沒有呼吸，然後回到電話上。

A: Check to see if your friend is breathing. Then come back to the phone.

B: 我有無線電話，所以沒問題。

B: I have a cordless phone, so no problem.

A: 注意聽救護車警笛，他們靠近時到外面去，告訴他們到了正確地方。

A: Listen for the siren of the ambulance. Go outside when you know they are close and show them they're at the right place.

B: 好。

B: Alright.

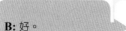

Word Bank 字庫

convulsion [kən`vʌlʃən] n. 痙攣，抽搐
siren [`saɪrən] n. 警笛

Useful Phrases 實用語句

1. 我兒子嚴重撞到頭。

   My son bumped his head hard.

2. 他的頭顱破裂了。

   His skull is fractured.

3. 他沒呼吸。

   He's not breathing.

4. 他跌倒並且失去意識。

   He fell and is unconscious.

5. 他受傷嚴重。

   He is badly wounded.

6. 傷口很深。

   The wound is very deep.

7. 我兒子吞下一個硬幣 [清潔劑]。

   My son swallowed a coin [detergent].

8. 我兒子被魚骨頭噎住了。

My son is being choked by a fish bone.

9. 他看來臉色發白而且正在出汗。

He looks pale and is sweating.

10. 我父親心臟病發。

My father is having a heart attack.

11. 我父親中風了。

My father is having a stroke.

12. 我女兒被熱水燙傷了。

My daughter was burned by hot water.

13. 他在流很多血。

He is bleeding a lot.

14. 她在嘔吐。

She is vomiting.

15. 我姊姊要生產了。

My sister is going to give birth.

16. 有個小男孩溺水了。

A little boy is drowning.

 Language Power 字句補給站

◆ 緊急救護情況 Medical Emergencies

electric shock	電擊
wounds	傷口
drug overdose	吸毒過量
burns	燒傷
seizure	突發 (如癲癇)
choking	噎到的
drowning	溺水的
poisoning	中毒的
earthquake	地震
internal bleeding	內出血
heart attack	心臟病

asthma attack	氣喘發作
stroke	中風
first aid	急救
CPR	心肺復甦術

12.4 犯罪報案
Reporting a Crime

12.4a 報案有人闖入 Reporting a Break-in

A: 緊急服務。

A: Emergency services.

B: 我的房子被闖入。

B: My house was broken into.

A: 你的地址是？

A: What is your address?

B: 卡爾路 878 號。

B: 878 Cal Drive.

A: 小偷還在房子裡嗎？

A: Is the thief still in the house?

B: 沒有。

B: No.

住所
郵電通訊
日常活動
銀行與保險
交通
食品與飲食
購物
社交活動
教育
休閒活動
醫療
緊急情況

A: 我已通知最近的巡邏車。

A: I've alerted the nearest patrol car.

B: 謝謝。

B: Thank you.

A: 請待在電話上直到員警抵達。

A: Please stay on the phone until the policemen arrive.

Word Bank 字庫

alert [əˋlɝt] v. 使警戒，通知
patrol car n. 巡邏車

12.4b 竊盜 Thefts

Dialog 對話

A: 我要報案。

A: I want to report a crime.

B: 發生什麼事了，先生？

B: What happened, Sir?

A: 有人偷了我的錢包。

A: Someone stole my wallet.

B: 你可以形容那個人嗎？

B: Can you describe the person?

A: 可以，他是個有點高有點瘦的青少年。

A: Yes. He's a teenager, kind of tall and thin.

B: 在何時何地發生的呢？

B: When and where did this happen?

✐ Word Bank 字庫

report [rɪ`port] v. 報告
crime [kraɪm] n. 罪

average
thin
brown
jacket
jeans
male
middle-aged
short
black
straight
sideburns
Asian

住所　郵電通訊　日常活動　銀行與保險　交通　食品與飲食　購物　社交活動　教育　休閒活動　醫療　緊急情況

Language Power 字句補給站

◆ 描述某人特徵 Describing Someone

性 別(sex)	☆男(male) ☆女(female)
年 齡(age)	☆年輕(young) ☆中年(middle-aged) ☆老年(old)
身 高(height)	☆高(tall) ☆中等(average) ☆矮(short)
體 重(weight)	☆重(heavy) ☆中等(average) ☆瘦(thin)
髮 色(hair color)	☆金(blond) ☆紅(red) ☆褐(brown) ☆黑(black)
膚 色(skin color)	☆白(white) ☆黃(yellow) ☆深(dark) ☆黑(black)
衣 著(clothing)	☆夾克(jacket) ☆短褲(shorts) ☆牛仔褲(jeans) ☆靴子(boots) ☆帽子(hat)
身 材(body build)	☆瘦小(small) ☆中等(average) ☆胖(heavy-set)
人 種(race)	☆白人(Caucasian/white) ☆亞洲人(Asian) ☆黑人(African-American/black) ☆西班牙裔(Hispanic)
眼睛顏色 (eye color)	☆藍(blue) ☆綠(green) ☆褐(brown)
髮 型(hairstyle)	☆長(long) ☆中等(medium) ☆短(short) ☆捲(curly) ☆波浪(wavy) ☆直(straight) ☆及肩(shoulder-length)
外貌特徵 (special features)	☆疤痕(scars) ☆刺青(tattoos) ☆留鬍子(facial hair) ☆鬍髭(mustache) ☆鬍鬚(beard) ☆鬢角(sideburns) ☆山羊鬍(goatee)

住所　郵電通訊　日常活動　銀行與保險　交通　食品與飲食　購物　社交活動　教育　休閒活動　醫療　緊急情況

住所

郵電通訊

日常活動

銀行與保險

交通

食品與飲食

購物

社交活動

教育

休閒活動

醫療

緊急情況

12.4c 搶劫與傷害 Robberies and Assaults

Dialog （對話）

A: 你發生什麼事了？

A: So what happened to you?

B: 我站在公車站，突然有個男人帶著一把刀抓住我。

B: I was standing at the bus stop when suddenly this man with a knife grabbed me.

A: 你可以描述他嗎？

A: Can you describe him?

B: 可以，他穿著一件黑皮衣、牛仔褲，金髮、藍眼，比我高。

B: Yes. He was wearing a black leather coat, and jeans. He had blond hair and blue eyes. He was taller than me.

A: 他的髮型呢？

A: How about his hair style?

B: 短髮，不，是普通長度，看起來髒髒的。

B: It was short, no wait, it was average length, and it looked dirty.

A: 你還注意到別的嗎？

A: Did you notice anything else?

B: 有，他有一顆門牙斷掉。

B: Yes, he had a broken front tooth.

A: 好的，請坐在這裡，放輕鬆，如果你想到什麼就告訴我。

A: OK. Just sit here and relax. If you think of anything else let me know.

Word Bank 字庫

grab [græb] v. 抓住
jeans [dʒinz] n. 牛仔褲
average [`ævərɪdʒ] adj. 一般的

Useful Phrases 實用語句

1. 我被攻擊了。

   I've been assaulted.

2. 我需要緊急服務。

   I need emergency services.

3. 有人跟蹤我。

   I'm being stalked.

4. 我聽到隔壁有槍聲。

   I heard gun shots next door.

Language Power 字句補給站

◆ 犯罪Crime

assault	攻擊
thief	小偷
stolen	被偷的
break-in	闖入
burglary	闖空門，竊盜
burglar	竊賊
robbed	被搶
robber	搶匪
attacked	被攻擊的

住所｜郵電通訊｜日常活動｜銀行與保險｜交通｜食品與飲食｜購物｜社交活動｜教育｜休閒活動｜醫療｜緊急情況

shot	被槍擊的
stabbed	被刀刺傷的
stalked	被跟蹤的
bleeding	流血的
injured	受傷的
missing person	失蹤人口
kidnapped	被綁架的
kidnappers	綁架犯
ransom	贖金
harassed	被騷擾的
rape	性侵
witness	目擊者
self-defense	自衛

12.5 尋人
Looking for Someone

Dialog 對話

A: 我要報案尋人。	**A:** I want to report a missing person.
B: 是誰走失?	**B:** Who is missing?
A: 我女兒。	**A:** My daughter.
B: 你的名字是?	**B:** Your name, please.

住所 郵電通訊 日常活動 銀行與保險 交通 食品與飲食 購物 社交活動 教育 休閒活動 醫療 緊急情況

A: 湯姆林。

A: Tom Lin.

B: 你女兒走失多久了，林先生？

B: How long has your daughter been missing, Mr. Lin?

A: 約24小時。

A: Almost 24 hours.

B: 請描述你的女兒。

B: Please describe your daughter.

A: 她5呎5吋高，大約112磅重。

A: She is 5 feet 5 inches tall and weighs 112 pounds.

B: 她眼睛什麼顏色？

B: What color are her eyes?

A: 深褐色，她有亞洲人特徵。

A: They are dark brown. She has Asian features.

B: 我知道了，你最後見到她是在何時何地？

B: I see. When and where did you last see her?

A: 昨晚大約此時。

A: Last night, about this time.

住所
郵電通訊
日常活動
銀行與保險
交通
食品與飲食
購物
社交活動
教育
休閒活動
醫療
緊急情況

Notes 小叮嚀

失蹤的定義在美國是必須超過24小時，因此在此之前警局不會有太多尋人動作，但如果事證明確，警局會馬上採取行動，找尋失蹤人口必須詳細描述失蹤者特徵，能盡量及快速提供警局所需資料，能找回失蹤者機率越大。

12.6 找尋失物
Looking for Missing Properties

12.6a 遺失護照 Lost Passport

  Dialog 對話

A: 我找不到我的護照。

A: I can't find my passport.

B: 你有找過你白天的袋子嗎？

B: Did you look in your day bag?

A: 我已找過每個地方，不見了，我弄丟了！

A: I've looked everywhere. It's gone. I lost it!

B: 我們最好聯絡我們最近的大使館。

B: We'd better contact our nearest embassy.

A: 對，我要馬上換新的。

A: Right. I'll need to get it replaced immediately.

B: 那裡的人也會發給你暫時的文件。

B: The people there can issue you a temporary document, too.

A: 我最好現在打電話給他們。

A: I'd better call them right now.

 Word Bank 字庫

embassy [`ɛmbəsɪ] n. 大使館
replace [rɪ`ples] v. 代替，更換
issue [`ɪʃʊ] v. 發出
temporary [`tɛpə͵rɛrɪ] adj. 暫時的
document [`dɑkjəmənt] n. 文件

12.6b 尋找皮夾 Looking for a Wallet

 Dialog 對話

A: 嗨，這是失物招領處嗎？

A: Hi. Is this the Lost and Found?

B: 是的。

B: Yes, it is.

A: 我丟了皮夾。

A: I've lost my wallet.

B: 你何時丟掉的？

B: When did you lose it?

A: 昨天下午。

A: Yesterday afternoon.

B: 昨天有兩個皮夾進來。

B: Two wallets were turned in yesterday.

A: 我該怎麼做？

A: What should I do?

B: 你要對我形容你的皮夾。

B: You'll have to describe it to me.

A: 好，是個黑色皮夾，有個小按釦可以合起來，牌子是 Callmans。

A: OK. It is a black leather wallet with a small snap that keeps it closed, and the brand name is Callmans.

B: 你可以告訴我裡面有什麼嗎？

B: Can you tell me what is inside?

A: 我的駕照在裡面且上面有我的照片。

A: My driver's license is in there and it has my photo on it.

B: 好，我去看我們有沒有。

B: OK, I'll go back and check if we have it.

A: 謝謝。

A: Thanks.

Word Bank 字庫

lose [luz] v. 遺失
turn in 遞交
describe [dɪˋskraɪb] v. 描述

Useful Phrases 實用語句

1. 我要把這個交給失物處。

   I want to give this to the Lost and Found.

2. 我想有人丟了這個。

   I think someone lost this.

3. 有人發現我的皮夾嗎？

   Did someone find my wallet?

4. 是個黑色的皮夾。

   It's a black wallet.

5. 裡面有兩張信用卡、大約300元及我的駕照。

   There were two credit cards, about \$300, and my driver's license inside.

Tips 小祕訣

　　駕照遺失可能產生各種個資盜用、詐騙 (identity theft, identity fraud) 風險，須向警方報案取得證明，並通知汽機車部門 (DMV) 駕照遺失及盡速申請補發。

12.6c 遺失信用卡 Missing a Credit Card

Dialog 對話

A: 哈囉，信用卡服務中心，我能為你服務嗎？

A: Hello, Credit Card Services. How may I help you?

住所
郵電通訊
日常活動
銀行與保險
交通
食品與飲食
購物
社交活動
教育
休閒活動
醫療
緊急情況

B: 我遺失了信用卡。

B: I've lost my credit card.

A: 我需要向你問些資料。

A: I'll need to get some information from you.

B: 好。

B: OK.

A: 你的大名是？

A: What is your full name?

B: 羅勃王。

B: Robert Wong.

A: 你的地址及電話是？

A: What is your address and phone number?

B: 林肯街508號，坎培市，加州95008。

B: 508 Lincoln Ave. Campbell, CA 95008.

A: 謝謝，我螢幕上有你的資料了，我需要問一個安全問題，你的寵物名字及拼法。

A: Thank you. I have your information on my computer screen. I need to ask you a security question. What is your pet's name and how do you spell it?

575

B: 我的寵物是露西娃娃，是兩個字，拼法是L-U-C-Y D-O-L-L。

B: My pet's name is Lucy Doll. It's two words, and it's spelled L-U-C-Y D-O-L-L.

A: 謝謝，你何時遺失卡片？

A: Thank you. When did you lose the card?

B: 我不確定，但我想是昨天下午。

B: I'm not sure, but I think it was yesterday afternoon.

A: 好，我現在取消你的卡片，新卡今天會寄去你的地址。

A: Fine. I have now cancelled your card. A new one will be sent to your address today.

B: 好。

B: OK.

A: 你可以告訴我最後一次刷卡是什麼時候嗎？

A: Can you tell me the last time it was used?

B: 可以，最後一次使用是三天前在「讀者書櫃」書店。

B: Yes, the last time it was used was three days ago at The Readers Bin Bookstore.

A: 知道了。

A: I see.

B: 你知道新卡要多久寄到我家？

B: Do you know how long it will take for it to get to my home?

A: 是寄快遞，所以會在一兩天內到。

A: It will be sent as priority mail, so it should arrive in one or two days.

B: 我要打電話開卡嗎？

B: Will I need to call and activate it?

A: 要，說明書會隨著卡片寄到，你打的開卡電話是免付費的。

A: Yes. The instructions will come with the card. The call you make to activate the card is toll free.

B: 我知道了，謝謝你的幫忙。

B: I see. Thank you for your help.

A: 不客氣。

A: You're welcome.

Notes 小叮嚀

　　發現信用卡或提款卡遺失要盡快掛失，發卡機構多有24小時服務處理這類事務，如果能在電話掛失後，將信用卡號碼、何時發現遺失卡片及何時致電發卡機構掛失以信件寄出會更周全。

　　如果持卡人在遭冒用前就掛失，按照聯邦公平信用及帳單交易法 FCBA (the Fair Credit and Billing Act) 中規定，發卡機構不能向持卡人請求支付任何冒用信用卡的費用；如果在掛失前就已被冒用，此規定明定持卡人最大損失 (liability maximum) 為 \$50，即持卡人最多支付 \$50 給發卡機構；如果是信用卡號碼被盜用，而沒有持卡人簽名，持卡人不需支付任何因被冒用而衍生的費用。

Appendixes

附錄

附錄

1. 溫度換算表 Temperature Conversion Chart

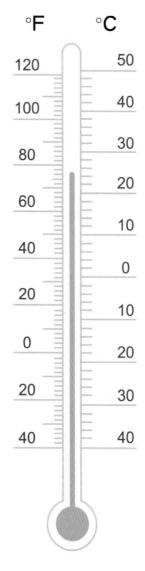

$°\text{C (Celcius)}=(°\text{F-32})^5/_9$ $°\text{F (Fahrenheit)}=^9/_5 °\text{C+32}$

2. 美國駕車須知 Driving Tips in the USA

◎美國人的駕駛習慣

美國人 16 歲就可以考駕照，在大多數地區，沒車子就等於沒有腳，哪裡也去不了，自己開車作為交通工具是獨立的第一步，因此優良的駕駛紀錄是很重要的。入境隨俗，美國人的駕駛習慣不可不知，才能確保出門平安，且不會拿到罰單。

1. 換車道時要回頭 (過肩) 查看，確定盲點內無車輛。
2. 禮讓主幹線車輛先行，不可爭先。
3. 碰到停車再開 (stop) 標誌，一定要使車子完全停止，確定可以通過再開。
4. 四面都有停車再開標誌時，要讓先到車輛先停先走，不可爭先。
5. 有行人穿越馬路，一定要禮讓，不可亂按喇叭或閃頭燈。比中指是嚴重的挑釁行為，不可不慎。
6. 紅燈可以右轉，要小心行人。若有 No right turn on red. 就要等綠箭頭燈亮，才可右轉。

◎被警察攔下怎麼辦？

美國高速公路又寬又直，一不小心就會超速。大多數城市時速限制多為 55 英里，多數駕駛駕車時速約在 65 英里左右 (即速限加 10 英里左右)。超過的話就有可能被高速公路警察 (Highway Patrol) 取締，拿到超速 (speeding) 罰單，違規處罰除了罰款，還可能包括上法庭。如果警察被取締時態度不佳，有可能被戴上手銬，送進監牢，及上法院裁決。沙漠地區或人煙較少處，限速常為 100 英里。 要注意地面警察雖較不常出現，但可能有直昇機警察突然出現取締違規車輛。

酒駕及超速在美國及加拿大及其他地方都是嚴重的交通違規，兩者的罰金都很重且可能要入獄，而且駕駛紀錄差，影響到以後一輩子的保險費。記住車內絕不可以放打開的酒，酒類最好放後車廂。危險的駕駛行為 (即使沒有超速)，可能會被警察以魯莽駕駛 (reckless driving) 逮捕並起訴，而魯莽駕駛通常是因為酒駕引起的。

臺灣警察巡邏時常常開著閃燈，可能導致國人對美國警車閃燈習以為常。「國家地理頻道」曾播出 4 位臺灣在美打工大學生，警察緊追其後閃燈 (加廣播) 還渾然不覺繼續開車，最後被阿拉斯加公路警察持槍攔下。切記在美國萬一被警察閃燈，務必盡快停車。車停好後，靜坐在車內，等待警察。切勿打開車門走出車外或在車內慌亂尋找物品，警察可能會誤認為你在尋找槍械或藏匿毒品而用槍指著你，這是

非常危險的。

美國是可以合法買賣槍械的國家，有些州並不要求買槍者註冊登記，因此全國真正槍枝數字無從得知，必須依靠估算。依照雪梨大學公共健康學院 2012 年所提供的估算 (GunPolicy.org)，擁有 3.1 億人口的美國人已擁有超過 3.1 億槍枝 (含合法與非法)，即每 100 人擁有 101.05 枝槍械，槍枝氾濫問題極為嚴重，警察因此對違法者執行勤務時非常嚴厲，他們必須防範違法者攜帶槍械，隨時可能採取之攻擊。

被攔下取締時可以主動禮貌地向警察打招呼 (Hello, Officer. May I ask what the problem is?) 警察不喜歡無禮及愛挑釁的人。在國外因為沒碰過這種情形或不知自己為何被攔下，通常會一時無法反應，但千萬不要裝成不懂英文，警察通常會問外地人是否懂英文，此時要誠實以對。(Yes, Officer. I speak a little English.) 聽不懂時，告訴警察 (I'm sorry, Officer. I don't understand.) 別裝懂，隨便說 yes 會給自己帶來麻煩。如果剛來不久，可以告訴警察 (Officer, I'm sorry. I'm from another country. I'm not familiar with the rules here.)。

按照警察指示，拿出所需證件 (駕照 driver's license、行照或租車同意書 registration or rental agreement)。如果證件在手套箱或後車廂，要告訴警察 (The rental agreement is in the glove compartment/trunk)，獲得警察同意再打開，以免警察誤會而極度警戒。如果持有國際駕照還沒換美國駕照，中文駕照也要帶著備查。保持禮貌，配合警察，對於小的違規，可能只會被口頭警告 (verbal warning)，而不會被開罰單。

3. 美國假日 Holidays in the USA

美國人的休假時間算是少的，從耶誕節到新年期間是美國的年假，家人們聚在一起享受佳肴、交換禮物或出遊。一年中的休假假日並不多，如果有週休二日加上少數放假或補假的星期一才有 long weekend，許多節日並不休假。

Official Holidays 國定假日 (為休假日，若碰到週末，則週一補假)

1. New Year's Day - Jan. 1 新年 (一月一日)
2. Martin Luther King Day (MLK Day) - 3rd Mon. of Jan. 馬丁路德金恩誕辰 (一月的第三個星期一)
3. Presidents Day - 3rd Mon. of Feb. 總統紀念日 (二月的第三個星期一)
   包括 Lincoln's Birthday - Feb. 12th 林肯誕辰 (二月十二日)
   Washington's Birthday - Feb. 22nd 華盛頓誕辰 (二月二十二日)
4. Memorial Day - last Mon. of May 陣亡將士紀念日 (五月的最後一個星期一)
5. Independence Day - July 4th 獨立紀念日 (國慶日) (七月四日)
6. Labor Day - 1st Mon. of Sept. 勞動節 (九月的第一個星期一)
7. Columbus Day - 12th of Oct. 哥倫布紀念日 (十月十二日)
8. Veterans Day - 11th of Nov. 退休軍人節 (十一月十一日)
9. Thanksgiving Day - 4th Thurs. of Nov. 感恩節 (十一月的第四個星期四)
10. Christmas - Dec. 25th 耶誕節 (十二月二十五日)

Not Official Holidays 非國定假日 (不休假)：

1. Groundhog Day - Feb. 2nd 土撥鼠節 (二月二日)
2. Valentine's Day - Feb. 14th 情人節 (二月十四日)
3. Saint Patrick's Day - March 17th 聖派屈克節 (三月十七日)
4. April Fool's Day - Apr 1st 愚人節 (四月一日)
5. Easter - A Sunday in Mar. or Apr. 復活節 (春分滿月後的第一個星期天)
6. Mother's Day - 2nd Sunday of May 母親節 (五月的第二個星期天)
7. Father's Day - 3rd Sunday in June 父親節 (六月的第三個星期天)
8. Halloween - Oct. 31st 萬聖節 (十月三十一日)

4. 房租契約範例 Rental Contract Sample

下列房租契約可說是標準版契約，涵蓋房東房客需協議之項目。租屋契約的條件是可以溝通的，溝通的幅度端看房東想多快出租。

 房租契約範例 Rental Contract Sample

In consideration of the agreements of the Resident(s), known as:

(房客姓名)_____

The owner hereby rents them the dwelling located at (地址) _____
_____ for the period commencing on the____ day of
_____ , 20_____, (開始日期) and monthly thereafter until the
last day of_____ , 20 _____, (結束日期) at which time
this Agreement is terminated. Resident(s), in consideration of Owners permitting them to occupy the above property, hereby agrees to the following terms:

RENT 房租：To pay as rental the sum of $_____per month, due and payable in advance from the first day of every month. Failure to pay rent when due will result in the Owner taking immediate legal action to evict the Resident from the premises and seize the security deposit. 每月$_____租金每月1日到期，未付款房東立即採取法律行動，款項由押金扣除。

LATE FEE 遲付罰金：Rent received after the first of the month will be subject to a late fee of 10% plus $3 dollars per day. 遲付罰金為每日10% 房租加 $3。

APPLIANCES 家電：The above rental payment specifically EXCLUDES all appliances not permanently affixed. Appliances located at or in the property are there solely at the convenience of the Owner, who assumes no responsibility for their operation. In the event they fail to function after occupancy is started, the Resident may have them repaired at no cost to Owner or request Owner to remove them. 租金不含非固定家電，房東無責任保證家電之使用，房客開始起租即

不得向房東要求修理或移除家具。

4 MAINTENANCE 維修：Resident agrees to maintain the premises during the period of this agreement. This includes woodwork, floors, walls, furnishings and fixtures, appliances, windows, screens doors, lawns, landscaping, fences, plumbing, electrical, air conditioning and heating, and mechanical systems. Resident acknowledges specific responsibility for replacing and/or cleaning filters on a/c and heating units. Any damages caused to units because of not changing and cleaning filters will be paid for by the Resident. Tacks, nails, or other hangers nailed or screwed into the walls or ceilings will be removed at the termination of this agreement. Damage caused by rain, hail or wind as a result of leaving windows or doors open, or damage caused by overflow of water, or stoppage of waste pipes, breakage of glass, damage to screens, deterioration of lawns and landscaping, whether caused by abuse or neglect is the responsibility of the Resident. Resident agrees to provide pest control in the event it is needed. 房客同意租屋期間維護房屋內外所有設備，包含更換、清潔冷暖氣濾網，任何因此產生的損壞由房客負責。任何吊掛丁在結束租期時必須拔除，房客因疏忽或濫用造成未關門窗財產損失或花圃、水管、水漬等損害由房客負責。房客同意提供害蟲防治。

5 CLEANING 清潔：Resident accepts premises in its current state of cleanliness and agrees to return it in a like condition. 房客接受房屋清潔現況，並同意歸還時恢復類似情況。

6 SECURITY DEPOSIT 押金：Resident agrees to pay a deposit in the amount of $ _____(金額) to secure residents pledge of full compliance with the terms of this agreement. Note: THE DEPOSIT MAY NOT BE USED BY TENANT TO PAY RENT DURING THE TENANCY! The security deposit will be used at the end of the tenancy to compensate the Owner for any damages or unpaid rent or charges, and will be repaired at resident expense with funds other than the deposit. 押金不可抵租金，房東在結束租期後用押金來修補房客造成之損失或未付房租，若押金不足支付，房客要付費。

PETS 寵物：Resident agrees to pay a non-refundable pet fee of $20 per month per pet. All pets found on the property, but not registered under this agreement will be presumed to be strays and disposed of by the appropriate agency as prescribed by law. In the event a Resident harbors and undisclosed pet, they agree to pay a pet fee for the entire term of the agreement, regardless of when the pet was first introduced to the household. 每月每一寵物收費 $20，不可退費，若發現未登記在租約內之寵物，將視為流浪動物由法律規定之單位處理。不論何時開始收養寵物，房客同意按合約全期支付寵物費。

PESIDENT OBLIGATIONS 房客義務：The Resident agrees to meet all of resident obligations; including:

A. Taking affirmative action to insure that nothing exists which might place the owner in violation of applicable building, housing and health codes. 保證不讓房東違反建物、房屋及健康規定。

B. Keeping the dwelling clean, and sanitary; removing garbage and trash as they accumulate; maintaining plumbing in good working order to prevent stoppages and/or leakage of plumbing, fixtures, faucets, pipes, etc. 保持居家整潔，清理垃圾，保持水管暢通。

C. Conducting him/herself, his/her family, friends, guests and visitors in a manner which will not disturb others. Resident warrants that he/she will meet the above conditions in every respect, and acknowledges that failure to do so will be grounds for termination of this agreement and loss of all deposits without further recourse. 房客及其家人、朋友行為不騷擾別人。違反者租約終止、押金沒入，不得異議。

OWNER STATEMENT 房東聲明：All rights given to the Owner by this agreement shall be cumulative in addition to any other laws which might exist or come into being. Any exercise or failure to exercise, by the Owner of any right shall not act as a waiver of any other rights. No statement or promise of Owner or his agent as to tenancy, repairs, alternations, or other terms and conditions shall be binding unless specified in writing and specifically endorsed. 所有其他法律條款賦予房東租約以外權利，房東未使用之任何權利不表示喪失，房東或仲介對房客修繕或其他承諾、條件，除書面聲明背書外，沒有規範效力。

PARTIAL PAYMENT 部分付款：The acceptance by the Owner of partial payments of rent due shall not under any circumstance, constitute a waiver of the Owner, nor affect any notice or legal eviction proceedings in theretofore given or commenced under state law. 房東收受部分租金，於任何情況下不造成房東喪失權利，也不影響通知房客或按照州法強制搬家的進行。

UTILITIES 公共費用：Residents shall be responsible for payments of all utilities, garbage, water and sewer charges, telephone, gas or other bills incurred during their residency. They specifically authorize the Owner to deduct amounts of unpaid bills from their deposits in the event they remain unpaid after the termination of this agreement. 房客負責租期內的水電瓦斯垃圾電話費用，若未付，房東從押金扣除。

PERSONAL PROPERTY 個人財物：No rights of storage are given by this agreement. The owner shall not be liable for any loss of personal injury or property by fire, theft, breakage, burglary, or otherwise, for any accidental damage to persons, guests, or property in or about the leased/rented property resulting from electrical failure, water, rain, windstorm, or any act of God, or negligence of owner, or owners agent, contractors, or employees, or by any other cause, whatsoever. 房東不負責任何因火災、偷竊、闖入、強盜等造成之生命財產損失，或此房屋因停電、水災、氣候及不可控制因素造成之損失。

TERMINATION 解約：After one month rental payment has been received, this agreement may be terminated by mutual consent of the parties, or by either party giving written notice of at least 15 days prior to the end of any monthly period. Any provision of this agreement may be changed by the owner in like manner. All parties agree that termination of this agreement prior to _____(日期) regardless of cause will constitute a breach of the tenancy as agreed on page 1 and all deposits shall be forfeited in favor of the Owner as full liquidated damages at the Owner option. 一個月之租金收到後，雙方同意下即可解約，或任何一方以書面在每月結束的15天前通知。租約中任何條款改變可以相同方式進行。雙方同意在

_____之前解約，不論原因，視為房客違約(如第一頁)放棄押金權力，房東有權選擇用押金作為清償損失。

METHOD OF PAYMENT 付款方式：The initial payment of rent and deposits under this agreement must be made in cash, or cashier check drawn on a local financial institution. Thereafter, monthly rent payments may be paid by check until the first check is dishonored and returned unpaid. Regardless of cause, no other additional payments may afterwards be made by check. Checks returned will not be redeposited. The Resident will be notified by a 3 day notice, and will be required to pay the amount due, including the bad check charge, in cash. Resident is aware that owner may report past rent, damages, utilities or other costs owed by Resident to credit reporting agencies. Resident understands this reporting could affect Resident's ability to obtain credit for future housing. 租金及押金以現金或當地機構的支票支付，若有一張支票跳票，不論任何理由，房東即不再收受支票，3天內房客會被通知，必須以現金支付房租及跳票手續費。房東可據此報告信用機構，房客因此可能影響將來住居之信用。

DELIVERY OF RENTS 郵寄租金：Rents may be mailed through the U.S. mail to _____ _____(地址). Any rents lost in the mail will be treated as if unpaid until received by Owner. It is recommended that payment made in cash or money order be delivered in person to the owner office at the above address. Only rents received by mail or in person on or before the due date will qualify the tenant for a discount! 未寄到租金視為未付租金，建議以現金或匯票付租金，親自送到上述地址房東之辦公室，只有到期日之前或當日收到的租金才有折扣資格。

RETURN OF DEPOSIT 押金退還：Security deposits will be deposited for the Resident benefit in a non-interest bearing bank account. Release of these deposits is subject to the provisions of State Statues and as follows: 條件
A. The full term of this agreement has been completed. 租約到期
B. Formal written notice has been given 已給正式書面通知
C. No damage or deterioration to the premises, building(s), or grounds is evident. 建物及地面沒有明顯損害。

D. The entire dwelling, appliance, closets and cupboards, are clean and left free of insects, the refrigerator is defrosted, and all debris and rubbish has been removed from the property; the carpets are cleaned and left odorless. 房屋、家電、廚櫃沒有蟲害，冰箱除霜、垃圾清除、地毯清潔無異味。

E. Any and all unpaid charges, pet charges, late charges, extra visitor charges, delinquent rents, utility charges, etc., have been paid in full. 沒有任何未付費用。

F. All keys have been returned, including keys to any new locks installed while resident was in possession. 鑰匙(包含新鑰匙)全部歸還

G. A forwarding address has been left with the owner. 留下聯絡地址 Thirty days after termination of occupancy, the owner will send the balance of the deposit to the address provided by the Resident, payable to the signatories hereto, or owner will impose a claim on the deposit and so notify the Resident by certified letter. If such written claim is not sent, the owner relinquishes his right to make any further claim on the deposit and must return it to the Resident, provided Resident has given the Owner notice of intent to vacate, abandon, and terminate this agreement proper to the expiration of its full term, at least 7 days in advance. 解約後30天房東要寄出剩餘押金至房客提供之地址，或房東以掛號寄給房客扣除押金之書面聲明。若房客在合約滿期至少7天前提出要搬家，但房東未在解約後30天時限內寄出處理押金聲明，即放棄扣除押金權利，押金需全數交還房客。

17 GAS, ELECTRIC AND WATER 瓦斯水電：Resident agrees to transfer the gas, electric, and water service charges to their name immediately upon occupancy and to make arrangements for meter readings as needed. 房客同意搬入後立刻安排換名跳錶事宜。

18 THREE(3) DAY INSPECTION 三天審查：Under the terms of this discount lease/rental agreement, Residents will be provided with an inspection sheet. It is their obligation to inspect the premises and to fill out and return to the Owner their inspection sheet within 3 days after taking possession of the premises. It will be presumed that the house is functioning in a satisfactory manner in all respects after the expiration of the 3 days. Resident agrees that failure to file such a statement shall be conclusive proof that there were no defects of note in the property. After that time, the Resident is obligated to provide for routine maintenance at this own expense, or to lose the discount. 在此有折扣的契約下，房客有義務於3天內檢查房屋、填寫及交回明細表，未提出異議，視為無問題。

OWNERS AGENTS AND ACCESS 仲介及入內：The owner may be represented by an agent who will carry identification. Resident specifically agrees to permit the owner or agent(s) access to the premises for the purposes of inspection, repairs, or to show the property to another person at reasonable hours, on request. Resident will also allow signage in the yard. 房客同意在適當時間內，房東可託付有證件的仲介入內檢查、修繕或帶人看房，及在院子留下標誌。

REPAIRS 修繕：In the event repairs are needed beyond the competence of the Resident, he or she is urged to arrange for professional assistance. Residents are offered the discount as an incentive to make their own decisions on the property they live in. Therefore as much as possible, the Resident should refrain from contacting the Owner except for emergencies or for repairs costing more that the discount since such involvement not by the Owner will result in the loss of the discount. ANY REPAIR THAT WILL COST MORE THAN THE AMOUNT OF THE DISCOUNT MUST BE APPROVED BY THE OWNER OR THE TENANT WILL BE RESPONSIBLE FOR THE ENTIRE COST OF THAT REPAIR. Any improvement made by the tenant shall become the property of the Owner at the conclusion of this agreement. 因契約有折扣，房客自己做判斷儘量不要打擾房東，除非重大緊急或會超過折扣的修繕(這些修繕需由房東同意，否則房客要自付費用)，任何修繕契約滿期後歸屬房東。

DEFAULT BY RESIDENT 房客怠忽：Any breach or violation of any provision of this contract by Resident or any untrue or misleading information in Resident application shall give the Owner or his agent the right to terminate this contract, evict the Resident and to take possession of the residence. The Resident agrees to a forfeiture of the security deposit and Owner may still pursue any remaining amounts due

附錄

and owing. 房客有任何違反契約條款或提供不實身分、資料將導致解約，押金沒入，房東得追討欠款。

22 RENEWAL TERM 續租：At the end of initial term herein, as per page 1, Owner may elect to renew for another term but at a rental increase of 3% to 5% of current rental rate may apply depending on the market index.租期已屆(如第一頁)，房東可決定續租，但可能依市場行情漲3% 到5%。

LEGAL CONTRACT 法律契約：This is a legally binding contract. If you do not understand any part of this contract, seek competent legal advice before signing. 這是法律契約，如有疑問，簽名前要做法律諮詢。

ACCEPTED THIS _____ day of _____ 20 _____ (接受日期), at

_____(地址)

Resident (房客簽名)

_____

Resident (房客簽名)

_____

Owner (房東簽名)

_____

5. 美國臺北經濟文化辦事處 (可下載外交部APP)
Contacting TECRO (Taipei Economic and Cultural Representative Office in the United States)

☑ 駐美國臺北經濟文化代表處
Taipei Economic and Cultural Representative Office in the United States

地址：4201 Wisconsin Ave., N W Washington, DC 20016-2137, U.S.A.
緊急聯絡電話：(1-202) 669-0180
一般事項，請於上班時間聯繫；護照、簽證及文件證明等領務事項，請洽 (1-202) 895-1812 其他一般事項，請洽 (1-202) 895-1800
傳真：(1-202) 363-0999
網址：www.taiwanembassy.org/US/
電郵信箱：usa@mofa.gov.tw

☑ 駐亞特蘭大臺北經濟文化辦事處
Taipei Economic and Cultural Office in Atlanta

地址：1180 West Peachtree Street, Regions Plaza, Suite 800, Atlanta, GA 30309, U.S.A.
電話：(1-404) 870-9375　　　　傳真：(1-404) 870-9376
網址：www.taiwanembassy.org/US/ATL/
電郵信箱：tecoatl@teco.org
急難救助：行動電話 (1-404) 3583875
　　　　　美國境內直撥 1-404-358-3875

☑ 駐波士頓臺北經濟文化辦事處
Taipei Economic and Cultural Office in Boston

地址：99 Summer St., Suite 801 Boston, MA 02110, U.S.A.
電話：(1-617) 737-2050, 259-1350, 259-1372 傳真：(1-617) 737-1684
網址：http://www.taiwanembassy.org/US/BOS
電郵信箱：teco@tecoboston.org
急難救助：行動電話 (1-617) 6509252
　　　　　美國境內直撥 (1-617) 6509252

✓ 駐芝加哥臺北經濟文化辦事處

Taipei Economic and Cultural Office in Chicago

地址：Two Prudential Plaza 180 N. Stetson Ave., 57&58 FL Chicago, IL 60601, U.S.A

電話：(1-312) 616-0100　　　傳真：(1-312) 616-1486

網址：http://www.taiwanembassy.org/US/CHI

電郵信箱：tecochicago@yahoo.com

急難救助：(1-312) 636-4758

✓ 駐關島臺北經濟文化辦事處

Taipei Economic and Cultural Office in Guam

地址：Suite 505, Bank of Guam Bldg., 111, Chalan Santo Papa Road, Hagatna, Guam 96910, U.S.A.

電話：(1-671) 472-5865　　　傳真：(1-671) 472-5869

網址：http://www.taiwanembassy.org/US/GUM

電郵信箱：tecogm@kuentos.guam.net

急難救助：行動電話 (1-671) 988-7088
　　　　　美國境內直撥 (1-671) 988-7088

✓ 駐休士頓臺北經濟文化辦事處

Taipei Economic and Cultural Office in Houston

地址：11 Greenway Plaza, Suite 2006, Houston, TX 77046, U.S.A.

電話：(1-713) 626-7445　　　傳真：(1-713) 626-0990

網址：http://www.taiwanembassy.org/US/HOU

電郵信箱：tecohou@sbcglobal.net

急難救助：行動電話 (1-832) 654-6041
　　　　　美國境內直撥 1-8326546041

✔ 駐檀香山辦事處

Taipei Economic and Cultural Office in Honolulu

地址：2746 Pali Highway, Honolulu, HI 96817, U.S.A.

電話：(1-808) 595-6347　　　　傳真：(1-808) 595-3161

網址：www.taiwanembassy.org/US/HNL/

電郵信箱：tecohnl@hawaii.rr.com

急難救助：行動電話 (1-808) 3518818

美國境內直撥 1-808-3518818

✔ 駐堪薩斯臺北經濟文化辦事處

Taipei Economic and Cultural Office in Kansas City

地址：3100 Broadway, Suite 800, Kansas City, MO 64111, U.S.A.

電話：(1-816) 531-1298, 531-1299

傳真：一般事務 (1-816) 531-3066

領事事務 (1-816) 531-6189

網址：www.taiwanembassy.org/US/MKC/

電郵信箱：kcteco@taiwan-kcteco.org

急難救助：行動電話 (1-816) 522-9546

美國境內直撥 (1-816) 522-9546

✔ 駐洛杉磯臺北經濟文化辦事處

Taipei Economic and Cultural Office in Los Angeles

地址：3731 Wilshire Boulevard, Suite 700, Los Angeles, CA 90010, U.S.A.

電話：(1-213) 389-1215　　　　傳真：(1-213) 3891676

網址：www.taiwanembassy.org/US/LAX/

電郵信箱：info@TECOLA.org

急難救助：行動電話 (1-213) 923-3591

美國境內直撥 (1-213) 923-3591

☑ 駐邁阿密臺北經濟文化辦事處

Taipei Economic and Cultural Office in Miami

地址：2333 Ponce de Leon Blvd., Suite 610 Coral Gables, FL 33134, U.S.A.

電話：(1-305) 443-8917　　傳真：(1-305) 442-6054，(1-305) 442-6054

電郵信箱：tecomia@bellsouth.net

網址：http://www.taiwanembassy.org/US/MIA

急難救助：專線電話 (1-786) 253-7333

　　　　　美國境內直撥 1-786-253-7333

☑ 駐紐約臺北經濟文化辦事處

Taipei Economic and Cultural Office in New York

地址：1, E. 42nd Street New York, NY 10017, U.S.A.

電話：(1-212) 317-7300　　　　傳真：(1-212) 754-1549

領務專用電話：(1-212) 486-0088

領務專用傳真：(1-212) 421-7866

網址：www.taiwanembassy.org/US/NYC/

電郵信箱：teco@tecony.org 、consular@tecony.org (領務專用)

急難救助：行動電話 (1-917) 743-4546 (假日)

　　　　　行動電話 (1-212) 317-7300 (平日)

　　　　　美國境內直撥 (1-917) 743-4546，(1-212) 317-7300

☑ 駐舊金山臺北經濟文化辦事處

Taipei Economic and Cultural Office in San Francisco

地址：555 Montgomery Street, Suite 501, San Francisco, CA 94111, U.S.A.

電話：(1-415) 362-7680　　　　傳真：(1-415) 362-5382

領務專用電話：(1-415) 362-7681

領務專用傳真：(1-415) 364-5629 (限美國境內使用)

網址：www.taiwanembassy.org/US/SFO

電郵信箱：tecosf@sbcglobal.net

領務專用信箱：tecosfconsular@sbcglobal.net

急難救助：行動電話 (1-415) 265-1351

　　　　　美國境內直撥 (1-415) 265-1351

☑ 駐西雅圖臺北經濟文化辦事處

Taipei Economic and Cultural Office in Seattle

地址：One Union Square, 600 University St., Suite 2020, Seattle, WA
98101, U.S.A.

電話：(1-206) 441-4586　　　傳真：(1-206) 441-1322

網址：www.taiwanembassy.org/US/SEA/

電郵信箱：info@teco-seattle.org

急難救助：行動電話 (1-206) 510-8588

附註：

◎「外交部緊急聯絡中心」國內免付費「旅外國人緊急服務專線」電
話 0800-085-095 (諧音「您幫我　您救我」)，自國外撥打回國須自付
國際電話費用，撥打方式為：(當地國國際電話冠碼) +886-800-085-
095

◎「旅外國人急難救助全球免付費專線」電話 800-0885-0885 (諧音「您
幫幫我、您幫幫我」，目前可適用歐、美、日、韓、澳洲等 22 個國
家或地區)，為國人在海外遭遇緊急危難時洽助之用，非緊急事故請
勿撥打。

◎護照、簽證及文件證明等問題，請於上班時間撥打外交部領事事務
局總機電話 (02)2343-2888

◎外交部一般業務查詢，請於上班時間撥打外交部總機電話 (02)2348-
2999

國家圖書館出版品預行編目資料

開口就會美國長住用語/黃靜悅, Danny Otus Neal著.
——三版. ——臺北市：五南，2014.09
　　面；　　公分

　　ISBN 978-957-11-7763-2（平裝附光碟片）

1.英語　2.會話

805.188　　　　　　　　　　　　　　　103015552

1AC3

開口就會美國長住用語

作　　　者	黃靜悅、Danny Otus Neal
發 行 人	楊榮川
總 編 輯	王翠華
企劃主編	鄧景元、李郁芬、朱曉蘋
責任編輯	溫小瑩、吳雨潔
內頁插畫	吳佳臻
地圖繪製	吳佳臻
封面設計	吳佳臻

出 版 者　五南圖書出版股份有限公司
　　地　　址：台北市大安區 106 和平東路二段 339 號 4 樓
　　電　　話：(02)2705-5066　傳真：(02)2706-6100
　　網　　址：http://www.wunan.com.tw
　　電子郵件：wunan@wunan.com.tw
　　劃撥帳號：01068953
　　戶　　名：五南圖書出版股份有限公司

法律顧問　林勝安律師事務所　林勝安律師

出版日期	2009 年 6 月　初版一刷
	2009 年 11 月　初版二刷
	2011 年 2 月　二版一刷
	2011 年 6 月　二版二刷
	2014 年 9 月　三版一刷

定　　價　480 元整　　　　　※版權所有・請予尊重※

TIME ZONES OF THE UNITED STATES

PACIFIC
（太平洋時區）

MOUNTAIN
（洛磯山時區）

CENTR
（中央時

WA

OR

ID

MT

ND

SD

NE

NV

UT

WY

CA

CO

KS

AZ

NM

OK

TX

HAWII-ALEUTIAN
（夏威夷-阿留申時區）
Honolulu   HI

ALASKA
（阿拉斯加時區）
AK   Juneau